AN OTHERWORLDLY ENCOUNTER...

"Miss Appleton?"

He laid his hand on her shoulder, intending to give her a well-deserved dressing-down, but she turned quickly and wound up in his arms. His chastising words caught in his throat as he gazed into her eyes, eyes that had convinced lesser souls they'd seen a ghost. As if on its own accord, his mouth lowered to hers, unable to resist the soft, sweet temptation.

Their kiss was luscious, spicy, and entrancing like a great wine, full of innocence, yet rich with erotic promise. Gabriel groaned, wanting badly to taste more of her. Desire wrenched through him with almost as much force as his anger as he felt the petal softness of her lips beneath his....

The sweetness of her response tore all logic from his brain. Gabriel wanted this woman desperately, and he had to have her. He was lost in a sea of pure sensation, pleasurably drowning in a woman he'd sworn to hate.

ACKNOWLEDGMENTS

Special thanks to: Wendy McCurdy, Stephanie Kip, and Karen Solem, for their talent and assistance.

Connie Flannery, Linda Cajio, and Marlene Murdock, for their advice and support.

And to my daughter Erin, for her enthusiasm and belief in me.

A HINT OF MISCHIEF

KATIE ROSE

BANTAM BOOKS
New York Toronto London
Sydney Auckland

A HINT OF MISCHIEF
A Bantam Fanfare Book / April 1998

FANFARE and the portrayal of a boxed "ff" are trademarks of Bantam Books, a division of Bantam Doubleday Dell Publishing Group, Inc.

All rights reserved.
Copyright © 1998 by Katie Rose
Cover art copyright © 1998 by Franco Accornera
No part of this book may be reproduced or transmitted in any form or by any means, electronic or mechanical, including photocopying, recording, or by any information storage and retrieval system, without permission in writing from the publisher. For information address: Bantam Books.

If you purchased this book without a cover you should be aware that this book is stolen property. It was reported as "unsold and destroyed" to the publisher and neither the author nor the publisher has received any payment for this "stripped book."

ISBN 0-553-57771-9

Published simultaneously in the United States and Canada

Bantam Books are published by Bantam Books, a division of Bantam Doubleday Dell Publishing Group, Inc. Its trademark, consisting of the words "Bantam Books" and the portrayal of a rooster, is Registered in U.S. Patent and Trademark Office and in other countries. Marca Registrada. Bantam Books, 1540 Broadway, New York, New York 10036.

PRINTED IN THE UNITED STATES OF AMERICA

WCD   10 9 8 7 6 5 4 3 2 1

FOR CHRISTOPHER

A HINT OF MISCHIEF

CHAPTER 1

New York, 1872

THE FLAMES FLICKERED mysteriously from the crystal chandelier, throwing strange, glistening lights on the women below. The fire roared, but little warmth seemed to penetrate the gloomy house. Shadows hovered in the corners, growing suddenly larger, like monsters leaping across the floor, then contracting, waiting for just the right moment to take over the room. An aching chill settled over the large gothic mansion as the wind howled outside, whispering secrets of lost ships, death, and destruction.

Inside, two women were seated at a table, a solitary taper burning between them. An old lace cloth covered the table, dripping over the corners like the web of a mammoth spider, and dust-encrusted draperies clung to the windows as if afraid to let go. The old lady, with her hair the color of spun sugar and her sweet smile, gazed anxiously into the guttering candle flame, while the younger woman across from her closed her eyes and hummed thoughtfully. Three brilliantly colored tarot cards were faceup on the tablecloth, and before them, a magical crystal ball.

"Is it Jack? Have you made contact?" The older woman leaned closer, excitement shining on her face. She twisted the lace of the expensive gloves in her hands, knotting them between her ringless fingers, and tried to ignore the frightening presence of the house. "I've heard of your powers. Martha Cummings told me how you helped her. And the Greyson sisters, why, their tale of contacting their long-lost brother is amazing!"

The other woman did not respond. She appeared to be listening to some hidden voice within herself. Rocking back and forth, she repeated some secret chant, concentrating on the images before her. Outside, the wind moaned, ending in a sorrowful wail that seemed to die in the loft of the trees.

Shivering, the older woman picked up one of the cards as if to distract herself. "What do these mean? Have you selected them for some purpose? This one with the woman holding the bird is pretty, isn't it? Why, it rather looks like me. Good gracious, this one with the swords is rather frightening!"

Jennifer Appleton opened her clear gray eyes and sighed in mute frustration. The dim candlelight revealed a face, although not beautiful by conventional standards, brimming with character, from her thickly lashed gaze to her short, square chin and burnished gold hair. The freckles she'd hated as a child still dusted her nose, while her Cupid's-bow mouth had never become more firm with age. Now her nose wrinkled with impatience and her eyes seemed to bore through the dotty society woman before her.

"Mrs. Forester, I must insist that you remain silent! I cannot promise that I can contact your dead husband, but I will certainly try. If I can't, I still may be able to discern some advice for you, or a message from the other side. But you must let me concentrate!"

"Oh, I am sorry, dear," the old woman said softly. Her fingers stopped fretting with the gloves. "Please call me Mary. I will try to be quiet."

Jennifer closed her eyes once more. Rocking back and forth in the chair, she began humming again, the sound strange and haunting in the shadowy gloom. The hair rose on the back of Mary's neck as the house seemed to take on a life of its own, echoing Jennifer's quiet tune. Frightened, she leaned closer, the gloves finally still.

"I see someone," Jennifer whispered. Mary gasped, her fingers tightening on the arms of the chair. Jennifer's head rolled back and forth, and her eyes focused on the crystal ball. "I see him! Tell me, is he a handsome man, dark of face and hair?"

"That's him! Jack, oh, dear Lord, Jack!" The older woman gasped. "What does he say? Does he look good? Is he all right where he is?"

"He says he's fine," Jennifer moaned softly, closing her eyes once more. "He wants you to know that he loves you and misses you. . . ."

"Oh, my dear husband!" Mary's eyes filled with tears. "Tell him that I love him, that I miss him, also!"

Jennifer nodded. Pain seemed to fill her, for she hugged her arms to her torso, her moan trailing off into a wrenching sob. Her brow furrowed, and when she spoke, her voice had deepened, sounding strange and guttural like a man's. "Mary . . . my sweet Mary. I know you love me, but the time has come for you to move on. Remarry, my love, and find happiness."

Stunned, Mary Forester held her handkerchief to her lips as she heard her husband's voice. "Jack! It is you! How can you say that? Oh, Jack, there was never anyone else for me! How could I love again?"

Jennifer groaned as if the emotions that filled her had become too intense. On cue, a harpsichord wailed somewhere in the old house, and a ghostly sound emanated from the walls. The chandelier trembled overhead, throwing dancing prisms of light about the room.

"Oh! I'm frightened!" Mary trembled, covering her face with her hands. "What is that?"

"You have angered him." Jennifer sighed. Her own voice was back. "You must listen to counsel from the other side. It is quite an effort for them to cross back over and try to communicate."

"I'm so sorry!" Mary looked frightened as the eerie music continued.

"Your husband refuses to speak again. He says you will be with him one day, but you must follow his advice. Be happy. Seek another spouse. He knows your heart is true, and he will look for you when it is your time. But he warns, do not do anything rash. If so, he will not be able to find you again."

"Yes, I will listen. I will do as Jack says."

The music faded away. Jennifer opened her eyes, looking around the room as if unable to remember where she was. Her disoriented gaze fell on Mary Forester, and she slumped into the chair, as if the effort of moving even her head had cost her dearly. She smiled in gratitude as her sisters, Winifred and Penelope, entered the room, turning up the gaslights and bringing tea.

Mary rose and hugged Jennifer. Her eyes misted with emotion. "It was my Jack. Through you, I spoke to him. How can I ever thank you?"

"It was nothing," Jennifer whispered humbly. Her voice betrayed a raspy quality, and she gratefully accepted a teacup from her sister.

"Nothing! It was magnificent! Jack spoke to me, and advised me to wed again. Can you imagine that?"

"I think that's excellent advice." Jennifer's younger sister, Penelope, grinned. "After all, one husband is hardly enough for any woman!"

"What she means is, you need to think seriously about what you heard," Jennifer said, giving her sister a sharp glance. "It has been my experience that ghosts seldom speak unless they truly need to convey a message. You've been fortunate enough to hear such a message. Please listen."

"I will." The woman nodded.

"Actually, it would be advisable for you to marry, as long as your interests are protected." Winifred, the older sister, said, a serious look on her face. "I've been reading up on women's rights. Some states have enacted legislation to permit a married woman to own property separately from her husband. Such conditions would be ideal for you, as an officer's widow, undoubtedly with means."

"Winifred is studying law," Jennifer explained as Mary's brow wrinkled in confusion. "She can help you with some of these issues."

"I see." Mary sipped her tea, then looked up at the three sisters gratefully. "I'm so relieved to have come. You see, another man has asked for my hand, but I didn't feel right about accepting because of Jack. I was . . . thinking of taking my own life," she continued, taking a deep breath and wiping her eyes. "I just couldn't cope anymore. But now—"

"Now you are free to wed," Jennifer said gently.

The woman rose, taking Jennifer's hands in her own. "You don't know what this means to me. Money couldn't begin to compensate for the peace you've given me."

Jennifer's smile froze as she envisioned the woman paying her with some heirloom that meant nothing to anyone but her. She watched in anticipation as the woman fumbled with the jet buttons of her pocket, then withdrew a checkbook. She scrawled something on the ledger, then folded the check in half and handed it to Jennifer.

"Please, take it. You know, I won't accept 'no' for an answer! I am a wealthy woman, and all of the ministers and physicians I have consulted together have not provided me with the peace you have. You've saved my life, really and truly."

Jennifer breathed a sigh of relief as she pocketed the offering, and Mary picked up her cape. "Now, I must be going. I will highly recommend you to my friends. You are a saint, my dear, a veritable saint. God bless you all!"

Mary disappeared through the door just before the three sisters burst into laughter.

"You were wonderful, Winifred. I swear I can still hear that music! And the chandelier moving worked out fantastically, Penelope!" Jennifer's eyes teared from chuckling.

"And you outdid yourself with the messages from her husband." Penelope grinned, glancing into the mirror and smoothing an invisible lock of hair. "I wanted to marry the old geezer myself!"

"The harpsichord was a nice touch," Winifred agreed. "And we got lucky that Aunt Eve was out. I don't know how much longer we can keep fooling her that we are putting on plays for our friends."

"I don't know where she thinks the money comes from." Jennifer shook her head. "For Aunt Eve, it's just sort of magically there."

"It almost wasn't tonight. For a minute there I didn't think Mrs. Forester was going to pay you. She seemed like a nice woman, but we've been taken advantage of more than once," Penelope remarked indignantly. "You'd think when you provide an honest service, you'd at least collect honest pay."

"Penelope," Winifred remarked dryly, "we are charlatans. You and I make the noises, I play the harpsichord, and Jenny does the rest."

Penelope seemed taken aback for a moment, but recovered quickly. "But there's more to it than that! Jennifer does give them a reading! We understand what it's like to lose someone you love! Why, we provide comfort, amusement, entertainment, and hope, all for the price of a box of bonbons. We are these ladies' confidantes, friends, alienists . . ."

"Legal advisors," Winifred added.

"And marital ministers, all in one! Tell me Mary Forester didn't feel better when she left here." Penelope turned a demanding eye on her sister.

"You're right, Penny, I daresay." Jennifer drew up a another chair. She sat back down, then planted her feet on the vacant seat before her as if it were a footstool. "Thank God for us all that I read that newspaper account of how popular spiritualism has become. Otherwise, I don't know how we would have kept body and soul intact after our parents died, we were so poor." She sipped Winifred's tea, glancing around at their aunt's rickety house. "But all that's changed. Now we can pay our creditors. Penelope, you can afford a new dress, and you, Winnie, all the books you want. I even think there's a possibility for that college money you so desperately wanted, and maybe, if everything goes as planned, Penny can make her debut!"

The three sisters hugged each other. In the dim light, it was obvious that Penelope was the beauty of the Appleton sisters. Golden blond, with a china doll complexion and huge blue eyes, she was well aware of her charms and practiced them on every male without qualms.

Winifred was her polar opposite. Tall, slender, and dark blond, her eyes were a perplexing hazel and had a way of staring coolly through a suitor's ardent words. She was the scholar, always buried in a book, and if the local girls called her a bluestocking, she couldn't have cared less.

But if Penelope was the beauty and Winifred the brains, Jennifer was the soul of the Appleton sisters. It was she who held them together, who refused to let them get sent to an orphanage. It was Jennifer who convinced their eccentric Aunt Eve to let them stay with her in her rundown mansion, Twin Gables, on the East Side of New

York. And it was Jennifer who saw a way to make the current occult fascination into a business, an occupation they managed to keep hidden from their aunt.

The door opened and Aunt Eve stepped inside. An elderly widow with soft white hair peeping from beneath her bonnet and a huge bustle adorning the back of her black dress, Aunt Eve looked like a genuine fairy godmother. She beamed at the girls, removing her bonnet, and if she noticed the eerie trappings and tarot cards that had mysteriously appeared in the room, she didn't mention them.

"Celia Weathermere sends her regards. She is such a lovely woman, and her son is so nice! He's always asking for you, Penelope. He wanted me to bring his card, but I refused, as it would have been most improper. Was the play successful this evening?"

Jennifer nodded, rising to help Aunt Eve with her shawl. Penelope rolled her eyes at the mention of Celia's son and offered a fresh cup of tea, while Winifred sent Eve a genuinely warm smile. They were all grateful to this woman for her kindness, even if Eve did seem a little bewildered at times by her rambunctious charges. It was Aunt Eve's most fervent wish to see them all happily wed, and she constantly quoted etiquette books in an effort to guide them along the path to marital bliss.

"No, thank you, dear, I think I'll just go on to bed. Penelope, you look a little peaked. Perhaps a dose of my medicinal tea will help. And Jenny, you look dead tired. Don't stay up too late. Good night, dears."

As soon as their aunt retired, Jennifer dipped into her pocket and deftly opened the check that Mary Forester had given her. When she saw what Mary had written, she choked on her tea, forcing Winifred to rush to her side and pound her back. Her eyes watering, she held up the check for her sister to see.

"My word!" Winifred leaned closer, adjusting her spectacles. "It is written for one hundred dollars!"

"Hurrah!" Penelope danced around the room, while Jennifer sent her a stern look.

"We can't possibly accept this," Jennifer said, rereading the check as if the numbers might disappear. "I told her my rate is ten dollars."

"Well, she obviously thinks you are worth more, and who are we to disagree?" Penelope argued prettily. "The lady wanted you to have it. She's rich, and she gave it to you of her own accord. We could do so much with that money."

"Legally, Penny is right," Winifred remarked after a long pause. "You rendered a service, and Mary Forester agreed to pay a prescribed fee. If she chose to give you more of her own free will, you are not wrong to accept it."

Jennifer sighed, then pocketed the check once more. "I suppose you're right, and we do need the money. Mary Forester is certainly wealthy enough, and knows what she wants to do with her own money. I just have an odd feeling about this. Somehow, I don't think this will be the end of it."

THE STATELY NEW York brownstone looked shuttered and quiet. Gabriel Forester stood at the door of his mother's house, admiring the polished white marble steps that gleamed softly in the fading sunlight, the brass doorknob and hinges, the Georgian-style window that curved over the door like an arched brow. The house was nearly identical to a dozen others that crowded the street. All of them were well kept and clean, reminders of the benefits of prosperity and wealth.

Yet, although there was nothing sad about the house in its appearance, Gabriel felt an overwhelming pain as he walked slowly up the steps. He hadn't been here in over two years, hadn't wanted to come back after his father's death. He took care of his mother, loved her, but he was able to deal with neither his own memories, nor his mother's preoccupation with her husband's passing.

But he couldn't avoid the place forever. He had known this day would come, that his mother couldn't continue to visit him at his offices. She needed his advice on some investment matters, and there were just too many documents for her to carry. He had to go to her home, his home.

The butler lost his sedate expression when he opened the door, and a broad smile creased his face. "Master Gabriel!" He recovered quickly, then resumed his formal stance. "The mistress will be so glad to see you. Do come in, sir."

Gabriel accompanied James into the parlor. He averted his eyes from the mantel, where his mother had insisted upon placing every photograph she possessed of John Forester. It looked like a shrine, an eerie memorial suited more to a church than to a home. He'd said as much, but his mother refused to take them down, claiming they brought her comfort. He stood with his back to the fireplace, fighting the riot of emotions that threatened to overwhelm him.

John Forester had been a gentleman. There was no other word that could so aptly describe him. He never turned away a man looking for help, even if he gave up his own dinner to provide it. He didn't understand his son, who was far more interested in finance than art, investments rather than intellectual discussions. He reminded Gabriel of the plantation owners in the south, content to sip mint juleps while the world crashed around them.

Fortune had initially been good to his father, for he'd invested early in marble mining, never realizing that the newly formed New York aristocracy would demand the elegant stone for their doorsteps, their floors, their offices and churches. Yet even with an overwhelming backlog of orders, he had nearly run the company into the ground. When it was almost bankrupt, Gabriel took over, and made the cuts and reductions in cost needed to survive.

Although he experienced tremendous success, his father never forgave him. A year later, when John Forester died of heart failure, some speculated that it was brought on by the crisis in his business. Although his mother never gave the slightest indication that she felt that way, she'd never been the same. Mary Forester had arranged the funeral, smiled at the guests, and accepted their condolences, but she withdrew within herself like a flower forever closed. She was only a shell of the woman he'd known all his life.

He heard his mother's footsteps and turned, fully expecting to see the broken woman who appeared at his office every other Monday morning. He braced himself, picturing her black dress, her parchment-like face wrinkled with sorrow, her bonnet enveloping her like a shroud. His mouth dropped when she practically bounced into the room, her eyes alight with excitement, her cheeks blooming. She looked like a healthy young girl instead of a grief-stricken old woman. She hugged him, and he smelled violet water, a scent that always reminded him of her and this house.

"James, fetch some tea! I prayed just this morning that you would come today. You see," she looked at him shyly, "I have something to tell you."

Stunned, Gabriel sank into a chair, shaking his head. "Mother, are you . . . well? You don't have a fever?" He felt her hand, but it was cool.

She giggled, the sound like rippling water. The servant returned, silently laying out tea. She smiled at him, and continued when he left the room. "No, silly, I'm just fine! Wonderful, perhaps. The most magnificent thing has happened. But let me start with my news. I'm going to marry Robert Wood." She sat across from him, dressed in lemon-sprigged muslin, looking like a schoolgirl with a wonderful secret.

"What?" The teacup he'd accepted tumbled to the floor and he gaped at his mother. "Isn't he a pauper?"

"Robert Wood has been a very good friend to myself and your father," his mother said defensively. "I had initially refused him," she continued, "out of respect for your father's memory. But the most wonderful thing happened! I saw Jack and spoke to him. He wants me to wed, can you imagine?"

"What?" Gabriel couldn't take his eyes from his mother. He couldn't believe what he was hearing. For a moment he thought she had gone mad, and he closely examined her eyes for dilation. They looked fine. Her breathing had quickened, but from excitement rather than illness. "You . . . spoke to my father?" he asked cautiously.

"Yes. Oh, I'm sorry. I've ruined my story by starting at the end. But that's all old news. This is the happiest day of my life!"

Gabriel tried to concentrate as his mother, brimming with joy, explained her recent encounter. "Remember that spiritualist I mentioned to you? She really is an amazing girl. I went to see her last week and she contacted Jack. I'd been so afraid that he would think . . . that I no longer loved him." Mary paused for a moment, her eyes filling with tears. Gabriel saw the old expression return to her face and he leaned forward, touching her hand.

"Go on, dear. Tell me what happened."

Mary nodded, touching her eyes with her handkerchief. "Anyway, the spiritualist acted as a medium and brought him back to speak to me. He insisted that I wed again, and said he understood completely! Oh, Gabriel, if you only knew what it meant to see him one more time, and to know, really know, that he is content with this! The woman gave me such peace of mind, I paid her extra!"

"How much extra?" Gabriel fought the fury that swept over him. He was beginning to understand, all right, and he didn't like what he was understanding at all. Good God, this spiritualist, this charlatan, had taken full advantage of his poor mother's grief!

"Oh, just a hundred dollars. Gabriel, why are you looking at me like that? It was worth every cent!"

"Dear—" Gabriel struggled to stay calm. He recalled the suspicious check, the odd numbers he'd seen in the bankbook, and Mary's secret new friends. Outrage flooded through him. He'd heard of these spiritualists, who took advantage of grieving widows and milked them for every last dime. He forced himself to speak evenly, but inwardly swore it wouldn't happen to his mother. "Don't you realize you've been cheated? This phony tea-leaf reader has absconded with one hundred dollars of your personal savings! Tell me everything. How often did you see this woman? Who is she? Where does she live?"

"Jennifer Appleton is worthy of a fortune, a king's ransom, I would say," Mary insisted. "There is nothing phony about her. You have to meet her, Gabriel, then you would understand. She is gifted, a very holy woman. There is no one like her."

"Miss Appleton, whatever she is, is not worth the security for your old age," Gabriel said grimly.

"I am secure," Mary said naïvely. "I have a house, a future husband, and James. What else do I need?"

"You have a future husband who is penniless, you're pouring money into some charlatan's pocket, and if you continue at this rate, you won't be able to afford James. Thank God I've paid for the house, or you'd probably lose that as well." Gabriel rose in frustration. He accepted his hat from the butler, who had deftly appeared, and put it on with angry determination.

His mother rose in alarm. "Gabriel! You frighten me with that look! Where are you going?"

"I'm going to pay Miss Jennifer Appleton a visit. Don't worry, I won't do anything rash. I just want to explain a few things to her. By the time I'm finished, you are the last person she will swindle."

CHAPTER 2

"PENELOPE, I DON'T see why I have to participate in such nonsense. I think my hair looks fine as is."

Jennifer scowled as Penelope approached with a pair of curling tongs in her mittened hand. Her sister looked like a woman on a mission and she determinedly held out the tongs, which glowed from the fire.

"Because your hair is as straight as a stick and totally unsuitable," Penelope replied, not put off at all by Jennifer's reluctance. "Curled bangs are all the rage, and you would look so much nicer with a little softness around your face. Now put your chin up."

"She is right, dear," Eve said, lending her support to Penelope's cause. The parrot, a two-foot-high bird that screeched intermittently and pulled on young ladies' hair, squawked in apparent agreement. Eve was forever trying to coax the bird to speak, but he remained as obstinately silent as ever, even as she offered him a nut. "And you do need to get out more, and meet some nice young men!" she continued. "The Rutherfords' ball next month will be just the thing! I don't know how you managed invitations, but all the right people attend, and all of the most eligible gentlemen. I daresay you will have a wonderful time."

Jennifer stuck her tongue out at Penelope, but let her apply the little papers to her hair. "The only reason I'm going along with this is for business," she said stiffly. "We were invited because Mary Forester sponsored us. We've gotten quite a few invitations due to her recommendations. She is a wonderful testimonial, and through her I can find quite a few rich new supporters. That makes great sense to me."

"She is spreading the word all over town," Winifred confirmed. Glancing up at Aunt Eve from the text of *The Law Review*, she continued in an emphatic tone, "By the time we get to the ball, everyone will have heard how successful our *performance* was."

Jennifer peered up at her aunt, carefully watching her reaction. Aunt Eve offered the parrot another nut, then smiled at her nieces. "I think it's so nice that you girls are entertaining yourselves with these theatricals. And what a clever idea! Who would have thought that a traditional evening entertainment would yield money? Most young ladies paint china or teach as governesses, but this is so much nicer. I daresay, even *Good Morals and Gentle Manners* would approve."

Jennifer sighed in relief, and Winifred went back to her books. The bird watched suspiciously as Penelope applied the tongs to her sister's hair, and a strange little hiss sounded in the worn parlor. Winifred sniffed, then glanced around the room, her face puckered.

"What is that odd smell? Aunt Eve, did you leave the teakettle burning again?"

Penelope gasped as smoke curled from the tongs. She quickly clamped down on the handle, forgetting her mitt, then screeched in pain. Dropping the handle of the tongs, she sucked on her finger, dancing from foot to foot.

"Will you get these things off me?" Jennifer attempted to do so herself, but only wound up with a scorched finger as well.

"I'm trying." Penelope picked up the mitt and removed the tongs. Everyone heard her indrawn breath as she surveyed the damage.

"Oh, my heavens . . ." Winifred began, dropping her book. She stared at Jennifer, pity and sympathy written across her classic features.

"What? What's wrong?" Jennifer gasped as she picked up Penelope's mirror. "My hair! Look at it! Look what you've done! My poor hair!"

"I know! I guess the tongs were too hot!"

"But I thought you knew how to do this!"

"I saw Margaret Flemming do it, but I didn't see how long she heated the tongs! Oh Jenny, I'm so sorry! Your beautiful hair!"

The sisters gathered around her consolingly, while Jennifer surveyed her burned curls. A sob tightened in her throat as she saw the frizzled ends and smelled the horrid stench. Not vain by any means, she was still female enough to feel dismay as her one real beauty lay destroyed, wrapped around the ends of the hateful tongs.

As her sisters and aunt commiserated with her, the door burst open and a blast of north wind came with it. Aunt Eve shivered and reached for her spectacles as a young man strode into the parlor. Penelope gasped, then looked again with renewed interest, while Winifred surveyed the new arrival shrewdly. Jennifer spun to face him, outraged, but something about his manner kept her from giving him a well-deserved dressing-down. His gaze swept across the four women.

"Sir, what is the meaning of this?" Aunt Eve asked sharply.

The man ignored her, turning intuitively to the woman he sought. "Which one of you is Miss Jennifer Appleton?" he demanded, although he was already staring right at her.

"I . . ." Her voice quavered. Somehow she managed to squeak, "I am Jennifer."

"Good." The man ignored the indignant squawking of the parrot. "I am Gabriel Forester, and I've just come from my mother. I understand you convinced her that you have some sort of powers, and that you can contact the dead. She even believes that you were able to speak to my father, and that his ghost appeared in this house! I think it shameful that you would take advantage of my mother's grief, and I intend to expend every last ounce of energy required to see you exposed as a charlatan and a fake."

He slammed a fist down on the table. Jennifer jumped, her heart in her throat. She glanced at Aunt Eve, but thankfully, her aunt seemed more bewildered than anything else. Her gaze swung back to Gabriel. Although she was terrified, a part of her was also fascinated. It didn't escape her notice that Gabriel was extraordinarily handsome, almost angelic. He had dark wavy hair, an astonishing face, a firm chin, a classic nose, and an incredibly sensuous mouth.

Yet he was also coldly furious. His beautiful blue eyes blazed, and his jaw was as tight as a harp string. A red flush covered his face, a vein protruded from his neck, and his hands were knotted so firmly that he seemed tempted to strike someone. So magnificent was his rage that even fearless Jennifer had trouble responding. Having no brothers and few male acquaintances, she knew nothing of men or their tempers, nor did she have the first idea of how to calm him. He seemed to be fighting to control his anger, and Jennifer prayed that he would be successful. In a moment, she seemed to get her wish, for the florid suffusion of his face faded and wonder replaced the wrath. He stared at Jennifer in disbelief, then leaned closer, as if not certain he could trust his own eyes.

"Miss," he asked, his voice rich with astonishment, "what in God's name have you done with your hair?"

Jennifer's hand flew to her tresses, and she self-consciously fingered the fried bangs. Flushing crimson, she tried to smooth them to one side. To her credit, she never lost her composure.

"I had a little accident with the curling iron." She shrugged, as if such happenings were commonplace, then rose to confront him. His arms were still braced against the table on either side of her waist, but she determinedly ignored them, as well as the heat she could feel from the intimacy of his stance. "Is there anything else you'd like to know?"

She had audacity. Fury died in him as he saw her gallant attempt to remain in control. He had to admit he was surprised at her appearance, and not just because of her hair. Gabriel didn't know what he'd expected, but a gypsy with earrings and tattered clothing would probably have suited better than this trio of attractive young ladies and a little old woman who looked like everyone's grandmother. The latter appeared terrified; nevertheless, she stood up, clutching her salts bottle, and stared him down like an aging mother hen determined to save her chicks.

"Mr. Forester, I believe you've had your say. I must ask you to leave my house this minute! This is disgraceful, barging in here and accusing my niece of some kind of sorcery . . . I know your mother, and she would be ashamed to think her son behaved in such a manner!"

"Come, Auntie," Winifred said, sending Gabriel a scornful look and putting her arm around the elderly lady, who was trembling. "Please don't upset yourself so. He's not worth it. I'll get you some tea. Mr. Forester, please remove yourself before we return." With a dignified air, she led Eve to the kitchen.

Embarrassment flooded through Gabriel. He thought of himself as a gentleman, and had a reputation as such. He wasn't used to upsetting sweet old ladies. He could scarcely imagine his mother's reaction when she heard, and he winced at the thought. His mortified gaze swept back to Jennifer.

"I'm sorry to have upset your aunt, but I have no intention of going anywhere without my mother's money," he said meaningfully, pleased to see that in spite of her obstinate stance, there was a tremor in her pretty hands. "She told me that she paid you, and I want that money returned."

"Mrs. Forester came here of her own free will," Jennifer declared. "She understood my fee, and contracted me for a reading. There are many other spiritualists in New York, and she could have made these arrangements with anyone. I provided her with direction, comfort, and sympathy, which she seemed to need badly. She was considering ending her life when she came here, and I am proud to say I was able to give her a reason to live. She chose to pay me more than my fee, but that was her decision. If her money isn't worth her life to you, then I think you need to reexamine your own values."

His rage returned, intensified by her implication that he had failed his mother. Gabriel was so furious that for a moment, he couldn't speak. When he finally managed to get the words out, they were a growl through clenched teeth. "Miss, my patience is nearly exhausted. I was hoping to be able to reason with you, but I can see that is impossible. You have bilked my mother out of her money under the most vile of pretexts, using the love she had for her late husband as bait. That I cannot abide. The money aside, I can neither stand by and see you succeed in such a way, nor watch you continue cheating others like this. As if someone could really contact the dead! Miss, you will hear from my attorney!" With that, Gabriel slammed the door behind him, and the whole house trembled.

Outside, the chill air did little to cool Gabriel's rage. He stood on the street, glaring at the spooky gothic house, wishing to hell that Jennifer Appleton were a man so he could wring her neck. But she wasn't a man, she was a woman, and a charming one at that.

He had to stop her. She'd practically admitted that she was a fake when she tried to justify her fee to him. But she never once claimed to have seen his father, nor to be able to contact the dead. She was more clever than most fortune-tellers, in that she stuck as close to the truth as possible. That in itself would make her hard to convict in court.

His fists tightened as he recalled the other things she'd said. His mother, suicidal! Anxiety swept through him, immediately replaced by renewed outrage. Of course she was making that up. If his mother had been depressed, he would have known. While it was true that Mary hadn't been herself, she hadn't seemed that upset. Guilt knotted his stomach, and he immediately pushed aside the notion. No, Jennifer was just using his self-blame and his concern for his mother, knowing that it would confuse him. Like any worthy opponent, she held a good card and knew how to play it.

He saw her shadow pass in front of the curtains. Her dark silhouette was curvaceous and enticing, something he hadn't wanted to notice in the house and didn't want to notice now. He saw her pause at the lamp, her face illuminated by the light, and he thought it the loveliest picture he'd ever seen. Even though her sister was more classically beautiful, it was Jennifer's fire and personality that made her so bewitching—something she obviously knew, he thought. And used. So intent was he on watching her that he didn't notice the policeman who strolled up the walk.

"Can I help you, laddie?"

Gabriel winced at the brogue, then turned toward the man. He was a burly, ruddy-faced Irishman. White hair peeped from beneath his cap, and heavy jowls resided beside a stern mouth. His nightstick twirled as he paused beneath the streetlight and looked curiously at Gabriel.

"No. I mean, I was just trying to straighten out a business matter."

The policeman's expression became suspicious as he took in Gabriel's expensive coat and polished shoes. He glanced toward the house. His eyes widened at the sight of Jennifer's softly curving silhouette.

"I see. Business matter? Why don't you come along with me to the station, laddie."

Gabriel pulled his arm away. "You don't understand! Do you realize that these women are charlatans? They say they can contact the dead!"

"The dead, you say? Look, fella, I don't want no trouble, but there's been reports of a Peeping Tom in this neighborhood. I'd like to ask you a few questions if you don't mind."

"I most certainly do mind! I am a law-abiding citizen, and these women are taking advantage of poor, innocent people! If you did your job, this wouldn't go on!"

The policemen turned beet red, and Gabriel suddenly questioned his own wisdom. But it was too late. The officer blew a whistle, and was quickly joined by an equally burly comrade who took Gabriel's opposite arm.

"But!—"

"You can explain it all to the chief, lad. Now, we don't want to have to use force, but resisting arrest is a serious charge. Come along quietly."

The two officers lugged him toward the station, while Gabriel argued fruitlessly. He shook his fist at the window, blaming one woman for all of this. He saw the curtain move, and in his mind's eye, he could see her laughing behind it.

"THE POLICE GOT him!" Jennifer chuckled as if she'd just witnessed the best joke of the season. She laughed so hard she cried. "Thank goodness that policeman was outside! This couldn't have been better! I'll wager he's fit to be tied!"

"That scoundrel! A spot in jail would teach him some manners! I am astonished that Mary Forester would have raised such a son." Aunt Eve shook her head and tsked, sipping the hot tea that Winifred had provided. "What on earth was he talking about, ghosts and some such?"

"I think he meant our theatricals," Winifred said quickly, giving her sisters a sharp glance. "We performed Dickens for Mary Forester. Perhaps she was alarmed."

"That's still no excuse for his behavior." Aunt Eve sniffed. "No calling card, no flowers, no appointment! I don't know what the world's coming to."

"I think he's handsome," Penelope remarked with the air of a true connoisseur. "Did you see those eyes? They looked like a winter sky." She sighed dreamily.

"You think every man in sight is handsome," Jennifer said. "Imagine him accusing us of taking advantage of his mother!"

"The fact that he is obnoxious doesn't make him any less handsome," Penelope said indignantly, miffed at Jennifer's implication. "He seemed very taken with you, though."

"Taken? I think he wanted to strangle me." Jennifer self-consciously touched her burned curls, wincing as she replayed the scene in her mind. Although she wouldn't admit it, she was secretly pleased with Penelope's observation. Gabriel Forester was handsome, but more than that, he did something to her. Her body still tingled just from the memory of his close proximity, and she was seized with a longing to feel those arms around her in a much more intimate embrace.

"Yes. As a matter of fact, I think he was very interested, even though he doesn't want to be. I believe if you showed the slightest reciprocation, you could have that man eating out of your hand, which would also make him less likely to cause us trouble," Penelope said practically.

A sudden thought made Jennifer look up from the

window. The same thought came to Penelope at the same time, and Jennifer's face lit up.

"Do you really think . . ." Jennifer asked shyly, watching her sister closely, "that a man like that would ever be interested in someone like me?"

"Good heavens, yes!" Penelope exclaimed, coming to stand behind Jennifer. She put her arms around her sister. "Dear, he would be blind not to be taken in by your charm! Are you going to try to entice him, then?"

Jennifer blushed, but a small smile crept over her face. "He is handsome. And I think it's nice that he's so concerned for his mother. Many young men aren't nearly so gallant these days."

"Jennifer Appleton!" Aunt Eve exclaimed, rising to her feet in astonishment. "You cannot seriously be thinking of encouraging that man's attentions!"

Jennifer looked at her aunt, then at Penelope and Winifred, who appeared solemn, then back to her aunt. She sighed and shook her head in the negative.

"No, of course not! How could you think such a thing?"

"I daresay not!" Aunt Eve huffed, fluffing out her shawl in an uncanny imitation of the parrot. "Gabriel Forester is no gentleman, that much is for certain!"

Jennifer nodded, appearing properly chastised. She and Penelope bid their aunt good night, then slowly climbed the stairs. As soon as they were out of earshot, Penelope closed the door and turned to her sister with a huge grin.

"Well? Are you going to do it?"

"Why not?" Jennifer grinned back, her mischievous face brightening at the thought. "After all, he is good-looking, and rich as can be. I am attracted to him, too, much as I blush to admit it. It makes perfect sense. And as you say, if Gabriel, well, comes to care for me, he is less likely to press charges."

"Jenny! It's such a wonderful idea! We'll have to be careful—I sense he could be a formidable enemy. But he is still a man for all that."

"So you'll help me?"

"Of course! It will be great fun. Darling, I've been dying to do this for years. I'll fix your hair, we'll get you some rouge . . . just a touch, don't make that face. We'll get you a few pretty gowns. Gabriel won't be able to help himself!"

Jennifer wasn't so certain, but found herself excited by the prospect. She withdrew one of Aunt Eve's etiquette books from the desk, then flipped it open to the section about courtship. "First, we need a plan. We know nothing about him, other than that he's Mary's son."

"We need to know where he goes, what he likes, who he sees," Penelope agreed. Her brows flew up in inspiration and she dove into the stack of invitations in the crystal bowl before her. "I have it!" She waved a cream-colored envelope decorated with cabbage roses. "It's an invitation to call at the Billings'!"

"The Billings!" Jennifer's nose wrinkled. "Why, they are the most boring girls I've ever known!"

"Yes, but they know everyone. And they remember us from when we were children, before Mama and Papa died. I hear they always have the best gossip. One session with them, and we'll know everything we wish about your Mr. Forester." She rubbed her hands together at the thought. "By the time we're through, Gabriel Forester will be nothing more than a love-struck swain. The man doesn't stand a chance."

CHAPTER 3

THE FOLLOWING AFTERNOON, Penelope stood outside the Billings' town house with Jennifer, who was impatiently tugging at her too-small gloves. Penelope dutifully rang the bell, and when a servant answered, placed her violet-sprigged card on the tray. They were ushered into a hallway while they waited to see if the Misses Billing were "at home."

Jennifer fidgeted, and Penelope rolled her eyes at her sister. This meeting was the first step to securing their place in society, a goal that was extremely important to her. She reached up and tucked a few burned curls under Jennifer's bonnet, smiling as Jennifer scowled. Jennifer could be so exasperating at times, but for all that, Penelope loved her.

"Now don't wrinkle your face. We must look our best! The Misses Billing will be a great asset to us. We were fortunate to get an invitation to tea. It was only due to Mary Forester's help, and we can't waste the opportunity."

Jennifer nodded. "I know, I just hate this sort of thing. I never know what to talk about with girls like these. They seem like magpies, chattering about dresses and such. But don't worry, I'll be nice."

Penelope chewed her lip in concern, knowing that the reddened result would only make her more attractive. But she *was* worried. Jennifer just didn't seem to understand social niceties. She didn't like pretty gowns, didn't appreciate good lace gloves or rich perfumes. Although her sister possessed a natural beauty, she didn't seem interested in her appearance, nor did she want to try to look more beautiful. It was something Penelope never understood.

"Now, when we get inside, stand against the wall so they can't see the tear in your hem," Penelope ordered. "And don't fidget with your gloves."

"This way, ladies." The house servant returned to usher them into the parlor, and Penelope sighed with relief. The Misses Billing had invited them to tea, something that wouldn't have happened just a few months ago. Penelope reminded herself that if her parents had lived, they would be on equal footing with the Billings of the world, but that wasn't the case now. Now, it was only thanks to Jennifer's talent and Mary Forester's endorsement that they harbored any chance at all of entering polite society.

Jane and Elizabeth Billing entered the room, both of them looking plump and well rested, without a care in the world. Jane approached first, her hands extended.

"Penelope! I haven't seen you since we were in grammar school, with that dreadful Mr. Whitcomb! I still feel his ruler on my poor hands. And this must be Jennifer! Come in, we've heard so much about you!"

Penelope smiled and extended her hand, enviously taking in Jane's gorgeous silver tea dress, and Elizabeth's sunny yellow one. Jane's gown, obviously new, was swathed with three kinds of lace that framed the bodice, then tapered off sweetly into a frothy petticoat. Elizabeth's gown was less ornate, but just as expensive, with its taffeta trim and ruching. But both were dressed in the height of fashion, their hair cleverly arranged in upswept hairstyles. Penelope tried hard not to look down at her simple, twice-mended muslin. Her own figure, while better than Elizabeth's, wasn't nearly so artfully displayed, and she deeply envied Jane's kid slippers. She tried not to think of the injustice of it all as Elizabeth patted her cheek fondly, then perched upon a high-backed horsehair love seat with her sister.

"Do tell me everything you've been doing, especially the séance business. Can you really contact the dead? We were so sorry to hear about your parents' accident. I believe Mother sent flowers, but wished we could do more. How is Eve?"

Penelope smiled graciously and replied in just the right manner, grateful that Jennifer had followed her orders and was keeping quiet. A student of the wealthy, Penelope had garnered enough information from the tabloids to know all of the latest doings. She furnished just enough detail about the fortune-telling to arouse interest, and yet remain respectable. She saw Jennifer's approving glance, and she went on eagerly to discuss costume, gardening, and all matter of mundane things that she knew would intensely interest the Billings.

Penelope grew worried once more as they discussed the merits of starch for petticoats and French lace gloves. Jennifer's foot began to tap the floorboards impatiently, but thankfully, the sisters didn't seem to notice. She prayed that Jennifer wouldn't say or do anything inappropriate, and struggled to think of a way to turn the conversation toward their purpose. Fate was with her, for Elizabeth put her cup aside and leaned forward, as if to impart the best gossip.

"I just heard that Charles Howe is back in town. He is not only gorgeous, but he has quite an income from his law firm and the family shipping business. He and Gabriel Forester are good friends, although they are exact opposites. Charles is so gay and funny, while Gabriel is so serious." She giggled. "I haven't told this to anyone, but Charles and I . . ."

"No!" Penelope squealed, giving the girl a hug. From the corner of her eye, she saw Jennifer perk up, her interest returning. "Are you really? Does anyone know?"

"Elizabeth!" Jane said disapprovingly. "You know Mother told you not to say anything until he proposes!"

"I know," Elizabeth said, little deterred. "But although it's not official yet, I can share my excitement, can't I? We've been keeping company for the last three months. Yesterday he sent me roses! If that doesn't show the serious nature of his intentions . . ."

"They were yellow, Elizabeth," Jane said sternly. "Yellow is for friendship. You read too much into these things."

Elizabeth looked like she was ready to cry. Penelope sensed sibling tension in the air, and patted Elizabeth's hand consolingly.

"I'm sure everything will work out just fine. You mentioned Gabriel Forester. I think we know him—isn't he Mary's son?"

"Yes." Elizabeth sniffled, her feelings clearly still injured. "I think him handsome, as well. Apparently, so does someone else. Rumor has it that Gabriel has been seeing Allison Howe."

"No!"

"Yes!" Elizabeth nodded, dabbing her nose delicately with her lace hankie.

"How fascinating," Penelope said. "Do you know Mr. Forester well?"

"Why, yes. Gabriel is a friend of the family. He is handsome as could be, but determined and ruthless. His family's in marble, and they own several newspapers. The Foresters are well respected and wealthy, but Gabriel is the businessman of the family. He was very close to his father. His death hit him hard." Elizabeth sighed.

"I think I recall him," Jennifer said casually, taking Penelope's lead. "Doesn't he live near the park?"

"Yes, he has a splendid town home on the upper East Side, although he is seldom there. Our older brother Stephen is a friend of his, so we hear of him quite often."

Penelope nodded. "I suppose, being a wealthy society man, that he frequents the men's clubs, gambling establishments, and resorts."

"Very seldomly, although I hear both he and Allison are attending the Barrymores' garden party. Gabriel actually spends most of his time at the office. He's very serious, as I was saying, especially about business. And Allison is a good match for him. She is complacent and proper, and has all the right connections. Her family was one of New York's first, and could further his aspirations. Gabriel isn't very affectionate toward her. I think he sees her as a business advantage."

Jane sighed. "I hope my future husband feels more for me than that. Gabriel Forester is a cold one." She shuddered.

"I hear the Barrymores' gardens are lovely," Penelope remarked idly. "I remember them from when we were children."

"Oh, they are!" Elizabeth gushed. "Are you going to be there? Perhaps we could meet. I'd love to introduce you to some of our friends."

"I misplaced the invitation," Penelope said with a sigh, sending the startled Jennifer a sharp look. "I tossed it out with a bunch of uninteresting cards. I feel terrible about it, for we so would have loved to attend."

"I'm certain the Barrymores wouldn't mind in the least if you accompanied us," Jane said, obviously delighted at the prospect. "Everyone is talking about you and would love to see you again."

"Are you certain?" Penelope asked demurely. "I wouldn't want to cause you any inconvenience."

"Nonsense! I'll send the carriage for you. We can all go together. It will be a great party. We look forward to it."

Jane echoed her sister's nod. Penelope stood, and Jennifer instantly did the same. "Thank you. We shall consider doing just that. We really must be going, though. Thank you for the invitation to tea, and please feel free to call on us soon at Twin Gables." Penelope smiled sweetly. "We can show you the séance room."

The sisters looked entranced. "I suppose you have many other engagements today. We certainly shall call on you. And please, make sure you attend our summer lawn fête. Mother puts so much work into it. Absolutely everyone will be there!"

Outside, Penelope and Jennifer walked as quickly as they dared around the corner, not stopping until they were well past the twitching curtains. They hugged each other, laughing so gleefully that tears streamed down their faces.

"Success! Why, Penny, you're a hit! We can go to the Barrymores' party, in a carriage, no less! We'll be able to parlay this visit into dozens of invitations! And mentioning the séance room—that was sheer genius!"

Penelope let Jennifer hug her, but she was pleased for an entirely different reason. The Billings were keys to a world she desperately wanted to enter. And she, Penelope Appleton, had just unlocked that door.

Her happiness disappeared a moment later as another thought occurred. Penelope's smile faded, and the brightness of the previous moment was gone.

"What's wrong?" Jennifer asked.

"We can't go to the party," Penelope said, her voice choked with tears.

"Why ever not?" Jennifer asked impatiently. "We can

go with the Billings, you heard them offer. And the Barrymores would never remember—"

"We don't have anything appropriate to wear," Penelope interrupted, bringing her handkerchief to her nose. "You saw the Billings. Their dresses must have cost a small fortune."

"We have our good Sunday muslins," Jennifer said practically. "Yours is very nice, and the blue color suits you wonderfully—"

Penelope shook her head, the tears sparkling against her cheeks. "It won't do. They would spot us for frauds in a minute. No, unless we have decent costumes, we can't consider going. It would harm our cause more than do us good to show up like paupers."

Jennifer frowned thoughtfully. This was an obstacle neither of them had considered. An idea dawned and she turned slowly to Penelope. "We could . . . I mean, we really have no other choice."

"What?" Penelope cried impatiently.

"In the attic, we have that old trunk full of dresses. We always said someday—"

"You mean Mother's things," Penelope breathed, shocked.

Jennifer nodded. "She would want this, Penny. You know she would. Desperate times call for desperate measures."

"But it's so . . . morbid!" Penelope gasped, pressing her hands to her lips.

"I know. I don't like it either, but I can't come up with anything better. Can you?"

Penelope fought the guilt that swept over her. Jennifer was right—their mother would have wanted this. They had been saving her dresses for a special occasion, such as when one of them wed, but Penelope saw all too clearly that unless they were accepted into society, weddings weren't likely to occur. The time for sentiment had passed. She squared her shoulders and nodded.

"I'll get Aunt Eve to help me. The dresses were designed for hoops, so we'll have to alter them, but the material is all first quality. By the time we attend the party, the Appletons will look just as good as anyone. You'll see."

"I CAN'T BELIEVE they won't do anything! What good is a police force if it won't stand up to three young women?"

Charles Howe chuckled as Gabriel paced the floor, his normally unruffled composure at this moment extremely ruffled. He was seated in Gabriel's immaculate office; every book was in place, every vase perfect, down to a row of letters on his desk carefully positioned so each letterhead could be easily read at a glance. Gabriel himself looked as if he didn't belong. His shirt was not tucked into his trousers properly, his jacket was askew, and a crimson flush washed his face.

"It's not that they won't stand up to them," Charles said, enjoying himself immensely. "The police chief has known Jennifer and her family for years. He heard about her parents' untimely death, and the subsequent orphan state of the three girls. Naturally his sympathies are with Jennifer."

"Charles." Gabriel turned a furious look on his friend. "The woman is a menace. She cheated my mother out of her money with some ridiculous séance! And when I confronted her, she had the audacity to imply that I had neglected my own mother!"

"I see." Charles nodded, well aware of Gabriel's guilt where his mother was concerned. "What was the girl like?"

"Nothing like what I expected," Gabriel admitted, sinking down into a chair in exasperation. "I pictured a lowborn female, even a gypsy dressed in rags. Instead, she's remarkably pretty. In fact, her sister Penelope is one of the most beautiful women I've ever seen."

"Really?" Charles asked drolly. "You do remember that you and *my* sister have . . . an understanding?"

Gabriel scowled at him, observing the way Charles's shoulders were shaking with barely suppressed mirth. "That's not funny. The other one is bookish, and while Jennifer isn't a beauty, there is something about her. What she is, surprisingly enough, is a lady. I didn't expect that."

"I see. So what exactly did the police say?"

"They put me in the back room, insisting I was drunk. I think they also thought me a Peeping Tom, for they accosted me outside Jennifer's window. Do you believe that! I ought to sue them for character assault!"

"And what *were* you doing outside her window?" Charles asked blandly.

"I was—" Gabriel attempted to explain, but felt his own face getting hot once more. He heard Charles laugh, and shot him an unappreciative look. "Believe me, the last thing I have in mind is romancing Jennifer. What I want to do is stop her, scare the hell out of her. Are you certain we have no legal recourse?"

"As your lawyer, I can advise you that we certainly have recourse, especially if you can prove that she swindled your mother. By the way, how much money are we talking about?"

"One hundred dollars."

Charles blinked. "One hundred dollars? Your legal fees may run more than that!"

"It's the principle of the thing," Gabriel insisted. "And I don't want her continuing this, with my mother or anyone else."

"I see," Charles said, hiding a grin. "And do you have proof that she actually took advantage of your mother?"

"My mother paid her to contact the dead, which she believes happened!" Gabriel said hotly. "What more proof do you need?"

"Well, we do have a problem. Your mother doesn't seem to be complaining. In fact, no one is except you." Charles held up his hand to forestall Gabriel's protests. "That doesn't mean we can't do anything. What I will do immediately is write her a letter on my stationery. That should put her off, if she's like most women. They're frightened to death of anything legal. And if that doesn't work, we'll go from there."

Gabriel lifted a frustrated face, and Charles laughed. "Don't worry, Gabe. We'll take your Miss Appleton in hand. Don't worry about a thing."

"Where are you going? To see Elizabeth?" Gabriel asked as Charles picked up his stick.

"No. I'm going out to dine, then I'm returning to my offices," Charles said with a wry grin. "A threatening letter to three charming ladies will take all of my concentration, I'm afraid. The Appleton sisters should receive it by Thursday at the latest. Is that soon enough?"

Gabriel smiled, his relief evident. "Nothing can be too soon for me. I want this woman stopped, Charles. No matter what it takes."

"WHAT IS THIS?" It was Thursday when Jennifer picked up the letter that was lying on a silver dish. The creamy Eton stationery and elegant hand sent a slight shiver up her spine. "Charles Howe, Attorney-at-Law" was inscribed into the left-hand corner. It was obviously a missive of some importance, and she was instantly filled with dread. She sliced the envelope with her letter opener, and as she read the document, the color drained from her face. "Winifred, could you take a look at this?"

Winifred, who had been seated on the floor amid her

books, pushed back her spectacles and took the missive. She stood up, coming closer to the light, examining the watermark, and the elegant handwriting.

"What is it?"

"A letter from Gabriel's attorney. It says if we don't stop what we're doing, they will put us in jail! Winnie, can they do that?"

"I told you that man was no good," Aunt Eve sniffed. "Storming into a young lady's home without so much as a calling card! To think, trying to punish you girls for your little dramas! Why, they would have to jail every household in the city, for all young women are so engaged!"

"Oh, no!" Penelope cried, putting down the bonnet she was stitching. "We're ruined!"

"Hush," Winifred waved her hand impatiently as she scanned the document. The sisters watched her closely, and even Aunt Eve was silent. Winifred's lip curled in distaste as she took in the letterhead and the indignant signature. She scowled as she began the missive, guessing its intent before she was midway through. Yet her expression, bookish and intense, lightened line by line, and by the time she reached the end of the document, seemed almost merry. She folded the letter and grinned at her sisters with satisfaction.

"What? What is it?" Jennifer asked.

"Why, this is the least interesting piece of fiction I've ever read." Winifred chuckled, a sound so unusual that even the parrot squawked.

"Fiction! But it's from the law firm of Charles Howe. He is one of the most important attorneys in the city," Jennifer cried.

"Yes, but nothing he says has any real basis in the law." As her sisters looked at her in confusion, Winifred sighed. "You see, he obviously wrote this letter as a favor to Gabriel, thinking we were a lot of dull misses who wouldn't understand the terminology. Unfortunately for him, I've done extensive reading of legal briefs, so his language doesn't intimidate me. Moreover, what he doesn't say, and what is obvious, is that Mary Forester hasn't complained—only her son." As the trio still stared in puzzlement, Winifred threw up her hands.

"He hasn't a leg to stand on."

Jennifer's worried expression dissolved, and she joined Winifred in laughter. When their chuckles died, Jennifer wiped her eyes.

"I suppose he never counted on the Appletons having their own private legal counsel," Jennifer said with a grin. "So, Attorney Winifred, what is our course of action?"

Winifred, obviously pleased to be able to practice her skills, peered at the letter thoughtfully. "We have several means at our disposal. We can ignore the letter."

"That would be the most proper," Eve said wisely. "A lady never acknowledges an insult, but just pretends she didn't understand."

"But then they will think we are frightened," Jennifer said.

"That is true," Winifred agreed. "It is the cowardly way out, but probably the safest. As your lawyer, I must advise you of all of your options. The other thing we can do is reply, and perhaps point out the areas of weakness in the document. That might quell Mr. Howe, for he obviously doesn't expect such a response. But it might also show him that he isn't dealing with fools."

"He's liable to get angry," Jennifer mused. "Men, from what I observe, don't like to be proven wrong."

"And they tend to shrink from women they view as superiors," Aunt Eve added. "Why, in *Titcomb's Letters to Young People, Single and Married*, he makes just such a point." She eyed her three unmarried nieces with worry.

"Still, I think it our best response." Winifred took off her spectacles and nodded in satisfaction. "I don't see either man as one willing to stop with a letter. If we ignore it and continue, they are liable to keep threatening. Both men have considerable status, and might eventually wear down a judge. No, I think cutting this off at the bud would serve us best."

"And, it may incite Gabriel once more." Jennifer chuckled, catching Penelope's eye. "He might even have to come here again, to let us know how unhappy he is. Wouldn't that be a shame!"

The three girls burst into laughter. Aunt Eve looked at her niece sharply. "You aren't encouraging that man, are you?"

"Why, no," Jennifer said innocently. "I'm simply enjoying the thought of his discomfiture." Feeling her aunt's eyes on her, Jennifer turned quickly to her sister.

"So what, Attorney Winifred, will you do?"

Winifred shrugged, her intelligent gaze gleaming with anticipation. "I shall reply to Mr. Howe's letter, and simply point out the error of his ways. As a fellow attorney, he cannot possibly miss my intention, nor misunderstand the position he is in. He is, after all, threatening three unprotected young women without cause. I've heard enough about Charles Howe to know that his legal reputation is extremely important to him. No matter what favors he owes Gabriel, he will not jeopardize his own career for another man's battle."

She sank down at her desk and picked up her pen with a flourish. Gabriel Forester would not succeed in his attempt to frighten them. Jennifer had worked too hard to find them a means of survival. And she, Winifred, would call on every ounce of her intelligence to fight back. It was a challenge that she looked forward to.

GABRIEL WAS ENJOYING a rare game of billiards when Charles Howe stormed into his club. The door slammed behind him, and he sent Gabriel's partner a look of such intensity that the young man immediately put his cue stick aside.

"I think you have business?" the young man asked. At Charles's curt nod, he backed toward the door. "I'll go freshen our drinks," he said quickly, then disappeared.

"Charles? Is something wrong?" Gabriel straightened in the midst of lining up his next shot. Charles's normally fair complexion was an angry red. His eyes blazed, and his jaw was tightly knotted. He seemed hard-pressed to inhale, and when he finally did, he thrust a document at Gabriel.

"Take a look at that!" he demanded.

Gabriel picked up the letter, vaguely aware of the soft scent of lilac water still clinging to it. He breathed the sweet smell, then, seeing Charles's glare, quickly opened the note. The paper was feminine, trimmed in pretty flowers, but the contents were anything but.

"Dear Sir," it began. "I have in my possession a letter sent to myself and my sisters on your letterhead. I cannot help but assume that someone less talented than yourself must have drawn up such a missive, for surely a man of your extensive legal experience couldn't possibly make such ludicrous mistakes. I am happy to point them out to you and show you the errors of the writer's ways. I am certain you will share in my incredulity and concern. If you care to discuss this further, please contact me at Twin Gables. I am sure that you don't wish your illustrious career besmirched by publishing such a poorly written document, obviously meant to frighten three helpless women. Signed Cordially, Winifred Appleton."

Gabriel scanned the attachment, a listing of Charles's legal errors, but the language was too complicated even for his own businesslike mind to follow. Openmouthed, he turned back to Charles.

"But there must be an explanation! Could they have

hired someone to help them with this? I don't even understand what she's written."

"There is no doubt someone helped them," Charles said furiously. "I don't for a moment believe that a woman wrote this. It would take someone very familiar with the laws of the State of New York to write such a response. Good heavens! You don't suppose they have the backing of Horace or Shane? Only men of their stature could have composed this!"

Charles visibly paled, clearly concerned about his career. Gabriel sighed and shook his head, gesturing to the letter.

"Charles, you're letting your emotions rule you. How could an insignificant tea-leaf reader afford such counsel! The very idea is ridiculous."

Charles calmed somewhat, but he paced the floor of the billiard room, still puzzled. "Then what is the explanation? You don't think they have the backing of the newspapers? She threatens publication."

"No, I don't think they have any backing at all. These girls are as poor as church mice. They don't have any society connections, or we would have heard about them long before this. My mother claims they are of good parentage, but she is infatuated with the girls. Frankly, they are nobodies," Gabriel said, but his own outrage grew apace with Charles's. "Somehow, these women have obtained legal counsel, maybe some ancient lawyer who has been taken in by their mysticism and charm. They probably promised him a second life, or something, in exchange for the letter. That's all."

"Well, I'm going to confront Miss Winifred Appleton," Charles said decisively. "I have an appointment with her next week. I refuse to be cornered like this by a mere woman. The nerve of her, threatening me! By the time I get through with her, Winifred will think my letter a mere pleasant introduction."

Gabriel shook his hand, then cupped the eight ball as Charles stormed out. Tossing the ball into the air, he couldn't help but grin.

Jennifer had brought the wrath of the law down on her head. He'd see who had the last laugh.

CHAPTER 4

THE BARRYMORES' GARDEN party was one of the season's "must show" events. Held outside the city at the family's summer house on Long Island, the party was well attended by the heat-weary Wall Street businessmen and their companions. The women, dressed in the height of fashion, never seemed aware of the weather, even though the heavy dresses they wore, coupled with petticoats, bustles, and panniers, made them swelter in the summer sun. The men were also garbed in their best, eager to show off glinting diamond breast pins, polished walking sticks, and jacquard vests. If, by noon, the women melted like frosted cakes and the men were deluged with sweat, one would only remark that they looked "rosy" or "dewy."

Tables were piled high with food. Servants constantly refreshed the punch, the ices, the cake, and the meats, for food perished quickly in the heat. It seemed as if a continuous line of men carried out the silver dishes, while another line removed them in a meticulous circle. In the center of the table, scented candles repelled insects, while fabulous swan ice sculptures quickly became unrecognizable forms. Tents provided shelter from the sun, and even they were swathed with flowers and chiffon drapes. No opulence was spared, for the Barrymores, like other Victorians, were determined to flaunt their wealth.

Gabriel stood amid a group of his associates, sipping a glass of punch. Allison Howe stood at his side, acting the part of the perfect socialite. Blond and pretty, with thoughtful brown eyes and a winning smile, Allison was much admired among the men and women of her crowd. She was now afire, discussing women's rights with several of the other women, an occupation that the men found amusing.

A woman with a mind, Gabriel thought, silently acknowledging the sympathetic glances of his friends. Yet Allison, he knew, was interested in the suffragette movement because it was fashionable, not for any true beliefs of her own. Pampered from infancy, Allison had the supreme self-confidence that comes from a worry-free existence. She'd gone to the best schools, known the right people, and never experienced financial troubles. It puzzled him sometimes that he didn't love her, but Gabriel didn't believe in love. That was for sentimentalists like his parents. Yes, Allison was groomed to be the perfect society wife, which was exactly what Gabriel was looking for.

He sent her an absent smile, twirling his punch and admiring her social acumen. He couldn't help comparing her to that Appleton creature, the one who'd been plaguing his thoughts all too frequently. Jennifer would be lost at such a gathering, wouldn't even have been invited in the first place. Even now he was frustrated at how quickly she came to mind, and how easily he could picture those luminous eyes and pouting mouth. He chuckled silently, thinking again of Charles's wrath the previous day. He now had a powerful ally in his determination to stop Jennifer Appleton's thievery—the law.

Just as he grinned in smug satisfaction, the face that

he'd been envisioning came into view. For a moment, he was certain he was hallucinating, for there was no way someone like Jennifer Appleton could have entrée to a party like this. His hand jolted with shock as she moved closer, laughing prettily at something a swain said, and his punch swirled over the top of the glass.

"Gabe!" Allison said in surprise as his punch spilled ingloriously over Marybeth Stockton's pale pink dress. "Whatever are you thinking?"

Flushed, Gabriel quickly offered his handkerchief, embarrassed at his loss of control. "I'm so sorry," he apologized, then moved toward the apparition, still unable to believe his eyes.

It was her. The devil herself, Jennifer Appleton. She was dressed in a pretty dotted-white-on-white Swiss chiffon, a pink sash tied just below her breasts. The dress was a little old-fashioned, but of good material and lovely styling. He had difficulty pulling his eyes away from her, for as he had supposed, her figure was magnificent. It was generously exposed by the light quality of her dress, and he surmised she wore little beneath the gown. Although the heat made such considerations practical, it was scandalous nevertheless.

When she finally lifted her face, he saw that she bloomed with color. If the fright of the lawyer's letter affected her, it was not apparent in her easy manner, her full, lush giggles, nor her *joie de faire* as she swung a croquet mallet and deftly landed her ball just outside the wicket. She must have felt his observation, for her eyes met his and held him spellbound.

"Jennifer! You must come! Oh, please, they are asking for you!"

A beautiful woman approached her, and Gabriel identified Jennifer's sister. Penelope led her away to a group of women clustered beneath a shade tree with their ices and fans. Gabriel recognized Mrs. Merriweather and Mrs. Greyson, the Misses Billing and Miss Barry. He waited for their rebuff, but instead, they seemed genuinely pleased to meet "the Appleton." Their talk grew animated, and Gabriel drifted close enough to hear the conversation.

"Is it true that you brought Mary Forester's husband back from the dead? What was it like?" Eleanor Greyson asked, her stern face lit up with excitement.

"How do you do it? Can you feel the ghostly presence?" the normally reserved Margaret Merriweather questioned.

"Are you frightened, living alone, knowing that spirits have been in your house?" Jane Billing wanted to know, her voice pleading.

"How do you give such marvelous readings? I've heard of your powers from several sources!" Judith Barry gushed.

Stunned, Gabriel saw Jennifer wield her power like a queen deigning to speak with peasants. She answered their questions cleverly, making them curious for more. Idly he realized her intelligence outweighed her beauty, but more obvious was her formidable charm. That, Jennifer Appleton had in boatloads.

Incensed, Gabriel was about to accost her when Jonathan Wiseley stole up beside him, a glass of beer in one hand, a chocolate cake in the other. "Pretty girl," he remarked, chomping on the cake. "I hear she's taking New York by storm."

"What are you talking about?" Gabriel blazed, and the young man nearly choked on his beer.

"Well, didn't you know? The 'bewitching trio' has been seen everywhere. They had tea at the Billings', lunch at the Swathmores'. I hear they've been invited to every major outing this summer. No one seems to know much about them, except that their parents, who were of good family, died. Poor dears! But there's no doubt as to their success."

Gabriel saw the truth of the man's words as the women piled knee-deep to get a word with Jennifer. Far from being out of her element, she played the crowd like a conductor of an orchestra. Worse, she seemed to be enjoying herself immensely, for she fanned herself prettily, letting the heat climb in her cheeks. Soon men surrounded her, and Gabriel could hear them fighting over who would bring her a glass of punch.

"As I said, poor little orphans. I, for one, would certainly like to adopt one of them. Say, do you think they are free lovers like that creature Woodhull? That would be terribly convenient, wouldn't it?"

Gabriel opened his mouth to retort, but didn't trust himself to speak. For some reason, he was furious with Jonathan's comment, and even more furious with the men thronging around Jennifer. Turning rudely away from Jonathan, he approached her, and heard her trying to decide whether to attend the Esterbrooks' ball, or the Chambers Street festival, a decision she seemed to enjoy mightily.

"Miss Appleton, I beg a private word with you." Gabriel sent her a look that brooked no refusal. As the men booed, Jennifer shrugged her dainty white shoulders, then descended from the crowd. Gabriel took her by the arm and practically dragged her into the rose garden.

"Unhand me this minute!" Jennifer cried as soon as they were alone.

Gabriel released her, suddenly aware that he *was* still holding her arm. Jennifer Appleton stood in front of him amid the Barrymores' prized Silver Lace roses, looking incredibly beautiful. Instead of appearing frightened by his confrontation, she held her chin up defiantly, as if prepared to defend her ground at all costs.

She looked so adorable, Gabriel had trouble staying angry. He had to remind himself of exactly who she was—and what she was. "Miss Appleton," he managed sternly, "what are you doing here? Is it common for tea-leaf readers, who bilk elderly ladies out of money, to entertain at garden parties in such a manner?"

"And what, sir, is your objection?"

He could have sworn he saw laughter lurking at the corners of her mouth. He gestured to her gown. "I think you know exactly what I mean. That you are here, dressed like that, flaunting yourself before the men! How did you get invited to this gathering, or did you just crash the gates?"

She was so close, he could smell her lilac water, so reminiscent of the letter to Charles. She was even prettier here than at a distance, for she seemed to emanate an energy and vitality that were intoxicating. His own thoughts drove him to distraction. Part of him wanted to put her over his knee and beat some sense into her; the other part wanted to kiss her until she swooned.

"I was invited by Madam Barrymore herself, thanks to a recommendation by the Misses Billing," Jennifer said indignantly, although she didn't seem entirely displeased with the situation. "As to my dress, it is no different than Sally Vesper's gown, nor Marybeth's. And I wasn't flaunting myself; I find the company of this society very congenial. I also find *your* interest questionable, since you are here escorting a female."

He gaped at her, outraged that she should turn his questions back on him. "You are the most exasperating woman I've ever had the misfortune to meet! Do you know what they are saying about you? They think you are like Victoria Woodhull, a free lover as well as a spiritualist! Is that the reputation you want?"

"I see." She lowered her face, appearing appropriately demure, but Gabriel knew better. He could almost sense her restrained mirth. When she looked up a moment later, it was as if a halo encircled her fair head.

"I truly appreciate your concern. As a gentleman, it was most kind of you to instruct me in the error of my ways. I am reformed, sir, thanks to you. I shall be forever grateful."

With that, she rose on her pink slippers and placed a schoolmistresslike peck on his cheek. "Good day, Mr. Forester. I leave you the garden."

Gabriel's admiration mingled with his outrage and disbelief as Jennifer daintily curtsied, then swirled to walk gracefully out of the glade. Evidently, she saw him as some mawkish schoolboy that she could toy with. His thoughts went back to her legal reply to Charles's letter, to the incident with the police, even to his first confrontation with her. So far, she had bested him at every turn. He had to appreciate her audacity, even as it enraged his male ego. She badly needed a lesson, Gabriel decided. One that he would teach her.

"Miss Appleton?"

He laid his hand on her shoulder, intending to give her a well-deserved dressing-down, but she turned so quickly that she wound up in his arms. The merriment disappeared from her eyes and she looked at him with something else, something that made him think she didn't entirely despise him back. His chastising words suddenly caught in his throat as he gazed into her eyes, eyes that had convinced lesser souls they'd seen a ghost. As if of its own accord, his mouth lowered to hers, unable to resist the soft, sweet temptation.

She was luscious, spicy, and entrancing like a great wine, full of innocence, yet rich with erotic promise. Gabriel groaned, wanting badly to taste more of her. Desire wrenched through him with almost as much force as his previous anger as he felt the petal softness of her lips beneath his. Forgetting everything except need, he placed scorching kisses along her throat, then to the sensitive place beneath her ear, then finally, back to her mouth. He increased the pressure, urging her lips to part.

Slowly, she stopped resisting and her young, slender body seemed to melt against him, making him gasp with pleasure. His own heart pounded so forcefully that he was concerned it would frighten her, but she shyly lifted her hands to his neck and buried her fingers in his hair, silently encouraging him. Almost roughly, he pulled her even closer and began to explore her mouth, plunging in fully to taste the depths of her sweetness as she yielded to him.

Jennifer surrendered mindlessly to the hot swirling emotions that seemed determined to consume her. Jolt after jolt of electrical sensation raced up her spine and through her body, jarring her nerves, making her blood sing with a gushing warmth. Intoxicated by his kiss, she unwittingly increased their passion by leaning fully against him, wanting every sensation, every delicious pleasure he could give her. Her tongue mingled with his, then her head fell back, cradled in his hand as he groaned, devouring her completely.

"My God, Jennifer . . ."

The sweetness of her response tore all logic from his brain. Gabriel wanted this woman desperately. He had to have her. He was lost in a sea of pure sensation, pleasurably drowning in a woman he'd sworn to hate. . . .

"Gabriel!"

He was jolted back to reality as Allison's voice shattered the stillness of the glade. He pulled away quickly, furious at himself and his lack of control. He was also confused, stunned by the passion that Jennifer had engendered in him. He glanced down at her, fully expecting a slap or a scathing remark. Instead, she was staring at him with a look he would never forget: Her eyes were wide, shining with desire and wonder, and a kind of adoration that made him pause.

Quickly he reminded himself that she was an actress above all else, and an accomplished one at that. He heard Allison approaching, and knew it would be a matter of moments before they were discovered. Aware that Jennifer's dubious reputation would be completely compromised should they be seen together, he turned swiftly and headed toward the gate. A backward glance assured him that Jennifer had sense enough to dodge into the gazebo, where she could collect herself unobserved.

"There you are. I've been looking all over for you. What have you been doing?" Allison asked petulantly.

"I was just looking at the famous Barrymore roses. They certainly haven't done well this year. I am dying of thirst, though. Let's get some punch."

He led her back toward the party, ignoring the suspicious glances she gave him. Most likely, she had seen him accost Jennifer, and had seen them enter the garden together. In truth, he didn't know what he would say if she questioned him.

There was no explanation for his fascination with "the Appleton" creature. None whatsoever.

ON THE WAY home, Jennifer had been strangely silent. Penelope chattered the entire time, while Winifred made several keen observations about the party and their success. The three sisters crept into the rickety old mansion, closing the door as quietly as they could, trying to hush every possible sound and not disturb their elderly aunt. When they were in their bedroom, Penelope, dying of curiosity, confronted Jennifer.

"So? What happened? Don't look at me like that—I saw you disappear into the garden with handsome Mr. Forester!"

Jennifer blushed, pressing her lace-covered hands to

her face. "You don't think—did everyone notice?" She whispered.

"No, silly. I only saw because I was looking. I want to know everything! I can tell something happened. Just look at you! You're practically glowing!"

Jennifer looked as radiant as a bride on her wedding day, and her eyes fairly sparkled with suppressed excitement. She raised her arms, allowing Winifred to pull the voluminous dress over her head. When she reappeared, her face was screwed up in concern.

"Are you sure he isn't really interested in Allison Howe? He did escort her to the party, after all. And he did seem to be, well, close with her."

"Allison!" Penelope waved her hand in dismissal. "He doesn't care for Allison! You heard what the Billings said, and they would know. Besides, it's every girl for herself. All you're doing is giving Gabriel a chance to decide. There's nothing wrong with that."

The cloud lifted from Jennifer's face and she hid a mischievous smile. "Well, then, I'll tell you. First he was furious. He wanted to know what we were doing there, and even accused us of crashing the party!"

"How dare he!" Penelope said indignantly.

Winifred sent her a sardonic look. "Penelope, we weren't invited. The man was right."

Penelope pouted, then tapped her foot impatiently as she waited for Jennifer to continue. "So then what? Surely you're not so happy because he yelled at you."

Jennifer shrugged coyly. "Then he berated me again for taking advantage of his mother. He even lectured me on my dress, accusing me of flaunting myself before all the men! He really was furious."

"That's strange," Winifred remarked, folding Jennifer's gown carefully before removing her own dress. "He doesn't have any claim to you. Why should he care what you wear or who you talk to?"

Penelope practically danced with excitement. She clapped her hands together like a little girl, and tossed a pillow at Winifred.

"What is the matter with you? It means everything, don't you see? If Gabriel wasn't attracted to Jennifer, none of this would have happened!"

Winifred looked stunned by Penelope's conclusion, while Jennifer appeared hopeful. Unconsciously, in a gesture as old as femininity, Jennifer smoothed her hair, then glanced shyly at her sister.

"Do you really think—"

"Of course," Penelope said triumphantly. "The only thing better would have been if he kissed you."

Winifred looked at Jennifer, surprised to see the red flush creep up her face. Penelope thankfully had her back to them and Jennifer quickly tugged on her nightgown, grateful for the concealment offered by the thin fabric. By the time she had pulled it into place and Penelope had turned around, she was composed and practical once again.

"We have to find out more about Gabriel," Jennifer said firmly, returning to the task of stalking her prey with all the determination of Napoleon himself. "Mary Forester has asked me to tea on Sunday, and she mentioned Gabriel will be there, but I can't depend on her forever. We need to know more about where Gabriel goes, what he does, so that I can *accidentally* run into him." She rubbed her hands together in anticipation.

"We need to follow him!" Penelope blurted out. Winifred's eyebrows lurched up in alarm, but Penelope was little put out. "That way we can discover firsthand what he does."

"Penny!" Jennifer cried. "Do you really think we should?"

"Of course." Penelope looked at her strangely, as if surprised she would ask such a thing. "How else will we find out about him? I tried to get more out of the Billings, but they don't seem to know. Following him is the only way."

Jennifer sucked in her breath, then, with her eyes shining, nodded. "I'll do it. I'll start tomorrow."

Penelope clapped, while Winifred shook her head, conveying her uncertainty about this plan. Still, she knew better than to argue when Jennifer was determined. Changing the subject back to business, she surveyed the ledger. "We need more money coming in. There are a few more gowns in mother's trunk that you can make over, but it is imperative that we get some new outfits made for all these upcoming events. Penelope, you especially need a new bonnet and some silk gloves. I know we have some more séances to do. Jennifer, what is the schedule like?"

"We have Amelia Stryker tomorrow night, Carol Jenik the following, and Ellen MacPherson on Thursday," Jennifer said, shaking her head with worry. "I just hope we can keep Auntie out of the picture. She's been asking to attend one of our 'theatricals.'"

"That won't do," Penelope shuddered. "I don't know how she'd react if she ever knew what we really did. I'll make sure she's invited to tea by the minister, and there's the sewing circle tomorrow night."

"Do you really think we can fool her forever?" Winifred questioned.

Jennifer shrugged with the resignation of a person who handles one catastrophe at a time. "We haven't much choice, have we? Don't forget we have the appointment with Charles Howe tomorrow," she reminded her scholarly sister. "Auntie knows he's coming and will help with the tea. I'm sure Charles is looking forward to giving us the legal thrashing of our lives."

Winifred pulled herself upright, steel in her stern hazel

eyes. "I'll take care of Mr. Charles Howe. You, Penny, provide the charm. Jenny, you and Aunt Eve bring the food and distractions. I will answer his legal concerns in a way that will have his proverbial head spinning. I'm looking forward to it."

Jennifer and Penelope chuckled as Winifred rubbed her hands, flexing her fingers like a swordsman preparing for a duel. As the gaslights went out, Jennifer slipped into bed. Pulling the covers up to her chin, she waited until Penelope and Winifred were fast asleep. Only then did she allow herself to recall the kiss that she and Gabriel had shared in the garden.

She could still feel the warmth of his body pressed against hers, the pulsing ache that had begun inside her when he pulled her into his embrace, and the clean, rich taste of him as he boldly explored her mouth. Jennifer gasped anew as she experienced those feelings all over again, and she was filled with awe and a nameless need.

Privately, she could admit the truth: It had been incredible. Although she'd only been kissed twice before, once by Billy Donahue in school, another time by a pesky cousin, those kisses had been nothing compared to Gabriel's. When he'd pulled her into his arms and his mouth had devoured hers, she'd felt as if her curls had been singed once more.

So this is what it was all about. Jennifer thought of Penelope's excited whispers about passionate kisses—something scandalous, yet truly enjoyable, her sister had assured her. Jennifer never had any idea what she was talking about, and had attributed it to Penelope's hopelessly romantic nature. Yet in the privacy of her room, Jennifer could admit that she'd been close to swooning in Gabriel's arms.

She tried to go to sleep, but strangely, it eluded her.

Tossing and turning beneath the covers, she tried to make sense of it all.

She was the one who chose to set her cap for Gabriel Forester.

Why then, did his kiss turn her into a plate of quivering jelly?

CHAPTER 5

"HE'S HERE!" PENELOPE cried. She drew back from the curtain and smoothed her dress, then peered critically into the mirror. Jennifer thought of a soldier preparing for battle as her gorgeous sister dampened a small piece of flannel with lilac water, then slipped it beneath the buttons of her dress and into her corset.

Aunt Eve hurried about the room, adjusting a picture here, a vase of flowers there. "That's better. Fresh flowers and a warm reception will do much to enhance your cause, dearies. With three beautiful women to choose from, Mr. Howe will certainly be in a dither! Don't answer the door too quickly, now. You don't want to appear too eager."

Jennifer hid a smile. Although Aunt Eve knew that Charles was Gabriel's attorney, she'd fallen eagerly into their plans, determined that no man cause trouble for her charges. Glancing once more around the parlor, Jennifer turned up the gaslights so the room was as comfortable as possible, then fluffed up a pillow where they'd decided Charles Howe would sit.

Aunt Eve scurried into the kitchen and opened the oven door. Waving a towel back and forth, she made certain that the enticing aroma of cinnamon permeated the house. After pouring the hissing water into a delicate china teapot, she dropped a tea ball of the finest cut tea leaves into the pot. On second thought, she followed the tea with a generous portion of brandy, stirring the aromatic liquid and happily inhaling the fumes.

It was so important that they win over Charles Howe. Jennifer quelled the butterflies in her stomach as she realized one of the most talented lawyers in New York waited on their step. Charles could cause them innumerable problems, both legally and socially, if he chose to. He had enormous influence with New York society, was well liked and respected, and came from a good family. Charles's acceptance would go far to further their entrée into society, while his antagonism could bury them in one legal battle after another. Even more importantly, Charles was Gabriel's friend, and as such, would certainly have considerable influence over him.

The doorbell rang, and Jennifer glanced once more at her sisters. Penelope settled onto the love seat, a book in her hand. At Jennifer's frown, she glanced down and turned the book right side up, shrugging in apology. Winifred rushed into the chair by the fire, a brief on her lap, then nodded to Jennifer.

Opening the door, Jennifer successfully hid her apprehension as her gaze fell on Charles Howe. Tall and perfectly built, he was dressed in the height of fashion in a pearl gray lounge jacket with a matching waistcoat and a sparkling white shirt beneath. A diamond pin nestled between the folds of his necktie, winking in the sunlight, and he carried his hat and cane in his white gloved hands. Handsome and well-bred, with his straight dark hair falling across his brow in a dashing wave and his black eyes serious, he looked at Jennifer, surprise clearly written on his face.

"Jennifer Appleton?" He glanced at the doorstep as if to verify the address.

"I am Miss Appleton," Jennifer replied demurely, sweeping open the door and gesturing inside. Dressed in a simple rose-colored morning gown, with a pearl brooch at her throat, she looked serene and beautiful, as much unlike a gypsy wench as he could imagine. Her bangs had begun to grow back in, and a charming little fringe of curls peeped from beneath her lace cap. "Please come inside, Mr. Howe. Winifred is expecting you. I must say, we are grateful that you've taken an interest in us. Winifred is so excited about meeting you!"

Charles's mouth gaped as he stepped through the door. Twin Gables, a creepy old mansion, nevertheless looked warm and inviting inside, especially with three beautiful women gracing the parlor. Like a little boy in a sweetshop, Charles glanced around quickly, his gaze bouncing from Jennifer to the gorgeous blonde patting the love seat before him, to the unusual beauty gracing the corner. Stunned, he handed his hat and cane to Jennifer, then walked dreamlike across the room, taking the seat that Penelope so generously proffered.

The scent of lilac water, so reminiscent of the letter, hit him full in the face. As he glanced up, he saw the woman in the corner watching him with cat eyes, sizing him up as if he were prey. He shook himself, dispelling the ridiculous thought, then gaped once more as a sweet little old lady tottered in and placed a tea tray before him.

Delicious smells of cinnamon buns, poppy seed cakes, and chocolate wafted up to tease his nostrils, and the teapot steamed invitingly. As a bachelor, Charles didn't often know the delights of a home-baked tea, and his mouth watered as the woman, who could have been his own grandmother, poured him a cup.

"I'd like to introduce you to everyone here," Jennifer said, her voice dripping with honey. Charles turned toward her, sipping one of the best cups of tea he'd had in ages. A feeling of warmth rushed through him, and he took another deep drink of the tea, amazed at how rejuvenating the simple brew was. "This is my sister Penelope, our aunt Eve, and Winifred. Winnie is the one who answered your kind letter."

Charles's gaze swung back to the sister in the corner. The enchantress smiled, and he saw the dangerously keen intelligence in her eyes. He thought of the legends of Morgan le Fay, and quickly dismissed them, declaring to himself that it must have been the house that made him so fanciful. Still, he could not look away, not even when Penelope, the most beautiful woman he'd ever seen, chirped in his ear.

"Winnie was so impressed with your letter! And we adore Mary Forester. I'm so glad she has someone like you to look after her! Gabriel must be proud, to have a mother like her!"

Charles sipped more of the wonderful tea, then took a bite out of the cake. The cinnamon bun melted in his mouth, and he nearly groaned aloud in pleasure. Warmth and contentment flooded through him, and it took every ounce of determination he had to remember why he was there.

"Yes, Mary Forester is a good woman. That is why I was so concerned that she not be taken advantage of, in any way. Unfortunately, you young ladies are in a unique position to influence her. I'm here to see that no one prospers at Mrs. Forester's expense."

Some of the sternness he'd practiced came back into his voice, and he was grateful. Aunt Eve gasped. Penelope drew back from him, looking like she would cry, and Charles felt a moment's panic. Fortunately, Jennifer smiled charmingly, nodding in agreement.

"We feel exactly the same way. Thank God she came to us! A woman as sweet as Mrs. Forester could easily find herself the prey of the vultures in our city! I am so glad we could help her."

"My nieces are the very picture of decorum," Aunt Eve defended them pointedly. "I've tutored them myself from *Hill's Manual* and *Godey's*. They are very proper, nice young ladies and would never dream of causing trouble to someone like Mary Forester."

Aunt Eve left the room to fetch the sandwiches, her head held high.

"Mrs. Forester was actually thinking of ending her own life when she came here." Penelope sighed. "But now, she is happy, and contemplating her wedding! Can you imagine?"

Gabriel hadn't told him that his mother was suicidal. Charles also didn't know that Mary was considering remarriage, a situation he knew Gabriel would find difficult. Doubt filled his mind as he realized he'd only gotten half the story from his friend. The attorney found it harder and harder to stay angry, especially when Penelope leaned over him, handing him another cake and affording him an enviable glance at her generous bosom. Jennifer saw that his teacup stayed filled, while Winifred sent him odd glances from the corner. Forcing himself to sound gruff, he turned toward Winifred, who still fascinated him more than Penelope's obvious charms.

"I know that you helped Mary, and that she is grateful. But you did accept too much money from her. That is both wrong and illegal."

Winifred raised her gaze to his, and Charles felt the blood throb in his veins. She indicated the brief on her lap and when she spoke, he could feel a vibration that went straight through to his stomach.

"Mr. Howe," Winifred began, her eyes shining with anticipation. "Mrs. Forester and Jennifer had a contract. By that, I mean a legally enforceable promise. Jennifer agreed to perform a séance for her, and Mrs. Forester would pay what she felt was fair. Mrs. Forester agreed to these conditions of her own free will, and of sound mind. Even though it was verbal, that contract was just as binding as if I came to you for a legal service. If I was so delighted with your performance that I chose to pay you more, and you accepted, no one would have done anything illegal." She waved a brief at him, indicating a column of terse, legal script. "Fortunately, Bernard Goodman, of Vanderslice, Goodman, and Barry, has generously provided me access to his law library. I have read his briefs extensively. Surely you are familiar with *Howe versus Clafflin*? I believe the case was proven and discussed to the court's satisfaction."

Charles's mouth dropped once more. This time he ignored both Penelope as she refilled his cup, and Jennifer as she replaced his half-eaten cake.

"You didn't read the entire trial brief? There were several interesting discussions as a result of that case."

"Yes, I know. Such as whether Tennessee Clafflin truly meant to cure Rebecca Howe, or just provide spiritual comfort. Also, Rebecca Howe was responsible for her own health, and if she decided not to go to doctors, but to put her faith in spiritual healing, that was her decision. Nevertheless, she paid the agreed-upon price for services rendered. I believe the court found for Clafflin."

"You can't agree with that verdict! Rebecca wrote a letter to the *Ottawa Republican*, stating that Miss Clafflin made her far worse than before she began treatment. Surely you wouldn't disregard such a letter? People have been sued for far less."

"And people have been wrongly sued," Winifred said coolly.

Aghast, Charles settled on another tack. "Did you read *Seton versus Shoemaker*?"

"In its entirety." Winifred smiled. Placing the papers aside, she leaned forward, intensity gleaming in her gaze. "What is your view on that verdict?"

As the two argued legalities, Jennifer and Penelope exchanged satisfied glances. Aunt Eve smiled smugly as she brought a tray of ham sandwiches from the kitchen, and offered one to Charles. The attorney rose to his feet, grabbed a sandwich as if unaware of his actions, then waved it in the air to make a point. Winifred rose and faced him just as forcefully, her cool voice never rising, her logic backed with inescapable fact.

Jennifer was filled with admiration. Although she'd always envied Winifred's intelligence, she had never seen her so passionate. Perhaps it was because Charles shared her legal knowledge, or was her intellectual equal. Jennifer smiled to herself. As puzzling as the situation appeared, she had to admit that Winifred and Charles made a handsome couple. She gestured to Penelope and her aunt, and they silently left the room, leaving Winifred and Charles to their wrangling.

The sun had long since set when the three women returned to the parlor. Charles glanced up, seemingly amazed when he realized the time. Aunt Eve looked reproving, Penelope winked flirtatiously, and Winifred appeared eager to continue their discourse well into the night.

"Mr. Howe," Aunt Eve said, "I am sorry, but my nieces are previously engaged this evening. Perhaps we could enjoy your conversation once again, at supper later this week?"

Embarrassed, Charles turned to Jennifer, who held his hat and cane. "I'm sorry, I have overstayed my welcome. I have not been a good guest either, dominating the conversation in such a manner."

"Oh, I think some of us found it fascinating," Jennifer said, sending a warm smile toward her sister.

Charles turned to Winifred, bowing before her as he would a respected lady. "My apologies for writing that frightful letter. I understand now that none of you would ever hurt Mary, nor anyone else of our acquaintance. I am truly humbled by the opportunity to know you, and I would take it as a kind gesture if you would all attend the opera one evening as my guests."

It was obvious that he meant the invitation for Winifred, but generously included them all. Aunt Eve nodded her approval. Jennifer grinned, thrilled with this outcome, while Penelope clapped. Winifred rose and placed her hand in his.

"It would be my pleasure."

A pleased flush washed over his face. Jennifer saw Charles struggle to think of something witty or clever to say. Nothing came to him and so he bowed once more, reluctantly leaving the house.

Jennifer leaned against the door, nearly fainting with relief. A smile curved her lips as Penelope cheered for Winifred, and Aunt Eve gave her niece a warm hug. Winifred looked strangely beautiful, serene and content, yet as energized as if she'd spent the last hour kissing instead of arguing. Jennifer would have liked to tease her about it, but something in Winifred's manner didn't allow such intimacy.

Instead, Jennifer chuckled, totally pleased with the outcome of Charles's visit. She could just see Gabriel's face when he heard about this.

One down, one to go.

GABRIEL SLAPPED HIS gloves against his thigh in irritation, waiting for the carriage to arrive at his mother's house. It was Sunday, and he'd promised her that he would stop by for tea, a promise that didn't make him feel any better. While it was wonderful to see her so happy, she continued to ignore his warnings about her future groom, and about that Appleton creature, whom she'd apparently befriended.

Gabriel's mouth curved into a thunderous frown as he

thought of Jennifer for the thousandth time. Unbelievably, Charles had stopped by the previous night after visiting the Appletons, and informed him that as far as he was concerned, all bets were off. Somehow, the bewitching sisters had won him over and he wanted nothing more to do with harassing them. If Gabriel didn't know better, he could have sworn Charles was drunk, even though the man insisted they'd only served him tea. He was drunk, all right, Gabriel thought hotly, intoxicated by the Appleton herself.

Yet he couldn't completely fault Charles for succumbing to their charms, much as he would have liked to do so. His own behavior with Jennifer in the Barrymores' garden was inexcusable. Worse, he had no logical explanation for it, no way to satisfy his own self-doubt where Jennifer was concerned. Why he'd felt compelled to pull her into his arms and kiss her senseless, when he'd sworn to hate her, made absolutely no sense. He could still taste the sweetness of her kiss, feel the seductive yielding of her soft body against his . . . What was wrong with him? What was it about this woman that threatened to obsess him?

He had but one consolation. At least he wasn't liable to run into "the Appleton" again anytime soon. Jennifer and her sisters, while a curiosity, were far from being accepted into society. He still couldn't figure out how she'd finagled an invitation to the Barrymore affair, but she'd managed it right under everyone's nose, and was a spectacular success. Yet, although everyone was talking about the grace and charm of the three sisters, no one of any consequence had truly embraced them.

The carriage slowed to a halt, and Gabriel disembarked. James graciously showed him into the parlor. Gabriel could hear his mother's light laughter, and the sound of feminine chatter coming from the tearoom. His irritation increased tenfold when Robert Wood, his mother's fiancé, rose from his chair and extended a hand, obviously delighted to see him.

"Gabriel, my boy! Where have you been lately? The marble company is keeping you busy, I suppose? I understand you've done a wonderful job with the business."

Gabriel stared at the outstretched hand without taking it. Instead, his eyes ran over the man's threadbare coat, shoddy boots, and worn shirt. When he still didn't reciprocate the greeting after a long moment, Robert coughed in embarrassment, then dropped his hand to his side.

"Mary will be delighted to see you. I know she was expecting you for tea. Gabriel, I realize our engagement may have come as something of a shock to you, but I would like you to be happy for us. I think your mother is a wonderful woman, and I will do my best to deserve her."

Gabriel gave the man a cool stare. "I'm certain you will. Mr. Wood, let me make my position clear. I have nothing against you personally, but I do care for my mother's well-being. She tends to be a little naive in financial matters, and I am concerned for her future. I think that your circumstances may make it difficult for you to assist her."

The older man flushed, then his gaze dropped to the floor. "I understand. It is true that my finances are not what they used to be, but I have no intention of squandering my money or your mother's. I know that you've been helping her and advising her regarding her investments. I hope that you will continue in that endeavor, and rest assured that I have no interest in her money. My pension is more than enough for us to live on."

"Good." Gabriel reached out his hand, and took the other man's in a warm clasp. The two men reached a silent accord. Relieved, Gabriel turned and followed the sound of his mother's voice to the tearoom. His smile froze when he stepped into the lace-encrusted room.

"Gabriel!" His mother cried, delighted. She rose, planting a kiss on his cheek, the scent of her perfume enveloping him. "I'm so glad you've come! I believe you know Jennifer."

It was her. The Appleton creature. Gabriel couldn't believe his eyes as Jennifer looked up, her face demure, her eyes pure mischief as she greeted him politely. Outrage flooded through him, mingled with embarrassment and discomfort as she rose, extending her hand to him.

"Miss Appleton," he managed to croak somehow, his eyes sweeping over her simple beige morning dress. Desperately he tried to find something wrong, anything about her appearance to sneer at and give him an edge, but there was nothing. The lines of her dress, while not quite the latest style, were nevertheless in perfect taste, and the tiny pearl earrings that dangled discreetly behind her burnished curls were elegant and pretty. Her gloves were of good quality, if not the best, and her handkerchief was tucked daintily inside her sleeve with a tiny edge of lace peeping out. Even her slippers, though worn, were clean and well kept. Nothing about her attire or demeanor would betray the heathen within.

Gabriel's gaze flew back to Jennifer's face and he could have sworn he saw amusement there. Mortification flooded through him as he vividly recalled taking her in his arms, with Allison a few feet away. Jennifer seemed to remember the moment also, for she blushed, then lowered her eyes to the table.

"I'll go ask James for more tea. Gabriel, please keep Miss Appleton company for a moment, will you?"

Mary skittered away before he could object. He was trapped. Frustrated and angry, he put down his hat, while Jennifer folded her hands expectantly. The clock ticked loudly and Gabriel paced the room. Finally, he turned toward his adversary, determined to break the wretched silence.

"Miss Appleton, what in hell are you doing here?"

Jennifer looked at him in surprise. "I was invited to tea by your mother." She shrugged, as if this were an everyday occurrence.

"There must be some mistake. My mother invited me to tea."

Jennifer grinned, her dress rustled enticingly, and she looked at him with all the angelic innocence of his namesake. "Maybe she wants us to kiss and make up."

But that only reminded him of something he'd been trying for over a week to forget. Embarrassed, he faced her directly, and spoke with as much sincerity as he could muster. "I must apologize for my behavior during our last meeting. It was completely outside my code of conduct, and ungentlemanly to say the least. I sincerely hope I haven't compromised you in any way."

Jennifer looked surprised, and, to his amazement, slightly disappointed. She lifted her shoulders slightly, her face solemn, but her eyes continued to dance as if she found the whole situation funny.

"No one saw me, so you needn't worry. Your reputation is intact."

"It wasn't my reputation I was worried about. I just wanted to assure you that in spite of our differences, I wasn't trying to destroy your good name for some petty revenge."

"Then what were you doing?"

The question he'd been asking himself came from her lips. He struggled to come up with a response, but he hadn't been able to, even for himself. He looked at her, and the indignation he'd expected wasn't there. Instead, she appeared curious and interested in his answer, and, if he had to be honest, hopeful.

Confusion reigned within him, and once again he pictured a scene that he'd fought to erase from his memory: the vision of her after he'd kissed her. He couldn't have imagined the wonder and passion he'd seen in her eyes, though he'd tried a million times to convince himself it never happened. But something in her expression told him he wasn't far from the mark.

"James will bring the tea momentarily. You two aren't fighting, are you?"

Mary swept back into the room, looking like a cat with a dish of cream as she surveyed Jennifer and Gabriel. Gabriel picked up his hat and shook his head.

"No, but I'll be going. I have a lot to do today, and you two will no doubt enjoy yourselves more without my presence."

"Gabriel, you can't!" Mary looked crestfallen.

"I'm sorry, dear, but I really must. I'll stop by and take you to lunch this week. Good day, Miss Appleton."

Jennifer rose, and this time, he couldn't mistake the expression on her face. Fury shot through him even as she extended her hand once more.

She was laughing.

CHAPTER 6

AT EXACTLY FIVE P.M. the following evening, Jennifer glanced into the looking glass to check her appearance. Dressed in her aunt's bulky cape, she was content that her figure was completely concealed within the voluminous folds of the garment. After donning her biggest, darkest bonnet, she pulled down the veil so that only her chin showed beneath the filmy cloth. Smiling in satisfaction, she crept out of the house, certain no one could easily identify her.

A thrill of excitement swept through her as she hailed a cab. As the coach pulled up, she had to step back to avoid being doused by a torrent of water from the street. She managed to keep her shoes dry, however, and when the cabbie apologized profusely, then helped her inside as if she were an elderly widow, she knew her costume was sufficient. Giving the man the address of Gabriel's town house, she sank into the back, her nerves keen as the carriage lurched ahead.

She was on a spy mission, the same as any detective, but her objective was even more elusive than a murderer's trail. She needed to find out as much as she could about Gabriel's daily schedule, so that she could conveniently accost him when he least expected it. Excitement filled her at the very idea, even as a warning flashed through her mind. She had to make sure that she wasn't caught, or all would be in vain.

Penelope had wanted to come with her, but Jennifer realized it would be far easier to slip in and out of crowds alone. It would also be more difficult to remain anonymous with Penelope, for her beautiful sister stood out like the sun in any gathering. No, far better this way, and when she had some information, she would gladly make use of her sister's expertise to conspire against Gabriel.

A smug giggle escaped her as she thought of his reaction at tea the previous morning. Surely he knew of Charles's defection by now, and must be boiling at the very thought. She was even more pleased by his apology and assurance that he hadn't been out to ruin her with his passionate kiss in the garden. He didn't seem to have any explanation for it, and appeared very uncomfortable in her presence. Jennifer wasn't quite the expert on men that Penelope was, but even she knew enough to be encouraged by his awkwardness.

He felt something for her. He had to. In spite of her plotting, the feminine part of Jennifer was very pleased that handsome, thrilling Mr. Forester seemed to be, as Penelope said, taken with her. A part of her worried about why it had become so important, and why his opinion mattered, but she dismissed the concern quickly. Now if she could only manage to spend enough time in his presence, she truly might be able to bring him to hand.

That thought led to other, darker ones that had cropped up repeatedly since his heated kiss. Jennifer felt a tingle of anticipation, for Gabriel had already demonstrated to her that he was irresistibly masculine, and would certainly act upon his impulses. Secretly, she wondered what they led to, for her mother had never told her much, and her aunt only whispered warnings about gentlemen taking liberties and the dire results. She had surmised some from the whispered giggles of the other girls, but all she knew for sure was that his kiss had been exciting beyond measure. Surely anything else would be equally rewarding.

The carriage stopped outside Gabriel's door. Instructing the driver to wait, she settled down inside, away from nosy eyes. She knew that Gabriel walked in the park at lunchtime, but what he did at night was a mystery. She decided to follow him from his house in the cab, and see where he went.

She didn't have to wait long for her quarry to appear. Gabriel strolled down the street at exactly five-fifteen, then stepped inside the door of his town house. Jennifer counted out the minutes for what seemed to be an eternity, but he didn't reappear.

"Miss, I've got to go. I've other fares tonight, you know," the cabbie called out, obviously annoyed to be parked on the street when he could be making money.

Jennifer alighted, then pressed a coin in the man's hand. "Can you come back in an hour? We may need to follow someone."

The cabbie nodded, pleased with the coin she'd given him. "I will that, miss." He helped her down to the street.

As the cab pulled away, Jennifer sprinted across the street, then stood before the door. She supposed she could just wait and see if he came out . . . Idly, she glanced down the road, but it was a residential area with no restaurants or places where she could watch. The wind blew ominously, and darkness was already threatening. Her eyes fell to the doorknob. She didn't dare . . . surely, he had locked it anyway. Her hand slipped out of the cloak and she gently tried the knob, fully prepared to dodge the other way if he appeared. Unbelievably, the door opened, and she stepped inside.

It was beautiful. Jennifer's breath caught in her throat

as she surveyed the lovely house, and she removed her bonnet to get a better look. The foyer floor where she stood was marble, from his shop, she surmised, and glowed with emerald green and white tiles. A framed watercolor of a seascape graced the wall, as well as a gilt looking glass that must have cost a considerable sum. A china cabinet filled with expensive Delft porcelain gleamed from the end of the corridor, and elegant swags graced the curved Georgian windows. A dark hallway led from there into the parlor, and a round staircase curved enticingly toward the bed chambers upstairs.

Jennifer paused, her heart in her throat. She could see Gabriel's walking stick tossed carelessly on the stairs, and knew that he had gone in that direction. Did she have the audacity to follow him into his private bedroom?

Bracing herself, Jennifer started down the hall, hushing any sound she might possibly make. This was mad, she told herself, hopelessly mad, but she'd come this far and had too much gumption to stop. She took short, quiet breaths, stepping so carefully on each tile that even the touch of her boots didn't give her away.

Climbing the stairs was more difficult, but she was reassured as she heard him slamming a door somewhere above. The fifth step creaked and she paused, terrified. Her foot was poised to take the next step, and she held it in midair, her heart pounding so hard it seemed it would come out of her chest. Luck was with her, however, for no one appeared, and she made her way up the rest of the stairs undisturbed.

Gabriel walked past the hallway, completely oblivious to his intruder. Jennifer quickly ducked into an adjoining bedroom. Her eyes closed with relief when he continued past, and he entered the room exactly next to her. She could hear the metallic clanking of his toiletries, and the soft rush of water pouring into a basin. Unable to resist, she stepped closer to the doorway and peeked inside.

What she saw took her breath away. Gabriel had stripped to the waist and was mixing his shaving cream in a mug, then applying the soft white foam to his face. Fascinated, she watched him lean closer to the looking glass, then slowly, carefully, inch his razor across his cheek. The blade pressed against the angles of his sharply chiseled features, curving around the sensuous mouth that she remembered so well. Every muscle in his back flexed as he proceeded with his task, and his arm lifted again and again until every last inch of cream was gone.

Jennifer swallowed hard, unable to explain her own reaction. Although she'd never watched a man shave before, there was something about spying on him like this, and watching him pursue a strictly male occupation, that was incredibly exciting. Her eyes roamed over his bare back, and she wanted to touch those lean, dangerous muscles, feel their play beneath her fingers. Hot, unbidden thoughts rose within her, and she had to lean back inside the doorway, fanning herself in the still room.

The movement cost her, however. Gabriel paused, instantly alert. He pulled on his shirt, then called out into the house.

"Benton, is that you?"

"Sir?"

Jennifer swallowed her surprise as she heard another male voice respond. Apparently, there was a servant somewhere in the town house. She could hear the man's heavy steps on the staircase as he approached, then a pause as he stood at the door.

"I thought I heard something. Check downstairs, will you? There's been a rash of burglaries in town lately."

"Yes, sir."

Jennifer heard the servant walk away, then Gabriel strode out into the hall. Jennifer froze in her tracks, not daring to move. She heard him walk into the room across from her, then the one beside it. A moment later, he was at the door of the room where she was hiding. Stifling a gasp, she stepped backward and found herself entangled in a pair of dusty velvet drapes. Wrapping them quickly around her, she waited in silence.

The door opened, and she heard his footfall. She didn't dare look this time, knowing that one false move would prove her undoing. A thousand scenarios played through her mind, of Gabriel discovering her and hauling her out to her disgrace. He might even take her to the police, for he'd already complained to them about her. The dust tickled her nostrils, and she had to fight the impulse to sneeze. Holding her breath, she waited in excruciating silence as he glanced around the room, then slowly exhaled as he strode out and checked the room next door.

That was close, she thought, rubbing her nose. Unfortunately, the sneeze she'd been repressing happened instantly as soon as she relaxed. Horrified, Jennifer put her hand over her mouth a second too late.

Gabriel's footsteps hurried back into the room she occupied. A moment later, she felt his hand, as strong as steel, grip her upper arm and drag her out of her hiding place.

"It's you!" His eyes bored into hers, burning with fury. "Good God, woman, what in the hell are you doing here! And why are you dressed like that? This better not be what I think—"

"It's not what it appears!" Jennifer tried to explain, shaking furiously. She attempted to pull away, but he only tightened his grip, determined to get to the bottom of this before she darted past him.

"No? Then what is it? I ought to have you arrested for breaking and entering!"

He was so coldly furious that for a moment Jennifer couldn't speak. "I . . . was with my maid, and I got lost! I had been walking, it was cold, and I had borrowed Auntie's cloak. I saw you come in here, and I followed you! I thought you could direct me. I tried to knock, but I guess you didn't hear me."

His hand eased its constricting hold on her arm, and he seemed to consider her story. "So you were lost and wanted help. What were you doing, then, hiding in the bedroom? Why didn't you just ask me?"

His brow lifted archly, while his eyes seemed to penetrate to her very soul. Jennifer gulped, then looked at the floor. When she looked up again, her face was beet red.

"I . . . you were half dressed, and I didn't know what to do! I was so embarrassed that I just ducked in here!"

His eyes raked her, and Jennifer lowered her gaze back to the rug, silently praying that he would believe her. She'd told him enough of the truth to make it plausible, and realized she really was deeply affected by his near nakedness. He had donned a shirt, but it hung enticingly open, and his firmly muscled chest was burned into her mind.

When she glanced back up, she saw that his anger had been replaced by something akin to amusement. A twinkle appeared in his harsh gaze, along with something else, an expression she remembered from the day he kissed her in the Barrymores' garden. For a brief moment, she thought he might try to kiss her again, an idea that filled her with breathless anticipation. When he spoke, his voice was rough, yet tinged with laughter.

"I see. Like most well-bred ladies, you found the sight of a little male flesh overwhelming, I suppose. I'm almost tempted to find out if you really mean that, and if you are as innocent as you appear."

Jennifer's eyes widened, and her throat went dry. She suddenly realized her vulnerability, trapped alone with him in his bedroom. Something about the look in his eyes made her afraid of the predatory male impulse she sensed in him, even as she was excited by it. His hand dropped to her cloak, and before she could protest, he undid the fastening and let it slide from her shoulders. Backing up against the curtains, she swallowed hard as he took a step closer, his arms braced on either side of her.

Thankfully, there was a knock downstairs. Jennifer heard a male voice call out, "Master Gabriel, Miss Howe is here." Startled, her eyes met Gabriel's and she saw his own glance quickly at the clock. He cursed silently under his breath and pulled away from her, buttoning his shirt.

"Yes, I'll be down directly," he called downstairs. Then he looked at Jennifer as if suddenly aware of her predicament. He grabbed her cloak and wrapped it around her, then gestured to the velvet curtains. He spoke in a hushed voice. "Quickly! Inside the drapes. No one can find you here; it would ruin you. When I've gone, you can slip out. Do you understand?"

Jennifer nodded silently, then did as he instructed. Peeping through the curtain, she saw Gabriel snatch up his jacket, then start downstairs. Jennifer caught a glimpse of him fastening the cuffs of his immaculate white shirt, then tucking the tail inside his trousers. As if sensing her stare, he turned to look directly at her. Shutting the drapes firmly, Jennifer heard what she thought was a soft chuckle as he raced down the stairs.

"There you are!" Jennifer heard Allison's cultured voice. "Charles and I thought we'd pick you up rather than meet at the restaurant. I hope you don't mind. Are you ready?"

"Yes. Let me just get my coat."

Thankfully, the door closed and the house was silent. Jennifer stepped out from behind the curtains, then peered carefully out the window. A moment later, she was rewarded with a clear view of Gabriel walking out with Allison.

A strange, unsettling emotion arose within her as

Allison touched Gabriel's sleeve, then leaned on him as he helped her into the carriage. Jennifer reminded herself of Penelope's words, that Gabriel wasn't in love with Allison, but still it bothered her to see him escorting her out to dinner. She leaned against the window, feeling an ache in her body, the soft sting of her lips where she'd bitten them in anticipation of his kiss. Startled, she realized that she envied Allison. She wanted to be the one with him tonight. In the privacy of her own thoughts, she could admit the truth: She craved him the way she craved chocolate, only more so. Had he pulled her into his arms a moment ago and attempted to take liberties with her, she wouldn't even have tried to stop him.

Jennifer knew she should be appalled at herself, but the feelings were just too powerful to shame them away. Her skin still tingled where he'd touched her. Sighing, she toyed with the idea of following him to the restaurant, but she couldn't see how it would help her cause. Instead, she waited until she heard the servant go upstairs to his room, then she stepped back into the bedroom, thinking perhaps to find a journal or something that would tell her more about Gabriel's doings.

As she slid open his desk drawer, she broke into a smile. There, right on top, was his calendar. Flipping through the pages, she eagerly scanned all of his scheduled activities for the next month. Perfect! Grinning at her own cleverness, she slipped the book inside her cloak and crept downstairs. After making sure that the carriage had gone, she turned the door handle.

It was only then she discovered that it was locked from the outside.

"DID YOU FIND anything?" Penelope turned to her sister, then gasped at the sight of her. "My God, what happened to you?"

Jennifer wiped the black smudges from her chin, then wryly removed her huge hat. Her hair, pulled from its upswept knot, fell around her face in tangles, and her pretty hands were streaked with embedded dirt. She put the calendar to the side as she tried to neaten her appearance. "Just a little problem getting out of Gabriel's house. I had to climb through the root cellar. It wasn't a pretty sight."

"You poor dear!" Penelope was all sympathy as she poured water into the wash basin. "Here, get cleaned up and tell me what happened. You really went into his house?"

"Yes." Jennifer allowed a mischievous smile to come to her face.

"I would have been scared to death!"

"I was horrified," Jennifer admitted, slipping out of her dress and dipping into the wash water. "He caught me. I thought my heart would climb right out of my body."

"He was there!" Penelope stared at her sister as if she'd gone mad. "You were in the house while he was there? And he found you?"

"I had to," Jennifer explained as she soaped her skin. "The cabbie wouldn't wait, and there was no other choice if I wanted to find anything out. He was sort of nice about it, though. I told him I got lost, and thought he could help me."

"And he believed you?" Penelope asked incredulously.

Jennifer shrugged. "He didn't have time to question me too closely. You'll never guess who showed up."

"Allison?" Penelope hazarded, and when Jennifer nodded, she scoffed. "That little hussy! How dare she?"

Jennifer rolled her eyes in disbelief. While she appreciated her sister's loyalty, her logic was sometimes a little muddled. "Penny, I was the one breaking in. She was his escort."

"I know, but to go to his house . . . that just isn't

done." Penelope clucked in the same admonishing tone Aunt Eve used.

"It was all perfectly proper," Jennifer said, wondering why she felt compelled to defend Allison. "Charles was waiting for her outside. I have to confess, I felt very odd seeing them like that. You know, kind of ill."

Penelope reached out and put a hand on Jennifer's forehead. When she noted it was cool, she frowned, as if this was a puzzle too difficult for her. Finally, she raised her gaze to her sister's and a queer expression graced her features.

"Jenny! You're not falling in love with Gabriel, are you?"

"Good heavens, no!" Jennifer cried, appalled. "Why would you think that?"

"I just thought that maybe . . . you were feeling jealous about him and Allison." Penelope shrugged as if the very idea were insane.

"Not at all," Jennifer huffed, scrubbing herself fiercely. "It just . . . surprised me, is all." Tossing aside the washcloth, Jennifer toweled off with the same vigor she'd used to wash.

"Well, all it proves is that he's seeing her, which we already know," Penelope said practically. "Were you able to find out anything else?"

"Yes." Jennifer pulled on her gown, then eyed her sister gleefully. "I found his calendar." She indicated the book.

"You did!" Penelope snatched it up, leafing through the elegantly scrawled pages. "That's wonderful! Oh, Jenny, we're almost there!"

Jennifer nodded. "He has everything penciled in, from his social engagements to his business appointments. It will be quite a simple matter now to put myself in his path. Let's only hope that's all it takes."

"It will be," Penelope muttered fiercely. "I just know it will be."

GABRIEL CRUMBLED A fifth piece of paper onto his desk the following morning and tossed it into the wastebasket. He tried to concentrate on the rows of figures before him, but they looked like some strange hieroglyphics, devoid of any meaning. Exasperated, he gave up and snatched up his hat and stick, then nodded to his clerk as he headed toward the door of his offices.

"I'll be going to lunch, and then for a walk in the park, as usual. You'll be here when I return?"

"As always, sir." Edward Pershing looked at him with bewilderment, then ventured a question. "Is it something I did, Mr. Forester?"

"I don't have any idea what you mean." Gabriel tugged impatiently on his gloves. When he saw the clerk's crestfallen face, he softened his tone. "I'm sorry, I'm not angry with you. I just have a lot on my mind. I'll go over the accounts payable with you when I get back."

He slammed the door, missing Edward's frown. In truth, there was no reason for him to question his clerk's presence, for Edward was always there, seated at his desk, churning out reports. The man was organized, meticulous, and a hard worker, but today it seemed that everything nettled him.

Perhaps the cool air of the park would help. Gabriel grabbed a quick bite at a nearby restaurant, scowling at the waiter and earning a scowl in return. He left a generous tip to make up for his surly mood, but in spite of the well-prepared food, the lunch seemed to sit uncomfortably in his stomach. He left it only half finished and headed for the park.

Central Park had just been completed, and had quickly become his solace in the city. His walks were so important to him that he even penciled them into his schedule, knowing how much he needed the relief. As he wandered down the intricate paths, he felt as if he could finally breathe. The fresh air was invigorating, and the dense foliage provided a welcome screen from acquaintances. Built by two famous architects, Frederick Law Olmsted and Calvert Vaux, the park had a deceptively simple look of glades, lakes, and woods that was actually fully designed and executed, taking over twenty years to construct. For Gabriel, it was an oasis, a place where he could collect his thoughts and emotions.

It was all because of her, that hellion, that she-devil Appleton. Gabriel swore there must be something to her witchery, for he couldn't get her out of his head. He'd gone to dinner the previous night with Allison, and even her intelligent conversation couldn't dispel the image of Jennifer hiding amid his draperies like a stowaway, confessing innocently to being in awe of his nakedness.

It seemed that he couldn't escape, no matter how hard he tried. If Allison hadn't shown up when she did . . . Gabriel knew exactly what would have happened. He would have pulled Jennifer into his arms and made passionate love to her in his own bed, regardless of the consequences.

Even now his flesh still burned at the memory. He thought of her story about getting lost, and wandering into his town house for help. It was just ridiculous enough to be true, and totally in character. That no one took her in hand appalled him, and he realized the task might well fall to him. He was half tempted to put her in her place once and for all, and paddle her so hard she couldn't sit for a week, but he also acknowledged that he wanted her so badly he couldn't think of anything else. Jennifer Appleton had become a bad habit, and he found himself wishing he'd never laid eyes on her.

At least here he could be alone. Gabriel had walked this park every afternoon for the past few years, even in bad weather, for it never failed to have a soothing effect upon him. So when he turned a bend and found himself face to face with Jennifer, he was almost convinced he was still imagining her presence.

She was a wood nymph, a delicate creature sprung from a flower. Unaware of his presence, she bent over a particularly beautiful rose and deeply inhaled its fragrance. Dressed in a simple cotton gown with her hair pulled loosely back and a few burnished curls escaping, she looked like a woodland fairy. Only he knew she was the devil in disguise.

She straightened, sensing his presence, then turned to him with a smile full of delight. He could have sworn that she was happy to see him, even as she cast her eyes demurely down to the ground.

"Miss Appleton. What a surprise to see you here. Is it your habit to frequent this place, unescorted?" A sneaking suspicion flooded his mind that her presence wasn't accidental, that she'd somehow learned of his habit of walking in the park. Gabriel recalled that he had misplaced his calendar. Surely, she couldn't have . . . he dismissed the notion as the utmost conceit. Still, the suspicion would not go away, especially in light of finding her in his town house the previous night.

Her cheeks flushed with color, making her look even more attractive. "A pleasant surprise, I hope," Jennifer said politely. "I'm not unescorted. Penelope was with me. I told her to go ahead." She smiled shyly at him. "I apologize once again for startling you at your house. I deeply appreciate what you did for me, and only hope you can forgive me."

Gabriel stared at her for a moment, as if trying to make sense of what she was saying. He hadn't done nearly what he would have liked to for her, and he wondered if she was deliberately teasing him. Deciding it was better not to even open up that line of conversation, he stared straight ahead, trying to sound as unconcerned as possible.

"I think it best if you don't mention that again. Should anyone discover that you were alone in my house, unescorted and unprotected, your reputation would be ruined. That would be a scandal that even an Appleton couldn't dismiss."

Jennifer nodded somberly. "I understand, and am grateful for your confidence. You are truly a gentleman, Mr. Forester." Before he could react, she gestured to the beautiful grounds. "Isn't the park lovely? I do so enjoy a leisurely stroll. I come here quite often, you know."

"Do you?" Gabriel made no attempt to hide his irritation. "You know, Miss Appleton, I find that statement extremely interesting, since I've never seen you here before. I've come to this park every afternoon, and not once can I recall ever running into you. Yet in the past few weeks, I feel that I have seen you constantly. How would you explain that?"

"It's really quite simple," Jennifer said casually, though her eyes twinkled with merriment. "You didn't know me until recently, and as such, would not have taken notice of me."

He couldn't imagine ever having walked past her and not seen her. "I suppose that is possible, but I still find it odd. Especially since I don't think I would have overlooked you."

He wished he could have taken the words back as soon as he uttered them, for Gabriel realized he'd just complimented her. Jennifer looked up at him and her eyes brightened, making him curse beneath his breath. She was so damned pretty, with those mischievous eyes, and her lips were so soft and pink. He wanted to taste them once more, and as the unbidden thought came into his head, he couldn't banish it. No, he had never seen her here, of that he was certain.

He tore his eyes away from hers and determinedly

continued walking, intending to complete his stroll as if he'd never been accosted.

Jennifer fell into step right beside him. Gabriel could smell the sweet scent of her, could feel her presence like warmth on a chilly day. His icy dismissal didn't affect her the way he'd hoped; Jennifer just chattered on as if they were old friends.

"Isn't it all so beautiful? I really love the way the sunlight reflects on the water, and the way the moss grows on the sides of the trees. I've always liked summer so much, though Aunt Eve says I run like a vagabond, wanting to see and do everything, but it doesn't last that long and you have to make the most of it, don't you think?"

He tried to resist her, but couldn't. She was Diana, Artemis, and Athena, all in one. Stiffly, he found himself replying.

"Yes, it is lovely here. I hear it is getting so crowded on Sundays that it looks more like a promenade. That's why I prefer to walk here during the week."

"And have tea with your mother on Sunday," Jennifer remarked. There was a curious tone in her voice, almost as if she was reciting his schedule. Before he could think about the implication of that, she stopped and looked earnestly up at him, laying her hand on his arm. "I do so admire and like your mother. If nothing else, I want you to know I think the world of her. None of us would ever do anything to harm her."

He wanted to believe her, especially since it hadn't escaped his notice that his mother was happier since Jennifer Appleton came into her life. The two women had become friends, which should have provided some consolation, since his mother was no longer seeing Jennifer for séances. Yet he couldn't get past the fact that Jennifer was a fraud, and that she had taken money from his mother for a service she couldn't possibly have rendered. No one could. He withdrew his arm from hers, fighting the almost uncontrollable urge to pull her close.

"I'm sure that you don't think you're doing anything to harm her. However, in the long run, it most certainly will. I realize, though, that you must be under considerable financial pressure. I know that it isn't easy for young ladies to sustain a living on their own. Therefore, I thought perhaps I could help you a bit with investments. Maybe then, you wouldn't need to perform the spiritualism nonsense."

Jennifer's face fell. Disappointment was clearly evident in her tone and manner as she paused in the center of the path. "I see. Then your offer of help is conditional upon our giving up the séances?" When he nodded, she sighed. "I must decline, then."

"What?" It was his turn to be surprised.

"You have to understand," Jennifer said softly. "I am responsible for them all. We were orphaned at a young age, and Aunt Eve, unfortunately, can't do much to help us financially. Penelope wants to make her debut in society, and that costs money. Winifred's ambition is to go to law school, and Aunt Eve thinks the heavens rain manna. I have to make sure we always have an income, and the spiritualism is the best way I know how. I'm sorry."

Gabriel stared at her, as if suddenly seeing her for the first time. The monster, the "Appleton creature," was a poor, frightened girl who'd had enormous responsibility thrust onto her shoulders at far too young an age. That she should manage that burden, and succeed in spite of it, said something about her character, as did the fact that she'd refused to lie to him. She could easily have taken his investment advice, still continued her fraudulent act, and there would have been nothing he could have done about it. Yet she'd told him the truth.

Life grew more incredible and complicated by the moment.

"Miss Appleton," he nearly choked, the words galling. "It appears that I may have misjudged you. I . . ." He dropped his gaze, aware that it was too bewildering to look at her, especially when she stared at him as hopefully as she was at this moment. His vision fell to her feet, and to his amazement, he saw that she was clad in cloth slippers that, although pretty, were extremely impractical for walking outdoors. His frown grew thunderous as the meaning of that sank in, and he indicated her footwear.

"Miss Appleton, if you are so accustomed to strolling through the park, why are you so unsuitably shod? Those slippers will dampen and you will catch cold."

Jennifer lifted her skirt a mere inch, but it was enough to set his blood pounding. A frothy bit of lace petticoat peeped from beneath the light cotton, and white silk stockings were scandalously exposed. She examined her slippers as if she'd just seen them, then shrugged nonchalantly, dropping her dress once more.

"Aunt Eve is always scolding me for running out of the house on a whim. I didn't think to change my shoes. I just felt I needed some fresh air."

"I see. Then where is your carriage? Surely you didn't run all this distance in house slippers?"

"I—" Jennifer started to explain, then stepped into a huge puddle. Gasping in dismay, she withdrew her foot and gazed at the sodden shoe. The soft, supple cloth was soaked through, and the mud stained her stockings.

Gabriel muttered an oath. He was forced to put his arm closely about her, to support her while she hobbled on the wet shoe. He tried to ignore the subtle scent that filled his nostrils, the wonderful feel of her in his arms, and to not notice how incredibly small her waist was or how well she fit against him. He clenched his teeth, aware that his body was responding to her closeness, arousing him to a degree that he wouldn't have thought possible.

She looked up at him, and for a moment, he thought

he saw an answering warmth. She didn't seem at all displeased with this arrangement, and snuggled more firmly against him, affording him a wonderful view of her small but well-formed bosom. That led to more thoughts he couldn't entertain, for if he did, he'd be compelled to pull her into his arms and kiss her until she moaned. He was fully aware that she was alone and at his mercy in this glade, and that, for all the aggravation she'd caused him, he wouldn't really be to blame for taking his own back. Would he? Yet he had the feeling that he would not be the victor if he gave in to her—and his desire.

Practically dragging her to the entrance of the park, he called for a cab, hailing one from across the street. He helped Jennifer inside, then magically, the missing Penelope appeared. She hopped in with them, seeming unaccountably gleeful about the situation. Sliding as far away from them as he could, he stared sullenly out the window, more than a little put out by this latest encounter. When they reached Twin Gables, he was compelled as a gentleman to help Jennifer from the carriage and up the steps.

Gabriel even caught what he thought was a smug expression, which quickly became solemn when she saw him watching her. Jennifer leaned fully on him, appearing more than content to wrap her arm around his as if they were waltzing up the staircase. Scowling, Gabriel waited for Penelope to open the door, and he entered with Jennifer hopping beside him on one foot.

"My Lord! What is going on here?" Aunt Eve dropped her hand from the parrot cage and glared at the young people before her. When she realized it was Gabriel, her mouth rounded into a perfect O. "Mr. Forester! I thought I made it plain that you aren't welcome in this house!"

"Now, Auntie, I had a little accident. Mr. Forester was kind enough to escort me." Jennifer displayed the shoe, which was ruined from the mud and water.

"Her slippers are just ruined!" Penelope cried plaintively. "If it wasn't for Mr. Forester, I don't know how we would have gotten home!"

"How terrible! You must be soaked through, poor dear. We'd better get you straight to bed." She took Jennifer's arm from Gabriel, sending him a look that impaled him more cleanly than an embroidery needle. "I'm sure you had something to do with this situation, young man. Thank you for returning my niece. Good day."

Gabriel stared at her in astonishment. He was about to protest his innocence, but when Jennifer turned and gaily waved to him behind her aunt's back, he simply closed his mouth and shook his head.

No one would believe him anyway.

CHAPTER 7

THE FOLLOWING DAY, Jennifer looked up as Aunt Eve came into the house. Her elderly relative appeared more tired than normal, and the twinkle in her eyes had dimmed considerably. She removed her bonnet, then rubbed her temples, wincing from the pain.

"Is something wrong, Auntie?" Jennifer asked, genuinely concerned. She had become very fond of Eve, and it troubled her to see the old lady looking so wretched.

"It's just my headaches again," Eve whispered, as if even that nominal sound was too loud. "I've been to my physician, but he said there is little that can be done. I thought I'd go up to my bed and lie down."

"Maybe I can help." Jennifer rose to stand beside her Aunt. "I used to rub Father's head when he was ill. He got headaches also, you know. He always said it worked wonders."

"He did? No, I wasn't aware of that. If you wouldn't mind, dear, my head aches so much I can hardly stand."

Jennifer assisted her aunt to her bed, helping the old lady loosen her stays and remove her boots. When she was propped up on the pillows, Jennifer stood behind her and began to gently rub her temples, allowing the warmth from her fingertips to penetrate her aunt's head. Gradually, the lines of pain eased from Eve's face, and color began to return to her skin. Her cheeks, which had been dull and pale, became pink, and her withered mouth curved upward in a smile.

"Jenny, that feels wonderful! However did you learn such a thing?"

Jennifer smiled, continuing the massage. "Father used to say I had the angel's touch. It always helped his headaches, and his arthritis. I don't know how it works, but it does."

Penelope entered the room, smiling as she saw her aunt's beaming countenance. "Come in, dear!" Eve said. "The most wonderful thing has happened. Your sister cured me of the most dreadful headache ever!"

"I know. Jenny's always had that ability. I used to go to her whenever I had an ache or pain."

"She's remarkable! Why, she's better than any physician or magnetic healer I've ever seen!"

At her words, Jennifer glanced up at Penelope, who returned her look as inspiration dawned. Jennifer finished the massage, gratified to see her aunt slip into a peaceful rest. Grinning with barely contained excitement, the two sisters crept downstairs.

"Are you thinking what I'm thinking?" Penelope practically sparkled.

"Good Lord, I don't know why we didn't think of it before! I've always been a decent masseuse, but I never thought to parlay my talent this way! Magnetic healers are all the rage. Vanderbilt goes to them all the time, as does Jim Fiske! We can make so much more money, meet more prominent people, and pick up additional clients all at the same time!" Jennifer rubbed her hands together gleefully.

"Now we just have to figure out how to get the word out," Penelope said thoughtfully. "I suppose we could post notice in the newspapers."

"No." Jennifer dismissed the idea quickly. "All the charlatans do that. We need something more public, a place where we could meet men. They are actually more open to magnetic healing than women are, and it would do our séance business good to get more male clients."

Penelope snapped her fingers. "I've got it! What about the stock market?" When Jennifer turned a puzzled look toward her, Penelope rushed to explain. "Remember, the calendar? Gabriel goes to the market every Friday, as do most other wealthy businessmen. We can set up there and show off your talent! In the meantime, we can attract Mr. Forester's attention as well!"

Jennifer broke into laughter. Where there was a will, there was a way. And the Appletons certainly had the will.

THE NEW YORK Stock Exchange was a madhouse of old wealth, newly rich upstarts, brokers, and financiers. Ticker tapes clicked the numbers while brokers shouted "Buy!" or "Sell!," grabbing up stock shares and dumping them surreptitiously. Men swore horribly, rubbing their whiskers in agitation as they lost out on a stock, while others cheered with excitement as the prices climbed higher. Outrageously wealthy men manipulated the numbers for their own advantage, while others sought to follow their movements and accumulate their own wealth in the bargain.

Cornelius Vanderbilt dismounted his buggy, giving his horses a fond pat before entering the den of thieves. Though sick and elderly, the commodore couldn't stay away from Wall Street, and neither his religious wife nor his seventy-eight years could convince him to do so.

Today he walked slowly into the stone building, emerging from the ever-present shadows and hobbling like an elderly clergyman. His white hair blew in the wind, and his arthritis troubled him terribly. Conventional society still snubbed him, so he'd married a woman who was accepted everywhere. Yet being at home alone with her was more than he could endure. He needed the market, with its frenzied activity, to remind him that he was still alive.

He entered the male bastion along with many of his acquaintances, prepared to play the market, have a few drinks, and smoke cigars. What he wasn't prepared to see was three beautiful women creating a sensation on Wall Street.

Jennifer, Penelope, and Winifred stood off the main trading floor, surrounded by curious men. Clad in simple navy blue walking dresses devoid of any artifice, they appeared businesslike and practical, while their charm and beauty was noted by all. Penelope spoke gently to the voyeurs, obviously in her element, while Winifred kept a close watch on the strongbox before her. Jennifer stood behind a seated gentleman. Her eyes were closed, her hands rested on the man's shoulders, and a strange energy seemed to come from her slender form.

The market mayhem went on as usual, but between breaks, others gathered round to watch. Moaning, Jennifer rolled her eyes, emitting a strange, eerie sound, while her hands maintained contact between herself and her patron. The old man seated before her initially appeared amused, but as Jennifer closed her eyes once more and hummed, his expression turned to wonder.

"I can feel it! Lordy, I can feel something!"

"Jennifer is a magnetic healer," Penelope explained as the men pressed closer. "She channels her own energy into the client, allowing his body to use her own healthy vibrations to aid in the healing process. Jennifer is like a battery—her right hand is the positive, the left negative. It's really quite simple and very scientific."

The man in the chair rose, then stretched his limbs before him. His face brightened, and a huge smile curved beneath his beard.

"She's right! My joints feel better than they have in ages! Bless you, missy!" The grateful man placed a few dollars in Winifred's hand, then, on second thought, a note. "Stock tip," he winked. "I'm a broker for Hoffman and Clews on Broadway. If you ever decide to invest, let me know."

"I'm next!" a portly man shouted, elbowing his way through the crowd. "I have a stiff neck, and I could use a pretty lady's hands on it! In fact, I have something else that's stiff, and maybe we could discuss that!" He leaned closer to Penelope and leered, while she wrinkled her nose and waved away the whiskey fumes with distaste.

Winifred stood before the chair, giving the man a stern look. "Sir, we are not prostitutes or women of ill repute. We are ladies, established here in New York society. My sister is prepared to share her healing talents for the benefit of all, but let me make our motives clear. We are here to help heal, that's all. My sisters and I will not be addressed with disrespect."

Stunned, the second man muttered an apology, while the one that had been "cured" turned around, ready to defend the women. But there was no need. Winifred's personality had a force of its own.

The commodore, observing this phenomena, tapped his way through the throng. Men parted for him, allowing him to walk freely to the clearing and approach the three women. He took the chair, obviously pleased at the thought of ministrations by these angelic healers.

"Do your best, ladies," he said, grinning. "My bones are aching. If you can make me feel better, it will be well worth your time."

Penelope gave him her sweetest smile, and Jennifer began the performance once more. The commodore, who loved women almost as much as he did the railroad business, enjoyed himself mightily as Jennifer laid her pretty, white hands on him and Penelope whispered encouragements. The crowd gathered even more thickly as one of the wealthiest men on Wall Street submitted to Jennifer's magnetic healing.

Gabriel walked into the trading room and handed his hat and stick to a porter. He'd been planning to buy some shares in a few emerging businesses, looking to balance the fluctuations in the marble business with additional investments. He glanced through his notes, then scanned the room, looking for his broker.

Then he saw them. Gabriel's mouth dropped and he couldn't believe what his eyes told him was truth. Jennifer was standing behind Cornelius Vanderbilt, her eyes closed, her face knotted as if struggling with something. Lovely Penelope stood next to her, a radiant flower in the midst of chaos, while practical, intelligent Winifred removed a gold pen from behind her ear and scribbled on a notepad.

He'd lost his mind. It had finally happened. The visions he'd been having of Jennifer had become hallucinations. There could be no other explanation for what he was seeing—until Charles Howe came to stand beside him. His friend's expression mirrored his own.

"What in the hell are they doing here!"

Gabriel ran his hand though his hair in agitation, too stunned to speak. As the commodore rose and flexed his muscles jubilantly, the crowd roared. He swung his arm around Penelope and gave her an appreciative squeeze, then he turned to Jennifer. He lifted her hand and kissed it regally, as if addressing Queen Victoria herself.

Gabriel opened his mouth, closed it, then opened it once more. Outrage swept through him as another man took a seat. This one looked young and healthy, and the only thing he seemed interested in was the opportunity to have a beautiful woman put her hands on him. Gabriel's face flushed crimson as Jennifer's pretty fingers sank down into the man's cravat and her eyes closed once more. He remembered her face after that one moment of insanity when he'd kissed her . . . she wore that same, dreamy expression now.

Jonathan Wiseley stood before them, sipping the dregs from his coffee, his expression astonished. "You've got to hand it to them, don't you? Who would have thought the Appletons so bold as to pull a stunt like this one? Good Lord, there's Fitzhugh from the *Times*. This will be all over New York by morning!" He put his cup aside, ignorant of the dangerous tension that raged in the two men. "I think I'll go make their acquaintance. I could use a little energy healing myself!"

Jonathan walked off and Gabriel flexed his hand, as if debating whether or not to plaster the man's face with it. Charles seemed almost as incensed as himself, for his normally placid companion shook with impotent fury.

"Wait until I see Miss Winifred Appleton alone. I'll certainly call her on this one. I'm half tempted to drag her out of here this minute. Good God, look at the men around them!"

Gabriel didn't have to look. His own anger overwhelmed him, and he shoved his papers into his trouser pockets. "You won't have to say anything to Winifred," Gabriel gritted. "I know who the real culprit is here. Excuse me while I have a word with Miss Jennifer Appleton."

Gabriel stormed toward the girls, listening to the murmuring of the men. Although many of the comments were respectful, there were a few crude remarks and wagers on who would be the first to get the full healing treatment from the Appletons. Their words burned his ears as he shoved through the crowd to get closer, aware of the mounting tension and excitement. To his astonishment, Jonathan's prediction proved correct, for he heard the reporter interviewing Penelope.

"Can you tell us where your offices are? Are you ladies

really brokers or energy healers, as you claim? Has the commodore given you any tips?"

Penelope answered the man blithely, while Jennifer continued with the healing. Another satisfied customer stood up, paid out his money, then tried to kiss Penelope, who playfully slapped him away.

Blood pounded in Gabriel's ears as Jennifer's eyes opened. To his gratification, they widened when they saw him, and, if he had to analyze their expression, appeared a little uncertain. She turned toward her sister as if to warn her, but Penelope had already spotted him and seemed delighted.

"Mr. Forester! I thought that was you. How wonderful to see you! Surely you aren't in need of Jennifer's talents? We would be glad to make special arrangements for a friend!"

He was too furious to respond. He ignored Penelope and, glaring at Jennifer, clamped a hand over her wrist and dragged her from behind the chair into an adjoining office. Before she could utter a word, he kicked the door closed, effectively shutting out the protests from the men on the floor.

"You have no right!" Jennifer began, but her own voice trailed off into a frightened silence as Gabriel stepped toward her, backing her up. Her bustle hit the wall and with his hands on either side of her, Jennifer was trapped. She looked up into his eyes and the expression she saw made her swallow. Hard.

"I have no right!" Gabriel glared at her. "What right do you have to come in here, pretending to heal people with your hands, for God's sake! As if such a thing could happen!"

"It does happen!" Jennifer said hotly. "It is well known that magnetic healing works. Evidently, the commodore thinks so."

"Miss Appleton." He spoke through clenched teeth,

spitting out each word with icy emphasis. "I want you to go outside, pick up your things, and instruct your sisters to quietly accompany me to my carriage. There, I will instruct my driver to take you home. Do you understand me?"

Jennifer glared at him defiantly. "No."

Astounded, he stared into her stormy gray eyes, wondering where this slip of a girl found the courage to challenge him, and why he felt this uncontrollable need to possess her. The fiery rebellion he saw in her only added to his predicament, for somehow he wanted her to rebel, only so he could have the satisfaction of taming her. He wanted to bring her to hand, kiss her senseless, and make love to her all at the same time.

"You aren't my husband, nor my father," Jennifer protested, though she didn't sound as confident as she had a moment ago. "Who do you think you are, giving me orders?"

He had to admire her audacity, especially since he could feel her shaking beneath his hands. Her chin lifted and she faced him squarely, but her lips trembled and her eyes were as wide as saucers. He looked down, then realized he had made another mistake as he saw her curves, outlined beautifully by her somber costume. She was in his arms, the hellion who haunted him, and he was once more torn between passion and utter exasperation. Without wanting it to, the thought came to his mind: Allison never made him feel this way. Summoning all the restraint he could manage, he spoke quietly.

"Jennifer," he said, unwittingly calling her by her first name, "you are a friend to my mother, and unfortunately, since I know you, I feel a certain responsibility toward you. Are you aware that several hundred men think you are a prostitute of some kind? I heard them wagering on who will be the first to have you. If such a situation is what you desire, say the word and I'll leave you to it. Your only chance is to get out of here before the crowd turns into a mob."

Her face went white and, like a little girl, she seemed only now to fully comprehend what she'd gotten herself into. Shame washed through her, changing her visage from defiance to confusion. Numbly, she nodded, and only then did he step back, allowing her to move out of his way.

"You are right. I'll tell Winifred and Penny." She lifted her face, appearing genuinely contrite. "Thank you for your concern."

The innocence in her tone sent his senses spinning. She was the most outrageous woman he'd ever met. Pulling her dignity about her, she turned and walked out of the room like a queen. Admiration swelled within him, confusing him even more. In that moment, he knew the truth: Jennifer Appleton would only continue to haunt his dreams.

And there wasn't a damn thing he could do about it.

PENELOPE SMILED, SEEING Gabriel haul her sister off to the offices. Everything was going just as planned. No, better than planned, Penelope thought. Jubilantly, she watched Winifred count their earnings. They had made more money in one afternoon than they made in a week of séances.

"Pardon me, miss. Did anyone ever tell you how beautiful you are?"

Penelope turned around, prepared to give the man her ever-present smile. She almost had to laugh at his question. People had been telling her she was beautiful ever since she could remember. But something about this man gave her pause.

He was far older than herself, in his late forties or even fifties, she surmised. His hair was dark, but shot with silver, and craggy lines surrounded his eyes. He was portly, his face bore a perpetual ruddiness, but his suit was of the finest quality and the Italian leather of his boots shone. Even his walking stick was cut from mahogany, and inlaid with ivory.

Penelope gave him her warmest smile. The man had money; he positively reeked of it. Excitement tingled through her as she realized he was focused on her. If she were to wed someone like him, she would have everything she'd ever dreamed of. Penelope also dimly realized that she would no longer be a burden to her sisters. Why, she could even help them! He extended his hand with a hearty grin and she saw his fingers were covered with diamond and gold rings.

"I would like to make your acquaintance. My name is James McBride. I am a merchant, a wealthy one at that. I've been coming to the market every Friday for years, and never saw as fair a face as your own gracing this hall. I must say, it is a pleasure."

"Penelope Appleton." Penelope lifted her hand, allowing him to press it with his own. Winifred gave her a disapproving frown, which she ignored. Looking up into James's eyes, she saw the inevitable interest that followed, as well as speculation. Honing all of her considerable skills, Penelope shyly withdrew her palm when he held it a moment too long.

"If you'll excuse me, Mr. McBride, my sister is waiting."

She gave him a wicked flutter of her lashes, while her words were perfectly innocent and polite. He was enchanted, as he was meant to be.

"Miss Appleton, I should like to call on you sometime, maybe take you for a buggy ride. Have you ever participated in the races on Fifth?"

Penelope's eyes widened. She'd heard of those outings, where Jim Fiske and his carriage full of gorgeous mistresses raced up Fifth Avenue, wagering heavily against the Belmonts and Schermerhorns. Afterward, they dined on champagne and oysters in Central Park, the losers treating the winners. They were millionaires, all of them, and Penelope's pulse raced as if he'd kissed her.

"No, I never have." Out of the corner of her eye she saw Jennifer approaching with Gabriel, and she quickly withdrew from the man's engagement. "I'm sorry, but I've got to go."

"How will I call on you?" The man's face dropped in disappointment as he watched her turn away.

Penelope glanced back at him and gave him a seductive smile. "You'll find me." She winked, then fled toward her sisters.

James McBride watched her go. He would find her, he decided. If it was the last thing he did.

CHAPTER 8

"My goodness, Jennifer, look at this!" Penelope said the following day as she dumped a sack full of cards onto the table.

"What is it?" Jennifer sifted her fingers through the brightly printed cards, frowning when she noticed that they all bore male names.

"Callers. These are all men interested in having a magnetic healing performed for them. Look! There must be forty cards here!" Delighted, Penelope read the inscriptions, and placed the cards into piles.

Winifred shook her head worriedly. "I think our magnetic healing was too successful. Jenny, I don't think we should do this again. For three young women living alone with our aunt, to have so many male callers could seriously compromise our reputations."

Reluctantly, Jennifer nodded, remembering Gabriel's words. "Yes, I'm forced to agree. It was one thing to do this at the stock market in public, and even that was dangerous. It is quite another to take these men into our home. I'm afraid we'll have to announce that the Appletons have gone out of the healing business, but are quite open to séances."

"Pooh!" Penelope cried. "Do we really have to forgo it?" Her pretty face crinkled as she saw the cards slipping through her fingers.

"Yes, we have to," Jennifer said decidedly. "By the way, how did we make out financially? Was it a great success?"

Placing aside her gold pen, Winifred looked up at her sister, a queer grin spreading from one ear to the next.

"We made five hundred dollars."

"Five hundred . . . are you sure?" Jennifer asked, nearly dancing around the room in excitement.

Winifred nodded indignantly. "Yes, I'm quite sure, the figures are exact. I am very careful, you know. Our one-day stint at the stock market really paid off tremendously. Imagine, five hundred dollars for laying your hands on a man's head!"

"Well, it's a little more involved than that," Jennifer said, though she was just as pleased. "What shall we do with it?"

"Why, we could put this in the bank and invest it, and we could make one or two percent interest. . . ." Winifred scribbled furiously. "Why, we could increase our capital by five dollars a year by doing nothing! Isn't that wonderful?"

Jennifer frowned. "But it's not enough." When her sister looked at her in bewilderment, Jennifer shrugged. "It isn't! Penelope's going to be seventeen this year. She needs to be launched into society. You need college money. And I need to make sure we have enough to live on, including enough for Aunt Eve. A few dollars is nothing."

"Have you a better idea?" Winifred asked pointedly.

In response, Jennifer rummaged in her pocket. Retrieving a crumpled paper, she smoothed the note and placed it before her sister. Winifred adjusted her glasses and read the scrawled writing.

"It says 'Union Pacific Railroad.'" She laid it down and stared at her sibling. "What does it mean?"

Jennifer's eyes twinkled. "The commodore wrote that.

He suggested we invest in stock, and he personally recommended that one."

Winifred's brow wrinkled as she stared at the slip of paper. "You do realize the danger. Stocks are not like bank notes. While the potential profit is great, so is the risk. And there is one other difficulty." She looked over her glasses at Jennifer as if explaining the obvious to one of questionable mental health. "Women cannot trade."

"Why not?" Jennifer asked forthrightly. "You're the law student. Is there a law against it?"

Winifred puzzled for a moment. "No, not that I recall. But who could we get to take such an order? Who can we trust? And who will be our broker?"

"I have an idea," Jennifer whispered, every word brimming with excitement. "Do you remember Justin Caldwell from school?"

"Do you mean that snotty little boy you used to beat up in the schoolyard? The one that called me four-eyes?" Winifred removed her glasses, polishing them against the hurtful memory.

"Yes, the very one. He's an investment banker now, of all things. He only got the position because of his father, but he's legitimate all the same. If I use the commodore's name, I'll wager I can coerce him into investing for us. What do you think?"

Winifred nodded speculatively. "He's a wormy little chap, but I don't think he'd do anything illegal with our money. He'd be too afraid of his father's wrath, or yours, for that matter. Do you really think you can convince him?"

Jennifer grinned, rubbing her hands together. "Leave that to me. Justin Caldwell will help us, or he'll be spitting grass in the schoolyard again."

IT WAS LATE in the evening when Jennifer returned. She removed her coat, and nodded in response to Winifred's questioning look. Passing quickly by her aunt's room and ignoring Penelope's chatter, she pulled Winifred into the bedroom and shut the door.

"How did it go?" Winifred asked eagerly.

Jennifer produced a banker's statement. Winifred quickly scanned the document.

"Why, Jennifer, you were able to buy fifty shares! However did you manage it?"

Jennifer grinned while Winifred read the statement again, certain there must have been some mistake.

"You're absolutely correct! Not only did I persuade Justin to buy us shares, but I stopped by to see the commodore. He congratulated me for taking his advice, and he told me to hold on to the shares for a few more days. We're going to do well, Winnie, I just know it! We may not make millions, but we should have enough to pay off our debts and get started on our plans!"

Winifred, usually so reserved, hugged her unabashedly, and Jennifer flushed in triumph.

"You did it! Why Jennifer, you did something very few women have ever attempted! I'm so proud of you! This took not only courage and intelligence, but shrewdness as well! However did you persuade Justin?"

Jennifer felt an absurd sense of pleasure at her sister's praise. "When I first entered his office, he pretended not to recognize me. He looks as wormy as ever, with his oiled hair parted in the middle and his derby. When I told him what I wanted, he sank back in his chair and patted his belly, and in the most obnoxious voice imaginable, told me that women cannot trade, especially scandalous women like myself."

"He didn't!" Winifred's eyes widened.

"He certainly did. I don't know why I was surprised, because he always was a snob. In any case, I simply reminded him of our school days and suggested that his silk suit would not benefit from a trip down Memory Lane."

"You didn't!"

"I did. Just as he was getting ready to throw me out, I said the magic word: Vanderbilt. I thought he would faint, especially when I insinuated that the commodore and I were on very friendly terms. He'd heard about our stint on Wall Street, and when I told him of the commodore's fondness for spiritual healing, his eyes nearly popped out of his head. His hand actually shook as he signed the papers, and he wound up begging me to put in a good word for him. Seems his own clients don't have nearly the collateral that our good friend Vanderbilt has, and darling Justin was just drooling to get his hands on it."

"Did you promise to help him?"

"Of course not. I told him I would think about it. In any case, he couldn't buy our shares quickly enough. He placed the order while I waited, and even called his own boy to run it down to the exchange. So we Appletons are now the proud shareholders of Union Pacific, and Justin is my errand boy."

When they both had laughed so hard they cried, Winifred hugged her again. When she finally released her, she placed her hands on her sister's shoulders.

"Now, Jennifer, you must promise me one thing. You must take some of that money and do something for yourself. Even if it's just a gown or a special book, do something special, something just for you."

Jennifer smiled softly. "Don't worry, Winnie, I'm not that self-sacrificing. I have something special planned. And I know just the person to share it with."

"MR. FORESTER. THERE'S someone to see you." Edward Pershing thrust his head cautiously through the doorway.

"Just a minute, Edward," Gabriel said. "I am occupied."

"Mr. Forester will be with you momentarily," the clerk told Jennifer. He took his seat in the outer office.

Jennifer smiled and nodded, filled with curiosity. There was something about Gabriel's voice when he said he was occupied that made her think it wasn't a business meeting that had him so engaged.

Gripping her basket, she wondered if Allison was in the office with him. Her presence would ruin everything. Jennifer recalled from his calendar that Allison wasn't scheduled to visit, but then, no one had been. Whoever his caller was, it was a surprise visit. Much like her own.

Edward frowned, then jumped up from his chair in exasperation as his pencil broke. "Excuse me, miss, but I've got to run out for another." He tugged on his coat.

Jennifer shrugged in agreement, then waited for the man to quit the room. As soon as he was safely gone, she went to stand beside the door to Gabriel's office.

Her instincts had been correct—partly. Jennifer heard a distinctly feminine voice on the other side of the door, but to her relief, it wasn't Allison's. Overcome by curiosity, she knelt down to the keyhole and listened to the conversation.

"I must plead with you, sir, to forgive my husband's debts. I know I was wrong in coming here, but I felt I had no other choice."

Jennifer's eyes widened as she struggled to hear Gabriel's reply. Part of her admonished herself that this was his private business, that she should be above listening at keyholes, but the rest of her couldn't resist. Besides, she was still sort of spying on him, and as espionage went, listening at keyholes was part of the job.

"I am familiar with your account," Gabriel said, so softly Jennifer had to strain to catch his words. "But your husband owes me for several jobs, none of which he's paid."

"I know, sir." The woman spoke with a thick brogue.

"Mr. Forester, I am going to confess the truth. My Paddy has a thirst for gin. He's a good man when he works, but the devil himself when he's drinking. If you complain about his debts, he will go to prison, and there will be no money for myself and our wee one."

The woman began to sob softly. Jennifer winced, waiting to hear Gabriel abruptly dismiss the woman. She had heard about Gabriel's taking over the family business, and that he was a stern taskmaster with anyone who owed him. To her surprise, she heard his voice, comforting, and full of understanding.

"Mrs. Murphy, please don't upset yourself so. You've done nothing wrong. I understand your problem, so here's what I shall do. Tell Paddy to come see me at promptly seven A.M. on Saturday. I will allow him to work his debt off. That will benefit both of us. I'll collect some kind of payment, and hopefully, keep him out of the tavern for a few weeks."

"Bless your kind heart, sir! How will I ever thank you?"

"There is no thanks necessary, Mrs. Murphy. This is a business decision that is best for everyone. My clerk will see you out."

"May God watch over you, sir!"

Jennifer scooted back from the doorway not a moment too soon. A tearful Mrs. Murphy emerged, holding a handkerchief to her face. She barely nodded to Jennifer, rushing past her to the street.

Jennifer stared at the door in amazement. Gabriel, stern forbidding Gabriel who never forgot a debt, had a heart. Recalling the gossip she'd heard about him and his father, Jennifer had assumed that Gabriel scrounged for every dime. She was further impressed by the genius of his solution, for to let the man off easily would be doing him no favor in the long run. She nearly beamed at Edward, who had just returned. Giving her a frown, he put his newly acquired pencil on the desk, then popped his head inside the office once more.

"Excuse me, sir, but you have another visitor."

Gabriel glanced up, obviously irritated at the interruption. "Take care of it, Pershing. I'm putting together a large bid and want to finish it today."

Edward stood at the doorway, rubbing his hands together in bewilderment. "But, sir, I really think you should see her yourself."

"Dammit, Pershing, the last thing I need is another surprise—" Before he could continue his diatribe, Jennifer peeped in just below Edward's arm, giving Gabriel a lovely smile.

Gabriel groaned, resigned. "Let her in. Pershing, you may go." Gabriel watched as Jennifer stepped into the room. The clerk seemed loath to depart. Curiosity twitched in the man's mustache, and it was with great reluctance that he closed the door.

"Miss Appleton." Gabriel deliberately lowered his voice, hoping to give his clerk less entertainment. "What in God's name are you doing here?"

Jennifer smiled, looking exceptionally pretty in a violet-sprigged dress and pert bonnet. Lace gloves covered her hands, and dainty amethyst earrings danced from her earlobes. She shyly displayed the hamper she'd brought with her. "I wanted to thank you for what you did on Friday at the stock market. I thought about it later and realized that you are a friend, and that you really did help us. I am grateful."

She looked so fresh and adorable that it was difficult to maintain his stern demeanor. "Miss Appleton, I don't know if we could qualify our relationship as a friendship, and you are well aware of the reasons why. In any case, no such display is necessary. I accept your thanks, but I have a lot of work to do today. Pershing will see you out."

Jennifer looked crushed. Her bottom lip quivered as if she would cry, then she bit it, fighting to keep her composure. Her huge gray eyes, normally glimmering with mirth, now looked pained, and he swore he saw a soft sheen of moisture there. His suspicions were confirmed a moment later when she withdrew her handkerchief from her sleeve, hiding her face in embarrassment.

"I'm sorry, I just thought . . ." Her words came out in a confused rush. "I'm always saying or doing the wrong thing! I just wanted to be friends, to make up with you, but you really don't like me at all, do you? Don't worry, I'll get out of your way. I'm sorry if I bothered you."

Gabriel swore, coming to his feet. Every ounce of gentlemanly conditioning prodded him, and his conscience pricked him unmercifully. He felt as if he'd just stepped on a baby chick, especially when he saw the way her shoulders slumped, the picture of dejection. Sighing, he realized he couldn't refuse her, no matter how noble his intentions or morals.

"Miss Appleton, wait."

She turned immediately. In spite of her emotional state, she looked at him dry-eyed and expectant. He quickly dismissed his sudden suspicions, reminding himself that she had used her handkerchief. Capturing her hand with his, he attempted to smooth away the hurt.

"Look, I'm sorry. I appreciate your gesture. It's just that I have a lot of work to do, and it really isn't proper for you to come here. A lady does not drop into a man's offices unescorted unless they are all but engaged, as I'm sure you know."

"Then you'll come for lunch?" Jennifer asked hopefully.

He had to laugh. She was maddening, irritating as hell, but utterly enchanting when she wanted to be. He could almost understand how people thought she could heal them, or that they thought they saw the dead in her presence.

"I can't. I was going to send for the boy at the restaurant around the corner."

Her mouth drooped in disappointment. "But you always walk in the park. This way, you could eat there, too, and it would take less time." She brightened, opening the hamper and displaying the food inside. "Aunt Eve made us chicken and potato salad, fruit and cake. There's even some wine." Proudly, she indicated the bottle.

"But—"

Her lashes fluttered artlessly. "I won't take 'no' for an answer. If you truly meant what you said, then please come. Besides, it will do you good to get out for a few minutes. Then you can come back, fresh."

Once again, his resistance evaporated. He stared at her for a full minute, then nodded. "I'll get my hat."

Jennifer beamed at him. He snatched up his hat, wondering just what had happened in the last few minutes, and why he always seemed to lose control around this woman. He pushed open the door, and Edward scrambled to get back to his desk. He gave the clerk a stern look.

"Finish those reports by the time I get back. Miss Appleton and I have a business meeting."

Edward nodded, then stared curiously at Jennifer, who smiled back at him. Gabriel ushered her out the door, and down to the street. He held her arm as he would any woman he was escorting, but he saw by her look of pleasure that she obviously enjoyed the attention. Distracted, he glanced down at her hamper, then took the heavy bundle from her.

"I'll call for my carriage since we have all this food."

"Oh, we can take mine," Jennifer offered. "It's still there."

He nodded, then followed her to a gleaming carriage that waited near the curb. Two glossy black horses stood before the vehicle, tossing their heads impatiently, while a jaunty driver winked at Jennifer. She directed the man to the park, then climbed in beside Gabriel.

"Miss Appleton, this is a rather nice carriage," Gabriel commented, settling the hamper on the floor and glancing at the supple leather seats and polished brass fittings. "Surely you don't own this? Your financial situation must be improving dramatically."

"Well." Jennifer looked nonplussed. "We did do rather well on Friday, with the magnetic healing. Now, don't scowl like that," she continued quickly. "And then there were the stock tips."

"What do you mean, 'stock tips'?" Outrage began to well up inside him again. He had a pretty good idea of what she meant, but he wasn't any happier about it when she confirmed his belief.

"Vanderbilt and some of the others gave us some advice. The Union Pacific stock turned around very quickly, and we made a handsome profit."

"Miss Appleton." Gabriel gritted his teeth. "Do you mean to tell me that you refused my help but accepted the commodore's?"

Jennifer rustled her dress, looking down at the floor of the carriage, then out the open window, then back. Trapped, she finally confessed. "Yes." At his thunderous expression, she rushed to explain. "I had no other choice! Your offer was conditional upon a promise I couldn't make. The commodore's was—"

"In exchange for services rendered." He glared at her, and when she gave him a sheepish smile, he couldn't contain his fury. "Miss Appleton, why is it I'm always torn between wanting to beat you, and . . ."

"And?" She picked up, brightening.

"And wanting never to see you again," he finished quickly—damned if she'd catch him like that. "So you seem to have done very well for yourself. I apologize for my foolishness in thinking that I might have been able to assist you. Now that you have such powerful friends, my offer must have seemed really ridiculous."

Why her relationship with Vanderbilt and the rest of them should bother him, he couldn't explain. All he knew was that his masculine ego was crushed. He didn't want the Appletons dependent on him in any way . . . did he? Why then did he feel so outraged and betrayed?

"It was nothing of the sort," Jennifer pleaded. "I appreciated your offer, you know that. I just couldn't promise what you wanted. Even now, with the investments, we are not financially sound. We still need the income from the séances." When he refused to look at her, Jennifer laid her hand on his arm. "Please, Mr. Forester, let's not quarrel. I wanted to treat you today, to thank you. I don't want to upset you."

"It's a little late for that, miss," Gabriel said coldly, but he found the sting subsiding.

The carriage rolled to a stop and they disembarked. Gabriel was forced to help Jennifer down, slipping his hands around her as he swung her from the step. This time, she was suitably shod for the park, with new little leather boots, he noted. Once more he was aware of her small feet and dainty ankles. He had to let her go quickly, and even then he was still physically affected by her nearness.

She pointed out the spot she'd found and playfully spread out the picnic cloth, letting it puff into the air like a sail before settling down to the grass. It was a beautiful place, and a perfect day. Autumn was coming, and there was a bite in the air, and the normally hazy sky was clear and breathtakingly blue.

Jennifer peeped at Gabriel, aware that he was still furious with her. It seemed he always was, no matter what she said or did. This romance stuff wasn't nearly as easy as Penelope described it, though she had to admit, her sister's tactics worked. Why they did remained a mystery to Jennifer.

She unpacked the basket, enticing him with food and gay chatter. He seemed detached, as if fighting off her spell, wanting to keep her at a distance. He ate the food, responded politely enough, but some of the brightness seemed to have gone away. Jennifer knew he was angry about the stocks, but what should she have done? Refused what she knew was a reasonable way to make money? Sometimes, she just didn't understand men at all.

A street urchin wandered by with a basket, then stopped beside Gabriel and Jennifer. His face was smudged with chimney dust, and his hands were blistered and covered with dirt. Jennifer shuddered, thinking there but for the grace of God went she. She gave the boy a bright smile, which he answered immediately.

"Afternoon, miss. Would you be interested in buying a wee kitten? I have a basket full."

He opened the lid, and Jennifer glanced inside. Three beautiful kittens tumbled about, playing with a leaf that had fallen into the basket. Her heart melted as she lifted a calico from the litter and held it aloft for Gabriel to see.

"Oh, isn't he cute? Gabriel, look! He looks like a little tiger!"

The boy, sensing a soft touch, went for the kill. "Can you spare a dollar, miss? If I don't sell 'em, we'll have to drown them, for there ain't enough milk in the house for all."

"Drown them! Why, you couldn't! Let me see if I have any money . . ." She rifled through her reticule, counting out pennies, looking forlorn as the boy ingeniously held up the doomed kitten.

Gabriel sighed, then reached into his own pocket. "Here's three dollars, and that's highway robbery. Give the others away."

The boy nodded, snatching up the money, then depositing the kitten in Jennifer's lap. Jennifer smiled at Gabriel, giving him a look so full of longing that he had to swallow hard.

What in the hell was he doing? One minute he swore to have nothing to do with her again, the next minute, he was buying her presents. Worse yet, when she rose a moment later and placed her hand on his shoulder, he was nearly overcome.

"Thank you, Gabriel. I'll treasure him always."

If she had stopped there, things might have been all right, but she leaned close to him and placed a chaste kiss on his cheek. And Gabriel lost whatever control he had thus far managed to possess. The memory of the one kiss they'd shared had seared his brain, and it came to the forefront now. Pulling her into his lap, he slid his arm around her waist, bringing her as close to him as possible, then his mouth devoured hers.

It was shocking, unbidden, and pleasurably arousing all at once. Desire exploded inside Gabriel as he tasted the spicy sweetness of her once more, felt the smoothness of her skin beneath his fingers, heard the helpless moan of desire that sent his blood pounding. In the back of his mind he realized that no other woman had ever had this effect on him. Why in God's name did it have to be her?

Jennifer slid her arms around him, surrendering in a gesture older than time. He parted her lips, gently coaxing them to open, to give him more, and she did exactly that. He deepened the kiss, unable to resist the erotic temptation she promised. He no longer cared that they were in the park, that the kitten climbed merrily over them, nor that they could be discovered by an acquaintance at any time. He had to have this woman, Gabriel realized, though it made absolutely no sense at all.

Reluctantly, he eased from her, aware that if he didn't stop, he soon wouldn't be able to. Stunned by the intensity of emotion between them, Gabriel looked into Jennifer's eyes, and once again saw them shining with wonder and devotion. He cursed himself for a cad, unable to explain his actions satisfactorily even to himself.

"We'd better get back. I've got to finish that bid, and you should get the kitten home."

"Yes." Flushed with confusion, Jennifer got to her feet, hugging herself as if to replace the warmth that had just left her. She picked up the kitten, nuzzling the tiny creature with her cheek. The kitten purred and squirmed playfully, making her giggle. It was the most adorable sight Gabriel had ever seen.

"I'll name him Angel. For you," she said, smiling.

There was nothing angelic about what he was thinking. Gabriel wanted to stop her, to warn her that there could never be anything permanent between them, but somehow the words wouldn't come out. He'd hurt and rejected her enough, and he just didn't have the heart to step on her again when she looked so happy. Instead, he nodded stiffly.

"Come along. We have to go."

Obediently, Jennifer followed him. When they reached her carriage, he helped her up, then shook his head when she patted the seat invitingly.

"I have to go. I suppose you'll be at the Rutherfords' ball? It seems the Appletons are invited everywhere these days."

Jennifer giggled, then shrugged her shoulders and nodded.

"I'll see you then." He turned and walked away abruptly, unable to face the melting pleasure in her eyes.

JENNIFER PRACTICALLY SKIPPED into the house, bursting with joy. Her sisters and aunt looked up in stunned surprise as she unveiled the kitten, then let the little fur ball scamper across the room. The kitten made a beeline for the birdcage, and plastered himself to the brass door like a miniature leopard, stalking its prey. The parrot squawked indignantly, huddling in the corner, while Aunt Eve gasped in horror.

"My word! What is that creature! My poor Sam!" Aunt Eve rushed to comfort the parrot, while Penelope pried the kitten from the cage.

"Oh, he's precious!" Penelope said, petting his tiny head while he mewed. "Where did you get him?"

"Gabriel bought him for me." Jennifer beamed, swirling around the room, holding onto her skirt as if she were dancing. "I named the kitten after him. We went for a picnic in the park, and he didn't even attempt to leave early. And then he asked if he would see me at the Rutherfords' ball! Isn't that great?"

"That's wonderful! Oh, Jenny, I just knew he wouldn't be able to resist you!" Penelope exclaimed. "Did he ask you to go with him?"

"Not in so many words, but he definitely seemed interested."

"We'll have to make sure your new dress looks especially nice. Let me take care of this kitty, and we'll make all the plans. Isn't there some cream in the icebox?"

"Yes, I think so." Aunt Eve nodded, looking more than a little bewildered by the new addition to her household. "I'll go and check."

As she and Penelope disappeared into the kitchen, Jennifer whirled around once more. She turned to Winifred in a playful curtsy. When she caught sight of her sister's expression, Jennifer frowned.

"What's wrong? Don't you like the kitten?"

Winifred smiled, but the misgivings didn't leave her eyes. "Yes, I think the kitten grand. I'm just worried about . . . the situation."

"What situation?" Jennifer asked, her stomach tightening. Whenever Winifred worried, it was always for a good reason.

"With you and Mr. Forester. Jenny, I could be dead wrong, and I hope I am, but have you given any real thought as to what his intentions are? I can't picture him ever asking you to wed, given what he thinks of us."

The day seemed to suddenly grow black. All of the joy of a moment ago vanished, replaced by the disturbing doubts that now demanded to be heard.

"How do you know that?" Jennifer asked, stung by her sister's observation. "He seems to like me. Do you think it that impossible that someone like Gabriel could ever care for me?"

Winifred's face grew softer, and Jennifer saw pity in her eyes. She came to stand next to Jennifer, running her hands through her hair as she had done when Jennifer was a child. "Jenny, I don't want to upset you. You know I think the world of you, and I'll always be grateful for the way you pulled us all together. I've never seen you happier than in the last few days. I just think that Gabriel might want you for . . . a mistress, but not a wife."

"Why would you say such a thing?" Jennifer cried, but the memory of that kiss heated her cheeks. Surely that couldn't mean . . . she was forced to remember the passion that had flowed between them, and the look in his eyes. Her blush heightened as she recalled that he had never called on her formally, never sent her flowers or any token of his admiration, never even brought her a punch at the Barrymores' garden party, something that would indicate honorable interest.

Winifred looked as if she would rather be anywhere than here, having this conversation. "I have given the matter considerable thought. Mr. Howe even indicated that Gabriel was genuinely . . . attached to his sister, and everyone expects them to wed. Gabriel is a gentleman, and men like him marry for money or position. I just don't want to see you hurt, that's all."

"Well, Charles could be wrong, after all. And how do you know he wasn't speaking for himself? Maybe those are *his* ambitions."

Winifred paled, and Jennifer immediately wished she could take the words back. It had not escaped her observation that her sister might have more than a scholarly interest in Charles Howe. The night they'd gone to the opera, the two of them had argued law well into the night. Jennifer had never seen her sister more alive or passionate than in Charles's presence.

"I don't know. It's another reason, I suppose, that I caution you. I need to caution myself as well."

Jennifer hugged her normally reticent sister, touched by the emotion in her words. "Don't worry, Winnie. Everything will turn out just fine for both of us. I'll make it happen, wait and see. And tomorrow night at the Rutherfords' party, we'll be the belles of the ball. And Charles won't be able to resist you."

CHAPTER 9

THE PREPARATIONS FOR the Rutherfords' ball began early the following morning. Jennifer awoke to find Aunt Eve rushing about the house, preparing an enormous breakfast which she insisted they all eat, so as not to be hungry at the party.

"Real ladies are known by their delicate appetites," she cautioned, as Jennifer looked wide-eyed at the three eggs, four strips of bacon, toast, fruit, and coffee that was laid out before her. "Eat it all now, and then I've planned a sumptuous lunch. I've also got hard candies for you to carry in your pockets in case you get hungry. None of my nieces will be accused of gorging themselves at the party."

Jennifer groaned, forcing down the huge quantity of food. "I never thought being a real lady was so complicated," she complained. "The Billings make it look so easy."

"That's because the Billings have been carefully tutored their entire lives," Aunt Eve asserted. "But I intend to do my part and give you all the benefit of my experience. After all, I was quite a belle in my day. Now don't slouch, dear. You'll give yourself cramps."

Penelope giggled as Jennifer rolled her eyes but

obeyed her aunt and sat up. Even Winifred seemed to fall into the spirit of things, for although she had a book propped up before her, she tied her napkin around her neck and ate while she read.

Penelope rose first, wiping her lips with her napkin then tossing it aside. "I'll heat the irons and crimp the lace on our bonnets. Don't worry, I won't burn you this time," Penelope protested as Jennifer gave her a look. "You will let me do your hair and apply a touch of rouge?"

Jennifer scowled, while Aunt Eve nodded furiously. "That and perhaps a touch of belladonna in her eyes, to brighten them. Men so like bright eyes, you know."

"I'm not putting poison anywhere near my face," Jennifer protested. "I'll go along with the other horrors, like ridiculously tight stays and curls, but I have to draw the line somewhere."

"I see." Aunt Eve sighed as if the matter little concerned her. "I understand that Allison Howe has very attractive eyes, but I don't suppose that's of any importance."

Jennifer looked at her aunt in astonishment. Eve still bustled around the kitchen, refilling coffee cups and putting out biscuits. There was absolutely no trace of sagacity in her expression, yet her words couldn't have been that innocent. For the first time, Jennifer wondered how much her aunt knew, and how much she hid beneath her befuddled exterior.

"All right, I suppose the rouge is amenable. But no belladonna," Jennifer said reluctantly.

Aunt Eve nodded. "That's a good girl. And Winnie, do stop reading so much today. You'll strain your eyes, and a certain barrister won't want to look into them. Perhaps you girls should dress and take a stroll outside. It will help you digest and put roses in your cheeks. I'll start pressing handkerchiefs. A real lady is always known by her hankie and clean boots. I read that in *Hill's Manual*."

The girls were bustled out of the kitchen and out into

the streets while Aunt Eve prepared bathwater. It seemed as if the day was filled with one activity after another, all designed to enhance the evening. The afternoon meant a nap, after the enormous lunch, then baths, followed by the puffing of talcum powder and dabbing of cologne. Aunt Eve helped the girls tighten their stays, then snapped petticoats and adjusted stockings. There was much talking and laughing amongst the sisters, the anticipation of the ball fueling their discussions. Jennifer complained constantly, Penelope loved every minute of it, and Winifred bore what needed to be done in a matter-of-fact way. When they had settled the ball gowns into place, Aunt Eve stood back and beamed with admiration.

"You all look so lovely I could cry. Come, Jenny, see in the mirror! Penelope, that ice blue truly is your color, and what a pretty gown! Winifred, you are absolutely elegant."

Aunt Eve chirped with pleasure, and Jennifer glanced at her sisters proudly. Penelope was a vision in an ice blue chiffon with a scooped neckline, making her generous bosom all the more enticing. Eve had attached a row of fresh carnations to the back of the dress, which Penelope assured everyone was very much in vogue, and she wore a fashionable black velvet choker copied from Degas paintings, guaranteed to make the Billings green with envy.

Winifred wore a simple gold-hued gown that went well with her darkly burnished locks. Her hair had been swept up into a French twist, secured with a dozen hairpins, and looked very elegant. Her outfit contained far fewer flounces than Penelope's, but the simple style and almost masculine linen collar only enhanced her cool good looks.

Jennifer clapped as her sisters curtsied, then glanced in the mirror for one last primp. Her own dress, an ivory lace gown with clean lines and a small bustle, was a perfect fit and showed off her slender figure. Black velvet ribbons adorned the low-cut neck and puffed sleeves, and a small amount of the same material snaked in and out of her hem. She'd refused a long trailing train, wanting to dance freely and have fun. After much consideration, the dressmaker had agreed, especially since Jennifer was wont to trip over any lengthy pieces of fabric draped around her. She looked wonderful, innocent and demure, while her eyes danced with excitement. At Penelope's prompting, she applied a bit of rouge, and bit her lips to make them redder.

Aunt Eve looked at the girls and her eyes filled with tears. "I am such an old fool, but you all look so grand! I wish I were going with you, but I still just don't feel up to it." She sighed. "And I do have one last surprise for each of you." Bringing forth a lacquered box, she opened it and withdrew a sparkling pin for Penelope's hair, a gold bracelet for Winifred, and a string of real pearls for Jennifer. "I've been saving them," Eve said proudly. "Your uncle purchased them for me years ago, and I just knew the day would come when I could give them to you. Tonight would be perfect."

They thanked their aunt profusely, touched by her gesture. Jennifer allowed Eve to slip the pearls around her neck, then pulled on her long gloves.

The three sisters raced down the steps, chattering excitedly. Snatching on their cloaks, they bade Eve goodbye. The old woman stood in the doorway, huddled in her shawl, waving as the carriage pulled away from the curb.

The Rutherfords' house was an elegant white marble, located in the best part of town, on Fifth Avenue. Jennifer gawked as they passed the wealthy homes of the Astors, the Schermerhorns, and the other New York millionaires who practically owned the street. Excitement coursed through her as they stepped inside and quickly allowed the servant to take their cloaks, as Penelope instructed. They hadn't the money to buy good evening cloaks, but once they shed their everyday coverings, they emerged as beautiful as any butterflies.

The room was a dazzle. Chandeliers gleamed brilliantly, the gaslights flickering behind crystal beads and sending incandescent lights dancing across the black-and-white marble floor. Music played gaily, and women decked in gorgeous gowns swept through the room like angels. Men, looking suave and debonair, stood about the punch bowls talking about investments and politics, while others flirted shamelessly with their demure companions. Fresh flowers bloomed everywhere, peeping from gold sconces in the wall, filling every available vase, and adorning the dresses of the younger girls. It was beautiful, breathtaking, and exciting, everything a ball should be.

Penelope was asked to dance immediately, and she swept across the floor, holding her skirt in one hand, her partner's hand in the other as smoothly as if she'd been doing this forever. Winifred, preceded by her reputation, was soon surrounded by a group of scholarly ladies and men who found her a witty and knowledgeable companion. Jennifer greeted the excited girls who wanted to know everything about spiritualism, and was questioned endlessly about the sisters' appearance at the stock exchange and magnetic healing. While some of the older, wealthier women snubbed her and whispered behind their fans, the younger and more liberal seemed happy to meet her.

Jennifer's gaze continually swept the room, looking for Gabriel, but he apparently hadn't arrived. Her foot tapped impatiently as she watched the dancing, though she tried to appear interested in the conversation. Sally Weatherwill was just asking her another question about contacting the dead when Jonathan Wiseley pressed forward, his gloved hand extended.

"Do you dance, Miss Appleton? Or only talk to ghosts?" There was a teasing note in his voice, and Jennifer smiled and took his hand.

"No, I dance also. Thank you."

The young man swept her out onto the floor. Jennifer

felt awkward at first, not having had much experience waltzing, but Jonathan quickly put her at ease and showed her the basic steps. He held her a little too tightly for her comfort, but Jennifer managed, by a misstep or two, to put some distance between them. She noticed the attention she was receiving, and, to Jonathan's displeasure, was asked again to dance almost immediately.

It was as if some sort of code had been established, for as soon as that waltz ended, another swain asked her for a dance, and another after that. Word had gotten out among the men as well about the *New York Times* article, and Jennifer was peppered with questions as she waltzed, especially about her day at the market. She answered them deftly, smiling all the while so that her partners didn't know whether her response was serious or teasing, but Jennifer discovered that Penelope was right. Dealing with men was almost mathematical, and once one had the formula, it was quite easy indeed.

"Do you have room in your program for one more dance?"

Jennifer knew the voice before she turned around. There was only one man who could do this to her, one voice she'd know anywhere. Her breath caught and her heart pounded. She could feel the heat rise in her face. Composing herself quickly, she turned and greeted Gabriel.

He looked wonderful—and far more elegant than some of the dandified men—clad totally in black dress clothes with only a sparkling white shirt and simple cravat. His dark wavy hair had been swept back from his face, making his sharp features even more threatening—and attractive. His hand, clad in a pearl gray glove, swept down to her wrist and he lifted her program, displaying the astonishing number of names. He didn't look entirely pleased when he surveyed the list scrawled on her card.

"It seems you have been enjoying yourself this evening. I would suggest you be careful with men like

Jonathan Wiseley. He has quite a reputation as a cad among the ladies."

"I will take your advice," Jennifer said demurely, but her heart sang with laughter. Gabriel sounded almost jealous! It was too good to be true. She gave him a sideways glance and shrugged. "Although Mr. Wiseley is extraordinarily kind. He is also a wonderful dancer."

Gabriel opened his mouth to argue, but when he saw the glint in her eyes, he started to chuckle. "Miss Appleton, for some reason, you bring out the worst in me. If I didn't know better, I would think you are deliberately goading me."

"Do you know better?" Jennifer asked innocently.

Gabriel shook his head. "Where you're concerned, Miss Appleton, I admit I know nothing. Now are you going to dance with me? I had hoped that the kitten would entitle me to special privileges."

She took his hand, allowing him to lead her onto the dance floor, overcome with joy. "Angel entitles you to lots of special privileges," Jennifer demurred, remembering Penelope's warnings not to act too eager. "Aunt Eve wouldn't agree, though. It seems our little tiger likes nothing better than to tease her parrot, which we all encourage. Thank you for him. He is a welcome addition to the household."

"You're welcome. It was the least I could do, considering that the kitten was about to meet its untimely end, which I thought was very curious."

"How?"

"I saw the same boy in the park the next morning with another basket of doomed kittens. It seems he has a racket going."

"You're joking!" Jennifer gasped. "Do you mean—"

Gabriel shrugged, but his eyes twinkled. "It appears the little entrepreneur knows a good thing when he sees it."

Jennifer giggled as they swept across the floor. There

was something incredibly intimate about this, being so close to Gabriel, her gloved hand in his, his other settled firmly around her waist. She could feel the heat from his body, smell the masculine scent of him, and enjoy the feeling of being small and feminine in his strong arms. He was an excellent dancer, and her own limited capability bloomed in his experienced strides. To her mounting excitement, she noticed that he was enjoying himself, although she sensed the battle within him. Winifred's words came back to haunt her, but she dismissed them quickly. He was dancing with her publicly, and that had to be a good sign.

Glancing through the crowd, she saw Winifred engaged with Charles Howe, and Penelope talking flirtatiously with an older gentleman. Both of them looked beautiful, and were obviously having a good time. When the dance ended, Jennifer wondered if he would escort her to dinner, for that would signal his interest to everyone there beyond a doubt. To her intense disappointment, he bowed before her.

"Thank you, Miss Appleton. I'm certain you will be very much engaged the rest of the evening, from the look of your program. Perhaps I will see you before I go."

"But—" Jennifer protested, wanting to stop him, wanting to tell him she didn't want to dance with anyone but him.

"Yes?" He paused, but was already looking across the room. His gaze settled on one of the other guests, and Jennifer saw it was Allison Howe. Allison looked wonderful, dressed in an expensive gown that radiated money and taste. She was talking with Elizabeth Billing, and the two girls smiled as if sharing a joke. Allison's eyes met hers, and Jennifer saw what looked like pity in them before she turned her gaze to Gabriel and smiled warmly. Humiliation swept through Jennifer, though she cast her eyes down quickly so he couldn't see.

"Did you say something, Miss Appleton?"

"No. Thank you again for the kitten. And the dance."

She left quickly, afraid she would start crying if she didn't. Making her way through the crowd, she swallowed hard, fighting the tears that threatened. Winifred was right. Allison was the kind of woman Gabriel would marry, not her, and the sooner she accepted that, the better.

ALLISON HOWE SAW Gabriel leave Jennifer and make his way across the dance floor. A frown creased her face and she tapped her fan across her palm in agitation. Elizabeth Billing sighed, then turned to smile at her friend.

"Isn't Jennifer Appleton pretty? It's a wonder Gabriel dares to dance with her publicly. She is, after all, very notorious!"

Allison smiled brittlely at Elizabeth Billing's subtle taunting. Her aristocratic upbringing prevented her from venting her true emotions; however, her eyes narrowed and her voice was tinged with displeasure.

"I'm sure Gabriel can dance with any female he wishes, as can most of the men. I don't notice that any of the Appleton girls are short of dance partners."

"Yes, I agree. It is so nice of him to choose Jennifer, particularly since she is new to society," Elizabeth sighed, "and not altogether accepted. Mama forbade me to ask her to supper. It just wouldn't be good for my reputation, you know. I hear Gabriel spends a lot of time with her. That's odd, don't you think?"

"Gabriel has many acquaintances," Allison said, though the fan tapped harder. "He is a businessman, after all, and must consort with all kinds of people as a result."

"I don't know what business dealings he'd have with the Appletons," Elizabeth continued, her voice dripping with sugar. "Do mystics require much marble, do you think? Do you know they say she can really speak to the deceased? Mary Forester swears Jennifer helped her immensely. And she does magnetic healing! Why, it was in the newspaper that she laid her hands on the commodore himself and cured him!"

"I did see that," Allison answered, staring at Jennifer speculatively. "I think I shall have to pay Miss Appleton a visit very soon."

As Gabriel approached, Allison smiled sweetly and extended her hand. She glanced back at Elizabeth, and spoke quickly.

"I wouldn't look so smug if I were you, dear. I saw Charles disappear with Winifred Appleton quite some time ago. Do enjoy the dance, and I hope to see you at dinner."

Allison departed with Gabriel, while Elizabeth gasped, her fan fluttering indignantly.

"MAY I FETCH you a jelly, or an ice, perhaps?"

"No, thank you," Winifred answered with detachment. She saw Gabriel escort Allison to dinner and gave a worried frown. She was standing behind the elephant plant with Charles, where they had been arguing the benefits of women in higher education. Charles, seeing her expression, thought lack of refreshment had caused her distraction. He glanced behind him, then turned back to her. "Is something troubling you?"

"No." Concealing her emotions, Winifred gave Charles a cool glance. "I was just observing your friend dancing with my sister. Mr. Howe, could I ask you something personal?"

Charles's brow lifted, as if surprised that the normally reticent and completely enticing Winifred would presume anything. "Of course."

"Does Gabriel Forester have . . . an arrangement with your sister?"

Understanding seemed to dawn on Charles's features, and Winifred hoped she'd done the right thing confiding in him. But she could not bear to see Jennifer's glowing happiness in the arms of a man Winifred was certain would hurt her. If Winifred knew the truth, she could perhaps help soften the blow when it came.

"Gabriel has been seeing Allison for quite some time," Charles answered carefully. "Our families have been in favor of the match, particularly since we once feared for Allison's future."

"What do you mean?"

"Allison had a girlish crush on an entirely inappropriate man. My parents forbade her to see him, for he drank and gambled, and would have brought her to ruin. For that reason, they have encouraged her relationship with Gabriel. I personally have not."

Winifred shot him a surprised look. "Why not? He is your friend, isn't he?"

Charles nodded. "Yes, he is a very good friend. However, I'm not convinced the match would make either of them happy. Gabriel needs to really care for someone, and I don't believe he feels that depth of emotion for Allison. And I also don't think Allison will ever forget Miguel if she doesn't truly love someone else."

"I see," Winifred said thoughtfully. "Do you think they will become engaged anyway?"

She locked her eyes with his, not allowing him a polite evasion. Charles squirmed, but nodded reluctantly. "Yes, I think so." When Winifred didn't respond, Charles took her hand gently. "Miss Appleton, please don't worry about your sister's relationship with Gabriel. Gabriel is a gentleman. He would never deliberately lead Jennifer on, I'll see to it."

"Thank you, Mr. Howe." Winifred smiled and pressed his hand, genuinely grateful for his help.

Charles looked down at her, his eyes becoming dark and full of some strange emotion. Winifred couldn't identify it, but she knew it was vaguely threatening and exciting at the same time. "Miss Appleton, have I told you how absolutely beautiful you look tonight?"

"No," Winifred answered honestly, taken aback.

"Well, you do. You outshine all the other women here, with their frills and fripperies. In fact, I find you downright stunning." He leaned closer and placed a tentative kiss on her cheek.

Winifred's lips parted in astonishment. An odd, tingling pleasure coursed through her, unlike anything she'd experienced before. But her delight was not long-lasting. As if suddenly realizing what he'd done, Charles turned bright red and withdrew a few steps backward.

"I'm sorry," he stammered. "I don't know what made me do that. Please forgive me."

"Certainly," Winifred said, though her spirit was crushed. She was well aware of what he meant. Charles, like Gabriel, may have been attracted to her, but did not see her as a woman he would consort with publicly. For once her scholarly mind seemed to have deserted her, and she was like any other adolescent girl, experiencing her first heartache.

"I'd better get back before someone sees us here. Good evening, Miss Appleton."

Charles departed, and Winifred leaned up against the wall, grateful for the screen of the elephant leaves.

PENELOPE SMILED AS James McBride brought her another glass of champagne. "I knew I'd find you if I kept looking," he declared, pressing the fizzy wine into the hands of the beautiful blonde. "By God, I've had to endure nearly a dozen damned teas and soirees, hoping to find someone who knew you! It seemed while the world knew of Penelope Appleton, no one knew your social circle."

Penelope smiled mysteriously, then sipped her drink. "That's because I haven't got one," she responded teasingly.

James McBride looked at her uncertainly, then boomed with laughter. "Not if you don't count half the men in this room. They all talk of nothing but you, my girl. The gorgeous Miss Appleton, with the sister that can speak to the dead."

Penelope smiled at his lurid description. She knew he was only half joking, for the three sisters were notorious. Nevertheless, she sensed the man's fascination with her, and she shrugged as if none of it really mattered.

"Now you must let me take you into dinner, my dear. They have pheasant and beef Wellington, salmon and oysters. You'll enjoy it, I'm certain."

"I am sorry," Penelope said deftly, fluttering her lashes. "But I have already agreed to have dinner with another man." When she saw his crestfallen face, she gave him a bright smile. "But I haven't promised dessert!"

"That's my girl!" James beamed. "To make up for it, you have to come to supper with me at the Astors' party. It's next week."

"*The* Astors?" Penelope asked in astonishment. "I've heard about those parties, where the women find presents like gold bracelets in their napkins."

"And diamond tie pins for the men," he agreed. "I am good friends with William Astor. He surely won't mind if I bring a guest."

Penelope's heart quivered. This man, while a little older, promised entrée into a world she'd previously only glimpsed. Pressing her hand to his, she gave him a seductive smile.

"That sounds wonderful. I must beg leave, now, for I've promised every dance. I'll see you at dessert?"

She knew never to stay too long with any one man, to always leave him wanting more. True to form, James looked as if he had to physically force himself from pulling her back.

"I guess it'll have to do."

His eyes followed her as she swept gaily away. Penelope smiled, confident in herself and her abilities. Everything was going just as planned. She made her way to the powder room, a newfangled idea, where ladies could freshen their nose powder or secure their artificial hairpieces. As Penelope bent over the mirror to adjust her pearl eye powder, she saw a young girl enter the room.

"Oh, excuse me! I didn't know anyone else was here." She looked as if she was about to depart, and Penelope stopped her.

"No, please don't leave. I'm almost finished."

The young girl approached, looking wide-eyed at Penelope. "I know you! You're the pretty one, of the three sisters! The ones who are magic."

Penelope laughed at her description, and gave the girl a closer look. About sixteen, she was fresh and charming, very Irish in appearance, and dressed to the hilt. Penelope enviously noted the French lace dangling from her sleeves, and the outrageously expensive jewels that encrusted her throat. She smiled, knowing it was unfashionable to shake hands with other women, and introduced herself.

"I'm Penelope Appleton."

"Oh, I'm sorry. I'm Mary Rose McBride. I can't believe I've met you. Everyone will be so jealous. You really are very scandalous, aren't you? James McBride is my father. I saw you talking to him." She smiled. "I have to go now. I can't be seen with you, for I would be—how would you say it?—ostriched by my friends. Good-bye."

A cold chill coursed through Penelope as Mary Rose swept away. This girl, a year or so younger than herself, was the daughter of the man who was so boldly courting her!

Penelope leaned against the wall of the powder room, suddenly feeling quite ill.

CHAPTER 10

No one spoke in the carriage on the way home. A few times, Jennifer attempted to engage her sisters in conversation, but Penelope seemed distracted and Winifred oddly depressed. Her own voice sounded artificial and strained, so she gave up after a few moments, and the only sound that inhabited the coach was the rolling of wheels across cobbled streets.

When they got home, Aunt Eve opened the door, still bundled in her shawl. Excitement twinkled in her pale blue eyes, and she gestured to a comfortable fire. "Come! I want to hear all about it! I've got hot chocolate waiting, and your cozy slippers. I'm sure you were all a stunning success tonight!"

The three sisters looked at each other, then burst into tears. Jennifer hugged Winifred, consoling her sister without knowing why, while Penelope embraced them both. Aunt Eve fluttered about like a sparrow, hopping from one foot to the other, obviously at a loss.

"Oh, my dears this is terrible. Terrible! Don't cry like that. Penelope, your face powder is running all over your nose. And sweet Jenny, you never cry. Never! What on earth is wrong?"

The three sisters settled down by the fire amid much weeping, fumbling for handkerchiefs, and wiping of noses. Jennifer blew hers loudly, startling everyone into laughter, which, as sometimes happens, instantly replaced the distress. Eve shook her head in bewilderment as the girls rolled with mirth, and poor Jennifer looked mortified.

"I'm sorry, Auntie," Jennifer apologized for all of them. "It's just that tonight was a dreadful disappointment to us all. It seems we really aren't accepted by society. While the Billings tolerate us because we are great for gossip, none of them asked us to join them publicly for supper, or wanted to appear too friendly."

Penelope dabbed at her eyes, immediately cleaning up the face powder. "Yes, I noticed that, too. We have to do something to break in, otherwise the really rich, like the Astors, will always look down their noses at us."

"Even a man like Charles Howe, who is a cut above the rest, spoke to me privately rather than in front of an audience," Winifred agreed. "Although we've developed something of a friendship, I think he couldn't risk his reputation by being seen with an Appleton."

"Why, that's the most ridiculous thing I've ever heard!" Eve hugged her shawl more tightly around her diminutive figure, incensed that someone wouldn't approve of her darlings. "I will say something to Mrs. Billing in church next Sunday! The very nerve!"

"It isn't just the Billings," Winifred said softly. "It's all of them. We are beyond the pale, as they say. No lady really wants to befriend us, and no real gentleman could consider an Appleton worthy . . . to court."

"I see." This Aunt Eve did understand. No one desired that the girls marry well more than herself, and their orphaned state, coupled with their lack of dowry, was a problem that she'd been thinking about for weeks.

"I think it's because of our theatricals," Penelope said,

looking meaningfully at her sisters. "The society people, while fascinated with new ideas, still look down their nose at what we do. As long as we're labeled that way, I think we'll always have a problem."

"And what then should we do for income?" Jennifer asked. "If we give up the theatricals, we become poor as church mice and can't even afford the basics. We're talking about survival here, girls. Acceptance is nice, but it doesn't bring bread."

"Jenny is right," Winifred sighed. "It's a dilemma. We can neither give up the theatricals, nor will society accept them."

"Perhaps what you need to do is gain a sponsor." Aunt Eve rocked back and forth in her chair thoughtfully, as if she were knitting, but without the wool and needles. "Someone who is strong and powerful. Someone who will mentor you girls."

"Who?" Jennifer shrugged. "No one we know is powerful enough to turn society around."

Aunt Eve smiled, her wizened face wrinkling with delight. "There I think I can help you." Fumbling inside a desk drawer, Eve pulled out a ream of papers neatly tied with a red ribbon. The three nieces looked on as she slowly unwrapped the bundle and began sorting through the letters.

Winifred sighed. "Eve, dear, while we appreciate your help, this is our problem, and we'll have to come up with a solution. I'm sure we'll think of something." She patted her aunt's knee, while the old lady looked at her sharply.

"So you don't think poor old Aunt Eve has any connections, or can assist my lambs with their troubles? I don't suppose you girls have ever heard of Mildred Adams?"

"The New York socialite?" Penelope asked, perking up instantly. "Why, she must be in her eighties now! Mildred absolutely rules society," she explained to her puzzled sisters. "It is rumored that she had a scandalous youth, but she married well and became fabulously rich after her husband died. She presides over the really important balls and parties like a dowager duchess. Surely you don't know her?" Penelope turned an incredulous face to her aunt.

"Of course I know her," Eve explained. "Mildred and I were sent to the same boarding school as girls. A dreadful place, but we became good friends and correspond whenever we can. She's invited me to her parties frequently, but what would an old lady like myself do there? Too much noise. Here is her last letter."

Eve passed the document around to the sisters, who read it in equal astonishment. Jennifer finished first, passing it to Winifred. She shook her head, grinning.

"I can't believe it! And you think this woman would provide us her sponsorship?"

Aunt Eve nodded, adjusting her spectacles as the letter came back to her. "Mildred loves a challenge, and she would see this situation as exactly that. Her endorsement would give you ironclad approval. Unfortunately, it may be difficult to gain an audience with her immediately. It seems that she had a secret love, a man she was prevented from marrying. I understand he passed a few years ago and she hasn't been herself since. I have heard that she's been seeing mystics and spiritualists to try and contact his ghost." Aunt Eve shook her head. "As if such a thing could happen!"

Jennifer glanced at her sisters, who looked back with the same sense of excitement. It was all she could do to keep from clapping her hands and prancing about the room. Instead, she managed to keep some of the delight from her voice, and answer calmly.

"Well, then, perhaps we could perform a private little theatrical for her. I'm sure that will take her mind off things."

"Why, that's a grand idea." Aunt Eve beamed. "Grand indeed."

"I AM SO grateful that you accepted my invitation to tea," Allison said demurely as Gabriel took a seat in her parlor, placing his hat beside him on the ornate chair. "I know how busy you are these days."

"Allison, I apologize if you feel I've neglected you." Gabriel sighed, running his hand absently through his hair. "I have a lot on my mind recently."

"I see. The marble business, I suppose? I heard you talking to Charles about a city contract." Allison gestured to the Irish maid to put the tea tray on the table before Gabriel. She dismissed the servant, then poured the tea herself, handing the cup to Gabriel and managing to discreetly touch his fingers in the process.

Gabriel frowned. None of this was like Allison. She was usually direct and confident in her dealings with everyone. His eyes ran over her quickly and he noticed that she had donned her prettiest dress, a soft yellow muslin that complimented her hair and complexion. It was a dress he had openly admired, and he could only assume that she had worn it today for that reason.

"Yes, we were discussing the contract. It seems that our mayor has selected another company to get the lion's share of the marble business. Charles thinks we should try to win his favor before taking any action." Gabriel stirred the tea and attempted to smile fondly at the woman. "You aren't usually interested in my business, Allison. Is there a particular reason today?"

"I'm always interested in your concerns," Allison said. "You know I'm not like some other women, ignorant of business and money matters. Women have just as much intelligence as men, which is something Benjamin Franklin noted a hundred years ago. He even recommended that women take up bookkeeping, and learn to assist their husbands with the mathematical tasks of running a business, as opposed to the physical work."

"I am aware of Mr. Franklin's theories," Gabriel responded indulgently, although he was getting more and more uncomfortable by the moment. "But I don't need help with the bookkeeping. I have Edward for that." His joke fell flat as Allison gave him a blank look. Seeking to change the topic, he leaned forward and helped himself to a cucumber sandwich. "Did you enjoy the ball last night? You looked wonderful."

Allison nodded, taking the seat beside Gabriel instead of the one she usually occupied across from him. A faint trace of perfume reached him, something else unusual. She continued to smile at him.

"Yes, I had a very nice time. I especially enjoyed the dancing. In fact, I noticed you did also. How do you know Jennifer Appleton?"

Gabriel choked on his tea. Putting the cup aside, he wiped his mouth with a napkin, then laid it on the tea tray. When he spoke, his words were guarded.

"My mother has seen Miss Appleton for her spiritualist abilities, and they have since become friends," Gabriel explained. "You know my feelings about mysticism. I have warned Miss Appleton that I will not stand by and see my mother taken advantage of, by her or any other charlatan."

"I see." Allison refilled his cup, offering it to him again. "Your exchange didn't seem . . . unfriendly," she said sweetly. "Are you certain that is all there is to it?"

"Yes. I have even spoken to Charles about legal recourse, but he is against the idea of threatening the women. Evidently, he feels sorry for them."

"Ah." Allison nodded, as if answering a question within herself. When Gabriel glanced at her curiously, she shrugged. "As men, I can see where you both would be enchanted by the girls. They are beautiful, after all."

"Allison, I am not—"

"And charming, from what I've seen. Thank you, Gabriel, for being so honest. I don't mean to sound jealous or shrewlike. I just wanted to know the nature of your relationship, that's all."

Gabriel squirmed, as Allison meant him to. "I have no intention of pursuing a relationship with Jennifer—I mean Miss Appleton—in any manner. I have run into her frequently in the last few weeks, but that is coincidence only."

"I see. And where do you 'run into' Miss Appleton?"

"I've seen her at the park, at my mother's, and several other places."

"Isn't it odd that until a few weeks ago, none of us ran into Miss Appleton at all?" Allison commented.

"I have considered the same thing myself," Gabriel murmured. "But if you think I am seeking her out, I am not. I have no intention of befriending her, or pursuing any other kind of relationship with her. I will admit that Jennifer . . . interests me, as would any outrageous individual, but that's all."

"Then you won't mind if I call on her." Allison rose, continuing to smile as his mouth dropped. "You see, I respect your intelligence, Gabriel, and I may find Miss Appleton as interesting as you gentlemen seem to find her. In which case, I would welcome her friendship. However, if she is truly deceiving people, then I feel I should do something about it."

Gabriel was at a loss. Allison handed him his hat, clearly intending for him to go. As he walked through the door, he stood on the step and realized something very unflattering.

Without meaning to, he'd told Allison everything she wanted to know.

WHEN GABRIEL LEFT, Allison was more than a little angry at what he'd said, and worse, at what he hadn't. Although she wasn't the most perceptive person in the world, she saw one thing very clearly: Gabriel was infatuated with Jennifer Appleton.

She left the house and got in her carriage, quickly reassessing everything she'd discovered about the situation. The men openly admired the Appletons. Since the ball, Allison had made a few discreet inquiries, and they all spoke of Jennifer's charm and talent, Penelope's beauty, and Winifred's intelligence. While none as yet had risked public censure to court the girls, they were, as Jonathan Wiseley put it, the talk of the town.

Her brother wouldn't hear a word against them. When she complained to him about the rumors of Gabriel spending time with Jennifer, Charles cut her off at the quick. He admired the Appletons and felt sorry for them. He did admit that he'd written a letter to the girls, warning them of repercussions should they continue their trade, but he was sorry now that he had done even that. He suggested that Allison mind her own business.

The women's opinions were a mixed bag. Some of the younger women were obviously jealous, for the Appletons had caught more than one swain's attention, yet most wistfully acknowledged their beauty, charm, and wit. The older, more liberated women praised the girls, while the traditional matriarchs decried their unfeminine behavior. It was worse than Allison had suspected, for no one could give a plain, unemotional read on the notorious girls.

Her mouth tightened as she thought of the gossip that would result if Gabriel ever decided to pursue Jennifer. She, Allison, would become a laughingstock, especially since everyone expected Gabriel to wed her. It would look very much like she'd been thrown over for a woman who read tea leaves for a living.

It wasn't to be borne. Allison signaled her carriage driver to make another turn toward the less fashionable part of town. She had to stop this woman before the situation got any more serious, had to claim her right to Gabriel before the notorious Jennifer could work her charms on him. It would be a simple matter. Allison had already figured it out. If she could persuade Jennifer to perform a séance for her, she could then tearfully enlist Gabriel's help in reporting the matter to the police. Gabriel couldn't possibly refuse her, and the Appletons would be ruined.

The carriage rolled to a halt and Allison stepped out onto the walk before Twin Gables. Tugging at her gloves, she smoothed the immaculate material, then adjusted her dress before ascending the steps.

She tapped on the door, preparing herself for battle. The door opened, and an older Irish maid appeared, dressed in a uniform so starched it could have stood on its own. Her manner was equally stiff as she took Allison's card and led her into the foyer.

"Are the young ladies expecting you, miss?" the maid questioned, as would any servant of the gentry.

Allison shook her head in bemusement. "No, I came unannounced. However, they are acquainted with my brother, so I thought perhaps they'd see me."

"I'll see if they are at home," the maid said with a nod. "In the meantime, why don't you wait here?" She gestured to a chair.

Allison sank down into the chair, surprised at the appearance of the maid. The Appleton girls' fortunes must have come up considerably, for although most middle-class families had some kind of house servant, she'd understood that the girls hadn't been able to afford even this.

Yet a servant gave one respectability, and Allison reluctantly had to concede the girls that much.

The maid returned a moment later. "Miss Jennifer is out on calls, but Miss Winifred will see you. Please follow me."

Allison entered the parlor and glanced around in curiosity. It was everything she'd envisioned, from the gloomy draperies to the chandelier laced with spiderwebs, to the round table directly beneath it. She'd almost expected to see a gypsy crystal ball, but even without it the room gave one the feeling of magic, mystery, and unearthly doings, just as intended.

Winifred rose from her pile of books and extended a hand. Allison saw her ink-smudged cuffs, her crooked spectacles, and the pen tucked neatly behind one ear. Charles talked of nothing but this woman, she recalled, and even as she returned the firm handshake, she couldn't help but be fascinated by her odd appearance.

"I'm sorry to barge in without an appointment, but I wanted to meet with you and your sisters. I understand Miss Jennifer isn't in?"

"She will be back shortly," Winifred said, gesturing to the love seat. "Aunt Eve is ill, and Penelope visiting. Please, sit down."

Allison seemed disappointed, but did as she was told. "Can I ask what you're doing?" she asked curiously as Winifred buried herself in her books once more.

"I'm researching New York law to see if there is any statute preventing a woman from studying medicine." Winifred gestured to her notes. "I was trying to help an associate of mine get into college. Her application is being denied solely on the basis of her sex. Now, when you consider how many women were employed as nurses during the war, it seems doubly ridiculous to assume they are too dainty and frail for such work."

"I see." Allison frowned thoughtfully. "You know, I

am a member of the National Suffragette Association. Maybe our organization can help."

Winifred nodded, intelligence gleaming in her eyes. "I have found them helpful in the past, but only if I put all of the information into their hands. I don't fault them for this, for most women aren't legally trained, and male lawyers aren't eager to do such research for us without remuneration. That is why these women come to me. As a woman without male means of support, I completely understand the frustration and limitations of our laws where women are concerned."

"I agree." Allison sat forward on her chair, eager for the discussion. "Do you know women still cannot go into restaurants and order for themselves? Not only are we considered unable to vote, we have no word in our education, manner of living, even our lunch! Unless a woman marries well, she is doomed by the confines of her husband's money and talent."

"Exactly." Winifred nodded. "I suppose you are aware that we were orphaned as children?" When Allison gave a slight nod, Winifred continued. "We found ourselves crippled by the very laws designed to protect us as the weaker sex. The only acceptable work we could obtain was as governesses or companions, work that not only was insufficient to occupy our minds and talent, but would doom us forever to a subservient role. Financial disaster was just around the corner for all of us, for even our dear aunt was left penniless after her husband died in the war. If it wasn't for my sister Jennifer, I don't know what would have happened."

"With the séance business, you mean." Allison spoke softly, less sure of herself now.

"Yes. I am going to be candid with you, Miss Howe. I see you are a woman of intelligence, so I will explain things to you on a different level than I might someone else. It was Jenny who came up with the idea of spiritualism as a means of survival. Because of the war, there are many people who have lost loved ones and who have never really addressed their loss. Through Jennifer, some of them actually feel they can speak to their beloved husbands, sons, and lovers who have passed on. For that invaluable service, Jenny has found a way to make a small amount of money."

"I see," Allison said tentatively. "But surely you don't pretend to bring forth the dead?"

"People believe what they want to believe," Winifred answered cautiously. "Some people think it really is their loved one giving them advice, while others are content with a tarot interpretation. We don't promise to bring forth the dead, but if a client thinks that's what happened, it often brings them comfort."

"Tell me about what happened on Wall Street," Allison asked. "Can Jennifer really perform magnetic healing? That you dared to intrude on the male bastion of New York! I have to admit, I applauded you."

Winifred bowed her head, accepting the compliment. "Our stint on Wall Street was very successful. Aside from the healing, we were able to make some money by investing through traditional male avenues such as the brokerage firms. It was rather a keen trick to find an investment banker to take us seriously. If you have time, I'd be happy to share the story. It is quite amusing."

"I'd love to hear all about it," Allison said sincerely. "I have long thought that a woman should be able to handle her own finances. Your experience may be something I could relay back to my group."

Winifred signaled to the maid for tea, then proceeded to relate the story of the wormy Justin. Allison rolled with laughter as Winifred described Jennifer's caginess in convincing him that she'd been sent to his bank by Vanderbilt himself, even though a competing bank had offered to help her first.

As they laughed, Jennifer burst into the room, weighed down with packages. Winifred put down her teacup and eyed her sister with affection.

"Jenny, whatever are you doing? We have company, and you do look a fright. You've dragged your dress through the mud again."

Jennifer saw Allison, and her face changed to embarrassed curiosity. "I got some tea for Aunt Eve's cold," she explained. "I also found you a few books to help with your research, Winnie. They were half price at the college bookstore." She inclined her head toward Allison. "How are you, Miss Howe?"

"Very well. I had to come by and meet all of you myself. I saw you dancing with Gabriel at the Rutherfords' ball."

There was a prolonged silence, and Jennifer turned a becoming shade of pink. Her eyes dropped, and when they lifted, she looked as if she were prepared to take on the world. "I see. Miss Howe, Mr. Forester and I are friends—"

"I know," Allison said confidently. "Your sister has been telling me all about you girls. I must say, I had an entirely different impression of you before I came here today. I now understand your situation much better. Miss Appleton, do you think you would be interested in speaking before our suffragette group? Elizabeth Cady Stanton and Susan B. Anthony are, shall we say, leading the charge, but I think my group would be very interested in your tale of the Wall Street banker."

Jennifer looked nonplussed, then glanced to Winifred. Her sister shrugged, as if unable to advise her. "I would be delighted," Jennifer replied. "If you think they would be interested."

"I know they would." Allison beamed. "And I was wondering, could you give me a sample psychic reading? I would like to experience the Appleton magic firsthand, if you don't mind."

"Certainly, if you really want to," Jennifer said cautiously. "I don't have time for a full séance, but if a simple reading will satisfy your curiosity, I'll do my best."

"I'm certain it will be memorable." Allison said, reaching for her purse and withdrawing a few bills. "Memorable, indeed."

As soon as Allison left, Jennifer turned to her sister. "What do you suppose that was all about?"

Winifred frowned, her intelligent eyes squinting in thought. "It wasn't a simple social visit, that much is certain. I hate to say this, Jenny, but I think this woman sees you as a threat to her relationship with Gabriel. Charles Howe has warned me that his sister is not too happy with Gabriel's attentions to us. She is determined to wed him, and has no intention of letting anyone get in her way. Consequently, she can be dangerous."

Penelope entered the house, tossing aside her cloak and removing her gloves. "I thought I saw Allison Howe leaving. What was she doing here?" She wrinkled her nose at the prospect.

"We were just discussing her visit. Very odd, from all appearances," Winifred said. "I tried my best to divert her and steer the subject to women's rights, which I understand interests her, but she kept trying to discuss the séances. I think she plans to make trouble."

"Do you think—" Jennifer turned pale at the thought "—that Gabriel is in on it with her?"

Winifred shrugged reluctantly. "I wouldn't put it past him. It would be most unusual for a girl of Allison's background to attempt to threaten us on her own. I don't think it would be farfetched to assume that she and Gabriel are consorting together, and that she came here to spy on us."

"Oh, no!" Penelope cried. "We have three good prospects lined up this weekend. Mrs. Weatherwill will be here Friday. She is very wealthy, and goes to spiritualists all the time. She could be a wonderful client for us, but if Gabriel and Allison interfere, it could really set us back."

"I just can't believe he would do this!" Jennifer said. "He seems to have been softening toward me lately. I really thought—"

"Gabriel may not realize what she's doing," Winifred put in softly. "The woman is extremely bright. And you did give her a reading. If she complains to Gabriel, he might be compelled to go the police, particularly if he thinks we're now taking advantage of Allison. We could probably fight the charges, but socially, it would ruin us."

"I hadn't considered that," Jennifer said, appalled. "He was just starting to trust me! If Allison goes to him with a story like that . . ." She looked pleadingly at her brilliant sister. "What do you think we should do?"

"I don't know." Winifred shook her head, for once helpless. "I feel a little responsible, since I didn't discourage you from giving her the reading. I've had second thoughts about it ever since she left. Every one of my legal instincts is aroused."

The three sisters nodded. Jennifer had to admit it was a possibility. Allison and Gabriel could be pretending to befriend them, all the while setting them up for a fall. Her emotions threatened to get the better of her, but Jennifer forced them away. Survival came first, no matter what.

The three sisters pondered the situation for a moment, then Penelope's eyes brightened. "I've got it! Let's kidnap him!"

"What?" Jennifer appeared astonished, and felt Penelope's head to see if she was ill. Her sister flung her hand aside impatiently.

"Yes, why not? Only for a few days, until the séances are done. Aunt Eve is insisting on visiting an old acquaintance this weekend in spite of her cold, and will be leaving Saturday morning. We could invite Gabriel to dine with us on Friday night. Eve has been taking her medicinal tea every night, so nothing will wake her, and she'll be gone before she knows what's happened. No one expects Gabriel at the office until Monday. We could send him into the cellar for wine, and just turn the key on him! No one will be the wiser!"

Winifred frowned. "Kidnapping is a serious offense. We could find ourselves in real legal trouble if he pressed charges."

"Silly goose, he isn't going to press charges!" Penelope answered, very sure of herself. "What man would admit that three women kidnapped him? He'd be a laughingstock. And we're not really kidnapping him . . . we're detaining him for the weekend, as our guest."

"Gabriel does value his reputation," Jennifer said thoughtfully. "Penelope is right. He couldn't possibly admit to such a thing. And if he's helping Allison, it would keep both of them from causing trouble, at least until the séances are over."

Winifred frowned. "I don't like it, but I can't think of anything better. Perhaps, by keeping Gabriel captive, we could find out what they're plotting. But wouldn't it be better to wait until Saturday, when Aunt Eve is gone?"

"Gabriel has plans for Saturday," Jennifer said smoothly, not mentioning that she stole his book. "It's Friday or nothing."

Winifred sighed, then looked directly at her sister. "He will be furious, of course."

"Of course," Jennifer agreed, little put off by that fact. She turned the plan over in her mind. Although she was frightened by the thought of Gabriel's reprisals, there was one benefit that no one mentioned, which would help only her. To have Gabriel close by for several days would give her even more opportunity to make him fall in love with her. And that possibility was irresistible.

"All right, girls," Jennifer said, her eyes twinkling. "Let's do it."

CHAPTER 11

When Gabriel returned home from his offices on Friday, he removed his business clothes and dressed carefully for dinner in his best jacket and fine linen shirt. Using very little of the popular pomade, he combed his hair meticulously, then shaved once more. Finishing with a dusting of powder, he called for his carriage.

As he pulled on his gloves, he examined the cream-colored invitation that smelled of lilacs. He could now recognize Jennifer's flamboyant hand, with its neatly dotted *i*'s and crossed *t*'s. He opened the card, still amazed to see the elegant lettering inviting him to dine.

He had to admit, she had gumption. He'd been shaking his head ever since he received the invitation, amazed at Jennifer's audacity. His first impulse had been to toss the pretty card into the waste bin, but on second thought, he'd decided to accept. Curiosity, overriding his common sense, compelled him. He was simply intrigued enough by the invitation to wonder what the notorious Miss Appleton was up to now.

He didn't question his own motives, although he was also aware that Allison's interrogation had gotten him thinking. Jennifer was everything he decried, and everything he normally avoided. Yet she'd converted his mother, his best friend, and half of New York society into her camp, and was becoming more popular every day. It seemed that he couldn't attend an elegant soiree or a simple lawn fête without the bewitching sisters coming up as the topic of conversation. Worse, many of the women and some of the men were openly curious about Jennifer's ability to perform séances, and talked of making appointments. Yet Allison's subtle threats of befriending Jennifer alarmed him. He didn't think she would stoop to causing the Appletons trouble, but then again, he wasn't sure. Allison, he knew, could be very determined.

His carriage pulled up to the curb, and Gabriel sat inside, giving the driver the now familiar address. As he rumbled through the streets of New York, he wondered if any other man was on such a fool's errand that night, or if there was just himself. He was very much afraid he knew the answer.

The house looked much as he remembered, if anything, more spooky. The overgrown rose bush, he admitted, was a nice touch, and the kitten, which he'd supplied, looked oddly menacing on the front step. The windows were shuttered, as many of the other houses' were with the onset of colder weather, but the Appletons' looked completely closed up. It should be, he thought dryly. They certainly had enough secrets to hide.

As he approached the door, he wondered again what it was about this woman that enchanted everyone so. She had beauty, but her sister was even more beautiful. She had intelligence, but there again she was bested by a sibling. No, it was Jennifer Appleton herself, and her own potent charm, that was the force to be reckoned with. The memory of her in his arms, of her kiss, refused to leave him. It was as if he'd been intoxicated by a gypsy love potion, one that grew stronger with every passing day.

"Gabriel!" Jennifer opened the door and invited him

inside, appearing delighted to see him. "Come in! Dinner is almost ready."

Wonder seized Gabriel as he stepped inside the house and into the parlor, followed by the kitten. He thought he remembered it well from his first time there. Now, although he recalled the room as being worn and a little shabby, it looked immensely improved. Good velvet drapes adorned the windows, and a new rug graced the floor. Cobwebs still adorned the chandelier, but they had probably been left for effect. A new cranberry-colored lamp threw a rosy glow about the room, and sweetly scented apple logs burned freely in the fireplace. The parrot appeared to cower inside his cage, watching the tiger-colored ball of fur beneath with considerable trepidation.

Gabriel turned to his hostess. She was even more beautiful than ever. Her hair had completely grown back, and now framed her face with a cloud of ringlets. She appeared properly demure, but her eyes were still all Jennifer. They twinkled and danced as if she knew his thoughts, and enjoyed every moment of his dilemma.

"You're looking well, Miss Appleton," he reluctantly conceded.

"Thank you." Jennifer put her hands sweetly into his. "I am so glad you could come! We have pheasant and stuffing, new potatoes and corn, apple pie and coffee. Here it is, all laid out. Can I take your coat?"

Gabriel handed her the garment, glad to withdraw from her handclasp. That simple touch left him tingling, and he needed to be in full control of his faculties around this woman. He gestured to the room. "I can see that you've come up in more ways than one. I suppose your investments paid for all this also?"

"Now, let's not start that," Jennifer said, giving him a mischievous smile. "We're going to be friends now, aren't we?"

Friends. He gazed at her as she swept across the room

and put aside his coat. Clad in a tea gown of simple beige muslin, with white lace at the neck and sleeves, Jennifer looked elegant and pretty. Her glowing burnished curls were drawn up and swept back behind her ears, showing her creamy neck and throat to perfect advantage. A pale pink rose, the last of the season, adorned her bosom, and tiny garnet earbobs danced from her ears. Her slender figure, perfectly proportioned, was shown to keen advantage in the tight dress, and the small bustle in the back swayed enticingly.

Gabriel felt his blood pound, particularly when she led him to the round table in the corner. Only two places were set, and he glanced in confusion at the candlelight, the flowers, and the sparkling white linen cloth.

"Where are your sisters?" Sweat began to accumulate beneath his collar as he realized that, in all probability, she meant for them to dine alone.

"Penny and Winnie are out, and Aunt Eve is not feeling well. She has a cold." Jennifer shrugged. "It seems it's just us."

She looked at him from under thick lashes as if daring him to object. Dimly, Gabriel remembered Allison's words, and her subtly veiled hint that his interest in Jennifer was not entirely aboveboard. "Miss Appleton, this is most improper," Gabriel said stiffly, fighting the desire that raged inside of him. "You must know that young girls do not see men unchaperoned. Nor do they break into men's houses, consort at the stock market, or conduct séances. If someone discovered us tonight, it could ruin your reputation."

"My reputation is dubious at best," Jennifer replied, her voice sparkling with unreleased mirth. "Please don't be frightened, Mr. Forester. I have no intention of . . . taking advantage of you, if that is what you fear."

Gabriel took his chair, amazed at her boldness. He was tempted to take her in his arms and teach her a few things about taking advantage, but he was well aware of who would emerge the victor of such a battle. Still, it outraged his male ego that this little slip of a girl could understand him so well and laugh at him at every chance. She was just too much of an enticement, and he felt like a little boy, eyeing a confection that wasn't permissible, but always close at hand. He decided to take charge of the situation and state the ground rules, for his own sake as well as hers.

"Jennifer, I accepted your invitation because I think we need to have an amicable relationship. You are now friends with my mother, and although I've expressed my disapproval, both of you have ignored me. My presence here doesn't condone your behavior. I was hoping once again to talk some sense into you tonight. I'm sorry if I offend, but I want to make myself clear."

"No offense taken. You are entitled to your views." She shook his hand as any gentleman would, then took the seat across from him. "Can we at least put our differences aside while we eat?"

Gabriel nodded, satisfied, yet when she gazed at him with those meltingly pretty gray eyes, he knew he was lost. She poured the wine herself, and then served him, putting a nice portion of the perfectly cooked pheasant on his plate. Her hand brushed his in the process, and again the contact heated his skin. He wondered if she knew what she was doing to him, if she really was that clever—or was she as innocent as she appeared?

"Where is the maid?" he asked hoarsely, fighting the urges of his body. Why did she have to look so damned pretty. . . .

"Oh, she has the night off. She made the dinner, though. All we have to do is eat it. You don't mind?"

Gabriel shook his head, although he did mind. He knew he should get up right then and there and take his leave, for surely "the Appleton" was trying to seduce him. Perhaps this was her way of getting even with him, or attempting to control him. Whatever it was, it was potent as hell. And he found he could do nothing but see where it led.

He turned his attention to the meal, grateful for the distraction of the food. It was, admittedly, one of the best suppers of his life. He fought to keep his composure as Jennifer worked her charms on him, entertaining him with funny tales about her childhood with her two sisters. When she told him a story about being in church, wearing a coat with a huge hole in it, which she'd tried to cover while the other girls laughed, his heart went out to her.

"I can't imagine that," he admitted, observing how utterly charming she looked at that moment. "Were you really that poor?"

"After my parents died, yes. My father unwittingly left us in debt. We tried traditional ways to make money, like becoming companions and governesses, but that only led us further into poverty. It wasn't until the . . . séances, that we were able to pull ourselves out of the rut."

Gabriel felt an oddly protective instinct as he envisioned Jennifer, small and proud, clutching the torn coat and pretending not to hear the laughter behind her. It was this remarkable woman who'd held the family together, he realized in amazement. Responsibility that he couldn't even imagine had been placed on her shoulders at a time when perfumes and gowns should have been her concern. Yet she'd handled it with grace and aplomb. Whatever her faults, he suddenly appreciated, Jennifer had courage and strength.

"You know, pretty much the same thing happened with my father," Gabriel commented. "He was a real gentleman, the kind who wouldn't dare ask an acquaintance for payment. He nearly ran the business into the ground. By the time I took over, we were almost penniless."

"He must have been so proud, that you were able to right things," Jennifer said softly.

A pained look came into Gabriel's eyes, and he

shrugged. "Actually, I don't think he ever forgave me. He died a short while after, and several people conjectured that it was from disappointment. In me."

"That's terrible!" Jennifer said, pouring him more wine. "How could that be? You were only doing what you had to."

"He didn't see it that way. Debts of honor were just that to him, honorable. It never occurred to him that some people wouldn't pay unless coerced." Gabriel's lip curled at the thought, but he glanced at Jennifer and forced a smile. "Maybe now you understand why I'm so protective of my mother's money. In many ways, she's just like him."

Jennifer smiled sadly. "I know. She really is wonderful. And she's so happy with her fiancé. Gabriel, I'm so glad you've decided to accept him."

"How do you know that?" It was his turn to look surprised.

"She told me that you and Robert spoke the day she had me to tea, and seemed to have worked out your differences. It meant the world to her that you made the effort."

Gabriel nodded. He raised his eyes slowly to hers. "Jennifer, I have to admit something. Your presence in my mother's life has brightened it considerably. Initially, I wasn't convinced that your motives were honorable, but I've come to realize that however it started, she has benefited from your friendship. I want to thank you for that."

Jennifer knew how hard it was for him to admit this to her. She lightly pressed her hand to his in a gesture that was almost a handclasp. "Let me see to dessert." She rose, disappearing into the corridor that led to the kitchen.

Gabriel's hand burned from her touch. For a moment, he almost dared hope she meant something other than the obvious, then he scolded himself silently once more for being a cad. She was funny and intelligent, perverse and witty. She was unlike any other woman he'd ever met, twice as desirable, and twice as infuriating.

Jennifer was drawing him into her web, and like a fly, he was helpless to do anything about it.

"How is it going?" Penelope whispered as soon as Jennifer appeared in the kitchen.

"Wonderful," Jennifer said dreamily. "He is finally talking to me as if we were friends. He is so handsome, kind, intelligent, and sweet. I know he cares for me, I just know it!"

"Don't become so enraptured that you cry off our plan," Winifred reminded her. "Remember, you're to ask him to help you fetch the brandy from the basement. As soon as he enters the wine cellar, turn the key on him."

Jennifer nodded, and Penelope gave her a brave smile. Kidnapping Gabriel was going to take all the courage she possessed. Picking up the coffeepot, she headed toward the parlor.

JENNIFER RETURNED A few moments later with coffee and the pie. Gabriel had stretched out on the parlor couch, wondering what was keeping the girl. He had to admit he felt relieved when she reentered the room, for the séance trappings left him curiously uneasy. The parrot squawked, rustling in his cage, and the fire threw ominous shadows across the floor. Even the kitten seemed feral, and eyed him with that odd wisdom that cats always appeared to possess.

"I'm sorry, but the coffee wouldn't brew. It took me a little longer than I'd anticipated."

"Of course," Gabriel said, withdrawing a cheroot from his jacket. "That was an excellent meal, Jennifer. Thank you. Do you mind if I smoke?"

"No, not at all," Jennifer said, pouring him a cup of the pungent brew. "Would you like some brandy with that?"

"No, thank you." Gabriel accepted the cup, not wanting to let go when their fingers touched. He sipped the liquid, feeling the burn of the aromatic brew as it stung his lips. Putting aside the cup, he puffed on the cigar, reclining against the sofa. The kitten jumped into his lap, and he idly stroked its soft head. In spite of his air of contentment, Gabriel's uneasiness persisted. Something was different now, something in the way Jennifer watched him. She turned away quickly when his eyes met hers and Gabriel frowned, his senses alerted.

"Gabriel, would you mind going to the cellar for the brandy? I think we should have some. This occasion calls for something special."

"The coffee is fine," Gabriel said, still watching her carefully.

"I really would like to share a toast with you," Jennifer's tone was imploring. "Would you please come with me? I get frightened in the dark."

He couldn't resist, not when she asked like that. Gabriel nodded, putting aside the cigar. The kitten leaped to the floor and he took the lamp Jennifer proffered. After all, he was a grown man. What threat could a dark cellar impose?

The stairs were shrouded in black, and the guttering light of the lamp barely illuminated the step before him. Gabriel grumbled to himself, wishing now he had refused. Someone had to take Jennifer in hand, to keep her from her impulsive actions, he thought in irritation. Next time, he would be more firm.

The basement smelled dank and musty, and he now knew the source of the cobwebs in the chandelier. Something scurried along one wall, as if indignant that he invaded its territory. The air was cooler, and he was grateful when he reached the last step.

"The wines are in the room to the left," Jennifer called from behind him. "You have to open the door."

He complied, stepping into a room that, while cool, was at least clean and well kept. Wines lined the wall, neatly stacked inside a brick alcove. The elusive brandies were below them, and a chair and desk stood against the wall.

"This is an impressive collection," Gabriel mused, blowing the dust from a bottle and reading the label. "Surely you didn't buy this from your investments?"

Jennifer shook her head. "My uncle was a collector. He spent a lot of time down here, labeling bottles and recording when to drink them. Those are his notes." She gestured nervously to the books on the table.

The darkness apparently did frighten her, for Jennifer wasn't acting at all like herself. Thinking to spare her, he bent down to retrieve the brandy. At the same moment, he heard her scurry away, and the door behind him slammed with an ominous thud. A sickening suspicion came to him as he turned quickly, just in time to hear the bolt slide shut with a solid clink. Dropping the bottle, he sprang toward the door.

"Jennifer! I demand that you open the door this instant!" He pounded furiously, but could hear no response. Outrage swept through him as he realized the truth. Jennifer Appleton had tricked him as easily as a mouse walking straight into a trap for a piece of cheese. He had been kidnapped.

CHAPTER 12

"I WANT TO thank you for the reading." Mrs. Weatherwill buttoned up her cloak and fumbled in her purse for several large bills. "It was wonderful, dear! Fascinating. Why, I could have sworn my dear departed husband was with us the entire time! I swear I can still hear him, pounding and shouting!"

Penelope choked, while Jennifer accepted the payment. Thanking the woman profusely, she closed the door, leaning against it in exhaustion. Once more, the banging started in the cellar.

"We can't keep him locked up all night," Jennifer said, as soon as their client left. "It's too cold and damp down there in the cellar. He'll catch his death!"

"At least he stopped that banging for a little while," Penelope said between giggles. "I swear Mrs. Weatherwill thought her old husband's ghost was locked below!"

"Gabriel is a grown man," Winifred said quietly, clearing the séance materials from the room. "It is highly unlikely that he'll become ill or experience anything other than discomfort. However, we can put him in a warmer place to sleep. There is a bedroom in the back wing we can use, with a door that locks. I think it was once a servant's room."

"He'll leave if we open the door!" Penelope insisted, as if such a thought hadn't occurred to anyone else.

"Not if we give him an incentive to stay." Winifred glanced toward Jennifer, who covered her mouth with her hands in mirth.

"Not Uncle's gun?"

"The very same." Winifred put the crystal ball aside and opened a desk drawer. Reverently, she lifted the pistol that had already seen one war, and handed the implement to her sister.

"Don't you think we're taking this too far?" Penelope asked, staring in horror at the weapon.

"We haven't any choice," Winifred explained calmly. "We've come this far. We have to see it through."

"I don't have the faintest idea how to shoot," Jennifer said, balancing the heavy gun in her hand. "Is it loaded?"

"I doubt it. It doesn't matter that you don't know how to use it. He doesn't know that."

Jennifer nodded, testing the Colt revolver in her grip. She practiced holding it securely, then aimed it as if she were about to shoot. Glancing into the mirror, she saw that she looked fearsome indeed.

"We just have to make sure Auntie doesn't wake up," Penelope said, shuddering at the thought. "She's been dousing herself with her special 'tea' for her cold, which is more than half brandy, so that should help."

"Yes, it would be difficult to explain Gabriel as a houseguest," Jennifer admitted. Squaring her shoulders, she took a deep breath, then accepted the lantern her sister handed her. "I'm ready."

"Do you want us to follow you?" Penelope asked, although she didn't look eager to do any such thing.

Jennifer shook her head. "No, it will be better if I try

to explain things myself. If all of us gang up on him, we'll get nowhere." She braced herself, dreading the confrontation that was about to happen.

"He will be furious," Winifred said, echoing her own thoughts. "Be careful."

Penelope nodded her support, while Jennifer descended the stairs to the dim cellar. It was quiet, too quiet, she thought. A pang of guilt assaulted her as she imagined what he was thinking, then she firmly shook it off. If Gabriel was plotting their downfall with Allison, she couldn't allow herself to be weak. She had to do what she'd always done: take charge, and ensure their survival.

She screamed when the banging started again suddenly, then she exhaled in relief as she realized Gabriel was still securely locked away. He must be able to see the light beneath the door and hear her footsteps. Shivering from the invectives he spewed, Jennifer put the lantern down and spoke loudly.

"Gabriel, it's me. Jennifer."

The growl inside sounded savage and she almost lost her nerve. "Let me out of here! Goddammit, Jennifer, this had gone far enough! Wait until I get my hands on you, you conniving, little—"

"Gabriel, be quiet or I won't open the door." Jennifer had to shout to be heard.

Spending an hour in the dank cellar obviously had had an effect on him, for Gabriel finally did fall silent after a few more minutes of frustrated pounding.

He was even more furious than she'd expected. Jennifer swallowed hard, realizing the precarious position she was in. Refusing to give in to her terror, she forced her voice to sound calm.

"Gabriel, I will open the door, and I will let you go upstairs to a bedroom where you will be comfortable. However, I have a gun, and I will use it if necessary. Do you understand me?"

The silence that followed was more ominous. Jennifer could almost see him thinking, and weighing his alternatives. His voice was deceptively placid when he answered, though Jennifer wasn't fooled.

"There is no need for the gun. I will do as you suggest."

The moment she'd been dreading was upon her. Jennifer slid open the bolt, braced for a tigerlike spring from the man inside the room. Her hands shook as she held the revolver, which was pointed directly at Gabriel. Even in the dim lamplight, he could see the weapon clearly.

"I know what you're thinking, and I can only warn you that I am very nervous. This is my first kidnapping, you know. Please don't do anything rash, for I might shoot you unintentionally."

Gabriel nodded, his gaze focused on the way her hands trembled. She could scarcely hold the weapon, she was shaking so badly.

Jennifer wavered, then gestured toward the door. "If you'll walk ahead of me, I'll take you to the bedroom."

One brow cocked over his eye, and he sank back down onto her uncle's desk. An odd expression crossed his face, and he locked his eyes with hers. "No."

Jennifer's mouth dropped. "What do you mean, 'no'?" she asked, panic in her voice.

"I want some answers first," he continued in that deceptively silky voice. Jennifer was only vaguely aware that he was more furious than she'd ever seen him. There was a jaguarlike menace about him, and he eyed her like a dangerous quarry that had been cornered.

"What do you want to know?" Jennifer asked, her voice even tighter. Her hands were sweating and she was afraid she'd drop the gun then and there. It was only by wiping one hand on her dress that she managed to retain her hold on the weapon at all.

"Why have you done this?" he asked conversationally,

though she could tell he was contemplating wringing her neck. "Surely you don't intend to take further advantage of my mother by demanding a ransom? If that is your plan, forget it. I control her money."

"Do you really think . . . ?" It was Jennifer's turn to look astonished as his implication struck her. "I would never do such a thing to your mother!" she sputtered, outraged that he would even suggest it.

"Then I am at a loss. Would you mind explaining why I am locked in your wine cellar, or is this a curious custom of the Appletons to show hospitality?"

She'd rather he were raging, Jennifer decided. That she could understand better than this cold inquisition, which was decidedly more dangerous. The gun shook, and she had to wipe her hand once more. When she lifted it again, she gazed at him with a mixture of desperation and pleading.

"I can't answer any of that now. This gun is getting very heavy. Please just go upstairs. If you don't, I'll have to lock you in here again, and I don't want to do that. I think you'll be much more comfortable in a bed."

He seemed to weigh that answer carefully, although she didn't know his conclusion. However, some of the rage seemed to leave him, for she saw his expression lose some of its tightness. The thought of a bed must have enticed him after his stay in the wine cellar, for he nodded, then stepped closer to the door.

"Please, one step at a time. Don't make me shoot. I really don't want to hurt you."

He proceeded ahead of her, then stopped. Jennifer panicked, thinking he was about to flee. Instead, he stooped and picked up the lantern, then turned to her with a curiously amused expression.

"I take it you can't carry the lamp and train the gun on me at the same time? If so, it makes sense for me to carry it."

He was mocking her. Heat came to her face, but Jennifer refused to react. The condescension in his voice didn't deceive her for a moment. He was angrier than hell, but smart enough to use any device to gain an advantage.

"Just keep moving," Jennifer said, gesturing with the gun. "Now, please."

He proceeded up the stairs, following her directions as he reached the hall. He passed her sisters, who blocked the front door, armed with brooms and a mop. Even the kitten stood with them, snarling as if on their side. Gabriel's brow lifted in a mocking arch, and he went around to the back of the house with Jennifer, then down the winding corridor before reaching the bedroom.

"Stop here," Jennifer ordered, fumbling for the key in the pocket of her dress. They were outside the doorway of the servant's room, in a sparsely furnished hallway.

"Certainly," Gabriel answered politely. "By the way, were your sisters going to clean me to death, or defend the moat at all costs?"

Jennifer ignored his baiting, gesturing to the room. "Inside, please."

He stood outside the door, once more taking her measure. Jennifer trembled as his eyes raked down her, then shifted to study the hallway, and the solid oak door. He pushed the portal open and glanced inside the room. It was furnished with a bed, a dresser, and a washstand. He looked back at Jennifer.

"You first."

Jennifer gaped, then pointed the gun directly at his chest. He was less than five feet away, and the pistol seemed to dance all around the circumference of his immaculate shirt.

"The room is for you, not me!" she squeaked.

"Ah, but you see, I cannot accept your kind invitation to spend the night without really understanding your motive." He leaned against the wall, placing the lantern at his feet. "Miss Appleton, let me explain the way I see things. I came here at your invitation, to 'bury the hatchet,' as they say. I am treated to a wonderful dinner, with enjoyable company, and then, after coffee and cigars, am taken captive by my gracious hostess. Now, I can do one of several things. I can continue this idiocy, which no man with half a brain would consider, and walk out the door, or I can hear you out. Now which will it be?"

Jennifer choked. He was so calm, but she knew what an effort he was exerting to remain that way. Although his voice was properly joking, she saw the fury in his eyes. She couldn't even imagine what he'd do if she released him in his present state.

"Gabriel, I understand that you're angry, and I'll be happy to explain everything once you are inside. I don't want to have to shoot you. Please don't make me."

"I wonder if you would." Gabriel smiled, though the expression never reached his eyes. He took a step closer. "I've known you for quite some time now, Miss Appleton, and I think your bark is worse than your bite—"

She meant to cock the gun to scare him. But somehow a bullet sang through the air, striking the plaster and shattering it into a thousand tiny pieces. Jennifer was thrown against the wall by the impact, and Gabriel scrambled out of the way, staring in astonishment at the smoking barrel still aimed at him. He turned his head and saw the fresh bullet hole, less than five inches from where he stood.

"What the hell—You could have killed me!" He stared at her as if she were insane.

"Gabriel, please go inside," Jennifer pleaded, shaken to her very soul. The realization that she could have hurt him almost made her faint, but she managed to remain standing.

He stepped inside the bedroom, obviously convinced she'd lost her mind. Jennifer pulled the door closed and locked it immediately. Her heart pounded in her chest as she heard him shouting threats and promises of retribution. Trembling, she sank to the floor and rubbed her sore hand, which still ached from firing the weapon.

Kidnapping wasn't as easy as it looked, she thought ruefully. As she made her way back down the corridor, she shuddered at the noises coming from his room. Thankfully, they became more and more muffled as she returned to the main part of the house, and disappeared altogether when she reached the parlor. There, she saw Winifred and Penelope, practically bursting with questions, and behind them, Aunt Eve. The elderly woman stepped forth in confusion and the girls parted, both of them gesturing wildly behind the aunt's back.

"What is going on here, miss?" Eve demanded, sniffling into her handkerchief. "A body can't get any sleep, even after drinking my nighttime tea! I thought I heard scufflings, even a gunshot! Why, the only gun in the house is your uncle's Colt, and I keep it right in this drawer . . ."

The girls panicked as Aunt Eve started for the drawer. Jennifer stepped in front of it, the hot gun gripped in her hands behind her, while Penelope turned her aunt toward a chair.

"You must have been dreaming, Auntie!" Jennifer said quickly. "Gunshots! Why, do any of us look like we've been shot?"

Aunt Eve glanced from one girl to the next, then visibly relaxed. "No, you all look perfectly healthy. I must be losing my mind in my old age. What on earth then could I have heard?"

"I am sorry," Jennifer said. "I guess our theatricals didn't go so well tonight. We were trying to do . . . MacBeth's ghost scene, and it got a little out of hand."

"Ah. Shakespeare." Eve shook her head as if displeased. "No wonder, then. You really should focus on nicer material, you know, something more suitable for young girls.

Shakespeare is so tragic, you know. But I could have sworn the noises I heard came from the cellar . . ."

"That must have been the ice boy," Penelope said quickly. "He's getting so careless these days! I had to scold him more than once for slamming the cellar door. He's promised to be more careful."

Eve nodded, her white brows lifting. "That's quite right, my dear. You must set a good example for these young lads, otherwise they grow into street urchins. Now, if you girls don't mind, I will go back to bed. My cold has me positively exhausted."

"Would you like more of your tea?" Penelope asked helpfully.

Eve smiled. "Why yes, how nice of you. If you could bring it up to me, child, that would be wonderful. I sleep so well after." She patted Penelope's head, then disappeared up the stairs.

"That was close." Jennifer wiped her brow in relief. "We're going to have a tough time hiding Gabriel from her, if she should wake up again. He's so furious, it would be like letting a tiger loose if we were to free him right now."

"All the more reason to let him cool off tonight," Winifred said calmly. She looked at her sister appraisingly. "You didn't have to shoot him, did you?"

"No!" Jennifer said, aghast at the thought. "I only wanted to scare him. He wasn't taking me at all seriously. I didn't do too much damage. Just a little broken plaster."

"That's good. Penelope and I nearly fainted when we heard the shot. That's probably what woke Eve. We'll just have to take special care that Auntie doesn't see him, or hear him again. The sooner Gabriel accepts the situation, the better."

Jennifer nodded in agreement, though part of her wondered if Gabriel would ever accept the situation. If their positions were reversed, she knew she wouldn't. But there was little she could do about it now. Gabriel was their prisoner, and whatever the price, she knew she'd be the one to pay it.

Following Winifred upstairs, Jennifer put on her nightdress. No sooner had she pulled it over her head when the banging started once more. Penelope sprang out of bed, and even Winifred looked worried.

"It sounds louder now," Penelope whispered.

"Probably because the house and street are so quiet," Jennifer said. "I'll go see to him. We don't need Auntie waking up."

Penelope nodded, and Jennifer slipped on her robe. Her bare feet curled against the cold floor, but there wasn't time to look for her slippers. The banging stopped for a brief moment, but started up again before she could take a breath. Quickly, she lit a candle, then stepped lightly downstairs for the gun, praying her aunt wouldn't awaken.

The corridor was even more eerie in the dead of night. Jennifer swallowed convulsively when she heard Gabriel's growls. He quieted when she reached the doorway. Jennifer knocked lightly.

"It's me. Jennifer. What's wrong?"

Silence followed, deadly and still. Jennifer waited, her hands shaking, the candle guttering as she tried to still the flame. Good Lord, what if something was really wrong? What if he was ill, or had hurt himself in his rage? Slipping the key into the lock, Jennifer heard the bolt slide open, then she put the key in her pocket and picked up the candle. Cautiously, she opened the door an inch at a time, holding the gun before her for protection.

He was there, sitting on the bed. Jennifer put the candle on the floor. When she straightened, she barely had time to gasp as he lunged toward her. The gun dropped to the floor as he slammed into her, throwing her up against the door behind her. The bolt clicked shut, and she realized belatedly that she had locked herself in the room with him. Horror filled her as she saw him grin with satisfaction. She was pinned between him and the door, the gun glinting a good three feet away from her. She was trapped.

CHAPTER 13

"LET ME GO!" Jennifer squirmed as Gabriel braced his hands on either side of her, effectively cutting off any remaining hope of escape.

"Not on your life," he said coldly, obviously pleased with this reversal. "Now, Miss Appleton, since you find yourself in the same prison as myself, let's see how you like it. Before I even consider letting you up, I want to know what's really going on here. Why have you been following me the last few weeks, and why am I here?"

There was no way out. Jennifer swallowed hard, aware of the vulnerability of her position. Gabriel was pressed up against every inch of her. The thin eyelet covering over her nightgown provided little protection against him, and the batiste gown itself, even less. From the expression on his face, she realized he was just beginning to become aware of how little she wore and, worse yet, how much was exposed. If only she could trick him, get away from him long enough to get the gun. . . .

"I'll tell you everything," Jennifer said, gasping between words. "But could you please let me go? I can't talk like this."

"That's too bad, because you're going to have to. I'm

not that stupid, Jennifer. I know what you're thinking." To prove it, he kicked the gun, and it slid beneath the bed. "Now start talking."

She had no choice. Jennifer knew when she was out of cards, and this time, she was down and out. "It all started when Allison came to visit," she squeaked, feeling his hands slide down to grasp her waist. Her breasts were pressed fully against his shirt, and she could tell by his expression that he was aware of it, as well. "She said she just wanted to meet with us, but then she asked me for a reading and Winifred got suspicious—"

"Allison? Wanted a tarot reading?" He lifted away from her slightly, seeming to listen to her for the first time.

"Yes. We thought it odd, especially since she ignored us at the Rutherfords' ball. Winnie thought you two were plotting. I defended you, however," Jennifer declared loyally.

Gabriel scowled, apparently unimpressed. "But not to the extent of giving me the benefit of the doubt," he thundered. "So why lock me up?"

"There was a séance planned tonight," she explained, her face flaming in embarrassment. "We had to make sure you weren't going to interfere . . ."

"So you jailed me like some common thief." Gabriel shook his head in amazement, while Jennifer squirmed beneath him. "How long were you planning to keep me captive?"

"I don't know, just until we were sure . . ." Jennifer felt his arm tighten around her, and she gasped. "The weekend."

"You were going to kidnap me all weekend?" It was his turn to look astonished. His expression turned quickly to outrage, and Jennifer's eyes grew wide with fear. "My God, woman, you tempt me to . . ."

His hands tightened around her waist as he pulled her

from the door and into his arms. Desperately, Jennifer struggled against him, not knowing what he planned to do, but not wanting to wait around and see. Her robe slipped from her shoulders in her struggles, and she gasped as she felt the flimsy material slide traitorously to the floor. Her bare shoulders gleamed in the dim light, and her hair loosened in the struggle, to fall around them enticingly.

Panic welled up inside of her as she saw his expression, and she knew she was in a very different kind of trouble. The fury on his face had changed to something else, something even more frightening to Jennifer. His eyes looked smoky, eager, and intense, and there was some kind of primitive male need rising in him that she could only sense. All pride and defiance left her, and she knew there was nothing to do now but surrender. "Please let me go! I didn't mean to cause you any trouble. I was just following you because . . . because I like you, and I wanted you. You can laugh at me all you want, but that's the truth."

Understanding dawned on his face, and Jennifer blushed in humiliation. She never meant for things to go so far, never meant for any of this to happen. She wanted so much to be like a real lady for him, someone of his own class, someone he could be proud of. Yet, once more, fate had taken that choice out of her hands.

He eased his grip on her, but he refused to release her from his embrace. Jennifer struggled weakly, appalled at herself and what she'd just admitted. Gabriel held her firmly, but his hands soothed her, comforting her, caressing her back and shoulders as if she were a desolate little girl. He gently ran his finger over her profile, then his finger stopped when it reached her lips. She paused, almost afraid to take a breath as his thumb rubbed gently against her moist lips, then slowly, tenderly, he lowered his mouth to hers.

It was a compassionate kiss, filled with sensitivity and kindness, meant to comfort and reassure her. Jennifer tried to resist its potency, but it was impossible. All of the suppressed emotion she'd felt for this man rose up within her, and she responded to him with an ardor that was achingly poignant and devastating to him. Pleasure, shocking and exciting, raced through her blood as he deepened the kiss, his tongue fully tasting the depths of her sweetness. From a distance, she heard his groan of desire, a sound that was strangely exciting. Wonder filled her, and she surrendered to him, dizzy with sensation.

Gabriel eased his mouth from hers and gazed into her eyes, tipping up her chin so that he could fully see into their mysterious gray depths. "My God," he murmured, seeming as stunned as herself by what was happening between them. "You surely are an enchantress."

"I think you are beautiful," Jennifer said, her voice achingly real and filled with awe. Her hands traced down his shirt, feeling the muscles beneath, and she gazed up into his face with reverence, as if seeing the dark curly hair and blue eyes for the first time. "You're like an angel," she breathed.

"Jennifer, my sweet Jennifer," he whispered, then took her into his arms. His mouth took hers, possessing her completely with his fierce need. Passion, pure and simple, ignited between them, and the kiss changed from one of seduction to an explosion of white-hot desire. Intoxicated, Jennifer melted against him without inhibition, wanting more of the emotions he was stirring in her. His hand lowered from her waist to the small of her back, urging her even closer, but she needed little convincing now, and she threaded her fingers through the hair on the nape of his neck, wanting to experience everything to the fullest.

Shuddering with pleasure, Gabriel slid his hand upward to the front of her gown, then cupped her breast.

Jennifer gasped, feeling the nipple rise beneath his fingers. A ragged moan escaped her as her body responded to him, and she pressed herself more fully into his hand. The delicious ache she'd felt for him earlier had now increased tenfold, culminating shockingly between her legs.

"Gabriel, please," she whispered breathlessly, not knowing what she craved, but needing it all the same. She surrendered to him fully, pressing herself against him, wanting everything that he promised.

"Sweetheart. Jennifer, my darling." He released her slowly, and she could feel the reluctance within him to leave her even for that short moment. Feverishly, he began unbuttoning his shirt, his eyes never straying from her face, his own burning with desire. "I think it's time I got rid of these."

Jennifer watched in fascination, crossing her arms and shivering against the cold. She knew she should stop him, should tell him that she'd never been with a man before, but her own blood was afire. She was lost in the intoxication of his kiss, and his caresses, and she didn't know how to begin to stop. His chest emerged, and she saw the lean, hard muscles beneath his shirt, and the dark matting of hair that traced enticingly lower to where his trousers began. He doffed those as well, and Jennifer turned away in shocked embarrassment as he came to stand before her, naked and magnificent.

"I think it's time we undressed you, too," he whispered teasingly, easing her gown from her heated body.

"I don't think—" Jennifer tried, but her words were lost as he placed scorching kisses on every inch of skin that he bared. By the time he'd taken the gown from her, she was writhing and whimpering in his arms. Chuckling softly, he lifted her up, then placed her on the little bed. The blanket felt scratchy beneath her hot flesh, but that only added to the heady sensations that consumed her. It seemed every inch of her was tingling, especially as Gabriel traced kisses along her neck to her elbow, then to her hand. He lathed her palm with his tongue, and she squirmed on the bed, clutching fistfuls of the blankets with her other hand, awed that her body should have so many hidden sensitive places. His tongue traced dizzying patterns back up to her elbow, then down from her throat, then lower, weaving a hot erotic tapestry around her.

"Gabriel," she panted. "I don't know if I can stand it . . ."

"I know," he whispered. "Just a little more. My God, Jennifer, you're so damned beautiful. I want to wait, but I don't know if I can—"

When he turned that same attention to her breasts, licking her nipples into diamond-hard points, she pleaded with him earnestly. His hands crept lower, caressing her legs, her inner thigh, making the heat burn impossibly hotter. Soon she was arching against him, begging him for release from this sweet torture as she felt him poised at the moist, hot entrance of her body. Answering her plea, he pressed forward, and she gasped as he thrust deeply within.

And stopped in surprise. "Jennifer? Are you all right?"

Jennifer bit her lip and nodded. Gabriel eased back instantly at her discomfort, and now spread teasing, wonderful kisses along her heated neck and throat, then lower, bringing her back to the same burning need she'd felt before. Soon all thoughts of resistance left her, and she clasped him closer to her, wriggling beneath him, responding eagerly to his expert touch. Withdrawing slightly, he entered again slowly, carefully stoking her pleasure until a fire raged within her.

Jennifer moaned, lost in the sublime feeling that swept over her. When she began to squirm once again beneath him, Gabriel couldn't resist. He thrust more deeply into her, trying to hold back, while his body urged him onward. Jennifer rose up against him and arched to meet his hot thrusts. An almost painful pleasure exploded within her and she cried out his name in wonder. Gabriel groaned, and he held her even tighter as he reached a shuddering climax.

Jennifer saw his beautiful face, suffused with pleasure, and she smoothed the curls from his forehead. At this moment, she felt much more complete than she'd ever felt before in her life. Wonder and awe filled her as Gabriel held her tenderly, his expression full of reverence. He kissed her gently, then rose a bit to stare down at her.

"Jennifer. My sweet Jenny. My God, what a woman you are."

A wave of incredible pleasure swept over her at his words. She sighed, feeling his arms wrap around her in contentment. Bliss filled her, along with a sense of euphoria. *So this is love.* She knew it, the way one knew all true things when seeing them for the first time.

She smiled at him shyly, unused to having a man's naked body so close to hers. It was intimate, strange, yet wonderful all the same.

"Gabriel, I didn't know . . . I had no idea," she breathed, trying to convey the rapture that possessed her. "I never knew that love could be like this."

He went still at her words. Confusion filled his face, and he seemed to recall something that bothered him. "Jennifer, are you saying . . ." he looked down at her, as if trying to piece together a puzzle, "that you've never done this before?"

"No." She shook her head, trying to decipher whether that was the response he was looking for. He stared down at her, and his expression became guarded. Something was wrong. She could feel it, yet she didn't understand why. Fear sparked inside of her, and she gazed up at him, trying to comprehend his thoughts. "Is that bad?"

"No." He sank back into the bed, stunned by his realization of the truth; Jennifer had been a virgin. Until him. A million thoughts went through his mind, thoughts that he just couldn't make sense of. Why had she done this? Why him? Suddenly aware that she was waiting for an explanation, he spoke quickly. "No, it's not bad at all. Most men like being the first. I just . . . didn't expect it."

She stiffened beneath him, his meaning abundantly clear. He hadn't thought her an innocent. She was the notorious Jennifer Appleton, unlike other girls. She never would be anything else to him. Anguish cut deeply within her, hurting far more than any physical discomfort. She rose, clutching the sheet to her breasts in embarrassment, trying to quell the ache growing inside her.

The look on her face went straight to his heart. "Jennifer, please—"

"Could I have my robe?"

Gabriel was at a loss. He hesitated a moment, but then found the garment on the floor, puddled where it had fallen a moment ago in the midst of pure passion. Handing the robe to her, he waited until she was dressed, then attempted once more to break the awkwardness between them.

"Jennifer, let's talk about this—"

"I'd rather not." Pulling the garment around her, she tied it securely, then felt inside the pocket for her key. Thankfully, her pride came to her rescue and she shrugged as if the encounter had meant little to her. "There really isn't anything to talk about, Gabriel. We both know what happened was a mistake. After all, I'm the notorious Appleton. What's one more stain on my reputation?"

"You know it isn't like that!" He rose from the bed, wrapping a sheet around himself, and started toward her. "You can't possibly think—"

Somehow, she managed to both evade him and answer him calmly. "I apologize for the kidnapping, and for all the other trouble I've caused you. I'll unlock the door, and you can leave in the morning. There really isn't anything more to be said. Good night, Gabriel."

"Jennifer!" he roared, but she swept out of the room and was gone.

THE FOLLOWING MORNING, Jennifer came down to the breakfast table slowly, her heart heavy. She had debated the idea of waiting until everyone had finished, then slipping into the kitchen for a bite, but she knew her sisters. They would be curious about her nonappearance, and would question her relentlessly. Showing up was definitely the lesser of two evils, particularly since she didn't want to answer queries about her late-night encounter with Gabriel.

She took her place at the dining table, grateful that Winifred and Aunt Eve were distracted by Penelope's chatter about the new rage in hairstyles. From the glint of the polished coffeepot, she could see that her eyes were still swollen, and she prayed no one would notice. Her only consolation was that Gabriel was gone, and she wouldn't have to face him. Accepting a cup of the strong brew, she sipped the coffee, nearly choking when Eve spoke.

"I didn't sleep at all well last night. I kept hearing that odd clamoring. Goodness knows what it was! Almost like someone knocking on the door in the middle of the night. Can you imagine?"

Winifred looked at Jennifer sharply, while Penelope shrugged. "I've had dreams like that before. Once I even got up to see what it was, although I was still asleep."

"I remember," Winifred said quickly. "You wandered right into the arms of that poor grocer boy, who had shown up early. I daresay the lad's been in love with you ever since."

"Pooh," Penelope said while everyone laughed. "That's what he gets for waking me up."

"I don't think this was the grocer boy," Eve continued. "In fact, I could have sworn I heard you, Jennifer, as well. It just doesn't make sense . . ." Eve's speculations changed quickly to a gasp, and she looked over Jennifer's head in astonishment. "My word! Why, what is he doing here?"

Jennifer's heart slowed to a thud and she glanced once again into the coffeepot, stunned to see Gabriel rounding the stairs. He strode straight into the dining room and surveyed the company with casual ease, as if he did this every day. Panic filled Jennifer as Aunt Eve nearly fainted and Penelope's mouth dropped. Only Winifred scarcely looked up from the morning paper, determined, Jennifer supposed, to hide safely within its pages.

"Good morning, ladies. Breakfast looks wonderful. I'll have three eggs, over easy, and bacon and toast. And coffee." He lifted a cup from the sideboard and poured himself a generous serving, then took a seat at the table.

"Young man, this is outrageous!" Aunt Eve sputtered, while Jennifer hid her face in her napkin. "Who do you think you are, barging in here like this, and not for the first time! This just isn't done!"

Gabriel looked from one guilty face around the table to the next. Understanding dawned, especially when Jennifer sent him a pleading look, then dove beneath her napkin again. Winifred's paper ruffled determinedly, and Penelope jumped up and down once as if a tack had been placed on her chair.

"I'm sorry, madam, I suppose your nieces forgot to tell you. I was invited to breakfast. Rather forcibly invited, as well."

"What?" Eve looked around the table. Penelope had turned a particularly attractive shade of rose, while Winifred seemed inordinately interested in the society page, which she normally derided. Finally, Jennifer laid down her napkin and faced her aunt, determined to tell the truth, no matter what the cost.

"He's right, Auntie. We did invite him. I'll tell you the truth, even though you may no longer want us here when you know it all."

She took a deep breath, unwilling and unable to continue the charade any more. But before she could spill everything, Gabriel smiled charmingly at her aunt and started talking.

"What she means is, your three nieces have gone out of their way to convince me that they have my mother's best interest at heart. As you know, I've had a quarrel with them for quite some time over their relationship with my mother. Jennifer invited me here so I could see firsthand that they mean her no harm. I must say she's convinced me by her kind invitation that she and her sisters are true ladies, and as such, would never hurt anyone."

Aunt Eve looked pleased, then nodded affectionately toward the girls. "That they are, my lambs! I understand, though a breakfast invitation is highly out of the ordinary."

"So are your girls, Mrs. Appleton. So are your girls."

Eve nodded, then rang for the maid. "An extra serving of eggs, please. We have a special guest. And bring out that fine jam I've been saving. This seems like a wonderful occasion for it."

Jennifer groaned, burying her face in her hands. Gabriel sank back into his chair, initiating conversation with the other sisters and treating Aunt Eve to a few stories about her old friends that delighted her. When Jennifer could stand to peep at him, she noticed he looked perfectly groomed and dressed, as if he hadn't spent the night making passionate love to her, or being jailed in the wine cellar. He gestured as he spoke, and she gazed at his hands, remembering the way they'd felt on her skin the previous night, and her own uninhibited response. Her face flamed, and her stomach knotted with hot embarrassment.

She had to get out of here, but Jennifer knew if she bolted, she would attract entirely too much attention. She exhaled, unaware that she'd been holding her breath in horror ever since his unexpected appearance. The maid brought him his meal, and to Jennifer's annoyance, he held reign like king in his own court. His handsome looks won him the attention of the servant, Penelope beamed over him as she did any man, and Aunt Eve seemed to change her opinion entirely about him. Winifred wisely kept to herself, and Jennifer scowled, wishing she could truly perform an incantation and whisk him away.

He seemed to read her thoughts, for he glanced up after a moment and gestured to her full plate. "Doesn't the meal agree with you, Miss Appleton?"

Jennifer choked, particularly when everyone looked her way. "Yes, it is fine. I'm just not very hungry." Using the excuse, she rose from the table. "I'm going to market now, Auntie. Have a good time on your trip."

"Surely, my dear. You look a little peaked, Jennifer. You can take my shawl. I don't want you succumbing to the ague."

Jennifer nodded, snatching up her coat, then placing Eve's shawl over her shoulders. Escape was uppermost in her mind. Last night was a memory that throbbed painfully, like a wound with a thorn embedded inside, and she wanted nothing more than to walk off that ache alone. To her disbelief, Gabriel rose at the same time. "I'll accompany you. My carriage is at the livery, and I have some things to do in town as well."

Jennifer sputtered. "But I was planning to walk—"

"Nonsense," Aunt Eve said quickly. "You don't look well, and since I've ordered our own carriage for my trip, it will do you good to accept Mr. Forester's kind offer. Besides, the weather is cold and damp."

Winifred dove beneath the paper and Penelope shrugged helplessly. Jennifer was trapped. She could do nothing but accept Gabriel's arm as he escorted her in a gentlemanly fashion out the door. Frustrated beyond measure at being forced into his company, Jennifer waited until they were outside, but she could see the curtain twitch and knew her aunt was at the window. She could do nothing but smile sweetly and accept his help into the coach.

No sooner did the door shut than she turned on him. "There is no need for you to come with me. I appreciate your covering up for us, for it would upset Aunt Eve tremendously to know the truth—"

"What, that I am your captive?" Gabriel grinned rakishly, calling to the coachman to drive to market. "I surmised she wasn't in on the caper."

"It's not funny!" Jennifer exclaimed. "I told you, we didn't mean for things to go so far—" She blushed hotly as soon as the words came out of her mouth. "What I mean is—"

"I know what you meant. Jennifer, we need to talk about this. I know you're hurt and upset about what happened between us, but please don't be. I know what an effort it must have been for you to admit your feelings to me last night, and I have a confession to make. I have many of the same feelings for you."

"You do?" Jennifer stared at him in astonishment. A tiny spark of hope began inside her, one that she didn't dare examine.

"Yes, I do. I care about you, though God knows I didn't want to. I also haven't the faintest idea what to do about it. In the meantime, I don't think it makes sense to pretend it didn't happen, or to sweep it under the rug, much as you would like to do that. There may be other repercussions as well."

Jennifer stared at him in confusion, then his meaning slowly dawned on her. She could feel the reddened blush creep up her face, and she looked away in embarrassment.

"I see you understand my meaning. Jennifer, I made love to you last night, not knowing you were a virgin. I didn't take precautions, nor did I discuss that with you, which was foolish. I just thought . . ." His voice trailed off and Jennifer looked at him sharply.

"You thought what? That I was experienced and would know about these things? That the notorious Jennifer Appleton was a . . . tart, as well? Let me out of this coach! I won't stay here another minute!"

She reached for the carriage door, but Gabriel stopped her. His hand clamped down on her arm, holding her tightly while she squirmed.

"No, you aren't running away from me this time. I confess, I did think that, and I apologize. Jennifer, you are unlike any other woman I've ever known. I didn't know what to think. Can you understand that?"

She did understand, though it still hurt. Jennifer realized he was being honest, but somehow that didn't help. She nodded, and he released her arm. She made a grand gesture of rubbing the abused limb, then she turned to him stiffly.

"I accept your apology, and my own responsibility for what happened. I'm sorry for everything, and I suppose I only have myself to blame for kidnapping you. Since you apparently don't have any evil motive, there is no need to continue any of this. Good day, Mr. Forester. I have my shopping to do."

She alighted from the coach, more than grateful when the coachman opened the door and held out his hand. She wanted nothing more than to get away, to comfort her own roiling emotions. Her insides felt tattered, and she needed to distance herself from Gabriel. To her amazement, he stepped up beside her as she approached the market stalls.

"I thought I said—"

"Miss Appleton, I believe you indicated that I was to be held captive for the weekend. As it happens, I have nothing planned that I can't miss, and I find the entire idea very appealing. You might as well take advantage of my help, for I am not going anywhere."

CHAPTER 14

"GABRIEL, YOU REALLY don't have to do this," Jennifer insisted, although she sensed she was wasting her time arguing with him. "I'm sure you could be doing a lot of more interesting things than going to market."

"Not at all," Gabriel said, walking very quickly to keep up with her. It took every ounce of his agility to stay by her side as she ducked and turned between the market stalls. New York's Fulton was a bustling place, full of bonnets and derbies, working-class hats and maid's caps, and it was no easy matter to continually pick out Aunt Eve's shawl. "I'm rather looking forward to it," he continued when he caught her. "I haven't been to market since I was a boy. Where do we start?"

Jennifer sighed, defeated. She was stuck with him. Determined not to lose her composure, she approached a familiar stall where a dark Italian man stacked row after row of potatoes, turnips, and other winter vegetables. He grinned when he saw Jennifer, and put his hand over his heart.

"It is she! My day is complete! How are you, Miss Appleton?"

Gabriel's face darkened and Jennifer had to laugh at

his scowl. She extended her hand, all part of the morning ritual, and Lorenzo placed a kiss on her glove as if she were royalty.

"I'm fine, Lorenzo. Now, I want a good price for the potatoes today, not like last week. You positively cheated me on those onions!" Jennifer sounded desolate, but a jaunty grin played about her lips as she handed him her list.

"Cheat! I never cheat, especially one so beautiful as you! I tell you what—I let you have five pounds today for a dime, how's that?"

"No more than a nickel," Jennifer said firmly. "And even that is highway robbery! Why, I could have ten pounds at O'Leary's for a nickel!"

"O'Leary! O'Leary! He wouldn't know a good potato from a rutabaga! Bah, O'Leary!" When Jennifer bestowed a melting look on him, the grocer shrugged helplessly. "All right, a nickel! But will you ask your sister to come with you next time? The beautiful one, with the hair like the sun! My God, that woman is magnificent!"

Jennifer nodded and smiled, knowing the poor grocer was in love with Penelope. Her sister barely noticed the man, but that didn't stop him from following her around like a smitten puppy. She watched closely as he selected the potatoes, objecting once when one of his choices was a little soft. Lorenzo shrugged as if it was all part of the game, then moved to the fruits.

"Would you ladies like some oranges? These are the last of the season, brought up on the train from the south. We won't have them much longer with winter coming." He displayed the soft orange globe enticingly. "They are sweet and wonderful."

Jennifer nodded, then got into a heated disagreement with him over price. Gabriel watched in awe as she whittled the man down on each and every item, getting fantastic prices, but always keeping the tone light and funny. It took quite a bit of talent, Gabriel thought, understanding now why the family allowed Jennifer this task. When the grocer handed her last month's bill, she scrutinized it like a hawk, going over each item and double-checking it. Lorenzo squirmed as she found an error and sweetly insisted that it be corrected before she parted with her precious coin.

Lorenzo grumbled and sighed, but took the coin and grinned, shaking her hand. Both parties appeared satisfied with the outcome of the game, although the grocer had one parting shot.

"Holy Mary, Mother of God, you drive a hard bargain! I will have to be firm next time, or you will make me a pauper!"

"And I will have to stay on my toes, or you will send me into bankruptcy!" Jennifer replied, though she smiled brilliantly.

The grocer grinned, then handed Jennifer a receipt. While she scanned the slip of paper, his eye met Gabriel's.

"Can I help you, sir?"

"No, I'm with the lady," Gabriel answered firmly, refusing to acknowledge Jennifer's glare.

Lorenzo looked at him curiously, taking in his expensive suit, his good linen shirt, and his wool coat. Then shrewdness replaced his curiosity, and, like any good salesman, he suddenly seemed determined to make the most of the opportunity. Reaching beneath the counter, he withdrew a small flask, then displayed the ornate bottle in all its glory. Jennifer snapped her purse shut and frowned as he opened the elaborate cask and held it enticingly beneath her nose.

"What do you think of that, miss? Wonderful, eh? This will make any man fall instantly in love with you!" He glanced at Gabriel with a meaningful look.

Mortified and desperate to quiet the man, Jennifer quickly took the bottle, then pretended to be absorbed in examining the label. "Martha Washington's Perfume Waters. I've never heard of this." She sampled the perfume, entranced by the heady aroma.

"It is, how you say, all the rage. I brought in some especially for you girls. Normally I sell at one dollar twenty-five, but I let you have at special price of one dollar five. What you think? Perfume for the beautiful lady, sir?"

Jennifer looked on in horror as she realized Gabriel was digging into his pocket. "No, we can't afford this. I'm sorry, Lorenzo, but you know we're on a fixed budget."

"Ah, but all ladies need something beautiful once in a while, do they not?"

"Yes, they do," Gabriel agreed. "I'll take it." Amid Jennifer's protests, Gabriel handed the man two crisp bills. Ignoring her look, he saw Lorenzo's face light up, and the man eagerly scrounged for paper to wrap the precious bottle. He returned with the change, and handed Jennifer the perfume.

"You will love it! That is a good man you've got, miss! A good man!"

Jennifer smiled brittlely, then returned to the carriage with Gabriel. Once out of earshot, she tried to hand him the perfume.

"Gabriel, I really can't accept this. I know you feel guilty . . ."

"No, I don't," Gabriel cut her off. "I bought that because you liked it, and all of you will enjoy it. Jennifer, there is nothing wrong with treating yourself once in a while. I admire your frugality, but you are entitled to some of life's little luxuries. After all your stock winnings, you should be able to buy yourself something. Since you won't, I will do it for you."

She looked at him in amazement, shaking her head ruefully. "You still don't understand, do you? Our stock earnings will help with some of our major goals, like Winifred's schooling and Penny's debut, but we are far from rich. What if Aunt Eve should become ill? Or if

Winifred should desire extended education? And what of our old age? I have to make sure we still stretch every penny so that we are protected."

Gabriel stared at her, aware that Jennifer was struggling with the kind of security issues that usually fell to the man of the house. "But surely you don't think this will continue forever? Penelope will marry, as will Winifred, I would think. And you." He reached up and arranged her shawl, which had become loose.

That touch brought back memories she didn't want to face. It was difficult to stand this close to him, to accept his simple gesture at face value. She felt vulnerable and unprotected, a feeling that, given the circumstances, wasn't very comfortable. Worse yet was his statement about her marrying. It didn't escape her notice that he wasn't offering himself, only suggesting that one day she would wed. A chill passed through her and a painful tightness constricted her throat. She shouldn't have expected anything else, not after what happened last night. Throwing herself into his arms had obviously only confirmed what he'd felt all along—that she wasn't a lady. The thought stung.

Stepping away from him, she arranged her shawl herself and shrugged as if none of it mattered.

"There is no one I can count on permanently. Even my own father, who loved us, left us in this situation. If and when my sisters wed, things will be easier, but I can never entirely depend on anyone else. Then there is Aunt Eve, whom I will always care for. How could I not, after all her kindness?"

Gabriel couldn't argue with her logic. "I understand all that, but there is nothing wrong with allowing someone to help you. Please accept the perfume. I don't mean anything by it, and there are no strings attached. I just want you to enjoy it."

Jennifer gazed at him for a long moment, trying to

discern what he really meant. He endured her perusal, returning her stare openly without squirming. She sensed that he was trying to somehow bridge the icy gap that she'd erected between them, that he sincerely wanted to give her and her family this gift. She didn't dare think it meant anything more. Reluctantly, she nodded. "Since you have already paid your money for it, and it is for all of us, I accept. Now I have to go to the butcher's and baker's, then look at some dry goods. You really don't have to come—"

"I wouldn't miss it," Gabriel insisted cheerfully, handing the perfume to his carriage driver for safekeeping. "I can't wait to see you whittle the butcher down on a few pork chops."

Jennifer grinned, but allowed him to accompany her down the street. They arrived at the butcher's, an immaculate shop filled with marbled cuts of meat, enticingly displayed fowl, and hanging links of sausage. The rotund butcher tossed a few scraps to a mangy dog outside, who scrambled to catch the treat, while the butcher continued chopping. He sang as he worked, expertly cutting the meat into a perfect portion, then wrapping it with brown paper and twine. He handed a package to the well-dressed woman before him, then turned to Jennifer.

"What'll it be, miss? I have nice fat bacon today, and a good pork roast."

"Do you have any bacon ends?" Jennifer asked, peering into her purse and counting out the coin.

"Saved a few especially for you. How are the ladies? I hope Mrs. Eve is well these days."

"She has a bit of a cold," Jennifer explained as the butcher retrieved a package from the icebox behind him. "But she loved the chicken you sent her last week."

The butcher winked, then leaned closer to her as if imparting a great secret. "One of those rich families had ordered it, but never showed up. Had I kept it too long, it would have spoiled." He shrugged cheerfully. "Their loss is your gain!"

Jennifer bowed, thanking the man, then went on to discuss the different cuts of meat. Gabriel was amazed at how differently she dealt with the butcher than with Lorenzo. She instinctively knew how to talk to people so they responded positively to her, and she genuinely seemed to like and respect them. In turn, the shopkeepers treated her with kindness, going out of their way to do her little favors or provide her family with an extra orange or slice of bacon. Unlike Gabriel's more affluent acquaintances, the working-class people seemed to have no objection to Jennifer's ignoble occupation, but understood her situation. It was no wonder, he realized, that the police were on her side, as were many of the local businesspeople.

She argued again when Gabriel insisted on purchasing a plump roast she'd been eyeing regretfully, astonishing the poor butcher, who hastened to wrap the meat as fast as he could.

"But that cost two dollars!" she protested in astonishment as Gabriel paid out the money. "I don't pay that for a week's worth of meat! Put it back," she told the butcher, who wisely pretended not to hear.

Gabriel led her out of the man's hearing by the elbow. "Jennifer, I insist. After all, I cannot subsist as your kidnappee on bacon rinds."

"You aren't really going to stay the weekend, are you?" Jennifer gasped.

"Absolutely. You wanted me, you've got me. That's all there is to it." Gabriel grinned at her aghast expression. Although he really didn't intend to stay another night, he did plan to teach the Appleton sisters a lesson, one they wouldn't forget. He continued in the same tone, "And since you provided dinner last night, it's the least I can do to reciprocate. It's about time you all had a decent meal. No wonder Eve is ill."

"That's not fair!" Jennifer cried. "I take good care of them all. And our meals are nutritious, even if they aren't costly."

"A little meat on the bones won't hurt anyone. Especially you," Gabriel added, his eyes filled with wicked meaning. "I seem to recall that you are a little too slender."

Jennifer gasped, sputtering. She walked away indignantly, refusing to be drawn into this conversation, one that would surely go in a direction that would only please him. His chuckle burned in her ears and she turned aside as the butcher reverently handed him the package. The man actually shook Gabriel's hand, obviously pleased that this noble gentleman had decided to help the poor Appletons.

"Next stop?" Gabriel asked, sounding delighted to have bested her.

"The baker. This won't take long. Gabriel, I insist that you wait in the coach—"

"Are you joking? I haven't had this much fun in ages. Let me do this one. I think I've got the hang of it."

"But—" Jennifer's protests fell on deaf ears as he stepped up to the spotless counter where the baker's wife placed hot, fresh bread loaves.

"What can I do for you, sir?" The plump woman asked, wiping her hands on her apron and giving Jennifer a less than friendly glance. A cloud of flour seemed to surround her, and Gabriel coughed, waving the air.

"I'll take some of those tea biscuits. And three of those loaves—they look wonderful. And some pound cake, those cookies, that lemon layer cake, and some tarts."

"Yes, sir!" The woman's eyes widened appreciatively, and she hurried to get his order. Jennifer fumed as Gabriel didn't attempt to argue with the woman about price, but cheerfully ordered just about everything he saw.

"We can't afford this!" Jennifer cried as the woman rushed to do his bidding. "I usually get the day-old bread, and the baker saves the leftover cakes for me. They're still good, and we all enjoy them."

Gabriel cast a disparaging glance toward the dry, crusty pastries. "Well, if I'm being held captive this weekend, I insist on eating well." He paid the woman amid Jennifer's objections. "Prisoner's rights, you know."

"Since when do prisoners buy their own meals?" Jennifer said, though her mouth watered at the sight of the tarts.

"This is a rather unusual kidnapping, and as such, calls for unusual measures," he said firmly, brushing her arguments aside. "I refuse to be mistreated while incarcerated."

"Gabriel, this is ridiculous." Jennifer stamped her foot in frustration. "This whole thing has gone far enough. We really couldn't kidnap you, you know that. And you don't have to do this—"

"I want to. And as far as not being able to kidnap me, that gun looked very real, especially when you nearly killed me. I think you girls did a magnificent job of taking me prisoner. In fact, I think the South might have won the war had the Appletons been on her side."

This teasing side of him left her defenseless. Jennifer stood by helplessly while he turned that devastating grin on the baker's wife. "I'll take those packages, ma'am. Have a good day." He bowed, while the rotund woman giggled flirtatiously. She glanced at Jennifer, then at Gabriel, and her smile grew broader.

"Sir, you've made my day. Here, take a few more cookies for the girls. Always liked the Appleton ladies, that I do."

Jennifer stared. "She's always hated us!" she said in bemusement once they were outside the shop, as he jauntily shouldered the package and headed toward the coach. "Ever since Penny came in and her husband nearly burned the entire morning's bread because he was staring at her. I don't get it."

Gabriel chuckled. "Maybe she's just thrilled to actually make a profit, for once. Lord knows, with customers like you, she probably barely breaks even."

"Humph," Jennifer said, shaking her head at the sight of the carriage, laden with packages. "Well, I certainly won't feel too badly the next time. She practically robbed you on those cakes!"

"Maybe, but I can afford it. Where to next?"

"Home," Jennifer said quickly. "Before you're bankrupt."

Gabriel chuckled, then extended a hand, helping her into the carriage. Inside, the wonderful smells of fresh bread, fruit, and pastries filled her senses, and the scent of the perfume still lingered on her dress sleeve. Although she'd never admit it to him, Jennifer realized she'd enjoyed herself. Gabriel had been funny and entertaining, as well as generous.

She glanced at him from beneath her lashes, then turned away quickly as he caught her looking at him. Casting her eyes downward in embarrassment, she could hear his laughter as the coach rumbled on. She had to remind herself to be cautious, and not let her guard down again for a second. She didn't want a repetition of what happened between them last night, and she especially didn't want to care any more for Gabriel than she already did. Unfortunately, he was making it very difficult to despise him.

They returned home to the "oohs" and "aahs" of her sisters when they spied their bounty, and Jennifer felt as if she were witnessing the return of the conquering hero. Gabriel, obviously enjoying himself to the hilt, displayed every enticing purchase to her sisters, basking in their admiration and gratitude. Jennifer scowled as Penelope giggled flirtatiously, dancing around with an orange in each hand, while Winifred rushed off to the kitchen to put away the roast.

No one else appeared to object as Gabriel hung up his coat and stoked the fire as if he'd been living with them for decades. When he flopped onto the sofa and put his feet on the step stool, Jennifer eyed him with mounting impatience. He ignored her and picked up the morning newspaper, instantly absorbed in the headlines. Even Angel, the kitten, seemed to capitulate, for he leaped into Gabriel's lap and rubbed against him, purring. Finally, Jennifer stood before him, blocking the warmth from the fire, and put her hands on her hips.

"Isn't anyone going to object to this? I let him go last night, and he insists on staying!"

Winifred's brows went up as she came out of the kitchen, wiping a betraying cookie crumb from her lips before speaking. "But we wanted to kidnap him for the weekend. We all think he and Allison are up to something. You agreed," she reminded her sister.

"Yes, but he doesn't have an ulterior motive," Jennifer insisted hotly. "I know he doesn't. We discussed it last night."

Penelope looked from Gabriel to Jennifer, then back again. Giggling, she shrugged, her shoulder lifting helplessly. "Then he's a willing captive. That makes it so much easier. We won't have to worry about that dirty gun going off again, and we can keep an eye on him all the same. And Aunt Eve needn't know. She left right after you did, and won't be home until tomorrow."

"But there's no reason for him to be here!" Jennifer protested. When her two sisters stared at her in confusion, Jennifer took a deep breath and struggled to explain. "I told him everything last night. He assured me that nothing was going on, and he wasn't in cahoots with Allison. I believe him."

Winifred stared at her intently, and Jennifer could feel the blush coming to her cheeks. Understanding seemed to dawn, for her sister's intelligent gaze took in Jennifer's swollen eyes and agitated demeanor. Her expression turned sympathetic, and she nodded, then reached for Gabriel's coat. Turning to him with a look that brooked no argument, she spoke in a businesslike tone.

"If that is true, then we all owe you an apology, Mr. Forester. We apparently have misjudged you. I sincerely hope we haven't caused you too much inconvenience. I wish you good day."

Jennifer breathed a sigh of relief. Winifred extended the coat to him, but Gabriel barely moved from his perch. He rustled the newspaper in annoyance, as if she had but disturbed his regular ritual, and looked directly at Jennifer.

"No."

"No?" Winifred looked astonished. No one ever challenged her when she spoke in that particular tone. Until now. She gazed at Gabriel in confusion as he politely explained his position.

"I believe I made myself plain to your sister. You have kidnapped me for the weekend, and I don't intend to go anywhere. If you have changed your mind, that's unfortunate. You should have thought of that before you laid down the gauntlet."

Winifred's mouth dropped, as if unable to believe her own ears. Jennifer sighed, her last hope dashed, while Penelope gasped in horror. Gabriel calmly folded the paper and gazed up at the three girls like a stern schoolteacher about to deliver a lecture.

"You young ladies are sorely in need of a lesson, and unfortunately, I have been elected to provide it. You invited me into your home last night under friendly pretexts, then while I was enjoying your hospitality, you imprisoned me in the wine cellar like some wild animal. The tables have turned, however, and now you will get a taste of your own medicine. You wanted my presence for the weekend, and by God you'll have it."

He turned from one pale face to the next. Although he still planned to leave after dinner, he was enjoying their discomfort. Perhaps they'd think twice before pulling such an outrageous stunt again, he thought self-righteously. His gaze stopped when he reached Penelope. Jennifer's sister was inching her way toward the desk when his eyes pinned her as securely as a botanist skewered his insects. "Don't go looking for your gun, Miss Appleton," Gabriel said, one brow lifting as she skidded to a stop directly before the desk. "It is upstairs, and unloaded. I have the ammunition. And if any of you try anything else and I am forced to leave, I will not hesitate to go to the authorities. Do I make myself clear?"

Penelope squeaked, while Winifred looked nonplussed. Only Jennifer appeared unsurprised and resigned to her fate. She sent him a pleading glance which he conveniently ignored, then he settled down onto the couch with his paper, utterly content. Feeling Jennifer's withering stare still on him, he looked up and smirked like a fox in a henhouse, perfectly satisfied with the situation.

"So now, Miss Appleton. When do we eat?"

CHAPTER 15

"WE HAVE TO get rid of him!" Jennifer insisted as the three girls huddled together in the kitchen. "If anyone should see him, our reputations would be destroyed!"

"No!" Penelope cried. "That can't happen! We've been working so hard to get accepted. We can't let him ruin everything!"

"Perhaps he was just joking, or trying to teach us a lesson, as he said," Winifred said pragmatically. "Surely he doesn't really mean to stay, now that we've set him free. Maybe he's just trying to frighten us."

The servant's bell rang behind them. Jennifer, Winifred, and Penelope stared at it in bemusement. The maid was off for the weekend, and there was no one else in the house. It had to be . . .

Jennifer entered the parlor and saw Gabriel with the bell in hand. He glanced up from his paper, as if annoyed at having to wait. Placing the bell aside, he gestured to the kitchen.

"While you girls are in there, I am hungry. A light snack before dinner would be nice. Maybe a glass of wine and some cheese. I believe you have an excellent vintage in the basement. I should know." He stared hard at her. As she gazed in disbelief, he snapped his fingers. "Hop to it! It is against the law to starve prisoners. Even Winifred can attest to that."

Grumbling under her breath, Jennifer returned to the kitchen and faced her sisters. "His Majesty wants wine and cheese. The nerve of him! As if we're really going to be his servants for the weekend."

"I think we'd better placate him," Winifred said softly. "Lord knows what he'll do if we cross him now. Until we can figure a way out of this, it is probably best to do his bidding." She saw Jennifer's defiant expression and Penelope's worried one, and she gestured to the parlor. "I'll take it to him. I'll try to talk with him again and explain how he could cause us trouble by being here."

"You can try," Jennifer said doubtfully. She knew it still nettled Winifred that Gabriel had out-debated her previously, and that she needed to win for her own self-esteem. "But I don't think you'll get anywhere."

Winifred took up a tray and put some cuts of cheese and fruit on it, then descended to the cellar for the wine. She selected a good bottle, blowing off the dust to ascertain the year, then returned to the kitchen and poured some into a goblet. Finally, she nodded to her sisters, squared her shoulders, and proceeded to the living room like a soldier prepared for battle.

Jennifer and Penelope peeped around the door as Winifred placed the tray before Gabriel. The man barely moved his feet from the stool, simply rattling the newspaper in acknowledgment of the offering. Jennifer wanted to smack him.

"Mr. Forester, may I have a word?"

Jennifer had to admire her sister's cool aplomb, for Winifred addressed him in the tones of a minister who was gravely concerned with the state of affairs. It was a different voice from the one she'd used earlier, when she'd ordered him out. Jennifer wondered if it would work.

It appeared to have an effect on him, for he laid the paper aside and picked up his wineglass. Jennifer could see his smirk of pleasure as he sipped the heady liquid, stroking his namesake kitten. He eyed Winifred with amusement, as if he were prepared to be entertained.

"Certainly. What can I do for you?"

"Mr. Forester, I want to apologize again for the actions of my sisters and myself last night. I am partly the cause of this misunderstanding, for I really believed you were involved in a scheme to discredit us."

"You've said as much," Gabriel nodded, appearing as cool as Winifred.

"I now entirely believe in your innocence, and as a gentleman, I am pleading with you to do the honorable thing. You must know that your presence in this house gravely jeopardizes our reputation. If anyone should find out that you spent the weekend here, all of us would be disgraced."

Gabriel put his wineglass aside and sank back in his seat, touching the tips of his fingers together as if thinking deeply. "Miss Appleton, don't you think you should have thought of that before you encouraged your sister to kidnap me?"

"Yes, I agree. But as you know, to err is human. I admit we made a costly mistake, and we have all been suitably punished for it. You have made your point, and we shall all take a lesson from this experience."

She was wonderful, Jennifer admitted to herself in awe. Winifred was surely made for the courtroom, for she argued with the precision of any defense lawyer. For a moment, even Gabriel seemed swayed by her inescapable logic. Jennifer wanted to applaud.

Her excitement died with his next words, for instead of rising and getting his coat, as she expected, he merely sampled a piece of the cheese, looking like a well-fed king in his own castle. He took another sip of wine, and when he finished, he smiled at Winifred benignly.

"I am glad you see the error of your ways, and I will certainly pay attention this weekend to see that the lesson has lasting meaning. You girls are entirely too willful and impulsive, and hold a strange disregard for other people's feelings if they are an obstacle to your success. Just as I believe your séances are detrimental to your clients, this kidnapping folly is another example of the same kind of behavior. But I will put your fears at ease. No one will know that I am here. I will tell no one, no one saw me, and I will depart before Eve returns. She of all of you is innocent, and I think she worries enough about you three without my adding to her concerns." He picked up the paper dismissively, then gave one more parting shot.

"While you are in the kitchen conspiring with your sisters, would you mind refilling my glass? I am truly enjoying this port."

Jennifer gasped in outrage, then quickly shut the door as he turned toward the noise. Winifred stomped inside a moment later, fuming from her encounter.

"That man! You cannot reason with him! Why, I used my best barrister appeal, and he simply refuses to listen!"

"You did great, Winnie," Jennifer consoled her. "It isn't your fault he's obstinate. I didn't think he'd listen, no matter what you said."

"What will we do?" Penelope cried.

She barely got the words out of her mouth when there was a knock on the front door. Penelope, Jennifer, and Winifred looked at each other quizzically, then Penelope put her hand over her mouth in horror.

"The Billings! I forgot I invited them to tea today! Oh, no, we're ruined!"

Winifred peeked out the side door. There she spied

Elizabeth's pert bonnet and Jane's elegant wool coat. She closed it as softly as possible and faced her sisters.

"It's them. Shall we pretend not to be home?"

"We can't do that! One cannot invite someone for tea, then conveniently disappear! That would be a slap in the face to them!"

Penelope wailed, while Jennifer squared her shoulders. "I'll talk to him. Maybe I can convince him to keep out of sight until the Billings leave. He did promise that no one would know he was here, and I don't think he means to disgrace us."

"Do you think he'll do it?" Penelope asked tearfully.

Jennifer glanced out the door to where Gabriel sat by the fire, the picture of contentment. "I don't know," she admitted. "But I can try."

Winifred patted her shoulder, and Jennifer took a deep breath, then walked through the door. Their captive looked up, unsurprised to see her, especially with the knocking that still sounded from the front of the house. He turned to her expectantly, and Jennifer swallowed hard, lowering herself to his eye level and gazing at him pleadingly.

"Gabriel, I beg a favor. I know you're still angry with us, and you have every reason to be. But Penny needs the parlor, she has guests. The Billings are here. I don't want to cause her trouble. Please, can you go upstairs? If any of what you said to me is true, please help us."

It burned to humble herself in such a manner, but she knew she didn't have any choice. She was in no position to order him around—he'd made that abundantly clear—and she was left with no choice except to throw herself on his mercy.

Gabriel gazed at her for a long moment, and Jennifer fully expected him to refuse. To her astonishment, he rose to his feet, and extended his hand to her, helping her back up. He then collected his paper and snack tray, and bowed slightly before her.

"I am at your service, miss. I told you before that I have no desire to cause any of you harm, especially you." His eyes burned into her meaningfully, and one brow lifted mockingly. "Where shall we go? Your room?"

His smirk didn't diminished the wave of relief that swept over her. "Come quickly," she whispered, then waved to Penelope, whose head was peeking out the door. Whisking him upstairs, she lead him into the guest room, the largest and most comfortable of the bedrooms.

"If you'll wait here quietly, I will be so grateful! Uncle left some books here, and the light is good. Can I get you anything else?"

She really was grateful and didn't hesitate to show it. Gabriel had them right where he wanted them, and no one was more cognizant of that than Jennifer. Silently she admitted they deserved it, and his cooperation meant more to her than she could express.

He lifted her chin, gazing into her eyes with an expression she didn't understand. Jennifer wanted to pull away, yet she was spellbound. His thumb idly caressed her full lower lip, and for a stunning moment, she thought he meant to kiss her again. Instead he smiled and spoke softly.

"You really love them, don't you? I wonder what would happen if you ever loved a man that way."

Jennifer's eyes closed and she waited for the feel of his mouth on hers. To her surprise, he released her, then stepped back as if to examine the room. Nodding, he turned back to her, the tyrant come home.

"This will do for now. I suggest you tell the Billings that their call can last only an hour or so, for I am starving. I can almost taste that roast. I do like my meat prepared medium rare." He dropped into a chair and grinned at her indignant glare.

"You—" Jennifer sputtered, mortified that she had been prepared to kiss him back, and that he had ordered her around like a servant. "You are the most vile, low-down skunk I've ever seen!"

"Now, now." He shook a finger at her. "I'll have a bath while I'm waiting, Miss Appleton. And I like my water hot. Since you don't care for the Billings, and won't have to sit in on the visit, I believe you're free." He lifted one brow, as if daring her to object.

Jennifer turned on her heel, hearing his laughter ringing behind her. Furious, she vowed that if she ever got out of this one, she would pay him back.

By God, she would.

"What are you doing?" Winifred asked as Jennifer hauled out the washtub.

"His Majesty has decided he wishes a bath." She scowled, filling the kettle with water. "He has also determined that his roast be cooked medium rare, and that he wants to eat soon. That man! I wish I'd never laid eyes on him."

"It is good that he agreed to stay out of sight," Winifred reminded her as she hastened to fill another kettle. "I'm sorry, Jennifer. I realize that part of this is my fault."

"It's all our faults," Jennifer said quietly. "We made a mistake, and it's coming back to haunt us. I don't know what we'll do tonight." When her sister looked at her questioningly, Jennifer explained. "We have Mrs. Hawthorne coming for a séance."

"That's right," Winifred agreed. "We've got to get rid of him. We both know how he feels about our business. I am certain he'll do everything in his power to ruin tonight's session."

"Maybe we should cancel," Jennifer mused. "And reschedule Mrs. Hawthorne."

"We can't. We're booked solid through the month,

and she is a new client. I don't think she'd appreciate being bumped, particularly at this late hour." Winifred stared at the wine bottle thoughtfully. She had selected another good vintage for dinner, certain that Gabriel would insist upon that as well as his roast. Her frown gradually curved up into a smile, and when she turned to Jennifer, her eyes sparkled with merriment.

"I've got it!"

"What?" Jennifer grinned, sensing what was coming.

"I'll put a sedative in his wine. He'll fall asleep directly after dinner, thus solving our problems! We can get him safely out of the way, hold our séance, and no one will be the wiser!"

"It's brilliant!" Jennifer cried as Winifred bowed, pleased as always to have her remarkable intellect recognized. Her own enthusiasm dimmed slightly as her sister retrieved the bottle, then began to pour it into a decanter. "Are you sure it won't harm him? We really have done him enough damage."

"No, silly. I'll use Aunt Eve's sleeping tonic. I think it's half alcohol anyway, and it never seems to cause her any ill effect. We'll have to be careful to make it look like we're all drinking the wine, though. He'll get suspicious if he's the only one."

"How do we manage that?"

"We'll use two identical decanters. We'll pass them continually around the table, so that Gabriel thinks we're drinking the same stuff. I'll cap the bad wine with the diamond-cut stopper, and the good wine with the solid one." Jennifer watched in admiration as Winifred poured a generous portion of the sleeping draught into one decanter, then filled it with wine. The second got wine only, and she stoppered them as she'd described. When she finished, the twin bottles stood on the sideboard.

Jennifer clapped. "Gabriel Forester has another think

coming if he thinks to best the Appletons. We'll just have to make sure Penny knows the difference as well."

"I'll warn her. Now you take up his bath, and I'll start getting the meal ready. Before we know it, our troubles will be sleeping."

"THIS ROAST IS excellent," Gabriel commented as he enjoyed his third helping. The Billings had thankfully departed on schedule, and dinner had been served exactly when Gabriel had commanded. Jennifer's outrage at preparing his bath was almost tangible, but there was nothing she could do other than fulfill his every request, protesting only when he teasingly suggested she scrub his back. He thought about demanding that she shave him, but experience had taught him to be cautious where she was concerned, and he had no wish to see his throat cut.

He had to admit he enjoyed his role as tyrant, and the occasional twinge of conscience he felt was easily dismissed because he knew he'd be leaving soon. And after all, the Appletons had treated him worse than any criminal, and deserved much more than the meager retribution he'd given them. The three women had run rampant far too long. And someone, Gabriel thought smugly, had to show them their place.

He refilled his plate, aware that Jennifer, Penelope, and Winifred were aghast at the immense amount of food he consumed. Gabriel noticed that they ate modest portions, and went to great lengths to save any leftovers for another meal. Frowning, he twirled his wineglass, aware that money, for the Appletons, really was a major concern.

He'd noticed other things during his stay, as well. Twin Gables, the family home, had at one time been a mansion, but had now fallen badly into disrepair. Gabriel had noticed that the roof leaked, and that the chimney was crumbling. Although the inside of the house was comfortable, there were drafts everywhere, the steps creaked, and water had leaked into the basement. Many of the bedrooms were unusable, so the three sisters shared a room. Even here in the dining room, there was water damage to the ceiling, and the chandelier swayed ominously. While the condition of the house was beneficial for their séances, it wasn't good for the inhabitants.

When he'd mentioned this to Jennifer, she'd merely looked at him in disbelief, then once again reiterated their financial situation. While he'd always believed her story—well, that part, anyway—seeing the deterioration of the manse only confirmed what she'd told him.

"Would you like more wine, Mr. Forester?"

Winifred addressed him politely and his gaze turned to Jennifer's bluestocking sister. A pang of pity struck him as he realized that Jennifer's ambition for her was not unrealistic: The woman had one of the finest minds he'd ever seen. Yet he acknowledged that even with a law degree, she'd have a hard time finding clients. For a brief instant, he understood what women like Elizabeth Cady Stanton were preaching about, and what a pity it would be to silence these gifts. He nodded in response to her question.

"Yes, I would. This wine is even better than the one I had earlier. It seems your uncle didn't share the Appletons' frugality."

"Uncle didn't need to," Jennifer explained, watching her sister pour the wine with a strange intensity. "He was relatively well-to-do until the war. Like many other widows, Aunt Eve didn't experience financial distress until after he died."

"I see." Gabriel sipped the wine, suddenly aware that all eyes were on him. Why were they all . . . he sniffed his wineglass. Surely they couldn't have . . . He glanced suspiciously around the table, then relaxed when he saw that the girls were all drinking as well. He was even more relieved when Jennifer refilled her own glass and sipped deeply of the contents.

"And your father?" he continued. "I know he died in an accident, but why didn't he leave an inheritance?"

"Father was heavily in debt," Jennifer explained. "We don't know what happened, only that it took us many years to pay back what he owed. It is something we've always wondered about, and something we'll never know the truth of. All Aunt Eve ever told us is that Father once loved someone he couldn't wed. Our mother loved him, so he married her, but he never seemed to have much ambition after that. We were astonished to learn about the disastrous state of his affairs. It was almost as if someone was out to ruin him."

Gabriel frowned, wondering if Jennifer's imagination was running wild, or if there was something to her theory. He'd heard of cases like this before, where one of New York's wealthy families, fearing their daughter's disgrace, forbade her to wed and set out to destroy the "improper" man so that he could never pose a threat. Could such a thing have happened to Jennifer's father? Or was it more likely that her father, like his own, just couldn't manage a business?

It was an interesting thought. Gabriel yawned loudly, wondering why it had become so difficult to think. His words sounded slurred even to his own ears, and, in spite of the small quantity he had drunk, he felt curiously weary. He reached for his coffee cup, but found himself yawning again.

"More wine?" Penelope asked sweetly, refilling his glass.

His previous suspicions came back to haunt him. As he looked around the table, he saw Winifred studying her plate as if it were of great interest. Penelope looked directly at him, her eyes full of watchful curiosity, while Jennifer glanced away guiltily. He rose unsteadily, outrage spreading slowly through him.

"You . . . you've poisoned me!" The words came thickly, and he cursed as his body moved clumsily away from the table. The parrot squawked, unmindful of the presence of the threatening kitten, while Angel leaped to his feet like a genuine tiger prepared to defend his mistress. Jennifer gasped as Gabriel lunged toward her, but his legs felt like dead weights and they refused to do his bidding. Instead, he collapsed onto the table. Sleep overcame him, and he fell immediately into its dark, dizzying depths.

"Is he out?" Penelope asked cheerfully, stooping to peer at Gabriel's face. A loud snore confirmed her belief. "That was close! Thank goodness he missed the potatoes! For a second there, I thought he would attack you."

Jennifer looked at the slumbering body in awe, her hands pressed to her lips. Gabriel was but inches away, and his hand still clasped the tablecloth directly in front of her. "Are you sure he's all right?"

"Of course he is," Winifred said indignantly. "I only gave him twice Auntie's draught. He's sound asleep, that's all."

"Let's get him upstairs," Penelope said quickly. "We don't have much time before our appointment, and the sooner he's out of here, the better."

The three girls hefted Gabriel's body in the direction of the steps. Jennifer took his shoulders, Winifred his torso, while Penelope got his feet. It was no easy task, especially since Jennifer had to walk backward, hauling his shoulders up the stairs one step at a time. Penelope giggled as his rump hit each step, in spite of Winifred's best effort.

"Can you lift him any higher?" Jennifer gasped, struggling toward the next step. "He's going to be black-and-blue tomorrow."

"I'm trying," Winifred grunted.

They all gasped as Jennifer lost her balance and Gabriel's head struck the stair. Filled with horror, Jennifer leaned closer, and saw to her relief that Gabriel was still breathing, and there was no blood.

"Looks like he'll have a headache, too," Winifred remarked dryly. "Come on, we've only got three more steps to go."

The sisters made one last supreme effort and dragged the body up to the landing, then into the guest bedroom. They stood back, breathing heavily from the exertion, while Gabriel slumbered peacefully on the bed as if he'd just fallen asleep there.

"Whew! He's a lot heavier than he looks." Penelope wiped her brow.

"Probably everything he ate," Winifred sniffed. "All right, ladies, let's get the dinner cleaned up. Mrs. Hawthorne will be here at midnight, and we need to prepare."

Jennifer nodded, but her eyes kept straying back to Gabriel. His dark curls had fallen over his forehead, and his thick black lashes barely fluttered. He looked like an innocent little boy, but there was nothing innocent or boyish about his strong, muscular body. Jennifer swallowed hard. He would be furious again when he awakened, she thought as she locked the door behind her.

It seemed to be becoming a habit.

CHAPTER 16

PAIN. THAT WAS all he could feel. Gabriel fought consciousness, knowing instinctively that what awaited him beyond sleep was the headache of all headaches. He could feel the blind throbbing from a distance, as if his brain were trying to burst out of his skull, and he moaned.

He lost the fight. Slowly, he came to wakefulness, and his groans became louder and more insistent. Wracked with pain, he raised his head a few inches, and nearly howled in agony. A nice-sized lump had formed on the back of his head, and when he pressed his fingers to it, he had no doubt as to the source of his anguish.

Collapsing back onto the pillow, he breathed slowly, trying to see in the total blackness surrounding him. It was then that he realized his pain was not limited to his head. No, that was merely where the worst of it hovered, torturing him like a python wrapping itself around his skull. Everything hurt, from his arms to his legs, and amazingly, even his posterior. Gabriel groaned once more as he made the mistake of running his hands down his torso to check for damage. It seemed there wasn't an inch of his flesh that didn't throb as if it had been stuck with hot needles.

What in God's name had happened to him? Had he been in an accident? He tried to force his mind to think, to get past the incredible ache and form coherent thoughts. He hadn't been in his carriage since that morning. He'd gone with Jennifer to buy groceries, had dinner, drank wine . . .

The wine. He sat up swiftly in bed, regretting the motion as soon as he'd completed it. Nausea rose in his stomach, and he had to force it down. His mouth was like cotton. None of this made sense. It was as if he'd drunk a gallon of hard spirits, even though he'd had only a few glasses of wine. My God, what had they done to him? Was it poison? But that didn't explain the pain. Had he pushed them too far? Had they beaten him out of revenge?

Fury pulsed through him, making his headache turn ravaging. The Appletons had turned the tables on him, poisoned him, and done something to him to make his body feel like it had been run over by a team of horses. He tried to sit again, but his rear end turned to fire. He gasped, then moved sideways to slip off the bed. Rising to his feet, he looked into the mirror and gaped at what he saw.

He looked like a specter. His face was pale, making the shock of dark hair falling over his forehead look coal black by contrast. His eyes were very patriotic, all red, white, and blue, while his lips looked painfully dry. He turned his head, trying to assess the damage, but couldn't see the lump. He didn't have to, however, for as he touched the tender area again, he judged it was the size of a small apple.

Could they have struck him unconscious? He pictured Jennifer sneaking up behind him, wielding the poker. My God, was there no limit to what these women would do, did they have no scruples or decency at all? Granted, he'd been lording his power over them, but that didn't justify something like this!

His pride inflamed, he gritted his teeth, determined that this time, he would teach Jennifer Appleton a lesson she'd never forget. If she wanted to play rough, without rules or morals, then he could play the same way.

What exactly he was going to do with her, he wasn't sure. He tried the door, wanting nothing more than to get his hands on the witch who'd done this to him, but it was locked. Thousands of needles of pain tortured him, his head throbbed even more, and his rear end ached unbelievably. Furious, he roared, pounding at the door, then stopping short as his head pounded back.

Never in his life had he been so angry. Red, hot rage blinded common sense, and he banged on the door again, then howled in suffering. One thought led him: When he got hold of her, when he got hold of her, when he got hold of her . . . His ire was so white-hot he couldn't complete the thought, but revenge was the only thing that mattered.

A key turned in the door, and he waited behind it, ignoring the talons of liquid fire that stabbed him repeatedly. A female form entered the room, carrying a lamp. Her back was to him, and she turned toward the bed, holding the lamp aloft, then gasped in surprise when she saw the bed was empty.

Blindly, Gabriel charged her. The lamp fell to the floor with a clatter, and she struggled in his arms. Cursing sulphurously, he released her, knowing instantly that he had the wrong sister. She fell against the door and it clicked shut. Unable to stifle a moan, he nevertheless snatched up the lamp and held it over her.

Penelope sat on the floor like a tangled doll, her dress rumpled, her hair escaping its prim knot. She stared at him, looking like a frightened child who is guilty of something and desperately afraid of being punished. Without remorse, Gabriel hauled her to her feet.

"Where is she? And what the hell did you three do to me? By God, woman, you'd better tell me the truth, or—"

Penelope squeaked as he took a step closer to her. "It wasn't my idea! I didn't know! We only thought . . . you'd sleep for a while."

"Sleep?" He snarled. "You poisoned me, didn't you?"

Penelope shook her head in denial, but when he grasped her arm, jerking her back and forth, she nodded, trembling with fright.

"It wasn't poison, only Auntie's sleeping draught! We didn't think it would hurt you, only cause you to sleep during the séance."

"What else did you do? Why do I ache all over?" he roared.

Penelope looked genuinely puzzled. Her eyes squinted, and she thought hard as she looked him over. When he rubbed his abused posterior, she gasped, knowledge coming into her eyes as they widened perceptibly.

"Well?"

"The stairs. We had to carry you up here. You are heavy, you know. Winnie thinks you shouldn't eat so much, and then—"

"Silence!" he thundered, and had the satisfaction of seeing her cower before him. At least he could still manage to frighten someone. He regretted his outburst a moment later, when his head pounded so hard he had to hold on to the bedpost to keep from collapsing. Massaging his temples, he realized what had happened. The Appletons, apparently deciding he was best gotten out of the way, had filled his cup with a sleeping draught, then hauled him up the stairs like last week's garbage. They had then deposited him onto the bed, and gone on their merry way, probably laughing and congratulating themselves on having bested him again. His only relief was the knowledge that they hadn't deliberately beaten him, although with the way he felt, they might as well have.

It wasn't to be borne. He snarled, ignoring his head, then gestured to the door while Penelope shivered in terror. "Open that goddamned door," he hissed. When she hesitated, he stepped even closer. "Penelope, I know who was behind this, and unless you wish to share your sister's fate, I suggest you do as I say."

Penelope's eyes were like saucers. She quickly obeyed. As she started to unlock the door, she paused as if uncertain who she should be more frightened of. "You aren't going to stop the séance?" she asked hopefully. "I promised I wouldn't let that happen."

Gabriel stared at her in disbelief. "I won't interfere with the séance, but I want that door opened. I'm not about to be caged up anymore like some animal. Do you understand me?"

He groaned in agony. Holding his head, he tried not to react to the blinding ache.

"It really does hurt, doesn't it?" Penelope asked sympathetically as she unlocked the door. "I know! I'll ask Jenny to help you when she's done. She can do magnetic healing, you know."

Gabriel smiled sarcastically. "Yes, and I can't wait to lay my own hands on the magical Miss Appleton. Now, where are you hiding during this séance?"

"Oh, Winnie and I work upstairs," Penelope explained, leading him down the hall. Like a little girl, she simply assumed all was well now that he was no longer shouting and threatening. All at once, Gabriel understood why Jennifer felt so strongly that she had to protect this sister. "Winnie works the harpsichord, while I make noises and do the lights."

"Let me see." Curiosity won over both anger and pain as Gabriel followed her down the corridor. She entered another hall, then rounded the corner into a vacant chamber. Once again he was amazed at the structure of Twin Gables, a rambling house that lent itself perfectly to their schemes.

Winifred looked up from the harpsichord, then gasped

in horror when she saw Gabriel. "What is he doing here?" she whispered fiercely.

"I insisted," Gabriel responded, the held his head to stop the incessant throbbing. When the worst pain had passed, he scowled at her. "Seeing as you took part in all this, I would suggest you stay out of my way, too."

Penelope shrugged. "He won't do anything. He just wants to see."

Winifred looked as if the entire world had gone mad. Gabriel could see her struggling to think of something, but for once, her incredible intellect offered no way out. Glancing through a crack in the floorboards, she put her finger to her lips and resignedly gestured to the room below. She gave him a pleading look. "Mrs. Hawthorne is here. Will you please be quiet?"

Once again he saw the loyalty of these sisters. Nodding, he refused the chair Penelope offered, and went to peek through the slat instead.

A well-to-do older woman sat at the table, her face streaked with tears, her lace handkerchief dabbing delicately at her eyes. Wretchedness seemed to overwhelm her, and she spoke softly to Jennifer.

"I only came upon the letters recently. I wasn't looking through his things! Really! Do you suppose that's why he was shouting?"

Jennifer nodded. "He probably thought you doubted his love," she said softly.

Gabriel realized that the woman must have heard him. Although his head still pounded, he could still reason logically enough to know that Jennifer, clever, poisoning Jennifer, had used his moans to her advantage. His lip curled in disgust.

"I didn't know what to think," the woman continued, sobbing. "He met this woman when he was away in the war. She was a nurse, and he fell in love with her while convalescing. I don't know what to do. How did I fail him? I feel as if my marriage was a sham, that I didn't know him at all."

"Let me see what the cards say." Jennifer shuffled a deck of odd-looking cards, then placed three of them before her. One of them had a heart with three swords thrust through them. "Here is your broken heart," she whispered, showing the woman the card.

"That's amazing!" the woman said through her tears. "How does that happen?"

Jennifer shrugged. "The tarot gives us a picture of what is happening in our lives, and can offer guidance and comfort. Let us see what else it says." Jennifer laid out several more cards, one on top, one below, and then two on either side.

One of the cards depicted a woman holding a cup. "Here she is," Jennifer pointed out. "She is in the healing profession. She is a woman of good heart and intention. She didn't want to cause you grief. She is sorrowful, for she loves your husband also, but cannot express that love."

"Was she . . . with him when he died?"

The woman raised her face toward Jennifer and for the first time, Gabriel could see her directly. In spite of the pain in his head, he nearly gasped out loud when he recognized the woman as Adele Hawthorne, a good friend of his mother's. Strangely enough, Gabriel knew the woman's story, for not only had she confided in his mother, but Jared Howe, Charles's father, had been in the same army hospital and had known of her husband's affair. Curious, he continued to peer through the crack.

Jennifer concentrated on her crystal ball, then a spell seemed to fall over her. She moaned, her eyes closing, and the room filled with an eerie vibration. Winifred struck up the chords of the harpsichord, and Penelope jiggled the chandelier wires. The woman below appeared awestruck in spite of her tears.

"Adele, my sweet Adele."

Gabriel's mouth dropped in astonishment. Jennifer no longer sounded like herself, but her voice had dropped several octaves and she spoke in a masculine tone. He forgot all of his aches and watched in fascination as the woman paused in her grief to stare at the figure before her.

"Robert? Is that you?" she asked in disbelief.

Jennifer moaned, and the room was once more filled with an energy that held Gabriel in awe. "Yes. I understand that I have hurt you. I never stopped loving you. Can you forgive me?"

Adele started to cry again. "Why? Why did you betray our vows? Wasn't I enough for you?"

"My sweet Adele, you always were. I met Marion when I was ill. She comforted me, nursed me, cleaned my wounds. I didn't want to care for her. God knows I fought it. But in the end, I succumbed. I don't expect your understanding, but I could rest better if you forgave me. Can you find it in your heart to do that?"

Adele sobbed. "But I have nothing to live for! My son was killed in that war; you, my husband, betrayed me. And now you are gone . . . how can I go on?"

"My sweet, don't talk like that. There is more I need to say to you. Marion has passed over also. She died working in that hospital, of fever she caught from the soldiers. She had a child. Our child. He is an orphan."

Gabriel rolled his eyes. Surely the Appletons hadn't stooped so low as this—to involve a child in some charlatan act! He knew what was coming, and he braced himself. Jennifer would give the exact location of the poor little orphan, Mrs. Hawthorne would "find" the mysterious child, and all would be well. It wasn't to be borne!

Predictably, the older woman looked as if she'd been struck by lightning. Jennifer moaned, then continued in the same odd tone. "That is why I couldn't leave her."

"A son!" Adele pressed her hands to her lips in wonder. "You had a . . . child?"

"I must go now. I still love you, and will always love you. Do you believe me?"

"Yes!" the woman whispered, nodding her head. "Yes, I understand and forgive you! But where is the child, your son . . ."

Jennifer moaned. Gabriel waited for her to "magically" supply the answer. To his bemusement, Jennifer shook her head. "I don't know."

"But . . ."

The mood seemed to change. Jennifer sighed, then fell into a slump. A moment later, she slowly opened her eyes. Winifred stopped playing the harpsichord, and Penelope let go of the chandelier wires. Gabriel had to hand it to them. Their props added to the show, but Jennifer was utterly convincing as a medium. Although he'd never admit it, he was captivated.

"Miss Appleton?" When Jennifer nodded, the woman threw herself at her, sobbing uncontrollably. "Oh, my dear, I saw him! I saw my dear husband!"

Jennifer comforted her, embracing the woman while she sobbed. "Did it help?"

"Oh, yes. He told me he still loves me. But he said there was a child! He had a son?"

Jennifer appeared surprised, then glanced down at the cards. "There he is." She indicated a page carrying a coin. "He is alone and needs money. I see him." She gazed up at the woman as if confused. "I really said that? About a child?"

"Yes! Do you know where he is?"

Once again Gabriel waited for her answer, which he was certain would be in the affirmative. Jennifer shook her head, squinting at the card with all her might.

"No, I'm sorry. I don't see anything else."

"Are you sure he's . . . alive?" the old woman asked in trepidation.

Jennifer stared at the card for a moment, then nodded.

"Yes. I think he is alive! I sense a lovely child, all brown hair and eyes. He is definitely alive."

The woman's eyes sparkled with tears. "Thank you so much! Although I am still hurt and disappointed in my husband, I feel I could forgive him one day. Being able to talk with him was such a marvel! I feel as if the weight of the world is off my shoulders. Thank you, my dear! You are truly an angel!"

The woman embraced Jennifer again, then dug into her purse for payment. Gabriel sank back against the wall, his aching brow furrowed with thought. No matter how ridiculous, he couldn't deny that Jennifer had brought this woman a measure of comfort that the finest physicians in the area hadn't been able to manage. His mother had spoken to him in hushed whispers about Adele's depression, the source of which very few knew. The woman had taken to her rooms, refused to wash or dress, and had let herself become almost catatonic in her grief. Yet looking at her now, one would never believe she was the same person.

It threw everything he believed into question. Gabriel looked once again at the woman below, beaming with life and determination, and pictured the poor wretched creature his mother had described. Even if it was all a concocted story, the woman obviously believed it and the session had brought her new hope.

Winifred's gaze caught his and Gabriel shrugged. "That was quite a show. But now won't you three feel guilty if that women scours the earth, looking for this fictitious child?"

"How do you know he's not real?" Winifred asked. "I've never seen Jenny say something like that before. She must have been very certain."

"Are you saying she really can talk to the dead?" Gabriel demanded angrily.

Winifred shook her head. "I don't know. All I'm saying is that Jennifer seemed to sense something tonight.

And even if she is wrong, do you really think it is harmful for Adele to know her husband really loved her? Or to have given her a reason to live?"

Gabriel couldn't argue with her logic. He had been moved by what he'd seen, especially the way the séance had brought peace to this poor, grief-stricken woman. Still, it didn't excuse Jennifer, nor was he ready to forgive what she'd done to him.

She burst into the room a moment later. "Can you believe what happened? I saw that child! My God . . ." Her voice trailed off as her sisters gestured wildly at something behind her. Whirling, Jennifer saw him standing near the door, his arms folded, his brow lifted in a mocking expression. Penelope lifted her hands helplessly.

"He made me open the door. He did promise not to stop the séance, and he didn't."

As Jennifer looked at Gabriel and saw the dark fury in his eyes, the promise of retribution, all color drained from her face. Giving a high squeak, she turned to rush out of the room, but he simply extended his arm, effectively preventing her from going anywhere. She skidded to a stop right in front of him.

"That's right, Miss Appleton, it is I, alive and well, no thanks to you. Unfortunately, your sleeping draught lasts quite a bit longer on little old ladies than on full-grown men. You might want to note that for future reference."

"We didn't—I mean, I didn't—"

"Forget it, Jennifer, I know exactly what happened. You had to do it, didn't you? Make a fool out of me one more time? You weren't content with simply jailing me, but had to poison me in the bargain! Well, this is the last time . . ." Without warning, he stooped and effortlessly scooped her up, holding her over his shoulder like a sack of potatoes, then turned to her sisters menacingly. "We'll finish this conversation in private. And I mean, *in private*. Do you two understand?"

"Put me down!" Jennifer pounded on his back, unable to see him wince as she struggled to get free. Astonished, Penelope and Winifred could do nothing but stand aside and nod as he hauled their sister across the threshold and down the corridor. A door slammed shut but they could still hear Jennifer's shrieks and Gabriel's rumbling.

Winifred turned slowly to Penelope. Her scholarly face knotted in thought and she tapped her cheek with a fingertip, as if she were trying to figure out the most abstract math problem. "Maybe the sleeping draught wasn't such a good idea," she said.

CHAPTER 17

"PUT ME DOWN, you oaf! Do you hear me?" Jennifer kicked and squirmed, accidentally striking the back of his head as she thrashed. Gabriel grunted in pain, and Jennifer received a smack on her rump for her trouble. Yelping, she stopped fighting as he carried her into the guest room and plopped her unceremoniously down on the bed.

"What do you think you're doing?" Jennifer asked, her eyes widening. It had occurred to her already that maybe poisoning him wasn't the smartest thing they could have done. Faced with the results of his ire, Jennifer was now certain.

Gabriel didn't respond. He simply slammed the door shut and locked it. Jennifer sank back on the bed, swallowing hard as he removed his gentleman's jacket and flung it aside. Next he untied his cravat, his eyes never leaving her. He undid his shirt buttons, then pulled the good linen garment from his body. Throwing it against the wall, he turned toward her, his eyes blazing in outrage.

"I want to know what exactly possesses you, and why you feel the need to torture me," he stated, his voice thick with ire. "Why, Jennifer? Am I some toy for your amusement, some example of the male species you need to torment?"

"No!" Jennifer rose from the bed, stunned that he would think such a thing. His naked chest filled her vision, and she had to fight to remember what he'd said. "We really thought you'd ruin the séance! You've made your thoughts clear on the subject often enough . . ." she finished weakly, aware that even to her own ears, her argument sounded lame.

"And if I wanted to cause you trouble, why haven't I done so already? I could have summoned the police numerous times, brought you to court, drained you financially with fines. Have I done any of this?"

His eyes blazed as he stepped closer. Jennifer swallowed hard. "No," she admitted, her voice barely a whisper.

"Then why?" he demanded. "Was it because I made love to you?"

"No!" Jennifer shouted, though shame and confusion welled up inside of her. Deep inside, she had to admit that some of her resentment toward him was because of exactly that, though it was mixed up with a million other emotions as well. Embarrassment stung her, and shock that he would dare bring that up. She felt the heat on her cheeks. "Gabriel, I'm sorry! We've both agreed that what happened between us was a mistake. It meant nothing! Putting you to sleep wasn't an act of revenge. We were only trying to get you out of the way. Everything sort of . . . snowballed from there," she finished weakly.

"It always snowballs where you're concerned," Gabriel ranted, full of self-righteous anger. He couldn't admit how much she'd stung him, with her assertion that his lovemaking was so easily dismissed. His pride inflamed, he took a menacing step toward her. "You're always plotting, always suspicious of my motivations, when I've been honest with you from the start! Well, I've lost all patience with you. This time you're not getting away with it."

"What are you going to do?" Jennifer asked, backing up as he stalked her. Her throat closed and she felt choked, a woman vulnerable and alone with a furious, half-dressed male—one that she found incredibly attractive. His steel blue eyes bore into hers, and he reached for her. The back of her knees hit the bed, and she struggled to stay on her feet. But instead of attacking her, as she had half feared, he took a cool cloth from the washstand and thrust it at her.

"Here. You did this to me, you fix it."

When he turned his back to her, Jennifer gasped in horror. "My God, what happened to you? You're black-and-blue—"

She bit her words off as the picture of him thumping up the steps came back to haunt her, and she pressed her hands to her mouth in shock. "Oh, no, Gabriel, we didn't do that, did we?"

He glanced back at her, furious. "Yes, you did. I understand I was hauled up the stairs after you drugged me. I thought I'd been in a prizefight when I first awakened."

"Gabriel, I'm so sorry. You have to know we didn't mean to hurt you like this."

"I don't know anything of the sort. Excuse me if I seem reluctant to believe you, miss, but women who poison their guests aren't exactly known for their truthfulness. Now if you don't mind, I'd like to be able to sleep tonight, without the swelling. I suggest you start with my back, and then we'll discuss where else it hurts."

Jennifer made a low, strangled noise, clearly visualizing the many times his derriere had struck the steps. She approached him with the same trepidation that she would an angry lion, clutching the compress and ready to bolt if he made a sudden move. His half-naked body, distinctly outlined in the dim light, looked strong, muscular, and far more sensual than she cared to notice. Unavoidably she thought of the previous night, when her hands raked that back in ecstasy. It was a thought she didn't encourage.

Lightly, she pressed the cloth to his back, then withdrew it instantly as he howled.

"Ouch!" He looked over his shoulder and glared at her again. "Do you mind?"

"Sorry. Let me try again—" She chose another spot and tried to place the compress on it. He jumped, hissing in pain, and she moved the cloth again, this time trying between his shoulders. Even that spot seemed sensitive, and he leaped nearly to the ceiling.

"Ow! Is that all you can do, torture a man? Forget it, I'll heal myself." He tried to snatch the cloth from her, but Jennifer held it firmly.

"I can't help you if you won't let me touch you!" Jennifer exclaimed, exasperated. A sudden thought came to her and she gestured to the bed. "Lie down. I want to try something."

"What?" Gabriel looked apprehensive, justifiably, Jennifer acknowledged. Laughing, she placed a pillow out for his sore head.

"Nothing painful, I promise."

"Why doesn't that reassure me?" Gabriel muttered, but allowed Jennifer to arrange him on the bed. "I watched your séance act," he sneered as she laid her hands on him and concentrated. "Pretty impressive, but aren't you afraid you've given her false hope?"

"How?" Jennifer asked, puzzled.

"Telling her that nonsense about a child. You can't know any of that, and suppose it isn't true?"

Jennifer stared down at him. Her expression was puzzled, as if he were trying to explain a riddle she couldn't figure out herself. "You know, it's so very strange, Gabriel, but I did see a child when I looked at the cards. Apparently, I also told her that when I was doing the séance, although I didn't remember it later. But something inside me tells me it's the truth—there really is a child."

"Jennifer, you can't—"

She shook her head as if still confused. Instead of arguing, she changed the subject. "Gabriel, if this is going to work, you have to be quiet. I can't concentrate."

Smirking, he did as she insisted, watching in fascination as her half-closed eyes focused on something far away. At first, he felt nothing, then strangely enough, an odd tingling began where her hands touched him. Apparently, Jennifer was an incredibly talented masseuse. She seemed to have a magical touch, and his body responded with a will of its own. The painful throbbing seemed to melt away, as if he were in a warm bath, and the aches slowly subsided.

Her hands slid sensually down his chest, and Gabriel felt his emotions veer completely in another direction. Desire, white-hot and searing, filled him, and he experienced a jolt of passion so intense that it took every ounce of discipline he had not to pull her into his arms. His anger, fully inflamed a moment ago, transformed into need. He looked up and saw that her full pink lips were even darker from pressing together in concentration, and looked incredibly appealing. Her thickly lashed eyes were closed against her alabaster cheeks like twin fans, and he wanted to kiss her into submission, making those eyes close with another kind of concentration.

Amazed at the emotion she stirred in him, Gabriel waited until her eyes opened and she glanced down at him. A pink flush stole over her, as if she knew what he was thinking, but she smiled softly.

"Is it better?"

"Yes," Gabriel said, surprised at his own admission. He flexed an arm and felt a only tiny pinprick of pain. Even his head was better, for the incessant throbbing had subsided, replaced by a dull soreness that was still much more bearable. "It really is," Gabriel said in amazement.

"See? Maybe now you'll credit I'm not a total charlatan."

Gabriel grinned, remembering the first time they'd

met and he'd thought her exactly that. His hand covered her pale one where it lay on his chest, and he turned toward her, his eyes smoldering with desire. "You're not a charlatan in every area, I'll grant you that much," he whispered hoarsely. "In some ways, you are very real indeed."

He took her into his arms then and Jennifer watched him come to her, breathless with need. The passion he'd so easily aroused in her the previous night came back like a pulsing ache, and the tension that had passed between them only served to fan the flames of desire even hotter. His lips covered hers and she was lost in the white-hot heat that ignited between them. She no longer cared that he would someday leave her for someone more appropriate; she couldn't see anything past the moment. He was hers now, and that was all that mattered.

Moaning, she assisted him as he struggled with her clothes, laughing as he cursed the many buttons and hooks that needed to be unfastened. Jennifer wanted to feel his burning flesh against hers once more, wanted to revel in that moment when they became one. He took his time with her, however, slowly stoking the fire within her until it burned out of control.

As her gown finally puddled at her feet, Gabriel took her mouth in another molten kiss, intoxicating her with the intensity of his desire. The tray she'd brought him earlier stood by the bedside, a single hothouse rose gracing the simple offering. Blindly, his hand crumbled the flower, then brought the soft petals to her skin, letting them flutter and skim across her like liquid fire.

Jennifer gasped, drowning in sensation. Gabriel lowered her to the bed, lavishing her with his mouth, then teasing her sensitive flesh with the rose petals. Her body cried out for release, the heat building shockingly between her legs. She arched up against him, no longer caring about anything but the tingling, burning ache within her.

"Gabriel, please," she begged, wanting the fulfillment his hard muscled body promised.

He withdrew from their embrace a small amount, then she felt him, poised at the moist warmth of her body. Rising to welcome him, she gasped as she felt him enter her that first small bit, then he plunged painlessly and fully inside her wet heat, filling her completely. A ragged moan escaped her as he withdrew and entered over and over, bringing her closer and closer to ecstasy each time. She cried out, shuddering as she reached it, feeling his answering moan as he could no longer hold back. Fused together for this sweet moment, they joined in blissful, astonishing pleasure.

It was several moments before Gabriel could move. When he did, he simply lifted his weight from Jennifer's body, then wrapped her in his arms. Jennifer sighed, enjoying the feeling of total contentment, and the warmth of his naked body next to hers. Smiling, she brushed a stray lock of hair from his face.

"How is your head? Is it all right?" Her fingers found the lump he'd gotten from the stairs.

Gabriel winced, then the pain seemed to ease from his face and he nodded, obviously amazed. "It's much better. You really do have some kind of healing talent, don't you?" When Jennifer frowned, annoyed that he would still question her, Gabriel chuckled. "Just make sure of one thing."

"What's that?" she asked, noting the teasing glint that came into his eyes.

"That this isn't part of the whole Appleton magnetic healing cure. That, my dear, I couldn't tolerate, especially on Wall Street."

Jennifer giggled, then settled down in his arms. It felt so right, to have him hold her like this, to enjoy the moment of peace between them. Awareness gradually came to her, however, and reluctantly she rose from his side.

"I've got to go. Penelope and Winifred are probably worried sick. They must think you've killed me, or beaten me, at least."

Gabriel grinned. "I felt very close to that earlier. I don't know when I've ever been that angry."

"Do you forgive me?" Jennifer asked, and Gabriel took her in his arms once more.

"You have a way of making it impossible to stay angry. Yes, I forgive you. But don't try anything like that again. I've already told you that I care for you, Jennifer. I would never deliberately hurt you. If you're worried about something, come to me. I think you'll find that I have some character, after all."

A small hope tugged inside of her, one that she wouldn't allow herself to give attention to. Nodding, she kissed him, then quickly removed herself from his reach and pulled on her dress. Rose petals fluttered to the floor, and she laughed, blowing one in the air toward him.

Gabriel watched her, enchanted, then in a moment, she was gone. Jennifer, he realized, had worked her magic on him completely.

GABRIEL AWOKE EARLY the next morning. For a moment, he lay in the little bed, disoriented, unable to remember where he was. Everything flooded back to him, culminating in his incredible lovemaking with Jennifer. He rose, amazed to find that her "cure," her magnetic healing, wasn't simply a prelude to what had happened between them afterward, but had lasting effects. His head felt clear, his limbs no longer ached, and even his derriere felt better. Apparently, his little charlatan did indeed have some real talent, aside from the one he admired most.

But why, oh why, did it have to be her? His emotions wreaked havok with his logic as he realized he'd never felt any of this toward Allison. He never felt compelled to kiss her until she swooned, to argue with her until she confessed he was right, to make love to her at the slightest brush of her fingertips. He admitted the truth to himself; he cared about Jennifer, deeply. He had never met a woman like her, and as angry as she made him, he was forced to admire so many things about her: her courage, her intelligence, her charm, and her wit. She teased him and defied him, tormented him and kidnapped him, locked him away, then made love to him with a passion that left him reeling. His society would never accept her, and he was practically engaged to another woman—one who was perfectly suitable. Why, then, couldn't he keep either his mind or his hands off Jennifer?

It was a question without an answer. Worse, he knew that the past two days had changed many of his perceptions about her, perceptions that had been very convenient. He had considered her a charlatan, yet in watching her performance, he understood what the Appletons gave their clients. Although he still wasn't convinced that she was a mystic, he couldn't deny that she gave comfort to the grief-stricken, and perhaps deserved some kind of compensation for that.

She truly was gifted when it came to healing—his own body testified to that. Who was he, then, to call her a fake, and demand that she cease to provide this help to others? Would society truly benefit if Jennifer stopped her practice? How many other Mrs. Hawthornes were out there, women who had lost sons and husbands in the war, men who had lost the love of a lifetime? Was it really so terrible for them to think they'd spoken to their loved ones once more, especially when the spirits seemed to invariably offer peace? But his own religious and moral convictions railed that it was wrong. The whole thing was terribly confusing.

Even more than that, having lived with Jennifer and her sisters, he saw the reason for her deceptions. Left orphaned and financially unstable, their choices had been grim. Did he really wish for them to become what society would accept, schoolmarms and companions, poor, penniless maids ripe for the first man who would wed them? It was a thought that he couldn't bear.

Dressing quickly, Gabriel quit the place, closing the front door softly behind him. Jennifer and her sisters would still be sleeping after their late night. He knew Eve was due back sometime today, and although he'd been able to justify his appearance at breakfast, he knew that explaining a weekend stay would be nearly impossible. As Winifred had so coolly pointed out, discovery of such a thing would ruin them, and although Gabriel had pretended otherwise, he had no intention of causing Jennifer— or the other Appletons—real harm.

He stood outside the house for a moment, noticing the poor condition of the place. Mentally, he calculated the cost of repairs. They needed mortar for the chimney, a new roof, some plaster work, and indoor refurbishments. His own estimate stunned him, but Gabriel put aside his tendency toward thrift. He had plenty of connections in the construction industry from his own business, and more than one carpenter and mason owed him favors. He could probably take care of the repairs for one tenth of what it would cost Jennifer, and he'd feel good about it in the bargain. He refused to question his own motives, other than to admit that he had to do something to help her, something to show her how he felt.

Whistling, he strode up the street to the livery to order his coach. He didn't notice the elegant carriage that slowed beside him, nor did he see Jonathan Wiseley as the man stopped his horses in astonishment. Gabriel continued walking as the sun rose in the east, whistling to himself, in all appearances a happy man. He crossed the road to the stables, and a moment later, drove down the street and was gone.

Jonathan gazed at the stables, then at the street where Gabriel had come from. Twin Gables rose at the center of the block like an elegant Victorian lady, aging and painted, but still charming all the same. A nasty suspicion crept into his mind, one that refused to go away. Waiting until he saw Gabriel's carriage go past at the crossroads, he alighted from his own vehicle to approach the livery. A sullen-looking boy chewed tobacco insolently, then spat at the curb as he approached.

Jonathan drew his gentleman's coat aside in repugnance, but managed a smile. He withdrew a silver coin from his pocket and dangled it before the youth.

"Yes, sir, what can I do for you?"

"The gentleman that just left. Do you know where he was staying, and when he left his carriage?"

"You mean Mr. Forester?" The boy's streetwise gaze narrowed in speculation. "Who wants to know?"

"A friend. Mr. Forester and I are acquainted."

"Then why don't you ask him yourself?" The boy smirked.

Jonathan produced another coin. The boy snatched them both up and put them furtively inside his coat. "Mr. Forester left his carriage Friday night. He was supposed to come back for it the same evening, but, except for a brief trip out with a lady on Saturday, it's been here ever since."

"A lady? Hmmm. And where was he going on Friday?"

"Twin Gables, sir. That's all I know."

Jonathan smiled. "That's more than enough, boy. More than enough."

CHAPTER 18

Aunt Eve bundled through the door with her bags in hand. Handing her parcels to Jennifer, she embraced Penelope, then gave Winifred's cheek a fond rub as she sank into her favorite chair.

"It's so good to be home! Did anything of importance happen while I was away?"

Jennifer choked, and Penelope smiled charmingly. "Not at all, Auntie, everything was completely normal. For us, anyway." She giggled irrepressibly.

Aunt Eve looked from one guilty face to the next. Jennifer hastened to put away her bags, while Winifred proffered tea.

"Tell us about your trip, Auntie," Jennifer said, sending Penelope a threatening glare. "We want to hear all about it."

In spite of her forebodings, Eve was soon comfortably ensconced back in her own home. The parrot squawked as Angel teased him unmercifully. The fire crackled, and the tea was hot and sweet.

"I had a wonderful time. Everything went better than expected." She looked at her nieces with the same expression she wore on Christmas morning, waiting to see their faces as they opened a specially planned present. "I didn't tell you girls, for I didn't want to raise your hopes too much, but I went to see Mrs. Adams."

"What?" Penelope nearly dropped her own teacup. "You stayed with her? How wonderful, and how scandalous!"

Winifred looked up from her book, interested in spite of herself, while Jennifer's mouth dropped open in surprise.

Eve chuckled, as if she were delighted to have shocked them. "Yes, I went to see Mildred. We had a wonderful visit! It is delightful to realize that some things never change, nor some people, for that matter. At first it was a little awkward and strange, but soon we were chatting away like two schoolgirls."

"That's great, Auntie," Jennifer said, amazed that this tiny, befuddled woman had managed to keep her own secrets so well.

"You should see her house," Eve continued, her eyes closing dreamily. "It's absolutely stunning. Everything was marble and gilt, all done in the most exquisite taste. I saw paintings by Rembrandt, Chippendale furniture, English china, and Irish linen. We dined on beef Wellington, and drank the best wines. We even had Napoleon brandy." Eve giggled girlishly, as if confessing a major transgression.

"That sounds marvelous," Penelope said, sighing. "It must be so nice to have all that money."

"That Mildred has, although I don't know that it brought her happiness." Eve's cheerful expression turned solemn, and she shook her head in thought. "I may have mentioned that Mildred once loved a man she couldn't have. She's never forgotten him. Funny, I don't think her parents ever suspected that she loved him like that. Even now, not a day goes by that she doesn't think of him."

"It's all so romantic," Penelope said.

"I think it's a little impractical," Winifred remarked. "What good has it done her except bring her unhappiness and longing? She would have done better to forget him and cut her losses."

"Do you think so?" Aunt Eve's blue eyes twinkled strangely. "His memory may torment her, but she also confessed that his love was the only real happiness she's ever known. In any case, I have good news for you three. She has promised to come visit, and to attend one of your theatricals! Isn't that wonderful?"

Jennifer and Penelope hugged each other, then enveloped their aunt in a tight embrace. Even Winifred looked pleased as she peered up from her books.

"Oh, Auntie, how can we ever thank you! Why this is more than wonderful. Good Lord, if Mildred Adams endorses us, we are practically assured society's seal of approval!" Penelope could barely contain her excitement.

"We would be accepted by the Billings, and the Howes. Why, we would be socially superior to them!" Winifred said, her scholarly finger tapping.

Eve nodded sagely. "Yes, and no man could object to any of you then! You could have your pick of beaux!"

Penelope and Winifred cheered delightedly, while Jennifer looked quickly at the floor. Thankfully, Aunt Eve didn't notice. The older woman's head dipped in embarrassment as the girls thanked her heartily. Wiping at her eyes, she smiled fondly at her nieces.

"I am so pleased to be able to help. Mildred will be here in a fortnight, and we have so much to prepare. We need to clean up the house, and you girls need new gowns. I must tutor you more on etiquette—Mildred has perfect manners and won't tolerate mishaps. Your behavior must be above criticism. That means no rough language, Jennifer, no posturing, Penelope. And Winifred, you must pretend to be interested in her conversation, even if you find it dull . . ."

Aunt Eve frowned, then rose from her seat and put her teacup aside. "What on earth is that?"

Jennifer, Penelope, and Winifred joined her at the window. Several rugged-looking workmen had appeared outside. One of them carried a bucket of cement, another had roofing tiles, while another carried carpenter's tools. The carpenter approached the door first and banged on it furiously. Astonished, Jennifer opened the portal.

"I understand you have a roof leak. Can you show me the attic?" He gestured to the stairs, then wiped his nose with his fist.

"But—we didn't order any work," Jennifer said, staring at him in confusion.

"Work's been paid for by a gentleman. Can you show me the attic?" He shuffled from one boot to the other impatiently.

"Young man, what is going on here? Who sent you, and what do you think you're doing?" Eve came to Jennifer's aid, staring at the workman as if she'd seen a specter.

The man pulled his cap from his head and rolled his eyes. "Lady, I don't have time to argue. I'm here on a Sunday, which is double-time. I don't think the gentleman who sent me will appreciate it if we waste his money, and I won't appreciate missing my supper. Now can you show me the attic?"

Jennifer turned to her aunt and shrugged. Eve gave a slight nod, a look of understanding coming to her eyes. Jennifer obeyed her silent signal and whisked the man up the stairs. When she returned, Penelope and Winifred stood beside Eve, scratching their heads. Eve looked at the three girls as if trying to sort something out.

"A gentleman! That must mean one of you has a rich admirer! Isn't that wonderful? Now, who?"

Jennifer immediately thought of Gabriel, Penelope wondered frantically about James, and Charles crossed Winifred's mind. Penelope and Winifred seemed able to dismiss their thoughts, for they both turned to Jennifer expectantly, as if the whole thing were solved for them. Jennifer shrugged, her shoulders lifting almost to her earbobs.

"I don't know, Auntie. Maybe they were sent by an angel?"

"Are you girls sure nothing unusual happened this weekend?" Eve asked, showing signs of a perception that amazed Jennifer.

"No, we have no idea," Jennifer said innocently.

One of the workmen banged on the roof, while another started a loud pounding upstairs. The girls skittered out of Aunt Eve's notice, leaving the older woman to look around her in perplexity. Sometimes she felt as if the entire world had gone mad.

.

"MORE TEA, GABRIEL?" Allison asked sweetly, refilling his cup before he could answer. Gabriel gave her an absent glance, his thoughts preoccupied with Jennifer.

The workmen had probably shown up by now, he thought, calculating the time. His smile grew broader as he mentally saw the girls trying to explain this to their aunt. He was sure Jennifer would adroitly avoid answering, but it would be amusing all the same. It wasn't often one had the opportunity to create a disturbance that was beneficial at the same time.

"Gabriel! Jane Billing just asked you if you wanted to look at the stereograph. She has a new collection of cards. Are you with us at all?"

Shaking off his pleasant thoughts, he flushed guiltily and glanced up. Allison was looking at him in frustration, while the Billings appeared insulted. Only Jonathan Wiseley seemed amused, and a disconcerting smirk played around the man's mouth.

"Sorry," Gabriel managed, then drank the too-hot tea.

Scalding his tongue, he tried to manfully cover up his distress, while hiding his annoyance at the same time. He had told Allison that he hadn't wanted to attend this tea, but she had insisted, claiming he never took her out anymore. Gabriel discovered that he was bored with these gatherings, which always seemed to include the same people, the same ideas, the same conversation. He saw his mother across the room, conversing with Mrs. Merriweather; he saw the Greysons, the Stocktons, and the Barrys. They were always there, discussing their vacations, the weather, the stock market, and society. When had he discovered it was all incredibly dull?

Since knowing Jennifer, a voice inside his head answered him. Gabriel felt the hot splash of tea as he replaced his cup, earning another frown from Allison. Had Jennifer truly bewitched him, or was it just his acquaintance with her and her eccentric ideas that made him view the world differently? Maybe it was her lovemaking, an experience that shattered everything he thought he knew when it came to sex. Or perhaps it was her unexpected virginity, a gift that she'd offered him freely, without asking for anything in return.

The thought unsettled him. This was his world, among society's best, not a world inhabited by séances and spirits. It was as if Jennifer had put a spell on him that made him no longer fit where he belonged. Gabriel swore he could still feel her hands on him, sliding down his chest to cure his ills, her eyes smoky and filled with passion . . . He stood up abruptly. He had to get outside, get some fresh air, and reorient himself.

"Gabriel, where are you going?" Allison asked indignantly.

"Just outside for a few minutes. I'll be right back."

He didn't see his mother's expression when he departed, nor did he observe the twinkle in her eye. Allison sank back onto the couch thoughtfully, holding the fragile china cup between her fingers as if afraid she would throw it. Jonathan chuckled, then sat down beside her, helping himself to another sandwich.

"Well, well. Trouble in paradise?"

Allison gave him a not-too-friendly look. "I should say not," she answered stiffly, aware that a woman of her class never discussed her problems publicly. "Gabriel has just been a little . . . distracted the last few weeks."

"Yes, I'd agree with that." Jonathan chuckled, the sound unpleasant in the lavish room. "Especially after the way he spent the weekend. I give the man credit for his stamina."

"Whatever do you mean?" Allison asked, trying to sound bored, but her interest was evident.

"It appears he spent the weekend at Twin Gables. I didn't realize that Gabriel was a fan of spiritualism, did you? Or perhaps there were other enticements." He gave her a sly glance.

Allison rose, her face pale. "That is the most incredible nonsense I've ever heard! How dare you suggest such a thing?"

Jonathan extended his feet and folded his hands across his chest, obviously pleased to be able to impart such gossip. "Perhaps you should ask him for an explanation, then. You see, I saw him myself. I was returning from the Athenaeum Club, rather late I'm afraid. I had a little too much brandy last night over cards. Imagine my surprise when I saw Gabriel retrieving his carriage from the livery at Twin Gables!"

"He . . . must have been nearby on business," Allison said quickly.

Jonathan shook his head regretfully. "Afraid not, my dear. I spoke with the stableboy. Surely you knew of his visit? I wouldn't want to be the one to say anything that would cause trouble . . ." His voice was thick with insinuation.

"No, no. You did the right thing. I am grateful for your confidence," Allison responded stiffly. Her mouth twisted as she realized that all of her fears concerning Jennifer were justified. In all likelihood, Gabriel had taken her as his . . . lover.

Allison clutched her cup, imagining the ridicule that would be heaped upon her when word got out. She could just see the glances, filled with pity, directed her way. Although Gabriel had never announced his intentions toward her, Allison had assumed that he meant to propose, an assumption she'd confided to more than one person. An embarrassed heat stung her cheeks as she remembered assuring the Billings that she would be engaged come Christmas. She would be a laughingstock when word got out about his infidelity, especially because it involved Jennifer Appleton.

Blushing furiously, she rose to her feet, a determined glint coming into her eyes. She couldn't let this happen. Jaded New York society would feast on such a juicy scandal, one that had the potential to ruin them all. Something had to be done about the notorious Miss Appleton, and quickly. Jonathan watched with interest as Gabriel reentered the Billings' drawing room and took Allison's arm. Allison gave him an adoring smile, and to all appearances they were the same loving couple they had been moments ago. Excusing herself, she crossed the room and approached Judge Winthrop, an old friend of the family.

Jonathan sank back into his seat, a satisfied grin on his lips. Entertainment, at last. It was, after all, what he lived for.

THE FOLLOWING AFTERNOON Jennifer stood outside Twin Gables, admiring the new roof. She could see the repaired shingles, the places where the new material stood out from the old like a patched garment, and the freshly mortared chimney. To an outsider, it may have looked only adequate, but to her, it was magnificent.

Gabriel had done this, she knew it in her heart. He had no idea what such a gesture meant to her, and she appreciated it far more than a bouquet of flowers or some trinket. Fixing the house was something they really needed, and to have someone take some of that burden from her was truly heaven. She felt genuinely satisfied that Aunt Eve would no longer shiver from the drafts. Smoke would no longer pour into the parlor from the faulty chimney, and they needn't worry about rain damage again. And with Mrs. Adams coming to stay, his improvements could not have come at a better time.

Hugging herself against the cold, she gleefully realized that the Christmas holiday was coming, and she'd already gotten the best present ever. A small, hopeful longing crept up inside her as she thought of Gabriel, and what his gesture may have meant. Had he sent her flowers or candy, she would have thought he felt only guilty, that he was just trying to pay off a mistress. But his gift seemed much more thoughtful and serious to her, as if he finally understood what she was up against.

That thought produced a warm rush of emotion inside of her. Even though Winifred had warned her, it was far too late to heed any advice. She was already head over heels in love with Gabriel. Common sense warned her to reel in her heart, but she just couldn't do that. Jennifer had worn her heart on her sleeve for as long as she could remember, and she couldn't change now. Her body glowed at the memory of his lovemaking, and the tender way he'd spoken to her, reassuring her he cared for her. Surely something good would come of all this—it just had to.

A police wagon rumbled down the road, slowing as it approached the house. Jennifer frowned, glancing down the street, looking for a reason for the vehicle's presence. She didn't see a fire, or a group of rowdies that would warrant the presence of the police, or a paddy wagon. To her amazement, Chief of Police Tim O'Roarke disembarked from the cart and approached her. His ruddy face appeared even redder beneath his white beard, like a benevolent Saint Nicholas, but his normally jovial eyes met hers with an expression that chilled her bones.

"Miss Jennifer." He nodded awkwardly, then glanced at the house. "Are the girls at home?"

"Yes," Jennifer answered. She tried to give him her best grin. "How are you? You haven't been to supper in some time. I was just asking Aunt Eve about you. She's only now come back from visiting, you know."

"I know." Tim shifted from one foot to the next, as if his own body were a burden. "She asked me to look out for the house whilst she was gone. A fine lady." He shook his head, as if ashamed of his own actions. "Miss Appleton, can we go inside?"

Dread filled Jennifer. Tim never called her Miss Appleton. Her common sense told her this was trouble—worse trouble than she'd ever experienced before. She took the policeman into the house. Penelope had just arisen, and was yawning, her hair tumbling attractively about her. Winifred was so absorbed in studying that she barely acknowledged his presence. Aunt Eve looked delighted to see him, and rushed forward, pressing her small hands into his.

"Mr. O'Roarke! How delightful to see you! Do come to breakfast. Jennifer and I were just talking about you. I have tea and scones, some good jam and a seedcake. Why, you look frozen through!"

The policeman looked even more embarrassed by Eve's gushing hospitality. He removed his cap, then glanced awkwardly from one woman to the next, his cheeks becoming impossibly redder by the moment. He coughed, as if choking on his own words, then finally spat them out.

"I'm sorry. I can't stay for tea, or breakfast. This isn't a social call. It is my terrible duty to inform you young ladies that you are all under arrest. Can you please get ready and step outside into the wagon?"

CHAPTER 19

ARRESTED! THAT IS ridiculous! Of all things! Please, sit down, Tim, and tell us what this is all about!" Aunt Eve stood before the girls like an aging warrior, prepared to defend them at all costs. Angel hissed at the intruder, while the parrot squawked, his feathers bristling.

"I'm sorry, madam. You know how much I admire you and the girls. But I don't have any choice. I have a warrant for the arrest of all three Appletons."

"What are the charges?" Winifred asked, her eyes squinting from behind her glasses like twin points of light.

The chief of police sighed, as if wishing he were anywhere but here. He withdrew a folded document from his pocket, then put on a pair of wire-rimmed glasses. His bushy white brows drew together as he skimmed the paper.

"You are being charged with performing charlatan spiritualism, accepting money for such practices, performing illegal tarot card readings, and . . . soliciting."

Penelope gasped, and pressed her hands to her mouth in horror. Jennifer had a sick feeling in the pit of her stomach. She glanced at Winifred, who didn't look at all surprised, but continued to question the officer pointedly.

"And who filed the complaint?"

"The name is Howe. A Miss Allison Howe."

There was a stunned silence in the room. Penelope squealed, her eyes flashing with righteous anger. "Allison! Why, I know what this is all about! She likes Mr. Forester, who happens to be smitten with Jennifer, and rightfully so." Penelope stood beside her sister loyally. "This is just spiteful jealousy on her part!"

"I'm sorry, miss, it doesn't matter why she complained, just that she did. I'm afraid I have to take you all in."

Aunt Eve waved a finger in the policeman's face. "That is utterly ridiculous! There has to be some dreadful mistake! My girls are not guilty of any such thing. I'm going straight away to see that young miss and get to the bottom of all this nonsense. Imagine, her slandering my lambs like that!" Aunt Eve huffed indignantly.

The police chief looked helplessly at the Appletons. "I'm sorry, madam. You know how much I think of the girls. We've turned a blind eye to their doings, knowing they had to make a living the best they knew how. But this time, there is nothing I can do. I tried to talk to the young lady who complained, but she refused to listen. She insisted on pressing charges, and has already seen the judge. Girls, can you please come with me?"

"No one is taking the girls anywhere!" Aunt Eve insisted. "Winifred, isn't there something we can do about this?"

Winifred rose from her perch near the fire and examined the paperwork, then returned it to the mortified police officer. "I'm afraid he's right, Auntie. The paperwork's all in order. There's nothing we can do right now."

Penelope sniffed in outrage. Jennifer pressed her hand comfortingly to her sister's arm.

"Why don't you get ready, dear? I'll think of something, don't worry."

Aunt Eve paced, followed by the tiger kitten, who seemed fascinated with the trail of her shawl. Winifred gathered up her law books, her great intellect already preoccupied with the legal possibilities of their situation. Eve glanced outside and saw the wagon, then turned to the policeman in horror.

"You don't mean to take them in that!"

Tim nodded reluctantly. "That is the accepted method of transport."

"Why, the scandal! Do you mean to take them down to the Ludlow Street jail in that conveyance, where everyone can see! You'll ruin the girls for life!"

It didn't seem possible for the officer to turn any redder, but he did. Jennifer held her breath, thinking surely the man's head would explode.

"I can't help that, ma'am. I feel terrible about all this. I know what it will do to the girls, driving down Broadway, making a spectacle. That's why I thought I'd take the side roads. 'Tis the least I can do."

Jennifer turned as Penelope descended the stairs. Her sister had donned her best gown, a sunny yellow muslin that showed off her figure fabulously. Her hair was swept up in a matronly bun that only enhanced the beauty of her angelic face. Donning her cloak, she turned toward the policeman with a whirl of her skirts. She appeared as noble as the heroine of any penny dreadful, and she extended her hands with a dramatic gesture, almost as if expecting a kiss.

"I suppose you wish to put handcuffs on me. Please try not to damage the gloves—these are my best."

"Now, Miss Penelope, I have no intention of handcuffing any of you—"

"Oh, but you must!" Jennifer said, an idea bursting

forth in her brain. She extended her own hands. "And make sure the wagon takes all the main streets."

"But I thought the side roads—"

"Nonsense!" Jennifer said exuberantly. "If we are to be a scandal, then let's be a grand scandal!"

Penelope's expression changed from hauteur to amusement as she understood Jennifer's meaning. Even Winifred grinned as she extended her hands, waiting for the harsh cuffs. The policeman shook his head, then withdrew to the wagon and returned with three pair of shining silver handcuffs. He attached them reluctantly to the girls, then scratched his head as they marched down to the wagon, holding their poor fettered limbs aloft.

Only Aunt Eve trembled with worry. The poor woman knotted her handkerchief between her fingers, following them out to the street, unwittingly creating an even more pathetic scene.

"I can't believe this is happening! How can you arrest innocent orphaned girls? Oh, such cruelty! There has to be something I can do, someone I can call upon, someone who will help. Winifred, dear, do we have any legal recourse?"

"I will read up on it, Auntie, don't fear. But we do need counsel to represent us. It would probably strengthen our chances if you could fetch a solicitor."

"Who, then, is the best?"

"Why, Charles," Winifred said, as if surprised by the question. She followed Jennifer out to the wagon, then glanced back at her aunt. "Charles Howe."

"Howe? Isn't that Allison's brother?" Aunt Eve cried.

Winifred nodded with a grin. "The very same."

Eve stood on the sidewalk, her eyes glistening as the wagon started down the street. Already neighbors had gathered upon seeing the police wagon, and stood horrified at the outrageous display of their three lovely neighbors being led out of the house like common criminals, as they would later tell the paper. As the paddy wagon rumbled toward the Ludlow Street jail, Jennifer looked tearful, Winifred appeared thoughtful, and Penelope waved to the gathering crowd like a princess imprisoned in her pumpkin. She blew kisses to her admirers who called out to her.

Smiling beneath her lace handkerchief, Jennifer settled back in her seat as Penelope played to the audience as if this were the finest hour of her life. "Don't you see?" She asked Winifred, who grew even more solemn as she leafed through her law books. "We can turn this around! As they say, bad publicity is better than none. I know some of the better reporters. With a little incentive, they'll all take up the cause of the Appletons!"

"Perhaps." Winifred found turning pages difficult with the hard metal bracelets. When her eyes met Jennifer's she shrugged. "I hate to be a spoilsport, but this could also ruin us. We may get out of the legal contretemps, but Aunt Eve is right. Socially, the New York elite will never forget this. They may be sympathetic now, but public opinion turns like the tide. We could find ourselves washed up."

Jennifer's smile faded. For once, she hoped her brilliant sister was wrong. Dead wrong.

Word had gotten out about the arrest of the Appletons before they reached the jail. By the time the wagon pulled up to Ludlow Street, a parade of supporters followed the wagon, and an even larger crowd had gathered at the jail. Men cried out "Jennifer!" or "Penelope!" as the girls exited the wagon, while the suffragettes held signs declaring "Free All Women!" A broad cheer exploded as the three beautiful women stepped into the street, followed by the burly policeman.

"There, there, move on." The police chief tried to disperse the crowd, but to no avail. Photographers scrambled to set up tripods, and reporters pushed to the front of the group. A loud "Boo!" ensued for the police chief as he tried to push the people back, and the reporters shouted questions at the lovely jailbirds.

"Jennifer, what do you have to say about the charges?"

"Is it true that Allison Howe, a friend of the family, filed against you?"

"Do you girls really contact the dead?"

"O'Roarke, do you think this arrest will reelect Judge Winthrop?"

The chief of police refused to answer any of their queries, but Penelope and Jennifer held court like two queens, the papers reported. Jennifer stood before the crowd, dressed as elegantly as any lady, her strange eyes flashing with passion. Her upswept burnished curls framed her face artfully, while her neat woolen cape with its demure velvet trim made her a pretty picture indeed. Penelope stood beside her, gorgeous as always, her cuffed hands waving flirtatiously. She was obviously determined to make the best of their situation, and the men especially remarked on her bravery and beauty. Winifred stood to the rear with her books, monitoring Jennifer's speech, surveying the mood of the people.

"We Appletons violently disagree with all of these false charges that have been pressed against us! As poor orphan girls, we have no male protector, no one to save us from the slurs of those who, for their own reasons, look to discredit us. We deny any and all charges of spiritualism, of fraud, or of any other kind of solicitation!"

"Why, then, would someone press such charges?" the reporter from the *New York Sun* shouted.

Jennifer smiled, and demurely lowered her lashes. "Two reasons. As women subsisting alone, we are a threat to those dependent on others. As our own success at the stock market demonstrates, women can provide for themselves. Is not such an example frightening to women who dare not take up such a challenge?"

The suffragettes cheered. Winifred nodded, admiring

Jennifer's skill at preaching to the choir. The suffragette influence was important to the city, and their support would be plentiful and vocal.

The reporters scribbled frantically, while more cameras clicked. One of the newspapermen glanced up. "And the other reason?"

Jennifer sighed modestly, as if reluctant to speak. A long moment passed before she shrugged her delicate shoulders resignedly.

"There are women who, perhaps, are not comfortable with what they perceive as our good looks. Both of my sisters and myself have been excluded from their society for this reason, shunned and whispered about, disdained and suspected, no matter how innocent our actions. I hate to speak of such things, but this is a story as old as womankind, I'm afraid."

The crowd broke out in excited whispers. Speculation was rife as Jennifer delicately suggested that the complaint against them was due to jealousy. The reporters fought for more quotes, shouting to the girls, while others pressed forward, curious to learn more of the story. The police chief, tired of waiting, insisted that the girls move forward.

"That's enough, you lads got your story and then some. I don't want you clogging up the jail, either. Leave the ladies alone. Clear the way, now."

Three other officers had joined them, obviously worried about the crowd. They pushed the reporters back, allowing the Appletons to walk through a path that opened like the Red Sea. They graced the path with their queenly presence, walking like Victorian Joan of Arcs toward their doom.

The papers loved it.

The crowd cheered them on, and Jennifer could hear them clearly even as the door closed behind her. As soon as they were inside, Tim insisted that the cuffs come off, and the officers bustled to do his bidding. The girls filled out the proper forms, and were then led to a cell directly behind the office.

As Tim held the door, he looked as unhappy as if he were the father of the three women ensconced inside. Penelope watched as the door slowly closed, then burst into tears as it clanged shut.

"Oh, I can't believe it! They really are locking us up in here! Let me out!"

"Please don't cry, Miss Appleton." The police chief handed her his own handkerchief. "We'll try to make you girls as comfortable as possible until we get this resolved. I'm having a good lunch prepared by the hotel, and dinner's been ordered from Grinnel's, and paid for by an admirer. Has your counsel been notified?"

"Aunt Eve is summoning Charles Howe," Winifred answered.

The police chief shook his head. "Brother against sister. Are you sure that is wise?"

Winifred nodded. "If Charles is uncomfortable taking the case himself, he will recommend someone else. I trust him completely."

Jennifer looked at her sister strangely. Winifred, who never got emotional, spoke with an understated passion that betrayed her depth of feeling. Jennifer just hoped that in this case she was right.

"WHAT? THE THREE girls arrested? By whom?" Charles Howe nearly leaped out of his chair as Aunt Eve stood before him like a worried fairy godmother, her blue-white head nodding urgently.

"The chief of police. He is such a nice man, and he didn't want to do it, but he had no choice. I can't believe it! They led my girls away in handcuffs, as if they were murderers! I was nearly beside myself as they were forced into that dreadful wagon! Every time I think of them, shut away in that cell..." Eve's voice was filled with tears. "I didn't know what to do. Winifred suggested I come to you."

"She did right." Charles swore as he threw a ream of papers into his case, then reached for his walking stick. "You don't happen to know what the charges are, and who filed a complaint?"

"Yes, I believe I do. They were charged with charlatan spiritualism, and solicitation, all utter nonsense if you ask me. As if someone could summon a ghost! The complaint, unfortunately, was signed by . . . your sister."

"Allison?" Charles stopped dead in his tracks. "Allison complained against the girls? Why? She is barely acquainted with Jennifer! I don't understand."

Aunt Eve shook her head despondently. "Penny said something about her being upset about Mr. Forester's relationship with Jennifer. I don't know this for a fact, of course." She looked at the lawyer pityingly.

Charles's face turned hard. His mouth twisted angrily, and fire sparked in his dark gaze. When he spoke, it was with much strain. "Unfortunately, I can well believe that. Allison has always been spoiled and inclined to get her own way. I have warned her in the past about declaring Gabriel's feelings publicly before he spoke to her himself, but I know she's done just that. She's probably afraid of looking like a fool if he cares for someone else, especially Jennifer. Wait until I get my hands on her."

His grip tightened on the case as if he had to fight to control himself from hitting something. Aunt Eve nodded tremulously.

"Will you go to the jail, then, and see that the girls are released? I have some money put away for their weddings that I suppose I could use for bail and to pay your fees. I was hoping to see the girls happily married someday . . ." Aunt Eve trailed off as her voice became choked with tears. No one needed to tell her that the girls' chances of making a good match had become nil.

Charles's scowl deepened as he realized the same thing. He seemed full of repressed emotion as he stopped, then took Aunt Eve's hand in his gloved one, and held it firmly.

"You must accept my apologies for the actions of myself and my sister. Between the two of us, we have caused tremendous difficulties for you and your family, and at this moment, I am deeply ashamed. Rest assured I will leave no stone unturned to right this dreadful wrong, and I certainly expect no compensation for that. Am I understood?"

Eve smiled, and tears sparkled in her eyes. "I am most grateful, sir. You are truly a gentleman."

"Will you accompany me to the jail?" Charles asked as he prepared to leave.

Aunt Eve shook her head. "I will come later. I was thinking of going to see your sister, and pleading with her to withdraw her complaint. Do you think it will do any good?"

Charles shook his head. "No, unfortunately, it may have an even worse effect. Also, legally, it could be construed that you were trying to influence her. I'll see to Allison."

Eve nodded, then covered her head with her shawl once more. "Then I will see you at the jail later. There is one more person I wish to visit. I think Gabriel Forester should know what has happened."

CHAPTER 20

"I DEMAND TO speak to whoever is in charge of this investigation! Now!"

The policeman looked up from behind his desk, where he complacently chewed a sandwich, and sighed. More visitors for the Appletons. In the past few hours, the office had been thronged with suffragettes, spiritualists, stockbrokers, and impassioned admirers. Counsel had already arrived and was advising the Appletons of their rights. Now, another polished-looking gent and a grandmotherly old lady stood before him, ordering him around as if he were some lackey.

"The chief of police is with the girls now, as is their lawyer. Now, why don't you have a seat right there—" He gestured to the bench.

"But you don't understand," Gabriel said in frustration. He'd come immediately with Aunt Eve, sick with guilt when he'd heard what happened. All the way to the station, he could picture nothing but his poor Jennifer, stuck inside a jail cell with only moldy bread and water. It was intolerable. "I am a witness, I can help you with the case. I have important information. These girls have been wrongly accused . . ."

"I'm sorry, but you'll have to wait. If I let every jackanapes inside who claimed he was here to help the girls, I'd be knee-deep in assistants. Sit down, or I'll have to throw you out." The policeman calmly chomped on his lunch, annoyed at the interruption. His eyes narrowed as he appeared to recognize Gabriel. "Don't I know you? Weren't you that Peeping Tom we caught a while back—"

Gabriel snarled. Before the policeman could object, he grabbed Aunt Eve's hand and burst through the doors, heading toward the cells where the prisoners were kept.

"Hey, you can't go in there!" The barrel-chested policeman jumped up, losing his sandwich in the process, but Gabriel and Aunt Eve were already halfway down the hall.

" 'Tis all right, Murphy. I know them." Tim O'Roarke nodded, admitting Gabriel and Aunt Eve while the officer scowled. "Come in and join the rest of us."

Inside, it was more like a party than a jail cell. Gabriel stared in astonishment at Charles and Winifred talking intently, Penelope preening before a gilt-edged mirror as if she were still at home, and Jennifer, his poor incarcerated heroine, lying comfortably on a donated couch. Food of all kinds sat on a table before them. Gabriel saw baskets of fruit, covered silver dishes, flowers, cakes, and homemade cookies, piled with cards from well-wishers, more than one of them male. Something hot and possessive rose in him, a feeling that was not relieved when he spotted a vase of roses from Vanderbilt himself.

"They've been arriving all day." The police chief shrugged. "Seems the Appletons have a few supporters."

"Gabriel!" Jennifer gasped, obviously pleased to see him. She sprang up from the couch and came to stand pathetically by the cell door. Charles and Winifred glanced up, giving him a cool look which made his stomach tighten, and Penelope grinned before going back to her primping. Aunt Eve held onto his arm as if to protect him.

"Girls, I am deeply sorry this has happened," Gabriel said, his voice filled with urgency. He clasped Jennifer's hand through the bars and held onto it tightly. "I came as soon as I heard. Jennifer, are you really all right?"

She nodded. "Tim has been treating us well, and keeping out the riffraff. Charles and Winnie are working on our defense. We're as well as we can be."

"They wrote us up in the paper," Penelope said with a sigh. "My hair must have looked horrible with all that wind! Do be a lamb and bring by the *Post* and the *Sun*, Gabriel. I'd like to see them."

"I'll bring all the papers, and anything else you want. Before that, I intend to go see Allison and persuade her to drop these ridiculous charges. When I think of what she's done—"

"I don't know if that's wise," Charles interrupted. "It may look as if you're trying to influence a witness. It might be better to wait."

"Charles," Gabriel said, dropping Jennifer's hand and struggling to rein in his temper. "I know she's your sister, but she has to be stopped. It's my fault she's done this, and I have to take responsibility for that."

Charles rose to his feet. His normally calm expression tightened, and his eyes flashed with fury. "I don't give a damn that she's my sister. Do you think I would try and protect her after this? I just meant that it might harm the case more than help it, especially considering your role in this drama."

"And what is that supposed to mean?" Gabriel faced Charles, his fists tightening in outrage.

"I don't think it would help for you two to start fighting," Aunt Eve said calmly, giving them both an admonishing look. "Imagine when the newspapers get hold of that."

Charles lost some of his righteous anger, and he extended a hand toward Gabriel. "I'm sorry. Mrs. Appleton is right. I'm just upset with the situation. Allison's part in all this has me furious as well as embarrassed."

Gabriel took the proffered hand and shook it, nodding to his friend. "I'm a little touchy on the subject myself. Look, I'm here to help. What can I do?"

"There's a pretrial hearing in the morning. That will determine if there is enough evidence to go to trial, and the judge will set bail. I'm putting together a defense for the girls, but maybe you could fill in some of the gaps for us. Do you know what caused Allison to do this? I don't want any surprises in the courtroom."

Gabriel glanced at Jennifer, who shook her head beseechingly. He understood her silent communication, but couldn't in good conscience obey her. It was far better for Charles to know the truth and prepare for it, rather than be blindsided.

"Yes, I do know." He saw Jennifer roll her eyes, and he continued without looking back at her. "Somehow Allison must have discovered that Jennifer and I . . . are attracted to each other."

"Oh, dear." Aunt Eve flushed, then withdrew her arm from Gabriel's and sat down. "I believe I feel faint."

"What else?" Charles persisted.

"I have witnessed one of the girls' performances, and am more than willing to testify that they have helped their clients, not harmed them. Furthermore, the woman they performed the séance for, a Mrs. Hawthorne, happens to be a good friend of my mother's. She sent me a note this morning, stating that Jennifer's vision has helped her locate her husband's orphaned child. She's on her way to get the boy, but is willing to testify that Jennifer is, indeed, a legitimate mystic."

"Good Lord." Aunt Eve fanned herself. For once her clever niece didn't seem to have anything to say for herself. Jennifer simply stared at Gabriel in stunned surprise.

"Anything else?" Charles continued ruthlessly, making another note. "There is one thing here that doesn't make sense, and that is why Allison would do this *now*. Is there anything that happened recently, anything that would infuriate Allison to the point of desperation? Something that so intimidated her, that she'd risk scandal?"

"Yes." Gabriel gave Jennifer one more apologetic look, then turned back to Charles resignedly. "I think Allison may have found out that I spent the weekend at the Appletons'."

"I am going to faint," Aunt Eve said, and she slid elegantly to the floor.

The police chief and Charles brought her quickly to a bench, while the guard rushed to fetch water. Gabriel administered the drink, gently slapping the blood back into her hands, while Charles brought her feet up, level with her body. Aunt Eve slowly came around, while Charles glared at Gabriel.

"You what? What the hell were you thinking? Do you realize that when this gets out, you'll have destroyed the reputations of these girls? When I think of poor innocent Winnie—" Charles glanced in fury at the cell. It didn't help his outrage to see Winifred's guilty shrug. "Gabriel, there had better be an explanation for this. Otherwise, as a gentleman, I must demand satisfaction—"

"Oh, it isn't like that," Penelope said quickly, wanting to correct his misconception before fisticuffs resulted. "We kidnapped him."

"What?" Charles asked, astonished.

"I'm going to faint again," Eve murmured, turning even paler.

"I think I am, too." The police chief sat down and removed his cap, scratching his head in perplexity. "You girls kidnapped him? A grown man?"

Gabriel sent Penelope a look betraying his lack of appreciation for her revelation. Penelope shrugged, then hastened to explain. "Was that the wrong thing to say? But we did. Jenny used Uncle's gun. At first we put him in the wine cellar, but then we felt sorry for him—"

"Penny, that's enough," Gabriel said quickly. He turned to Charles, who looked torn between outrage, shock, and horror.

"Unfortunately, Penny is right." Winifred nodded. She met Charles's gaze with a sheepish expression. "And it was all my fault. I thought Allison and Gabriel were in cahoots together. We had a séance planned, and I was afraid Gabriel would cause us trouble, so we kidnapped him when he came to dinner. When he wouldn't leave the next day, it was my idea to put a sleeping draught in his wine. Gabriel cannot be falsely accused here."

"Winifred, that's enough!" Charles insisted, appalled.

Gabriel held up his hand as everyone tried to speak at once, each of them protesting everyone else's innocence. Only Jennifer buried her face on the couch in mortification as one outburst overtook another.

"I have the real explanation here," Gabriel said, cutting them all off. "The fact is, Charles, I am in love with Miss Appleton. I spent the weekend at Twin Gables for that reason. I understand that this admission may harm the girls' reputations, but you might as well know the truth. I will do anything I can to make this right, and to help them. That's all the press or the court or anyone else needs to know."

The noise of a moment ago died as quickly as it started. Winifred's spectacles nearly fell off, Charles smiled as if finally proud of his friend, and Aunt Eve's color came back quickly. The police chief nodded, as if everything finally made sense, and Penelope giggled. Jennifer looked up from the couch, her mouth gaping like a shucked clam, as Penelope would tell her later. She stared at Gabriel as if really and truly seeing a ghost.

"Are there any more questions, counselor?" Gabriel asked stiffly.

Charles sank down on the bench beside Aunt Eve, taking the old woman's hand in his own. "Yes, only about a million. This does put a whole new light on everything, especially the fact that you've witnessed the girls' performance. I think you and I had better get together this evening and go over the briefs. We also have to raise money for bail. Judge Winthrop will ask for a lot, with this case being so spectacular. He won't want to risk upsetting the Christian vote, which will naturally be against the girls."

"Charles," Winifred protested indignantly. "I do insist upon seeing everything before court tomorrow. I have some ideas as well."

Charles gave her a stern look. "I'll deal with you soon enough, young lady. It sounds as if some of your brilliant ideas are what got everyone into this mess. I am truly disappointed in you, Winifred, truly disappointed."

Winifred flushed at his tone, but gathered her composure and rose, facing Charles directly. "I can understand your feelings, but that doesn't change the fact that I can assist with this case. I've already researched some decisions that will aid our cause."

Charles nodded coolly. "Fine. I'll be here before breakfast. I have a lot of work to do tonight to get this case prepared."

"You may want to look up *Clafflin versus the State*," Winifred said, then her voice trailed off as the lawyer gave her a furious glare. "I just thought it would help."

"Do they really have to be here all night?" Aunt Eve asked, her face creased with worry.

"Unfortunately, yes," Charles said softly, trying to comfort the old woman. "But don't worry, we'll do our best to get them out of here." Charles gave one last glance at the cell, where beautiful Penelope looked intrigued,

Winifred contrite, and Jennifer blushed prettily. He shook his head, then slung his arm around his friend's shoulder. "I hope you're free to give a deposition this evening."

Gabriel smiled grimly. "I don't have another thing planned."

PENELOPE TURNED TO her sister in excitement when the two men left, her beautiful face alight with happiness.

"Jenny, did you hear that? Gabriel publicly announced he loves you! And he wants to do right by you! Do you realize what that means?"

Jennifer looked at her sister as if her lovely blond head had finally fallen off. When Gabriel had declared his feelings for her to Charles, she had to admit a certain part of her had soared with joy. For one brief moment, she could believe it, and the heady emotion was almost more than she could bear. But reality came crashing back soon enough. Gabriel was first and foremost a gentleman. He would always do the right thing, and saving them from slander would be a priority in his mind. She scowled at her sister. "Of course that's what he said. He's taking the blame for all this so we won't look bad. Don't be a dimwit."

"Oh." Penelope sank to her seat in disappointment, the sparkle going out of her eyes. "Then you don't think—"

"No, I don't think it for a minute," Jennifer said. The memory of Gabriel's lovemaking crept into her mind, but she dismissed it firmly, feeling the hot color rise to her cheeks. "I think he is a gentleman, and as such, is trying to rescue us from our own misdoings. I certainly can't allow him to make such a sacrifice, or ruin his own name just to bail us out."

"Young lady, I have something to say about all this."

Aunt Eve came to stand by the jail cell, her expression stern. Although she seemed as lovely and fragile as ever, like a bone china figurine, her eyes sparkled with something other than kindness and addled bewilderment. For once she seemed to know exactly what was going on, and she faced her niece with an admonishing glare. "You and I have some things to discuss."

"Yes, I know." Jennifer raised soulful eyes to her aunt, overwhelmed with shame. She had never intended to hurt this old woman, whom she'd come to care for deeply. The revelations of this afternoon must have come as a great shock to her, and Jennifer cringed as she thought of the poor elderly woman actually fainting in Gabriel's arms. Taking a deep breath, she rushed to apologize.

"Auntie, I want you to know how sorry I am. I know we've betrayed you and let you down. I wouldn't blame you at all if you disowned us completely, and tossed us back out into the street. You've given us everything, and this is how we've shown our gratitude. I am truly ashamed." She extended her hand through the cell.

To her astonishment, Eve didn't accept her gesture, but continued to glare at her like a schoolmarm with a naughty student.

"That's all well and good, miss, but it doesn't fix anything. As far as throwing you into the street, you very well know better. There isn't a stone I wouldn't turn for you, or a fire I wouldn't walk through to help you. But when you stubbornly refuse to help yourself, that's when I will interfere."

"What do you mean?" Jennifer asked, truly puzzled. She glanced behind her and saw that Winifred and Penelope shared her confusion.

Eve snorted in an uncharacteristic gesture. "What I mean is, you must accept Gabriel's offer and allow him to make this right. If you and Gabriel were to wed—"

"What?" Jennifer protested, shocked.

"If you and Mr. Forester were to marry, the papers, the people, everyone would view this all very differently. Mr. Forester's actions would simply be seen as the result of his being totally besotted with you, his behavior determined strictly by emotion. He would appear as a romantic, rather than as a cad preying on helpless females, and a romantic is always loved, especially by the ladies. Your infatuation with him would look totally normal, and although people would initially be shocked, they would soon have to welcome you into society as his wife. Mary Forester and I could help with that, as would Mildred Adams. I'm sure when I explain to her what happened, she will see things the same way."

"But—"

"There are no 'buts,'" Aunt Eve continued firmly. "You have no choice other than certain ruination, for yourself and your sisters, as well as Gabriel. Allison's role in this, while questionable, is understandable. By seeing her publicly in what appeared to be an exclusive manner, Gabriel gave her the right to think he would ask for her hand. *A Gentleman's Conduct Toward Ladies* states just that."

Jennifer sank down on the couch. She hadn't thought of any of this, of how the scandal would affect everyone else. Penelope chewed her lip in worry, Winifred gave her an "I told you so" look that she deeply resented, and Aunt Eve still regarded her with that peculiar steely firmness.

"There is only one little problem," Jennifer said, relieved to have thought of it. When Aunt Eve looked at her questioningly, Jennifer shrugged. "He hasn't asked me. He offered to help, but I didn't hear him propose exactly, nor do I think he intends to."

Eve nodded resolutely. "That, my dear, we shall take care of. As a gentleman, Gabriel will understand it is his duty to make things right by you. He has compromised you, unwittingly, perhaps, but it is all the same. He must marry."

"So what do you think will happen?" Gabriel was almost afraid to ask.

Charles poured two fingers of brandy into a glass and handed it to Gabriel, then on second thought, poured another for himself. Downing the liquid, he collapsed into a polished leather chair and looked straight at his friend.

"It won't be good. Winthrop will probably ask for at least ten thousand apiece. To do less will seem as if he's affording them special treatment because of their sex."

"Ten thousand!" Gabriel gasped, choking on the fine brandy. "He may as well ask for a million! Even at ten percent bond, where the hell could these girls get that kind of money? They're hanging by a shoestring as it is."

"I don't know, but finding the money is the least of our problems," Charles said, ruffling his hand through his hair in agitation. "I have a relationship with this judge. He has a daughter about Jennifer's age, and I'm hoping I can use that to arouse his sympathy for the girls. The best I can hope for is a quick trial, so they don't have to spend much time in prison. I think Winthrop will agree, especially when he hears that the press is determined to make a circus of the whole thing."

"Charles . . ." Gabriel twirled the liquid in his glass, then forced himself to ask the question that had been haunting him all night. "Are they going to get off?"

Charles sighed. "I think I can build a decent case for them. Fortunately, Jennifer only read cards for Allison, and didn't perform a séance. Your mother's already sent me a note, saying that she'll gladly testify on Jennifer's behalf. That will help, seeing as she's availed herself of the girls' services. Surprisingly, I've received messages from quite a few of Jennifer's clients, all offering the same thing. I'll start interviewing them tomorrow, to see if we can use any of their testimony."

Gabriel rolled his eyes. "Wonderful. We'll have a courtroom full of little old ladies swearing that they've seen a ghost and that they paid Jennifer for that vision. Anything more concrete?"

"Yes." Charles gave Gabriel a sympathetic glance. "I'll have to discredit Allison. Your testimony will help with that. I'm going to try to leave as much of the story out as I can, but in either case, it's going to be nasty."

Gabriel nodded. "I thought as much. I'll reveal whatever you think wise. I have to admit, I feel responsible for Allison's behavior, which is partly why I wanted to see her. I thought maybe I could explain things, and make it easier for her to do the right thing."

"I don't think telling Allison you've fallen in love with Jennifer will help much," Charles said dryly. "I know my sister. Her ego won't permit her to allow such an event, and she'll only turn twice as vicious. No, I think it best if you stay away from her. I'm counting on my parents to help with that."

Gabriel sighed. "So it doesn't look too bad?"

"No. The only complaint that's been filed is Allison's, and I think I can take care of that. The suffragettes are on the girls' side, as is the press. The worst part of the whole thing will be the scandal."

"People will forget," Gabriel said. "As soon as the next scandal hits the papers."

"They won't forget this one soon." Charles tossed the newspaper at Gabriel. "See for yourself."

Gabriel put aside his glass and picked up the *New York Sun*. "BEWITCHING SISTERS JAILED!" He cringed at the screeching headline, then gaped as he saw the girls' picture on the front page. There was Penelope waving to the crowd and blowing kisses to the reporters, Jennifer ladylike and serene, and Winifred standing behind her looking bored. He quickly skimmed the article.

"The Appleton sisters, long known in the city of New

York for their charm and beauty, were arrested today and charged with charlatan spiritualism and solicitation. The complaint was filed by a Miss Allison Howe, who claimed she went to visit the Appletons and was subjected to a tarot card reading, for which Miss Jennifer Appleton charged her $10. The female brokers, who are said to be consorts of the commodore himself, have often been the subject of speculation and scandal, especially since appearing on Wall Street and performing 'magnetic healing' services. The city is rife with speculation as it was revealed that a Mr. Charles Howe, brother of the plaintiff, is defending the Appleton sisters. When asked for a possible motive for Miss Howe's actions, Miss Jennifer Appleton hinted that jealousy may have been the cause. Could a certain noted businessman whose family sells marble be involved in more than just a spiritual relationship with Miss Appleton?"

Gabriel tossed aside the paper in disgust. "How can they print such trash? Can't something be done about this? My family has an interest in some of the newspapers, perhaps that will help."

"I'm afraid it's too late for that. If anything, things will get worse. Remember, the reporters haven't had time to dig up much on the girls yet. Any breath of impropriety, any momentary indiscretion, is sure to make it into print over the next few weeks."

"Then they will be destroyed." Gabriel stood up and stared lifelessly out the window. His face was as set as granite.

Charles nodded. "Yes. Only a miracle could save them at this point. Even if the charges are dropped, which I think they will be, the papers will devour this. The story, unfortunately, has everything: politics, women's rights, scandal, religion. Here's where the girls' looks will backfire. If they were dowdy and unassuming, people would be more willing to forget. But given that they are on the verge of acceptance, that they have gentleman admirers, and that they are all lovely, the papers will be relentless. The Appletons' fall will become the talk of the town for years."

Gabriel said nothing for a few long minutes. When he did speak, his voice had a dead quality. "Is there nothing we can do? My God, I can just hear the Billings and the Weatherwills, and all the other old hens. They'll rip the girls to shreds."

"No, they just won't ever acknowledge them again. And any hope of Penelope's marrying well, or any of the girls for that matter, becomes null and void. Men will want them as mistresses, of course, but no one will take them seriously in any other capacity. Don't act so shocked, Gabriel, you know what people are like. Our society has strict rules, and the Appletons have violated every last one of them."

"Good God." Gabriel thrust his hands into his pockets, and stared out into the night sky. His mouth set grimly, and he seemed to be fighting to keep from violence. Charles had never seen him so upset. "We have to do something," Gabriel said when he could speak, though it was through gritted teeth. "I know my mother will stand by the girls, as will you and I. If we band together and force the others to accept the Appletons, eventually society may come around. I can't just stand by and see them ruined."

"There is one thing you can do," Charles suggested gently. When Gabriel glanced at him quizzically, Charles shrugged. "If you were to marry Jennifer, it would put a stop to a lot of this."

Gabriel looked at him incredulously. "Don't you think I've already thought of that? What did you think I meant when I said I'd do anything to make this right? Of course I'll marry Jennifer. It's the only thing to do."

Charles's expression softened with relief. "In that case,

we may be able to help them, really help them. Marriage always gives a girl respectability. No matter what the gossip is after that, people will construe it all as true love. You don't doubt that Jennifer will accept? I understand she can be pretty stubborn."

Gabriel smiled, but the expression didn't reach his eyes. "Jennifer will marry me, if I have to drag her down the aisle. Don't laugh, Charles, it may come to that. The only thing Jennifer values more than her sisters is her own independence. It's not something she will give up lightly, but she will give it up." Gabriel grinned with determination. "By God, she will."

CHAPTER 21

GABRIEL KNOTTED HIS necktie tightly, then straightened it to perfection. A quick glance in the mirror indicated that he looked exactly as he wished to look: elegant, and in control. His black cutaway morning coat, a little more formal than his lounging suit, was in the height of fashion, and his starched white shirt with its new shorter collar displayed his tie to the best advantage. Finishing his costume with pearl-colored gloves, he put on his coat and headed for the waiting carriage.

It wasn't every day a man proposed, he thought to himself in amusement. Even though his proposal was a little outré, he wanted to make it as memorable as possible. Having to ask Jennifer to be his wife while she was in prison already assured that, but nevertheless he knew women set store by such things. If nothing else, he would try to look the part of a gallant groom and make the moment as romantic as circumstance would allow.

His smile increased as he sank back into the leather seat of the coach, thinking of his future. It was amazing how everything had changed. It was as if the entire world had slanted sideways, and he could see everything from a totally different viewpoint. Even after his meeting with

Charles, when he promised to ask Jennifer to wed, he'd thought the task would simply be one of duty and obligation. Yet a sense of promise had welled up inside him and wouldn't go away.

Jennifer as his wife. The very idea was exotic and thrilling. He knew now that what he'd said yesterday was the truth, a truth his heart had been trying to tell him for weeks. He loved her—it was as simple and as complicated as that. How and when it had happened, he wasn't certain, but even from that first glimpse of her, sitting in the parlor with her fried bangs, he must have loved her. He couldn't remember a time when he didn't.

Better than that was the feeling his upcoming wedding gave him. All that time when he thought he'd eventually marry Allison, he'd been unable to picture anything but a life of sameness and ennui. Whenever he had those disturbing thoughts he'd simply pushed them away, assuming all men felt that way at the prospect of losing their beloved bachelorhood. But marrying Jennifer was a whole different vision. She tormented him, teased him, made incredible love to him, infuriated him—but never bored him. To his delight, he found he couldn't wait to get to the altar and make her, finally, his own.

The carriage rumbled to a halt at his mother's house. Gabriel grinned to himself as he thought of her reaction, then he walked up the steps, unable to forget how differently they'd both felt just a short time ago.

"Sir?" James stared at him in astonishment, trying to cover a yawn. He glanced down at the still gray street, where dawn had barely broken, then back to Gabriel. "Come in! I don't think your mother was expecting you . . ."

"She isn't. It's a surprise." Gabriel chuckled. "Tell her to come down directly, I haven't got all day. I have to go get engaged."

"I beg pardon, sir?" James looked as if he couldn't possibly have heard right.

Gabriel laughed once more, and the servant, for the first time Gabriel could remember, began to laugh with him. The two of them guffawed, and James actually slapped his back.

"A fine joke, sir! The madam will appreciate—"

"No joke," Gabriel assured him when he could speak. "Hurry, man. Tell her I need to see her. My future bride's in prison, and I have to help get her out. Now."

The servant looked shocked, then rushed up the steps. Gabriel whistled, feeling like nothing could stand in his way. For once, the pictures of his father didn't trouble him, and he experienced a pang of sorrow that the old man couldn't be here today. Somehow, he knew he'd approve of Jennifer, in spite of her background, which was an amazing thought indeed.

Mary Forester dashed into the room, still wrapping her dressing gown around her slender frame. Her soft white hair was in charming disarray, and she stared at her son as if to ascertain his sanity. "James just woke me. Gabriel, is it true—"

"Absolutely." Gabriel laughed. "I'm asking Jennifer to marry me today."

All slumber left Mary's gaze and she threw herself at her son, enveloping him in her embrace. "Oh, Gabriel, that's wonderful! You've made me so happy! Jennifer is so perfect for you. Eve and I thought we'd practically have to hit you over the head, but for you to discover it all on your own—"

"Wait a minute. You and Eve?" Gabriel stepped back and held his mother at arm's length.

"Never mind all that," Mary said quickly. "I'll get you grandmother's ring. Jennifer will love it, it's so beautiful. Oh, Gabriel, I'm so proud of you! You really are the white knight, riding in to her rescue. It is so romantic!"

Tears glistened in her eyes. Gabriel held her in his arms, while Mary returned his embrace tightly. For the first time, he fully experienced the depth of his mother's love, and found it incredible. She was truly happy for him.

"I'm such an old fool, it's just you've made me so happy." Mary finally broke away, then reached into her pocket for a handkerchief. She wiped her eyes, then smiled at her son. "When will you wed?"

"As soon as possible," Gabriel said. "I have to legitimize our relationship before the papers destroy the girls, so the sooner, the better. Perhaps on Christmas."

"That would be lovely," Mary agreed, her eyes shining. A momentary thought seemed to stop her and she looked at her son closely. "Gabriel, is that the only reason you want to wed? To do the right thing by Jennifer?"

Gabriel smiled at her reassuringly. "No. Even I'm not that noble. I really do care for her. Somehow I didn't realize it before, but I'm in love with Jennifer Appleton. I think I always have been."

"That's wonderful!" Mary hugged him again, nearly dancing him around the room. "Oh, Gabriel, if you only knew how long I've waited for this! You will, of course, live at your house. It will be so much easier, and convenient for the girls. Jennifer could still continue to work with her sisters, since it's just across town. I am so happy!"

Gabriel's smile faded, replaced by a small frown. "Mother, you don't think I will allow Jennifer to continue her work after this? I couldn't possibly permit my wife to be a spiritualist."

Mary stared at him incredulously. "Why ever not, Gabriel? That is an important part of Jennifer's life, and her family will still need the money. Even with our combined resources, it will be difficult to finance two other sisters of marriageable age, and their aunt."

"We'll find a way," Gabriel said firmly. "Mother, I am firm on this. Especially after today, Jennifer is out of the séance business. I will not have my wife pretending to summon ghosts back from the dead. It is all a farce, and a cruel one at that. Although I was willing to testify on her behalf that she didn't intentionally harm her clients, I haven't changed my mind about this. It is still wrong, and I will not support it."

The light seemed to have gone out of Mary's eyes, and she stared at her son sadly. "Have you discussed this with Jennifer?"

"No, but I will. Jennifer will agree—she won't have any other choice. As my wife, she'll have to obey me, like it or not."

Gabriel was flushed with indignation, his jaw set firmly. Mary studied him for a long moment, then nodded and patted the sofa. "Gabriel, sit down a moment. I think it's time I told you something."

Reluctantly, Gabriel sank down onto the couch, and his mother took her place beside him. She put her small hand over his. "When I went to see Jennifer, my life was worth nothing to me. You see, I had a tremendous amount of guilt, because I had so quickly fallen in love with another man after your father's passing. Robert had always been a good friend, and it seemed natural to turn to him in my sorrow, yet it quickly became something deeper. I didn't plan it, and I didn't want it to happen. Can you understand?"

Gabriel nodded. "Unfortunately, I know exactly how you feel."

Mary smiled tremulously, then continued. "I didn't know what to think, or how to feel. To marry Robert would have been wrong, I felt, in the eyes of so many, including you. Yet to live without him, to spend my old age alone, hearing nothing but the ticking of the clock, and crying at your father's portrait, was something I just couldn't bear. One particularly terrible night, I took an overdose of my arthritis medication. I thought if I just went to sleep and God took me, it would end everyone's troubles."

Gabriel stared at his mother in horror. "Then you really did try to—"

"Yes." His mother wiped her eyes quickly, then continued firmly. "I know what you must think of me, but please try to understand. I was desperate. I had no one I could talk to. Even my priest told me I should remain true to my husband's memory, and that anything else would be sinful. To live without Robert was to live without happiness, and I didn't want to do that."

Mary stifled a sob, then pressed the handkerchief again to her face. Gabriel felt a deepening sense of shame that his mother had had to face this alone. "Go on, dear," he gently encouraged her.

"When I went to see Jennifer, I was at my most desperate hour. The medication, you see, hadn't done anything other than make me ill, and Doctor Fielding lectured me very sternly. Jennifer was my last hope. When she appeared to summon your father's ghost, and gave me permission to follow my heart, it was as if the weight of the world lifted. Jennifer and her sisters made me see that neither God nor your father wanted me to be miserable. She gave me the strength to make the right decision. She let me choose joy."

Gabriel stared at his mother in astonishment. "Then you are saying . . ."

"Gabriel, I know your father never really appeared to me as a real ghost, but I have never doubted that he is with me and, through Jennifer, he made his wishes known. Yet what the girls gave me was worth so much more than a ghost sighting. I can't put a price tag on it. They gave me back my life, dear."

Gabriel stared at his mother, speechless. The enormity of her confession weighed on him, and he didn't know how to react. Everything in his intellect told him that he should reject all this—everything in his heart told him to stay open-minded. As if understanding his dilemma, his mother rose.

"I'll go get the ring. Just think about what I've said, dear. And if you truly love Jennifer, you'll love her for what she is, and not try to change her. No marriage ever succeeded that way. If Jennifer wants to give up the spiritualism herself, that's one thing. For you to force her, that's another."

His mother left the room, leaving Gabriel deep in thought.

"I DON'T CARE if she's sleeping. Wake her up."

Charles tossed his gloves aside, and growled at the humble housekeeper. The woman scampered to do his bidding, while he paced the room in agitation.

Allison had to withdraw her complaint. Charles had thought about it all night. Everything changed when Gabriel announced he would marry Jennifer. Somehow, he had to make his sister see that.

Allison appeared, obviously annoyed at being awakened so early. "What are you doing here? Why aren't you genuflecting at the alter of the Appletons?" She flopped onto a chair and ordered her coffee.

Charles gazed at his sister with a mixture of anger and pity. She was such a pretty thing, and hid her passionate nature beneath a cool facade. He remembered her disappointment a little over a year ago when she'd fallen in love with an improper man, and her parents had had to dissuade her. It was little wonder that she was so determined now, with so much at stake.

"Allison, I know you are unhappy that I've chosen to represent the Appletons, but I have no other choice. What you're doing is wrong, and morally, I have to stop you."

"Morally?" His sister sent him a superior look. "Why

don't you examine your own morals, brother dear? The real reason that you want to represent the girls is that you're attracted to that bluestocking Winifred. Why don't you just admit it and get it over with?"

Charles stared at her in astonishment. "Wherever would you get such a ridiculous idea?"

"It's written all over the both of you. Don't try to pretend, Charles, there is no point. So unless you have anything else to say to me, it is quite early and I haven't had my breakfast yet."

The maid brought coffee and sweet rolls and placed them beside the young woman. Charles's outrage increased as he thought of the Appletons in their jail cell this morning, all because of Allison. He faced her directly, stepping between her and her breakfast.

"Allison, you must drop the charges against Jennifer. Don't you see that you'll only face public humiliation if you continue this farce? The papers have already begun to question your role in all this. Should you continue, you will be a laughingstock."

She paled a little at that, but calmly reached around him and helped herself to a roll. "I am not worried, brother. You see, the church is on my side. These women should have been stopped long ago. What they are doing is illegal and wrong. No one can fault me for seeing that they get their just reward."

"Why don't you just admit the real reason you're doing this?" Charles snarled, unable to help himself. He hauled his sister to her feet, startling her out of her composure. "You are jealous that Gabriel has fallen in love with Jennifer! My God, woman, don't you realize how this will look? When the whole story gets out, you won't be able to hold your head up again!"

Allison stared at her brother in shock. "Love! Gabriel doesn't love her. He can't love her! Jennifer Appleton is a charlatan, a fraud, and a fake! A gentleman like Gabriel cannot possibly love a woman like that. I know it!"

Charles released her, giving her a sympathetic look. "Allison, please, you must listen to me. I know Gabriel gave you reason to think he cared for you, and that he would one day marry you. Gabriel knows this as well, and feels terribly guilty where you're concerned. But that doesn't change anything. Gabriel is in love with Jennifer, and he's going to ask her to marry him. Today."

"What?" It was Allison's turn to look stunned. Slowly, she lowered herself back into her seat. "No, you are wrong, you must be wrong. Gabriel would never—"

"Allison," Charles cut her off. "I saw him last night. He has every intention of getting his grandmother's ring and asking Jennifer to be his wife. It will happen today."

"My God." Allison put aside the sweet roll, obviously no longer hungry. She held her stomach as if it hurt, and stared up at her brother. "Are you really so certain?"

"Yes." Charles's voice was softer. "Gabriel wants to do the right thing, and he has to marry her now. I'm sorry. I know you love him—"

"Love?" Allison looked at Charles and laughed. "I don't love Gabriel. I never did."

"What? Do you mean—"

Allison sighed. "I know how it appears, but I've never loved anyone since Miguel. I was willing to marry Gabriel because that's what everyone wanted, but it wasn't love."

Charles breathed a sigh of relief. "Then even more so, you must withdraw the complaint. You have to let the girls go free."

"I think not," Allison said indignantly. When Charles looked at her in confusion, she struggled to explain. "Why should I? So Jennifer and Gabriel can run off and marry, and be happy? What about me, what they did to me? They made a fool out of me, and they will pay . . ."

To his amazement, his sister began to weep. Charles

felt a momentary helplessness. He and Allison had never been close, and he'd never seen her cry. Now he acted on instinct and stood beside her awkwardly, patting her back as she sobbed. When the tears subsided, he tilted her face up to his.

"Allison, I know you're angry, but this course of action will only hurt you. Think of yourself now. You can't win here. The Appletons have the suffragettes on their side, the Vanderbilts, even the McBrides. If you become tainted by this scandal, you will never find a husband. Your own life will be over."

Allison seemed to hear him for the first time. "Is that what you truly think will happen?"

Charles nodded. "Without a doubt. When word of the engagement leaks out, your motives will be ridiculously apparent. Even our parents will be publicly embarrassed. No man will want to be involved with you, let alone make you his wife. Your name will forever be associated with scandal. Allison, you can't do this. Please, for your own sake, withdraw the complaint."

Mortified, his sister rose to her feet. "Charles, I think you are right. My God, if the Billings got hold of this—"

"We will all help you. Everyone will make it seem that Gabriel asked you to wed, and you refused him. Only then did he, out of duty, turn to Jennifer. You can go to Europe for the summer, let the talk die down. By the time you come back, it will be over. If you help the girls now, they will help you save face, I know it. Please, Allison."

"Yes," she whispered, putting her head in her hands. Than she looked up at him, and her expression was filled with a dawning horror and understanding. "Why didn't I see this? Charles, you are right. Yes, I will withdraw! Tell me what I need to do."

Immense relief flooded through him. Charles took his sister into his arms. "You leave everything to me. I'll make it all as painless as possible, I promise."

Jennifer awoke in the cell, every inch of her body aching. She and her sisters had refused to don prison garb to sleep, and her stays had cut unmercifully into her flesh during the night. Groaning, she sat upright, rubbing her eyes as the guard approached.

"I've got a gentleman here to see you, Miss Appleton." The older man slipped the keys into the door, trying to hush every possible sound so that Winifred and Penelope wouldn't awaken. "He says it's important."

Jennifer nodded, then rose painfully to her feet. She slipped into her boots, and smoothed back her hair, grateful that she hadn't let Penelope talk her into one of those false hairpieces that were so popular now. Her own hair was in disarray, and she could just picture a roll of curls dangling down her back by a thread.

The guard let her into the visitors' room, and all thoughts of physical discomfort left when she saw the man sitting there. "Gabriel!" she squealed, and rushed into his arms. "What are you doing here so early?"

She pressed up against him, feeling the strength of his body, the warmth of his closeness. He smelled good, like shaving lotion and soap, and his arms held her tightly, making her feel safe. She never felt so much at home as when she was in this man's arms, and she reveled in that knowledge.

Gabriel chuckled, then gradually stepped back and held her at arm's length. His normally serious face looked concerned, and his gaze raked her from her head to her feet.

"Are you all right, sweet Jenny? Have they been treating you all right? Have you eaten—"

"Yes, I'm fine." Jennifer laughed. "If I had any more to eat, I'd be ten pounds overweight. We've gotten so many baskets of food and fruit that we're swimming in it. Penelope donated some of the baskets to the poor yesterday, there were that many. Don't worry, we're fine." She blushed a little when she saw his fine clothes, and glanced ruefully down at her own ruined costume. "Although I don't look as pretty and fresh as you do. Please forgive my dress. Prison is lacking in some respects."

"Jenny, I'm not worried about your dress." For the first time since she could remember, Gabriel looked awkward and ill at ease. His starched collar seemed to annoy him, for he pulled at it repeatedly, even though he was very used to formal clothes, and his suit seemed to fit him stiffly. "Please, sit down."

Growing concerned, Jennifer obeyed him and sank down onto the seat. She folded her hands and waited patiently as he paced the cell, seeming more determined to wear a hole in the floor than to tell her what was on his mind. Finally, he turned to her quickly, and she saw a multitude of emotions on his face: determination, relief, happiness, and confusion.

"Jenny, my sweet Jenny. I've come to several startling conclusions in the past few days. Ever since I met you, I've been unable to get you out of my mind. You've haunted me more than any fictitious ghost you've ever conjured. You've teased me, tortured me, laughed at me, and made love to me with a passion that left me dazed. I meant what I said yesterday—I am terribly, passionately in love with you."

Jennifer's emotions soared and she leaned closer to him, her hands braced on the seat. But her hopes were dashed with his next words.

"I've tried hard not to love you—the good Lord knows you are not the perfect woman for me. You are a spiritualist, for God's sake, and a charlatan at that. You know how I feel about all this—I've certainly expressed it often enough. You and your sisters have flouted society, made spectacles of yourselves at the stock market, and are rumored to be everything from modern-day witches to street tarts."

Gabriel stopped his pacing and stared at her, as if trying to make sense of all this himself. When Jennifer didn't offer assistance, he continued raggedly.

"I tried to avoid you and forget you, but to no avail. You were always there, whether physically or in my mind. Now you and your sisters are in dire danger of becoming outcasts. I am partially responsible for that, and I admit my role in all that has passed. Even if you and the girls are released, people will talk, and Penelope's chances of making a good match are null. Winifred's ambitions will be in jeopardy, and as for you—"

Jennifer looked at him expectantly.

"You know no gentleman will ask you to wed. So, after giving the matter much thought, I plan to follow through on my offer. You must know that the spiritualism has to stop, that you cannot go back to your previous life. So there is but one thing to do." He dropped to his knee and dug into his pocket. Jennifer stared in disbelief as he withdrew a small velvet box and popped the lid. Inside, a beautiful sapphire gleamed. "Jennifer Appleton," Gabriel asked, "will you be my wife?"

CHAPTER 22

GABRIEL WAITED IN breathless anticipation as Jennifer stared at the ring, although he was certain what her response would be. She really hadn't any other choice. Everything he'd said was true, and he was being as honest as possible. Only marriage could avert certain disaster, for herself as well as her family. Although he wished his proposal could be made under other circumstances, Gabriel knew he had to lay the groundwork as accurately as possible. Jennifer had to give up her role as voodoo priestess, and live a normal, wedded life.

She smiled at him, and only then did he notice the sadness in her eyes. "It is beautiful," she breathed, reverently touching the box. Regretfully, she closed the lid and handed it back to him. "I'm sorry, Gabriel, but I cannot accept. Thank you for your offer."

Gabriel stared at her in astonishment. "Why? What do you mean you can't? I don't understand—"

Jennifer laid her hand on his shoulder, her touch feather-light and comforting. "Gabriel, I appreciate what you're trying to do. You are and always have been a gentleman. But a marriage can't be built on obligation and duty. You don't really love me, and can't accept me, which are one and the same thing. I know the stain that will be on my name, and I know what a struggle it will be to get out from under this mess, but I can't let you marry me to avoid scandal. I am honored, but I truly cannot accept under the circumstances."

Gabriel stared at the closed box in his hand in confusion. "But you must! It is the only thing to do now . . ."

"Gabriel, tell me honestly. Have you ever come to terms with who and what I am? You don't have to answer, I see it in your face. You would be embarrassed every time someone brought up my past, or when someone sought my counsel. Especially now, after what happened with Mrs. Hawthorne. Don't you see? I really was able to help her! I can't ignore that, or pretend to be something other than what I am. Don't worry about us—the Appletons have always pulled through, and somehow we will again. But I want you to know I am beholden to you for what you've done, and what you've offered to do."

Before he could reply, the door burst open. Gabriel got quickly to his feet, brushing at his trousers, while Charles wrapped his arms around him in joy. Astonished, Gabriel couldn't speak for a moment, enveloped in his friend's bear hug. If Charles realized he was interrupting anything of importance, he didn't show it.

"Gabe! Great news! Allison has agreed to withdraw the complaint! Isn't that wonderful!"

"Wonderful." Gabriel could barely squeeze a reply out, Charles hugged him so fiercely. His friend released him a moment later, then turned to Jennifer, giving her a similar hug, which earned a scowl from Gabriel.

"Charles, that is incredible news! Are you certain?" Jennifer gasped.

"Yes, she is here with me now. She is speaking to the desk clerk. We should have this whole misfortune cleared up this morning. Miss Appleton, you must allow my apologies again for any discomfort afforded you or your family. Allison is truly sorry, and will do everything she can to make it up to you. I'll explain everything later. Gabriel, we may need your assistance if you're available."

"In a moment," Gabriel said. Charles looked curiously at him and saw the box he clutched in his hand. For the first time, he seemed to realize that his friend was replying rather stiffly, and was not in good spirits at all. Embarrassed, Charles correctly guessed what was taking place, and sheepishly exited.

Gabriel turned back to Jennifer, and replaced the box in his coat. She rose, extending her hand, but he refused to take it. Disappointment and pain lanced through him, and his heart felt as if it had torn in two.

"Gabriel, even more so now, you are released from any obligation. I hope you understand—"

"I think I understand perfectly," he said coldly. "The fact is, miss, your spiritual activities and notoriety are more important to you than I am. I guess the thought of a real home life, with children and family, isn't enough for you. I understand that, even while I deplore it, and only wonder why you encouraged me. If it was to add another feather to your bonnet, I applaud you. You have mine. Good day, Miss Appleton. I'm sorry to have inconvenienced you with my clumsy proposal. May you be happy in the life you have chosen."

"Gabriel!" Jennifer cried as he slammed the door behind him and was gone.

JENNIFER COMPOSED HERSELF as the guard waited patiently outside. Her heart felt as if it were breaking. Even though she knew she had done the right thing, that Gabriel really couldn't accept her for herself and to wed him under such circumstances would be disaster, she didn't feel good about the whole encounter. Why did everything have to be so hard? Why couldn't she just fall in love and marry, then live happily ever after like the girls in the fairy tales?

Because fairy-tale princesses aren't tarot card readers, or séance mediums, she reminded herself. And real life didn't have white knights to rescue damsels in distress. Jennifer sniffled back tears, trying to look normal as the guard opened the door.

"They'll be wanting you out front, miss. Something about the charges being dropped. I can give you another minute if you need it."

Jennifer wiped the wetness from her face and smiled gratefully at the man. She wondered how much he'd overheard. "That's all right. I'll be fine." She straightened her dress, then followed him out into the main lobby, where chaos reigned.

The room was filled with people, all talking excitedly at once. Thankfully, she didn't see Gabriel. Reporters waved notebooks, the desk clerk argued loudly, Charles was speaking with the chief of police, and Aunt Eve stood in the corner with Mary Forester, looking bewildered. Winifred and Penelope appeared ecstatic, and were busily filling out forms. When Jennifer entered the room, she was bombarded by the press.

"Miss Appleton, what do you think of the charges being dropped?"

"Was Miss Howe pressured by anyone?"

"Will you be going back to performing séance rituals?"

"Have you girls ever truly seen a ghost?"

Jennifer shrank back from the exploding lights. With as much dignity as she could muster, she answered the reporters calmly.

"We have done nothing wrong. Miss Howe's withdrawal of her complaint proves just that."

The reporters all scribbled furiously in their notepads, and fired more questions. Jennifer answered them in the same resigned voice, until finally, the police chief waved his beefy hand.

"All right, lads, that's enough. Miss Appleton has some papers to complete. Clear the room."

The reporters grumbled and left, most of them more than satisfied with the firsthand scoop. Jennifer joined her sisters, who hugged her enthusiastically.

"Isn't it wonderful? Allison withdrew," Penelope said cheerfully. "We won't have to go to court after all, although I was dying to wear my new winter velvet. I thought it would look nice for the papers."

Winifred stared at Jennifer, then spoke sharply to Penelope. "I don't think Jenny is interested in hearing about your dress. And just because we don't have to go to court, I think this is far from over. Unfortunately, there is a good chance that the scandal will ruin us. When word gets out that we've been jailed, no one will want anything to do with us. I'm afraid the worst of our troubles are still ahead."

Penelope pooh-poohed her words, but Jennifer and Winifred exchanged glances, both of them knowing that Winifred was right. They would be tried before a real jury of their peers: society. And neither had any doubt as to the outcome.

When Jennifer, Winifred, and Penelope returned home, they couldn't dissuade Aunt Eve from ordering hot baths immediately, and having a huge breakfast prepared. All three girls tried to tell Eve that they had been well fed and cared for, but poor Aunt Eve obviously envisioned her doves as being tortured in prison and wouldn't hear of anything other than pampering them.

"I've been so worried about you! Good heavens, cooped up like ruffians in that horrible prison! I couldn't sleep a wink last night. All I could picture was my little lambs, locked away like street trash! I'm so glad you're home."

Jennifer smiled wanly, finishing her pancakes as her hair dried by the fire. It did feel good to be home again, among her own familiar comforts, but she felt more than a little guilty where her aunt was concerned. She and Winnie had again expressed their apologies, which Eve simply brushed aside, but hearing that the old woman had spent a sleepless night on their behalf didn't help much.

The restless ache in her heart didn't subside as the day wore on. Winifred buried herself in law briefs, delighted that the police chief had let her take a mountain of old case histories as long as she returned them within the week. Enthralled with reading about real-life convictions, she was unapproachable for the better part of the day.

Penelope primped and played with her dresses and her perfumes, glad to be back among her own things. She had felt their stay in the jail was simply an adventure, and she refused to believe any of Winifred's dire warnings. Penelope was sure everything would sort itself out, and she didn't tire her mind in thinking about any other possibility.

Finding no refuge in her sister's cheerful presence, Jennifer took a book up to her room and tried to distract herself, but the persistent heaviness in her heart would not leave her. Finally, she gave into everything churning inside of her and flung herself onto the bed, crying her heart out.

A timid knock sounded on the door a few minutes later. Jennifer quickly straightened, then wiped her face, not wanting to worry anyone. "Come in," she called, expecting to see Penelope. Instead, Aunt Eve entered the room, carrying a pot of tea and two china cups.

"I thought you might want a little something," her aunt said, softly setting the tray on the table and pouring out a hot cup. "It always seems to help me."

"Thank you, Auntie." Jennifer choked back tears, then

sipped the steaming brew. The tea was difficult to swallow at first, but gradually she managed and found that it did help.

Aunt Eve poured her own cup and the two women, one old, the other young, sat side by side. Jennifer tried to retain her composure, but when her aunt put her hand comfortingly on her back, Jennifer broke. Sobs wracked her, and the older woman held her tightly.

"That's right, my dear, get it out. It isn't good to hold so much pain inside."

"Auntie, I feel so wretched!" Jennifer exclaimed, turning into the older woman's shoulder. Her aunt felt comforting, and smelled good, like lavender. Her lace collar scratched Jennifer's face, but even that was reassuring, reminding her that some things really didn't change. For a moment, Jennifer thought of her mother, a memory she had successfully buried because it was simply too painful. Now, she realized, she missed her terribly. "I know you wanted me to marry Gabriel, but I just couldn't. Auntie, he doesn't love me the way . . . a husband should," she continued, wiping fiercely at her eyes. "Dear heaven, if I could just stop crying!"

"It's all right, dear. It just amazes me how little the world has changed."

There was an odd wisdom in her aunt's voice, and for all the times she'd appeared befuddled, she didn't seem that way at all now. Jennifer lifted her face and tried to explain.

"He can't accept me, really accept me," she continued. "I was so hoping that eventually he would! But he only asked me to marry him out of duty. I am not the kind of woman Gabriel really wants."

"I see," Aunt Eve said softly, smoothing the hair from Jennifer's face. "So you think he feels nothing for you? That he was only being noble, asking you to wed?"

Jennifer thought for a moment. "I think he does care for me," she said slowly. "But I want more than that. He hates what I do, and would always feel embarrassed by it. I know it must have come as a shock to you as well, to know that we were really . . . what I mean is—"

"Spiritualists," Eve said it for her.

"Yes," Jennifer breathed. "I don't expect him to accept all of that completely, but I don't know what he thinks we should have done. We needed the money: It was as simple as that."

Eve nodded quietly. "Men like Gabriel who are born to a certain amount of wealth never truly grasp what it is like to be hungry. I have to admit, I didn't either until after your uncle died. Jenny, I have watched you since you were a little girl. You always had talent and ability, and you were a survivor. You could easily have knuckled under, with the weight of responsibility that fell on your shoulders, but you didn't do that. You used your talent, and found a way to help all of us. Surely Gabriel can't fault you for that."

Jennifer sighed. "I should think not, but I don't believe he really understands. How could he?"

Eve smiled softly. "I think your Gabriel has more character than you give him credit for. Give him time, my dear, and he'll come around. There are always compromises, when two people really care for each other. And this conversation has shown me one thing."

"What's that?" Jennifer looked at her fondly.

"That you are certainly in love with Gabriel. Otherwise his opinion wouldn't matter to you in the least."

Jennifer smiled, then wiped her face clear of tears. When she looked up, she saw her aunt watching her with a kindness and knowledge that perplexed her. A sudden, disturbing thought came to her and she had to know the truth. "Aunt Eve, did you know all of this all along? About Gabriel and the séances, I mean?"

Eve smiled, her dim eyes brightening with pleasure. "Well, of course, my dear. Sometimes it's rather nice to be taken for old and senile." When Jennifer looked at her in astonishment, her aunt laughed softly in a conspiratorial manner. "You can get away with murder."

CHAPTER 23

"ARE YOU SURE? There aren't any other postings for us?" Penelope practically scolded the mail boy, rummaging through the few pitiful letters that had arrived at the door.

The young lad scuffed the curb, then turned soulful eyes toward the beautiful woman. "Sorry, miss, but that's all there is. I asked 'specially, like you said, but the postman said that's it. There's one for you, though," the boy said hopefully, as if that would make it all right.

"I see. Thank you." Penelope pressed a coin in the boy's hand, then reentered the house with as much dignity as she could. Once inside, away from prying eyes on the street, she glanced at the letter addressed to her.

It was expensive stationery, creamy white and smooth to the touch. Penelope frowned as she examined the scrawling hand, but the writing was only vaguely familiar. Eagerly, she tore the missive open, hoping it was an invitation to a ball or a simple dance, but when she saw the contents, her heart squeezed painfully.

"My Dear Miss Appleton," it began. "I was very sorry to hear about your misadventure. What a terrible thing, to send three young ladies to jail! The New York police must have very little to do these days.

"Unfortunately, I must withdraw my invitation to dine with you on Thursday at the Hamiltons'. I'm sure you understand that it would be wrong for me to continue to see you under the present circumstances. It isn't myself that I am concerned for, but I have to think of my daughter, and what a scandal would do to her. I am truly sorry, and wish you only the best . . ."

It was signed, "James McBride." Penelope felt her hands begin to tremble and she cried out sharply. Tears started, almost of their own accord, and she stared through blurred eyes at the paper, unable to believe what she was reading.

"Dear! Whatever is the matter?" Aunt Eve came to her side and Penelope thrust the missive into her dress.

"Nothing," Penelope said, determinedly wiping her face. When Eve frowned, Penelope simply pointed to the other envelope the post boy had brought. "I was just disappointed that we didn't get any other mail. We haven't received an invitation in weeks, not to a winter dinner, a ball, or even a plain old gathering. I can't believe it!"

The parrot squawked in complaint, and the cat purred, wandering beneath the cage restlessly. Winifred looked up from the fireplace, where she sat with Charles Howe.

"Penelope, what did you think was going to happen? Did you really assume society would just forget everything, after our incarceration and the resulting scandal? Unfortunately, while Allison withdrew her formal complaint, she has been very vocal about attacking us publicly. The suffragettes, once sympathetic to us, have turned away, as have the church and the women's groups."

Charles blushed at the mention of his sister. "I am deeply sorry about Allison, but what Winifred says is true. In spite of my warnings, she is still spreading gossip about you girls, more to appease her own ego than anything else. She can't find it in her heart to forgive Gabriel for what she considers his betrayal, and has made you girls the scapegoats."

"It's nothing that we didn't expect," Jennifer said, folding the paper. She smiled at Charles, pleased that since their jailing, he had become a frequent visitor. Part of it was to show his support for the girls, since his sister was determined to destroy them, but Jennifer hoped Winifred was also part of the reason.

"Actually, it is worse than we anticipated," Jennifer said. "Listen to this: 'New Revelations About Appleton Girls: Church calls Jennifer Appleton the Mother of Evil.'"

"Such nonsense!" Eve said emphatically. "Why, I told the ladies at the Women's Church Society that they could just do without my embroidery if they continued to blaspheme you."

"My mother is also trying to influence her sewing circle and Ladies' Association," Charles said quickly, clearly eager to make amends for his sister. "She is making sure that any charitable works done by you girls, monies you've donated, and food that you've given to the poor, gets proper credit."

"And the police chief is doing his best to squelch any legal gossip that comes up," Winifred noted. "But I have to admit, none of this is really having much of an impact. Everything I feared has come to pass. Good women cross the street when they see us. Their daughters are afraid to acknowledge us, even if they wanted to, and their sons avoid us like the plague. Socially, the Appletons are ruined."

There was a long pause after Winifred's dire words. Penelope looked around the room, then burst into tears, truly despondent. Jennifer rose and stood beside her, stroking her head and attempting to comfort her, but Penelope was beside herself.

"We'll never get back in! We are destroyed! Who will court me?" Penelope asked plaintively. "None of the good men would dare defy everyone to seek me out! I'll be a spinster forever!"

Penelope dashed out of the room and ran upstairs. They could hear the pathetic tap of her little boots as she reached her room, then slammed the door shut. Jennifer sighed, then looked up at her aunt, and saw the reality that she'd been trying to hide from: They really were ruined. Not just for suitors, as Penelope said, but in every way. Business had fallen off sharply, and Jennifer knew the reason. People were starting to question whether séances and card readings really were the work of the devil. As ridiculous as that assumption was, it was enough to scare prospective customers.

Jennifer also worried about Winifred. Although she had been accepted into law school, aside from the question of funds, her future looked bleak. What client would put his legal future in the hands of a scandalous woman? Although Jennifer was deeply grateful for Charles's loyalty, and that he tried to involve Winifred in his own cases to keep her active mind busy, Jennifer knew that playing second fiddle to his first would never be enough for her intelligent sister.

For the first time ever, Jennifer was truly frightened. Every door seemed closed to them, and potential disaster lay ahead. More than once she had toyed with the idea of seeing Gabriel, begging him to marry her, only so she would no longer be a burden to the family, but she realized that wasn't really an answer. Gabriel, understandably, hadn't called on them. Charles had intimated that Gabriel was still very hurt, and was convinced that Jennifer had refused him because she enjoyed her notoriety more than a life with him. Yet even if she could convince him now, and if she were safely wed, what about the rest of them?

To Jennifer's surprise, Aunt Eve stood up and shook a finger at them. "You girls have to stand up for yourselves now, and not give in to this. You'll have to be the examples, and show your sister the way. You must accept any invitation that comes your way, look and dress your best, publicize your good deeds, and continue to let those who love you help. Wallowing in self-pity won't do anything. Mildred Adams is still coming, and she will be here in a few days. If you girls impress her sufficiently, she will put her stamp of approval on you. I, for one, will do everything I can to make that happen."

Jennifer looked at her aunt and a huge smile spread over her face. Relief poured through her as a plan of action came to her mind. "Yes, I'd almost forgotten! I think Auntie's right!" She turned excitedly to her sister. "We've agreed to give Mildred a spiritual session. Don't worry, Auntie, we won't do anything rash. We'll simply have to make it the best experience she's ever had!"

Charles shifted uncomfortably in his chair. Apparently, the idea of a séance didn't hold much appeal for him. "I think it might be better for you to wash your hands of the whole spiritual business at this point. It seems only to associate you with trouble. Gabriel, also, will never understand and only think his conjecture was right. Perhaps you should give it all up, and let the gossip die down."

"Yes, but then how do we make a living?" Jennifer cried. "Our stock purchases have done well, but recently, the market's taken a turn for the worse. If we abandon our readings, then what do we do? Accept positions as governesses and companions—if anyone would even hire us at this point?"

"That won't help Penelope much," Winifred pointed out. "That will put our station just above the serving class. No man would take her seriously as a marital prospect."

"And I don't know if Gabriel will ever forgive me,"

Jennifer said pointedly. "I can't allow us to become bankrupt because of his disapproval."

Winifred nodded reluctantly. Even Charles and Aunt Eve had to accede the point, and no one had a better suggestion. Jennifer continued softly, "Besides, if we abandon our work now, we admit defeat. We are, in fact, saying that the old biddies are right, and that we are engaged in something evil. Moreover, after what happened with Mrs. Hawthorne, I think I really am starting to develop some kind of special talent. I have to explore that, and see where it goes."

"Jennifer is right," Aunt Eve said after a moment's thought. "The women will look to what you girls do. Unfortunately, much of the world's opinion is made up not of fact, but of perception. If you girls act guilty, they will assume you are. No, better to go on as you have and hold your heads high than to act like convicted witches." The older woman shuddered.

"Then it's decided. I'm going shopping to see if I can find some better props—ours are looking a little wretched. Winnie, why don't you think about adding some new harpsichord music, and ask Penny to do something with the paintings in the room, like make their eyes move."

"I can do something," Eve said determinedly. "I'm not as addled as you young misses thought. Perhaps I can volunteer my special tea. That will help with the mood, and my presence may lend legitimacy to what you're doing."

"Good," Jennifer said, surprised and touched at her aunt's suggestion, and her eagerness to help with their work. "We have to make spiritualism fashionable again," Jennifer continued. "Once we do that, we're fashionable as well."

Everyone nodded in agreement. Jennifer put on her cloak, then gave them a brave smile. It seemed they were back in business. And no one knew more than herself how important it was to make this séance a success.

ALONE IN HER room, Penelope withdrew the letter from her pocket and read it again. Slowly, the portent of James McBride's words sank in, and she understood what they meant with a frightening clarity.

It wasn't going to happen for her. Everything that she had wanted, everything that she had struggled for, was gone in a flash because the Appletons were now socially unacceptable.

Penelope sobbed like a brokenhearted little girl. She cried for the jewels she'd envisioned, for nice carriages and gorgeous gowns. She cried for the dreams of sumptuous banquet tables, laden with rich food, surrounded by splendidly gowned women and elegant men. She saw herself in that picture, surrounded by beauty and the kind of security that only real money could buy. The vision dissolved the same way the Irishman's words, smeared from her tears, ran off the letter.

It just wasn't fair. She'd done everything right; she knew it. James McBride was beginning to care for her. She knew he was close to proposing, had been talking lately of building a new mansion on Fifth, so it would be easier to dine with their friends. Although she'd only slipped out of the house a few times to see him, not sure Winifred and Jennifer would understand, she could tell that he was succumbing to her charms.

And she genuinely liked the man. James made her laugh, treated her like a princess, doted on her every whim. If sometimes she felt a little uneasy when he paraded her before his wealthy friends like another glittering bauble he'd purchased, well, she understood that. She had planned to marry him, to be secure with his money, and to help her sisters and Aunt Eve as well, for James had more than they could spend in ten lifetimes. It was her secret ambition, her way to help the family, and now it was all gone.

Sobbing bitterly, she barely heard Winifred's sharp footfall, or the door close behind her. When she looked up and saw her sister, she opened her arms, wanting solace from the kind of pain she'd never experienced in her young life.

"Dear, what is wrong? I knew it was something more than the lack of invitations. I could tell." Winifred sat beside her sister and smoothed her pale locks from her wet, red face.

"Here." Plaintively, Penelope thrust the envelope at her sister.

Winifred opened the letter, and as she read, her lips got tighter until it seemed she would almost have to pry them apart if she ever wished to speak again. When she finished, she folded the paper into a tiny piece, then tossed it aside as if it were nothing more than the morning rubbish.

"Penny, I'm so sorry. I know you'd been secretly seeing this man, and even though I dreaded it, I understood."

"You did?" Penelope sat up, wiping her face, looking astonished. "How did you know?"

A wan smile came to Winifred and she held her sister in her arms as if she were a child still. "I saw you with him at the ball and I guessed. But Penny, as disappointing as this must be, I'm sure you didn't love him, did you?"

Penelope shrugged, fresh tears starting. "I don't know. I mean, I liked him well enough. He was good to me." She turned her tear-streaked face toward her sister. "But don't you realize what this means? James had enough money for all of us! You wouldn't have had to worry about me anymore, and for once, I could have helped all of you! And now it will never happen!"

"I see." Winifred nodded, then smoothed her hand along Penelope's back as her sister sobbed. When she finished crying, Winifred handed her a handkerchief, even though she knew Penelope would never be without her own. "Now here. Dry your eyes. Dear, none of us would want you to make such a sacrifice on our behalf. Whatever made you think such a thing?"

Penelope sat upright, mopping her face with the linen. She put it aside and stared at her intelligent sister as if she were daft. "Winnie, you are the brains. We all know that. You will always figure out a way to survive, because God gave you that gift. Jenny is clever. Like a cat, she will land on her feet because she will make it so. But I . . ." She stared off toward the mirror, and automatically began to neaten her appearance. "I realized that my contribution would have to be this way. And I really thought it would work. Now, no man will want me."

"That's not true." Winifred sighed, shaking her head at her lovely sister. "Penny, you are so much more than your looks, and don't ever think that you aren't again. All of us would have been severely disappointed had you sold yourself to McBride, just for money."

"You would?" Penelope looked at her sister incredulously. "But you always wanted to help me make my debut, to marry a rich man. . . ."

"We've always wanted you to wed, because that's what you seemed to want. But above all, we want your happiness, and marriage to a man you don't love will never bring you that. And McBride doesn't love you. This letter proves that. Penny, you can do so much better. Even living with someone like . . . Lorenzo would bring you more happiness if you loved him."

Penelope thought of the poor grocer boy who stared at her with such intense devotion. "But . . . I would still be poor!"

Winifred smiled. "Yes, but if you were happy, you'd manage. We haven't been unhappy, and yet we are poor. It's true, money does solve some problems, but it creates some too. And marriage is the single most important decision you'll ever make. To chain yourself for eternity to a man who doesn't love you, and who you don't love, will only buy you misery, no matter how much money he has."

Penelope nodded. Looking up at her brilliant sister, she felt some of the pain ease from her soul, and she forced a smile. "Winnie, I think you're right. Even Charles and Gabriel have supported us through this. James couldn't think much of me at all to drop me this way. My God, what if we were married? He might even have divorced me, which would have ruined me entirely! How could I have been so stupid?"

"You weren't. You simply made the same mistake a lot of girls make. The fact that you realize it shows me something else." When Penelope looked at her questioningly, Winifred smiled softly. "You're growing up. It's not always fun, is it?"

"No," Penelope shook her head. "It's not fun at all."

"I know. But I'm proud of you."

"You are?"

"Yes. This was a hard lesson for you, and I know you'll pull through. Come, Aunt Eve made us a lemon cake to cheer us up, and we have some exciting plans to talk about. Mildred Adams is coming for a séance, and we have some wonderful ideas on how to make it a success. We really need your help, and want your ideas as well. The Appletons are a team, you know!"

Penelope straightened, and seemed to actually grow taller. She smiled, more genuinely this time, and followed Winifred toward the stairs. As she passed the rubbish can, she threw James McBride's letter into it, and never looked back.

IT WAS TWILIGHT by the time Jennifer headed home. Inside her shopping bag she carried a broad assortment of goodies designed to lend an even spookier flavor to the house. Now that Aunt Eve knew what they were doing, it was even easier to decorate, since they no longer had to dismantle everything before her return.

Excited, Jennifer thought about the contents of her sack. She'd bought purple curtains, believing as Poe did that there was something ominous about the color. In an art shop, she'd found plaster busts of Napoleon and other dead heroes, which would lend an "otherworld" look to the séance room. There were also cheap oil paintings of family ancestors, long forgotten in the war, some with eyes that simply begged to be cut out and replaced by Penelope's. There was a mynah bird, who, with his glossy black coat and ability to really speak, would give the parrot a run for his money and remind visitors of the creepy poem "The Raven." All in all, it would create an atmosphere not to be forgotten.

There was only one problem. There was something missing, the one special effect that would really hone in on the séance flavor and give it an authenticity that was lacking. Jennifer left her sack in the carriage, then crossed the street to a row of gloomy shops. She didn't really know what she was looking for, she just knew she'd feel it when it was discovered.

Most of the more fashionable stores on Broadway were closed. Jennifer had wandered from the main thoroughfare and found herself in an unfamiliar neighborhood. Peering down the dismal alleyway, she saw one dark window after another. Gaslights cast an eerie halo in the fog, and the rain-drenched streets looked like they ran with oily boot polish instead of water. Shuddering, she was just about to give up and go home when she saw a single light gleaming right in the middle of the row of stores.

It was a strange little shop, complete with dusty windows and dim lighting. A black candle burned in the window, and Jennifer noted the odd effect it created, reminding herself to look for similar tapers. The door was also black and featured a knocker in the shape of an old man's face. It stared back at her with a fierceness that startled her. Grinning, she pushed open the door, knowing this was the right place.

Inside was just as gloomy as outside. Jennifer saw the proprietor, a cackling old woman with flowing white hair who nodded in her direction, then went back to reading her book. Rows of herbs, unusual vials, and strange instruments graced the shelves before her, while beautiful stones, crystals, and incense were displayed on a table. There were brightly painted tiger cats from Africa, and horrid masks designed to ward off evil spirits. Gargoyles grinned wickedly from the corners, and tiny skeletons danced in celebration of a Spanish festival. Jennifer saw over a dozen items she could easily use, but a worn leather book caught her eye and seemed to call to her.

Nonsense! she told herself, but something would not let her pass the volume. Reluctantly, she touched the book, feeling the pebbly texture of the worn leather cover. There had been a lock on the outside, but the key was gone and to her surprise, it sprang open by itself. Jennifer idly turned the pages, finding them of good quality and embossed with gold. It appeared to be a book of enchantments, some of them ancient sounding, all of them melodic and charming.

A vision grew in Jennifer's mind. They could easily add a spell to their work, giving the séance a truly authentic flavor. Immediately, she could see herself reciting one of these chants, then falling under the spirit's power. The effect, she judged, would be marvelous.

"How much is this?" Jennifer put the book before the woman. Opening her change purse, she frowned as she saw her coins had dwindled drastically. The old women looked up as if annoyed to be disturbed, then shrugged.

"Whatever you want to pay. It is, after all, yours."

Jennifer stared at the woman curiously, but decided

that, as a business transaction, this was too good to be true. She plunked down the last of her coin, fully expecting the woman to tell her it wasn't enough. But the old lady simply cackled once more, scooped up the coins into a hand as gnarled as a tree root, then went back to her reading.

Astonished, Jennifer took the book and walked out of the shop. Some things, apparently, were just meant to be.

Outside, nightfall had settled on the city. Jennifer walked through the streets with her book, looking for the carriage, but belatedly realized she was lost. It was like being in a labyrinth, for every street she entered only seemed to take her farther away from anything familiar. Fear crept over her, and she nervously clutched her book, grateful that she'd left everything else safely in the carriage. Rough-looking people huddled in the corners, while a group of workmen gathered over a flaming barrel, warming their hands against the cold. Footsteps sounded behind her and Jennifer gathered her cloak tightly and hurried down the street. She had just reached the corner when she felt a hand on her shoulder. Panicking, she whirled, only to find Gabriel standing behind her.

"Oh, dear God, you scared me!" Her heart thudded wildly and she struggled to catch her breath. Inwardly, she had to admit that she was grateful to see him. Relief flooded through her, even though she could tell he wasn't at all happy to find her wandering the streets like this.

"What the hell are you doing here? Do you realize where you are? You're almost in the slums on Baxter. There's nothing here but drunks and prostitutes, no police—I was on my way back from visiting a customer, otherwise I wouldn't be here after dark!"

"I was shopping and got lost!" Jennifer cried defensively. She saw him glance down at her odd book, and she hid it behind her back, but her gesture came too late. The intelligence in his blue eyes gleamed in the darkness, and she knew he had fathomed the reason for her to be in such a location.

"Get into my carriage. I'll take you home." He practically carried her into the fine-looking coach waiting at the end of the street. The driver, obviously nervous to be in the neighborhood, displayed his buggy whip as a few street urchins shouted from the gutter. Jennifer saw a huge rat dart past and disappear into the wall of a tavern, while a grizzled-looking man eyed them speculatively from the corner. Shuddering, she gratefully did as Gabriel suggested.

Once inside, she turned to him, ridiculously happy to see him. He looked as elegant and handsome as ever, clad in a dark woolen coat and a top hat that gleamed even in the dim light. He removed the hat immediately, due to her presence, and she wanted to run her fingers through his dark silky hair, and to touch the rugged edge of his jaw, watching it soften into a smile. She did neither. "You don't have to take me home. My carriage is somewhere near Broadway."

"Broadway!" Gabriel looked at her as if she were insane. "You're a good half mile from there. I'd rather see you safely home."

"But I can't. You see, I've got other purchases in the carriage and I can't leave them overnight . . ."

Gabriel's expression changed to derision and he glanced down at the ancient book beside her. "What else? Witches' caps? Pentagrams? Broomsticks?"

Jennifer heard the barbed irony in his voice and realized he was furious. Shrinking down into the seat, she shrugged. "A mynah bird, and some other things."

"I see. You really haven't learned anything from any of this, have you? You still intend to continue your role as gypsy? Do you have any idea what they're saying about you?"

"I don't care!" Jennifer cried. When she saw his expression turn icy, she sighed. He would never understand. "Gabriel, I have to try even harder now. If I can make this fashionable again, everything will be fine. Do you know Mildred Adams?"

"The matriarch?" Gabriel asked, appearing surprised.

"Yes. She's an old friend of Aunt Eve's. She's coming to stay, and we're putting on a séance for her. I have a lot of new props, including this book of chants. Don't you see? We mean to put on the best séance she's ever witnessed!"

"Yes, I do see," Gabriel said coldly. As the driver stopped behind her carriage, he helped her down. When she reached the ground, Jennifer looked up, and for a moment, thought she saw pain and regret in his eyes. The look was gone in a moment, replaced by his more familiar disapproving scowl.

"I will follow you home. Jennifer, I want you to be more careful. You are dabbling in something you really don't understand, and it could be dangerous."

"Dangerous!" Jennifer laughed. "Gabriel, you've seen what we do. There's nothing frightening about it. My word, next you'll be telling me to buy gargoyles to ward off evil spirits."

She tried to lighten the awkward mood between them, but Gabriel's expression didn't change. He handed her into her carriage, waiting until she was fully seated before turning away.

"Gabriel!" Jennifer called as he started to walk away. He stopped beneath the streetlight and looked at her expectantly. "Thank you," she whispered.

He stared at her for a long time, then climbed back into his own carriage. For a frightening moment, Jennifer knew what that look meant: He was memorizing her in detail, almost as if creating an invisible photograph to carry with him. And she knew why.

Gabriel had just said good-bye.

CHAPTER 24

THE FOLLOWING MORNING, Jennifer was thrilled to find that her sisters had caught her mood and were eagerly preparing for the grande dame's visit. Winifred had rolled up the carpets and hung them outside for a beating, while Penelope washed the linens, complaining good-naturedly about the damage to her hands. Eve had spent the better part of the previous day baking, and now displayed several sumptuous cakes, scones, and tea breads, all designed to make her friend feel welcome.

"Wait until you see what I bought," Jennifer said, and eagerly unveiled her finds. While her aunt was less enthusiastic, especially since her beloved parrot hated the mynah bird on sight, Winifred and Penelope were enthralled. Penelope immediately found a sharp razor and cut out the eyes of one of the oil paintings, then held it before her face. Everyone laughed, for the image really did seem to follow them eerily around the room.

"Now, for the pièce de résistance." Jennifer displayed the book like a ringmaster saving the best for last. Penelope put the painting aside and frowned, her nose wrinkling.

"Why, that's just a dumb old book!"

"It is more than that," Jennifer explained, flipping

through the pages in fascination. "It contains spells. You know, chants," she explained to her bewildered sister. "I think it will really add a nice touch to the séance."

"I see." Winifred nodded, her smile curving. She stood over Jennifer's shoulder, looking at the ancient-sounding poems. "Before you contact the spirit world, you'll recite one of these as if it were a conduit into the other plane. I like it. And some of these chants sound wonderful."

"Exactly." Jennifer smiled back. "Now, when will Mrs. Adams arrive?"

"This afternoon," Eve said, glancing at her letter. "Our carriage will transport her here. I expect her by two at the latest."

"Are you certain she'll still come after our jailing?" Penelope asked, worried. "She is, after all, high society."

"She had some misgivings, but I think I convinced her. We'll have to make sure her visit is a success, for all concerned," Aunt Eve said, her wrinkled forehead betraying her worry.

"We'll just have to make sure she has a good time," Jennifer said emphatically. "Perhaps, Auntie, you could take her on calls after lunch, giving us time to make up the room. We don't want to put everything out right away—the element of surprise always helps. We'll close off the séance room and finish everything, then bring her in at midnight." She rubbed her hands in anticipation.

Eve looked doubtfully at the assortment of scary props lying around her. "I just hope you girls know what you're doing."

"Don't worry, Auntie." Jennifer giggled. "If we know anything, we know this. Mildred Adams will leave here convinced she's seen a ghost. And nothing else we can do will top that."

The carriage appeared outside just before the lunch hour. All three girls eagerly watched at the window as the door opened, and the driver helped the old woman down to the street. Penelope squeezed Jennifer's hand as Mildred Adams stepped royally up the stairs, like Queen Victoria herself, gesturing for the coachman to help with her bags.

Aunt Eve rushed to the door, then paused, smoothing her dress. When it was perfect, she opened the portal slowly. Mildred gave her a brief hug, then entered the room with a spryness her age belied. Placing her bag on the floor, she glanced around the room, her eyes lighting on the girls. She removed her black veil, and her face, which had been described by every New York newspaper at one time or another, appeared exactly as they imagined. She looked like an aged Madonna, graceful and elegant in her features, but her eyes were wonderful. Dark brown and intense, they betrayed a hidden passion and determination that her subdued demeanor would have hidden. She had the stance of someone used to giving orders and being obeyed, which was confirmed as she instructed the coachman on exactly what to do with her bags, then handed her gloves and coat to the bewildered maid. But something in her formidable expression changed when she saw Jennifer, and she stared at the girl in stunned surprise.

"Mildred, I'd like to introduce you to my nieces. This is Winifred, Penelope, and Jennifer. Girls, Mildred Adams."

They all curtsied, just the way Aunt Eve had instructed. When Jennifer rose, she saw that the old woman still peered at her as if in shock. When Jennifer looked at her aunt questioningly, Mildred coughed to cover her embarrassment, then nodded briskly.

"Yes, yes. I had assumed you were Eve's nieces. You are all she talks of, you see. I understand you've gotten yourself in a nasty mess. No more than you brought upon yourselves, I would think. No respectable young woman of my acquaintance was ever jailed! If it wasn't for Eve's insistence, I would have seriously reconsidered my visit. Now I'd like to see my room, and have luncheon ordered immediately. The dust on the streets is dreadful, and I can still feel it in my lungs."

Penelope giggled, while Eve hastened to do her friend's bidding. They could still hear the old woman grumbling upstairs as Eve showed her the guest room. The old woman continued her litany of complaints, and Penelope had to cover her mouth to hide her laughter, while Winifred looked concerned.

"Not a pleasant old person, is she? It's a good thing we went to extra effort, although I doubt it will be appreciated. I don't think she approves of anything!"

Winifred's prediction proved correct. Mildred complained constantly through lunch. The roast beef was undercooked, the potatoes overcooked, the bread not freshly baked. Jennifer got exasperated, but noticed that Eve treated her friend deferentially, not at all insulted by the woman's manner. Vaguely, she remembered her aunt saying that Mildred had once lost someone she loved, and had never been the same since. Perhaps that, more than awe for her wealth, explained Eve's patience with the old dowager.

Finishing her own meal, Jennifer glanced up and found that the two women were looking expectantly at her. Eve smiled, indicating the séance room. "I was just telling Mildred how talented you are with your readings and séance work. Would you perhaps perform a reading for her while she is here?"

Jennifer hid a smile. Aunt Eve was a born salesman, and knew exactly how to whet Mildred's expectation. Frowning as if undecided, Jennifer shrugged. "I suppose. I haven't done many since . . . our jailing, but I think I can conjure something."

Mildred nodded, as if any other answer was unacceptable. "Good. I always take a nap after lunch, then I will go on some calls. There are a few interesting people in this neighborhood still, although not like the old days."

"Tell us about them!" Penelope cried, eager for gossip. "I want to hear all about your society, and who did what to who!"

"That's whom, my dear." Mildred nodded, wiping her lips with her napkin, prepared to hold court. While Jennifer, her aunt, and the maid hastened to clear the table, Mildred entertained them with stories about the rich and powerful. Penelope was enthralled, and Jennifer saw that the older woman had taken to her sister completely. Following her aunt into the kitchen, Jennifer smiled.

"I think she likes us, but she keeps looking at me strangely. Are you certain she's been to séances before?"

Eve nodded. "Yes. I think you remind her of someone." When Jennifer looked at her quizzically, Eve shrugged. "Let's get dessert, then I'll take her out later for calls. Everything is going perfectly so far. Are you prepared for this evening?"

Jennifer nodded. "Ready as I'll ever be."

"Good. Just continue to follow my lead and all will be well. She likes you girls already, I can tell. That is very unusual for her."

"I can imagine," Jennifer said dryly. "She doesn't seem to like much."

Eve smiled sadly. "She has her sorrows, but be patient. She really is a wonderful woman, once you get to know her."

JENNIFER HAD HER doubts about Mildred's wonderfulness, especially as she continued to grouse about everything. The linens weren't smooth enough, the bathwater wasn't hot enough, the fruit not quite as fresh as what she was used to, and the supper too ordinary. Jennifer's only pleasure was hearing that Mildred had snubbed the Billings, who recently had become Jennifer's most caustic critics. Now, with the séance upon them, she forced all thoughts of her own annoyance out of her mind and became calm.

"Is everything ready?" she called to Penelope, who giggled behind the wall.

"How do I look?" Her sister rolled her eyes, and the portrait once more appeared to come to life, staring about the room.

Jennifer laughed. "Perfect. Is Winnie set up with the music?"

The harpsichord groaned, and Jennifer nodded in satisfaction. "Good. She'll be here any minute. Now remember, don't play the music while I'm reciting the chant, or we'll lose the effect. I need everyone's concentration to make this successful." She removed the crystal ball from her black velvet wrap, and placed it on the table. "Ready."

Aunt Eve, hearing her cue, brought Mildred into the room. Immediately, the lights dimmed, and the harpsichord played softly from the room beyond. The older woman looked startled as she glanced about. The mynah bird, loosed from his cage, strutted above the new purple curtains like Poe's own nightmarish poem, while the parrot watched intently. The tiger cat paced back and forth near the fireplace, and the chandelier dripped with cobwebs. The wind moaned outside, and the oak tree tapped the window accommodatingly.

Mildred looked at Jennifer, momentarily surprised by her change of costume. Instead of her normal subdued clothing, she was garbed in a gypsylike outfit. Gold earrings dangled from behind a red veil, and the same garish material was swathed around her. Disdainfully, the old woman took a seat and glanced around the room as if something smelled bad.

"Don't think these surroundings make any difference," Mildred said coldly. "While it is all very clever of you girls, I can't say I'm impressed. Penelope, come out from behind that wall this instant! As if a portrait could move!"

Jennifer forced a smile while Penelope slid open the secret door and stepped sheepishly into the room. "I find the atmosphere is conducive to the spirit world," Jennifer explained. "They don't need the props, but we do. They help keep part of our brain, the logical side, busy, while our spiritual side is then free to reach out." She handed the woman the deck of tarot cards. "Could you please concentrate on your questions and shuffle the cards?"

Mildred complied, scowling all the while, obviously not convinced by her explanation. Jennifer realized the old dowager would be a tough nut to crack. Most of her clients would have been stunned by the decorations, which would have won half the battle for them, but Mildred was going to require plenty of extra effort.

The old woman returned the deck, still scowling in disbelief. Jennifer concentrated, trying to allow the sensations and feelings to come to her as they had with Mrs. Hawthorne, but Mildred's incessant scathing remarks and almost palpable disbelief seemed to shut the psychic door in her mind. Try as she might, the layout of brightly colored cards seemed to hold no meaning. Frantically, Jennifer hazarded a guess.

"This is the Knight of Wands. This would mean an older man, over thirty-five years, who is entering your life."

"There is no such man," Mildred huffed. "That makes absolutely no sense."

"I see. Then this card"—Jennifer raised one of a woman with a bird on her shoulder, surrounded by a lovely garden—"is a woman of independent means. I think—"

"That is perfectly obvious," Mildred said impatiently. "A newspaper could tell you that about me. I think your talents have been overestimated by the press, my dear."

Jennifer heard Penelope's sharp intake of breath. She had to fight to keep her own emotions under control, for she would have dearly loved to tell Mildred Adams to jump off the partially constructed Brooklyn Bridge. Deciding to forego the cards, Jennifer closed her eyes, focusing on the séance instead.

"I understand you wish to summon someone who has crossed over. Let us attempt to do so now. If everyone will be silent, I will recite a chant that will bring forth the spirit. Mrs. Adams, please concentrate on the image of the person you wish to see."

Mildred's lips curved in derision, but she did as Jennifer suggested. Winifred stopped playing the harpsichord, and Penelope took a seat.

Humming softly, Jennifer rolled her head, allowing the eerie mood to possess her. Staring into the crystal ball, she whispered the chant she'd borrowed from the book, allowing her words to be heard by the others in the room.

> "Night of darkness, night of evil!
> Part for us now, your cloak of onyx!
> Beyond lay the otherworld, where one has gone
> Lost and alone, his soul to wander.
> Come to us now, O spirit of the night!
> Join with us, and set this soul to right!"

The wind howled, and Jennifer felt a strange energy fill the room. The hair on the back of her neck rose, and her skin pimpled with goose bumps. Slowly, she opened her eyes, and saw Mildred Adams's face white with terror. Penelope had arisen and stood open-mouthed, her eyes popping like twin parasols. She pointed behind Jennifer, her mouth open, but no sound came from her lips, as if she'd been struck dumb. Jennifer whirled around in her chair.

A white steamlike mass hovered just behind her chair.

Gasping in shock, Jennifer rose, barely able to step backward as the mass began to take form. Within minutes, it had gone from the appearance of a cloud from a teakettle to the silhouette of a man. Jennifer could make out a masculine form garbed in an old-fashioned cloak, hat, walking stick, and boots.

"My heavens," Penelope breathed. "It's a . . ."

"Ghost!" For the first time in its miserable existence, the parrot spoke, squawking in fright at the emerging phantom.

A face began to emerge from the swirling fog, like a wax sculpture slowly hardening into shape. Recognition struck Jennifer painfully as she stared at the familiar figure, along with a wild hope she almost didn't dare express. Emotion, rich and enthralling, filled every cell in her body as her heart told her what her mind couldn't accept. Her exclamation choked in her throat and she could only gape in astonishment as the man fully materialized before her.

"Papa?" Jennifer whispered, but before the presence could acknowledge her, Mildred rose shakily from the table. Her normally stern face had become young again, and her disapproving mouth was smiling in wonder and a happiness that seemed almost holy. Her eyes had softened to those of a girl, and she held her hands to her heart, as if afraid it would escape from her frail body.

"Samuel? Oh, my Lord, Samuel! It is you! My love! You've come back to me!"

Jennifer and Penelope glanced at each other, as if to verify what they were seeing, then returned to the phantom that now stood perfectly formed before them. Jennifer's heart swelled as her father smiled, extending his hand toward her as he used to do when she was a child. Tears started sliding down her cheeks, and she heard Penelope sobbing behind her. Winifred stepped from behind the wall, all of them entranced with the glowing figure that had appeared in the room.

"Samuel! He's come back!" Mildred turned to Eve in excitement. "She did it! Your niece is really blessed!"

Jennifer sank down into her chair, feeling as if she would faint. Penelope touched her shoulder as if to comfort her, although her hand was damp and shaking. The ghost of their father smiled softly, reassuringly, sending a warmth spiraling through the girls. When he spoke, his voice was exactly the same as they remembered, as if no time had passed at all.

"My dear girls. How long I have wanted to visit with you!"

"Papa? Is it really you?" Penelope cried.

He smiled again. "I have watched and waited, and been with you so often. There wasn't a tear that you cried or a laugh that you enjoyed that I wasn't there for."

"How?" Jennifer asked, unable to believe what her eyes told her was true. "How did you come?"

"You brought me. You've perhaps heard of myths where mortals can cross over and bring us back? Your love and prayers did that. Your mother is also with you often, ever since that terrible day when our carriage crashed. Our only regret is the struggle you've had to endure, because of us. I was never successful when it came to money, and so couldn't provide a legacy that would have helped you now."

"That is my father's fault," Mildred sobbed. "He didn't want me to marry you, and he set out to destroy you. That's why your businesses failed, and why you were never able to get ahead financially. It is a knowledge that has weighed horribly upon my mind, especially when I learned that your girls had been punished, as well."

The girls looked at Mildred in amazement. Mildred Adams, wealthy aristocrat, one of New York's fifty, had once loved their father! It was all too amazing.

The phantom nodded. "All is forgiven. Your father did what he was supposed to do to protect his daughter, and you and I have loved each other, just as I loved my wife. There is no regret in this."

"Papa, are you . . . happy?" Winifred asked, her face streaked with tears.

The spirit nodded slowly. "I know it is hard to understand, but we all are like this. Luminous beings. You cannot remember, but you will. Dust you are. But I am so proud of you all! Winifred, you must follow your instincts. Learn, my dear, for you were given a mind meant for that. Penelope, listen to your heart, and not your purse. And Jennifer, my sweet Jennifer, don't be so afraid. There is always abundance for those who believe."

While Jennifer pondered his words, he turned to the two older women. "My dear Eve. I have especially watched over you and sent my love for taking care of my girls. I will be with you again soon. And Mildred," he said to the matriarch, who suddenly seemed fragile and small, "remember me and help my girls."

"Papa?" Jennifer cried as the vision before them slowly faded. "Papa!" She ran toward the swirling mist.

"Remember," the voice echoed. "Remember."

CHAPTER 25

ALL OF THE women were sobbing when the spirit vanished. Aunt Eve recovered first, and turned up the lamps, yet it was as if all light had gone from the room. The void left by Samuel Appleton's ghost was very real.

"I can't believe we saw him!" Penelope shook her beautiful head in wonder. "Papa! Was he really here, Jenny, or was it all the same dream I've had, over and over?"

"No, he was here," Jennifer said, embracing her sister. "He was really here."

"I have to admit, I often had doubts about a hereafter," Winifred said, her face alight with love and wonder. "But after tonight, I never will again. To think that we not only exist after our time here, but that our love lives on!"

"That's why we have to be so careful to whom we give that love," Mildred said softly. She looked like a young girl again, all harshness and disapproval gone from her demeanor. "We really do tie ourselves to each other through that emotion."

Jennifer thought instantly of Gabriel, and what Mildred's words implied. Could it be that through love, she was tied to him for eternity? It was something she couldn't bear to think about.

"When did you love our father?" Penelope asked, and Mildred smiled sadly.

"Before he met your mother. I think I should start at the beginning now and tell you all about it. Goodness knows, I never thought we'd have this conversation, but after tonight, anything is possible. I was barely sixteen when I met Samuel Appleton. I thought him the most handsome man I'd ever seen, but more than that, he was kind. He was a gentleman's gentleman, bright and ambitious, but he was also poor."

"And your parents forbade you to love him," Jennifer said, her voice tinged with pity for the young girl she pictured.

"Exactly. At first they thought it was just an infatuation, that I would outgrow it. They shepherded me to party after party, seeing that I met all the right men, but to no avail. My heart belonged to Samuel. When they discovered my correspondence with him, they forbade me to see him again and threatened to cut me off completely. I was frightened for him, you see, for this was another time and place and I knew what my parents were capable of. Unfortunately, I didn't know the whole extent until later. I had simply thought Samuel disappeared and no longer loved me."

"What happened?" Winifred asked.

"They convinced him I no longer cared for him. Even after he married, they destroyed him financially. They were always afraid that at some time, he would come back for me. They made sure that would never happen."

Mildred spoke bitterly, her face twisting like rumpled paper. Penelope soothed her, giving her hand a squeeze, while Jennifer sent her a sympathetic look.

"He was very hurt," Eve said, trying to soften Mildred's pain. "I thought he'd never get over it. He didn't marry for many years, yet he seemed to be happy later when he did. I know his children were the greatest joy of his life, but he never forgot you."

"That's good to know," Mildred whispered. "I didn't discover this until quite recently, when I happened upon some old letters of my father's. My only revenge was that I married a playboy, and that drove them nearly to distraction. Oh, I lived a grand life all right—summered in Europe, held parties nearly every week—but I never produced the heir they so desperately wanted. When they died, they left me so much money I became the reigning queen of New York, and I lived that role to the hilt. Soon after, my husband died. But I have never forgotten Samuel—which is why I was always so reluctant to come visit you girls every time Eve suggested it. I didn't think I could look into your faces, see him, and stand it."

Mildred looked directly at Jennifer, who suddenly understood the old woman's reaction to her. Of all the sisters, she had always looked the most like their father, and Mildred, of course, had immediately seen the resemblance.

Penelope stifled a sob. "That's so cruel," she said, then glanced at her sisters in bewilderment. "But then if you had married him—"

"Then you girls wouldn't be here." Mildred smiled, all anguish disappearing from her wizened face. "Now if you don't mind, I've wasted a good forty years feeling sorry for myself. I have a lot to make up for, and I think I know just where to start. You young ladies have yourselves in a bit of a bind. I will help you with that, but you have to follow my lead. New York's finest aren't always forgiving, and it will take quite a bit of effort on everyone's part to get you reinstated."

"How on earth will you do that?" Penelope asked, barely able to contain her excitement.

Mildred smiled again, and it was a young girl's face that looked back at them. "Society loves nothing more than intrigue. When it becomes known that you girls really did conjure a ghost, you will not only be fashionable, you will be so in demand, you will never sit out another dance again. No one will dare call you frauds after this. I personally will see to it."

Penelope clapped her hands, and Winifred laughed. Aunt Eve brought tea, and hugged her friend. Mildred had tears in her eyes. Only Jennifer looked concerned as she stared at the spot where her father's ghost had stood. In all her years of performing the séance ritual, she'd never truly believed there was a door to the spirit world that could be opened.

And now that she'd done it, she was more than a little afraid.

MILDRED WAS AS good as her word, for she'd barely packed her trunks and returned home when the newspapers began to scream their success. Jennifer stood beside Penelope at the newsstand, stunned to see her name emblazoned on every headline. Her hands shaking, she barely tossed the newsboy a coin before snatching up the *Post* and reading the story.

"Jennifer Appleton Summons Ghost! New York Matriarch Calls Encounter 'Incredible!'"

As Jennifer scanned the story, the newsboy stared at her, then pointed a grubby finger in her direction.

"That's her! The ghost lady! She's right here!"

Crowds at the market stand turned at his words. Jennifer glanced up and was besieged by people who, having seen the headlines, approached her with curiosity and awe. Women touched her skirts, begging her to make their beloved dead ones appear, while children asked for her autograph. Bewildered, Jennifer scribbled her name, while Penelope, also a sudden celebrity, was asked the same things. Men spoke to them reverently, removing their caps, as if they were goddesses, while the grocer boy stopped with his hands full of apples and watched apprehensively. When it seemed that the girls were surrounded, he plunked down his fruit and pushed his way through the thickening crowd.

"Move aside! Let the girls pass! Come on, if you want to know all about it, buy a paper! Get out of the way!"

Penelope's face softened in relief when she saw Lorenzo. Grabbing her hand, he pulled her and Jennifer, who blindly snatched her sister's skirt, through the throng and into the relative safety of his stall. There, at least, they found some protection from the crowd, which had now grown frightening.

"Mother of God, these peoples! I cannot believe—Are you girls all right?"

"Fine!" Penelope said brightly. "Lorenzo, they think we are famous!"

"Thank you so much," Jennifer said, glancing back at the crowd. They were snatching up papers and pointing in their direction. For the first time, Jennifer realized that a crowd could be trouble, and she shaded her eyes, looking for their carriage. "I think we're parked across the street. I don't know how we'll get through . . ."

"Don't you worry about that. There's a back way through my shop. Come now, before they get out of control."

Lorenzo's warning was not without merit, for sure enough, the people came rushing back, wanting to talk to the bewitching sisters. A policeman appeared, and his nightstick waved in the air as he tried to disperse the crowd, but word spread quickly that the Appletons were in their midst and the fans refused to leave. Lorenzo bustled them through the rows of vegetables and out the back. Then they were able to dash to their vehicle unnoticed.

"Whew! That was close." Penelope turned and smiled

in gratitude at the grocer as Jennifer climbed inside. "Thank you, Lorenzo. You saved us!"

He shook his head as if his efforts were of no concern. But when he raised his face and looked at Penelope his eyes were full of adoration. He waved to her, his heart on his sleeve as his face turned beet red. As the crowd began to realize they'd been duped, they rushed into the street, and Lorenzo, like a knight garbed in a green apron, shoved them back so the Appletons could make their escape.

"Thank heaven for your friend," Jennifer remarked as the vehicle safely cleared the crowd. Her brow furrowed, and she said, "The reaction of the people worries me. It was one thing when we were merely notorious, but now they act as if we're godlike. Did you see the look on some of their faces?" She shuddered, leaning back into the carriage so she wouldn't be recognized.

"Hmm." Penelope shrugged. "Maybe they just think we are special."

"I wouldn't put it past some of these people to think we can really conjure the devil himself. Lord, what this could lead to!"

Penelope nodded. "Maybe it won't be so bad. We'll be invited to everything. Jenny, think of the bright side . . . any party we grace will become an instant success! Why, if we can draw such a reaction in the market stalls, imagine what will happen at a soiree!"

"Well, we'll soon find out. Mildred is sponsoring us at the Christmas Ball. Everyone of consequence will be there, or so she says. My heavens, will you look at that!"

Jennifer's voice fell off as they approached Twin Gables. A crowd was gathering outside, hoping to catch a glimpse of a ghost or an Appleton. Jennifer saw Aunt Eve's worried face at the window, then the maid appeared, flapping a dish towel at the crowd, trying to shoo them away. As the sisters alighted from the coach, the people parted respectfully, but Jennifer could hear their murmurings as she walked up the path to the house.

"That's the one! She's the one who brings the ghosts!"

A reverent hush passed through the crowd as Jennifer approached. Fear began to grow inside her and she took Penelope's hand and hurried toward the house. Even Penelope appeared concerned, for as Jennifer had noticed, people weren't treating them simply as celebrities, but were speaking in hushed church tones as if the girls were more than mere mortals.

"Girls! I'm so glad you're back!" Aunt Eve rushed them inside. "I've sent for the police. They started gathering this morning, and it's getting worse. It seems as if everyone wants to see you!"

Jennifer glanced out the backdoor and saw a few people standing in the yard. Quickly she closed the curtain, relieved when she heard the officer outside, clearing the throng from their door. Penelope danced, sifting her hands through the dozens of invitations that graced the dining room table, then gasped in wonder at the flowers that had begun to arrive. A boy brought in holly and chrysanthemums, poinsettias and other Christmas flowers. Soon the hallway looked like a conservatory as word of the miracle spread quickly throughout the city.

"I'd say you girls got what you wanted," Aunt Eve said, though her face was lined with worry. "There won't be a soul in the city who doesn't know you."

"Perhaps it will die down when no more ghosts appear," Winifred suggested. "You know how people are. Right now we are a cause célèbre, but that could change overnight."

Jennifer nodded, but her own face reflected Eve's anxiety. Everything seemed to be getting out of hand too quickly, and she didn't have the slightest idea what to do about it.

The next few days wore on in much the same way. The

girls, overnight celebrities, were hounded by fans and the press. Even Penelope complained when they were fitted for their gowns, because the seamstress, her mouth full of pins, kept insisting that they try and contact her lost love. Penelope swore that they would, mostly to ensure that the woman didn't deliberately sew their dresses too tight. They were besieged at the market, their parlor was filled daily with callers, and even their pastor sought them out to discuss life after death.

Mildred was delighted with their popularity, particularly when Winifred was invited to attend Vassar. Winifred insisted it was due to her grades, but her newfound status didn't hurt, especially when the dean wrote and asked about the séance. The press asked what kind of shirtwaists they wore, and what kind of gloves they preferred. Overnight, they became fashionable, and young girls in the street began to copy Jennifer's tasteful gowns, Penelope's frothy dresses, and Winifred's restrained elegance. It was overwhelming, to say the least.

Yet as Jennifer dressed in preparation for the ball, she felt an odd restlessness plaguing her. No one knew for certain how her father's ghost came into being, nor what the repercussions might be. That frightened her more than anything, although Penelope and Winifred didn't seem to care. Still, the worry ate at her, and she felt terribly vulnerable.

She couldn't understand it, for things were certainly going exactly as they'd planned. The Appletons were at the height of their popularity, and after tonight's ball, Mildred had assured them, they would reach a new pinnacle. But as she stared into the mirror, holding the velvet ball gown before her, Jennifer could no longer hide from the truth.

It wasn't enough.

She was getting her every wish, seeing Penelope launched and Winifred's ambitions fulfilled, but the emptiness inside of her would not go away. A dawning realization came to her: The time she had been happiest was with Gabriel. The very feminine part of her longed to hold him in her arms once more, and experience that tremendously exciting magic he so easily wrought. Jennifer's cheeks stained red as she thought of that night when they'd kidnapped him, and he'd artfully seduced her into the sweetest surrender. Biting her lip, she recalled her fears afterward, that she might have carried Gabriel's child as a result of allowing him those liberties, but the thought no longer frightened her. Instead, it filled her with an odd longing.

Jennifer forced her thoughts aside. It was useless, utterly useless. Gabriel would never forgive her, and he would never understand. She resigned herself to her fate: Nothing could fill the void in her heart reserved for him— not fame, not fortune, not celebrity status. She missed him terribly, and the ache inside of her simply would not go away.

Jennifer stepped into the dress, waiting for their maid to finish with Penelope and assist her with the fastenings. Glancing over her shoulder, she smiled at her sister's girlish chatter, and at Winifred's dry comments. Both girls looked beautiful, and were so looking forward to the ball that evening that Jennifer refused to dampen their enthusiasm.

When she glanced back at the mirror again, she was startled to see another reflection staring back at her, that of a young girl. The girl had long, chestnut braids that looped back behind her ears in an old-fashioned style. Her dress looked old as well, almost colonial, Jennifer thought, and she wore a pinafore designed to keep her gown clean. Her face was small and pretty, her cheeks pale, but her eyes were luminous, sad and pleading. Jennifer was about to cry out when the young woman vanished as quickly as she appeared, and the mirror became glass once more.

"Winnie! Dear God, did you see that?" A cold chill went through Jennifer, and no amount of velvet could keep her warm.

"What is it?" Winifred came to her side and glanced at the mirror. Her puzzled expression clearly said she'd seen nothing, and for a minute, Jennifer couldn't do anything other than point.

"There. In the looking glass! I saw it!"

"You saw what, dear?" Winifred obviously thought Jennifer had her laces tied too tightly, and began to tug on them.

Jennifer pulled away impatiently. "It was a ghost! A young girl! I saw her in the glass!"

Penelope glanced up, then shrugged and went back to ordering the maid around. Jennifer took a seat, her knees shaking, her legs like jelly. Winifred, seeing her sister's expression, took one of her hands and tried to warm it between her own.

"Are you sure?" Her voice dropped, and instinctively, Jennifer knew why. The last thing they needed was the press to get hold of this.

"Yes. Winnie, you know I'm not fanciful. I saw her! I swear, I did nothing this time—no chant, no meditation . . . nothing! She just appeared as clearly as you!"

Tears started in Jennifer's eyes. The fright had shocked her badly, and she continued to glance back at the mirror, as if half expecting another phantom to appear.

"Maybe you saw one of us," Winifred said consolingly. "Like Penelope or the maid. Sometimes, at an odd angle, a reflection can look very strange."

"I wish it were that simple," Jennifer said. "Winnie, I know what I saw. Worst of all, I have no idea who this girl is, or why she was here. She was a ghost, for heaven's sake, a real ghost just like our father's!"

Winifred bit her lip, a gesture Jennifer knew signaled deep thought. "If you're really sure, then I don't think we should tell anyone about this. It's one thing to have spoken to our own father, for people would think he had reason to contact us. It's quite another to have unidentified spirits wandering around the house."

"What are you two talking about? We have to get ready," Penelope said, giving them a pretty pout which was completely wasted on her sisters.

Jennifer nodded. "Winnie, I think you are right. I will take your advice." She shuddered, then glanced at the mirror again. The reflection was only her own, yet she couldn't shake the feeling that she was being watched.

CHAPTER 26

THE CHRISTMAS BALL, held at the Belmonts' estate, was the season's "must attend" event. Jennifer alighted from their carriage with her sisters and Aunt Eve. She stepped onto a red carpet that had been rolled from the Fifth Avenue mansion down to the curb, ensuring that the guests' feet never had to touch the New York streets. Servants lined the walkway, shivering in the cold, yet perfectly attentive to the needs of the party-goers. One took her muff, another her cloak, another furnished a glass of champagne, and by the time they reached the grand hallway, they had already joined the party.

Inside, Jennifer was slightly scandalized at the portrait of a naked Bouguereau lady, displayed proudly for all to see. She was grateful that Mildred had coached them about the picture, for she knew August Belmont was ridiculously proud of the piece of artwork, and that any negative reaction from the Appletons would mark them as rubes. She heard Penelope's stifled giggle, but fortunately, her sister was able to control her reaction. The three sisters entered the ballroom, where the dancing had already begun.

Penelope was asked immediately, and Jennifer smiled

proudly at her beautiful sister as she swept across the marble floor, stunning in her midnight blue ball gown. In spite of the Christmas season, Penelope had refused to wear red or green, knowing that neither color did her justice. Instead, she was like a sapphire jewel in the midst of the crowd, and more than one gentleman remarked on her elegance and beauty.

Charles spotted Winifred and approached immediately, bearing tempting little sandwiches and, of all things, caviar. He indicated the plate to Winifred, and smiled at her questioning look.

"Fish eggs." He grinned, looking more charming than ever. "They're all the rage. By the way, you girls look wonderful. Everyone's talking about you—it's all I've heard all evening. Gabriel is supposed to be here tonight, but I haven't seen him yet. Jennifer, are you all right? You look a little pale."

Jennifer saw Winifred's concerned gaze sweep over her, but she nodded and forced a bright smile. "I'm fine. I think I'll take a walk and reacquaint myself with everyone. Enjoy the eggs." She turned quickly, seeing Winifred's glowing happiness at Charles's compliments. Although she was glad for her sister, her own loneliness only returned twofold, and she felt like a third wheel in their company. The thought of running into Gabriel completely unnerved her, for she hadn't expected that he'd be attending an event like this one. Would he even speak to her, or would he ignore her completely? He might even have an escort, and she'd have to endure the sight of him with another woman in his arms. The thought devastated her.

The image of the ghost she'd seen also wouldn't leave her, and even the good champagne did nothing to calm her nerves. It didn't help that she was the object of conversation everywhere, and it was only by ducking behind a marble statue of Venus that she was able to have a moment's peace.

"Miss Mildred Adams." Jennifer heard the servant announce the matriarch's arrival, and watched as the old woman entered the room like a queen. She barely turned her head, giving a smile only to those who were either very rich or very important, reserving her handshake for August Belmont and his beautiful wife. Jennifer watched her in awe, for Mildred seemed to know everyone, including the obscenely rich Astors and Goelets, the Drews and Jeromes. She even spoke to Jay Gould, treating him with a fondness that stood out, since everyone else reportedly hated him. Her head lifted, and in spite of her diminutive height, she spotted Jennifer immediately. The frown that came to her face was tangible, and Jennifer saw her cut her way through the crowd, making a path directly toward her.

"There you are. What are you doing, hiding back here like a housemaid? I'm only enduring half these conversations for your sake."

The old woman smiled, but looked concerned, especially when she saw Jennifer's expression. Forcing a smile, Jennifer put her hands into the older woman's.

"I was just watching everyone. It is a little intimidating, you must admit. Besides, I don't think I've gotten over what happened at the séance, and my nerves are a little on edge."

Mildred's wonderful gaze swept over her quickly, and she nodded, as if confirming something to herself. "I see. Who is he?"

"What?" Jennifer's mouth dropped, and the old woman chuckled, tugging at her gloves.

"I know perfectly well what's troubling you, miss. You see, I was young once, and in love, as I explained to you already. You look like a woman who's pining for a man, and that we cannot have. Who is he?"

"Gabriel. Gabriel Forester. I don't think you know

him. He doesn't travel in quite so wealthy circles." Jennifer indicated the glittering crowd beyond.

"Forester? Of course I know him. He'll be here tonight whether he wants to or not. That is, if he expects to do any business in the city next year. The mayor is here, along with his consorts, and most of the city contracts are negotiated here, over champagne cocktails. Don't look so shocked, my dear. You are, after all, a woman of the world. So what is the trouble with this Mr. Forester?"

"He doesn't approve of our . . . spiritualism," Jennifer explained. "He's so angry with me that even if he comes, he probably won't speak to me."

"Ah," Mildred sighed, nodding her head. "We'll see about that. In the meantime, there are some women I want you to meet. Madam Woods, you may have heard of her, wants you to speak at the Spiritualist Convention. It is a wonderful honor, and a national tour, an opportunity that will put you before everyone of any importance. Put your chin up, and get rid of that dull look in your eyes. Everyone is watching you tonight, my dear, and you absolutely must sparkle!"

Jennifer followed the old woman toward a group of brilliantly gowned females standing beside a fountain. When Jennifer approached, they turned to her, delighted, and thanked Mildred a hundred times for bringing her over. One of them extended a diamond-crusted hand and clasped Jennifer's, her smile beaming.

"I am Josie Woods. I heard all about your feat! Imagine, summoning a real ghost from the dead! My dear, I want to hear everything about it, and you will, of course, accept my speaking engagement? You will be compensated handsomely, of course, but more than that, there is the exposure. Every newspaper across the country will know of you. This could lead to just about anything you wish, including a seat on the suffragette council, publishing, you name it."

Jennifer nodded, stunned by the import of what was being offered to her. She would be rich and famous, have an opportunity to travel and to speak to thousands of influential people. The whole idea was heady, and she stared at the elegant woman, her eyes wide with disbelief.

"Me? You really want me?"

"Of course, my dear. You are far more qualified than anyone else we could think of. Everyone else is mouthing ideas, while you've actually performed a miracle! I don't think you understand the importance of what you've done. You will be a symbol to women everywhere, an example to them of what one woman can do! I applaud you, Miss Appleton!"

To Jennifer's amazement and stunned embarrassment, she actually began to clap, as did the other women in the group. Jennifer felt the color rise to her cheeks as others glanced her way, staring in admiration and envy. Bowing her head, she felt the intoxicating excitement creep through her as everything she'd ever dreamed became reality. For a brief moment, she even felt the part, and silently acknowledged the truth to herself: She'd done it! Glasses of champagne were raised to her, and the music stopped, allowing the applause to grow thunderous.

Jennifer bowed, and enjoyed it all. She saw Mildred's approving nod, Winifred's beaming happiness, Penelope's blown kisses. Charles saluted her, and even the Billings were forced to nod her way. It was better than champagne, better than anything she'd ever experienced. She allowed herself to bask in her moment of glory, then her eyes fell upon Gabriel.

He was standing on the far side of the ballroom, looking incredibly handsome in a black suit with tails, and a flawless white shirt. Jennifer's breath caught and she waited to see disgust or disapproval in his eyes, but he only raised his glass to her, toasting her as did everyone else.

That simple gesture tore at her heart, and when she was swept into the arms of another man on the dance floor, she wanted nothing more than to break off and leave. But she couldn't. She had fought for this, worked for it, and finally, had won. Her sisters' future was now secure, as was her own, and she was caught up in her own success. Yet at no other moment in her life had she felt so miserable, especially when she saw Gabriel dancing with a beautiful blonde. Jennifer's hand tightened in the man's who held her, and he looked at her questioningly. She only smiled, and forced her gaze away, pretending, as Mildred had advised, to sparkle.

She only wished it was as easy as it looked.

"THERE YOU ARE." James McBride finally managed to cut in on Penelope's dance partner, and secure a dance for himself. His hand slipped around her waist, and he gazed into her eyes, obviously satisfied to have captured his quarry. "I've been trying to claim a dance all night."

"The men here are very determined, to say the least," Penelope said coolly, wondering at his attention. She had neither seen nor spoken to James since she received that dreadful letter. Surprisingly, the memory of it no longer hurt, and when she looked at him, she felt very little emotion.

"Not as determined as myself. You don't become as rich a man as I am without patience. I can wait forever if I have to, and I always get what I want."

He gave Penelope a meaningful glance. She smiled distantly, and allowed him to lead her around the dance floor. As they waltzed, Penelope could tell something was on the man's mind. He cleared his throat awkwardly a few times, then attempted to draw her closer to him, but Penelope didn't encourage him at all. She was polite, but that was it. Finally, he stopped midwaltz and shook his head.

"It's no good; I've got to say my piece and get on with it."

Penelope looked at him strangely, then indicated an enclosed patio that opened from the dance floor. "I think there's a place there, if you feel you want to talk."

He nodded, as if grateful for her suggestion, then practically dragged her to the alcove. Rushing to keep up with him, Penelope managed to maintain her composure and sit quietly in a wicker chair. She looked up at him expectantly as he paced the tiny floor.

"You must know how I feel about you, Miss Appleton. I think I've made it apparent. I know you women set store by where and when this takes place, but I'm a man who's always acted on my gut feeling, and I'm not about to change now. I know I sent you that letter, and said we shouldn't see each other, but all that has changed. You see, a man like myself has to marry well. Even Vanderbilt couldn't wed the woman he would have chosen, because she wasn't acceptable."

"You mean Tennessee Claflin," Penelope said calmly. "The spiritualist."

"That's right." James waved a thick arm as if dismissing the conversation. "The commodore knows, as I do, how important it is to make the right decision when it comes to a wife. I wrote that letter when it seemed that you wouldn't be accepted, that everyone was calling you a charlatan, and worse. But now . . ." He gestured around the room. "Now you are as good as any queen, especially with Mildred Adams's blessing. Nothing stands in our way. I guess what I'm asking is, will you marry me?"

Penelope sucked in her breath. It was all there, waiting for her. This man was fabulously rich, she reminded herself. If she married him, she could have everything she wanted, everything she'd ever dreamed of. She would be accepted by the Astors and Goelets; parties like this one would be a weekly occurrence. She would assume her rightful place in society, her place destined not by birth but by desire. She would live like a princess, sheltered in James McBride's smile, forever untouched by want or need.

Yet, she had no qualms when she leaned forward and put her hands in his.

"James, I am honored, deeply honored. But I cannot be your wife. I'm sorry if I gave you cause to think otherwise. I will remember this day always with fondest memories, and only pray that you won't think too badly of me, for I very much treasure our friendship."

The Irishman looked stunned, and it was a full moment before he could object. "Why, then? I know I'm not a very handsome man, but surely . . ."

"Don't, please. It has nothing to do with any of that. I realize now that I need to love and be loved. We Appletons have everything we've ever struggled for now: money, position, acceptance. I thought that was what I was looking for, what I needed to be happy. But I feel this emptiness, this ache inside of me that needs to be filled, and my heart tells me that only loving the right man will do that."

James rose from the seat, a wry smile crossing his face. His eyes looked pained, but he didn't seem very surprised. "Well, well, my dear, I can't say I'm not disappointed. I do hope you meant the part about the friendship, for as surely as Erin is green, I'd like to remain a friend of yours. And one day, when you find the man you love, he'd better be worthy of you or he'll have me to reckon with!"

Thrusting a fist into the air, his ruddy face took on a deeper hue as Penelope stood up and kissed his cheek.

"Thank you," she whispered. "For everything."

He departed, closing the door of the patio behind him. As soon as he was gone, Penelope sat down in her chair and sighed. It wasn't every day one passed up the opportunity to be a millionairess.

Yet she didn't regret it at all.

"MAY I HAVE the next dance?"

Jennifer's heart pounded as Gabriel stepped into their circle just as the music ended. Her partner seemed loath to let her go, but manners dictated his actions for him and he reluctantly conceded. As a waltz began, Jennifer felt the tingly excitement of Gabriel's hand slipping around her waist. He held her more closely than any of her other partners, and she could only sigh, admitting silently at how right it felt to be in his arms.

"You have been quite a success tonight. I must congratulate you," Gabriel said softly. "Even if it is under false pretenses."

"What do you mean?" Jennifer asked, surprised. She had expected disapproval, but the cold resignation in his voice made her shiver.

"Come on now, Jennifer, this is me. I of all people know you put on an act. How you managed to convince Mildred Adams that she'd seen a ghost must have been quite a stunt. Did you have Penelope appear dressed in a sheet, or did Winnie pop up in a corpse's shroud?"

"Gabriel, you can't really think—!" At his disbelieving smirk, Jennifer felt her happiness at being with him dissolve into fury. She stamped her foot, halting the waltz, looking at him incredulously. "My heavens, you must take us for the biggest con artists ever, to be able to pull off something like that! As it happens, a ghost did appear. Everything Mildred said is the absolute truth!"

"Sure it is," Gabriel said sardonically, yet his eyes were furious. "Just as leprechauns hide pots of gold. You know, Jennifer, I don't know why I'm surprised by all this, but I am. Somehow, I'd come to think better of you, but taking advantage of old ladies' grief is your forte after all, isn't it? I suggest you keep dancing, Miss Appleton, or your well-deserved fame is about to become questionable. Everyone is looking at you."

Glancing over her shoulder, she saw that he spoke the truth. Forcing a bright smile, she swirled to the music, hiding the fact that she gritted her teeth. Why did this man have the power to infuriate her over all others? And why, for heaven's sake, did his approval still matter so much?

"What a wonderful actress you are!" Gabriel continued, dancing perfectly. "I can see how Mildred thought you conjured a ghost after all. You could make a man believe just about anything, Jennifer. You are that powerful."

Jennifer squeezed back the tears that threatened, determined not to give him that satisfaction. When she looked up at him, her eyes were shining and hard. "Gabriel, I'm telling you the truth. We really did conjure a ghost, my father's spirit. I have never lied to you. I don't know how it happened, just that it did. I don't expect you to be happy about our success, but I care about what you think and I want you to know the truth."

Gabriel stopped as the music ended and clapped along with everyone else. When he glanced down at her, Jennifer saw uncertainty and apprehension in his gaze. "If that is so, then I am really worried. Jennifer, the occult is not something you want to fool around with. No one completely understands this business, least of all you and I. It could be dangerous."

Jennifer smiled in relief. "You still care about me, don't you? I knew it!" She beamed, feeling a warm flood of emotion fill her, but her hopes were dashed with his next words.

"You misunderstand me. I am concerned for you, and want you to be happy. That's all I've ever wanted. It seems that you have a line of swains waiting for the next dance with the notorious Miss Appleton. Good-bye, Jennifer." Then he was gone.

Jennifer managed to smile as the next man took her hand, wondering why no one else seemed to see that her heart was breaking.

CHAPTER 27

"I ASSUME YOU know why I'm here."

"Actually, I don't." Gabriel glanced down in confusion at the card he still held. "Mildred Adams" was scrawled across the elegant stiff paper, which he noted was devoid of the pretty flowers and birds that adorned most of the younger women's calling cards. The New York matron had never been known to call on a middle-class gentleman, and Gabriel was curious as to her reasons today.

Mildred's voice cracked like a whip. "Are you or aren't you Gabriel Forester, of the Forester Marble Company?"

"Yes, I am." Gabriel answered, surprised. "Why? Are you interested in marble?"

"I might be," Mildred said, tapping her finger thoughtfully. She drew out her spectacles, and to his astonishment, appeared to examine him from head to toe. When she finished, he assumed he must have passed some kind of inspection, for she nodded her head. "Yes, you'll do. In fact, I think you'll do nicely."

Fortunately, Benton brought the tea at that moment, giving Gabriel a chance to collect his thoughts. Mildred, he recalled, had been to the Appletons for a séance. The session had reportedly impressed her to the point that she thought she'd seen a ghost. This much Gabriel knew. That she was a known eccentric he also knew. But her reasons for this visit perplexed him completely. He had no choice but to wait patiently, as he watched her add a second dollop of cream to her cup.

"You are aware that I have taken a special interest in the Appleton girls?" Mildred eyed him intently, watching every move and every reaction like a physician trying to discern the health of an individual.

"I'd heard as much," Gabriel admitted awkwardly.

"Then you should be aware that I am very concerned with the girls' social activities, who they see, what their prospects are."

"I see, but what has that to do with me—"

"Young man, do not be obtuse! You are aware, I'm certain, that Jennifer Appleton is in love with you, and is pining away because of it?"

"Jennifer!" Gabriel snorted. "Yes, I am well acquainted with Miss Appleton and her antics. I saw her at the Belmonts' ball. Not only is she not pining away, but she looked uncommonly happy and well to me. She certainly seemed to be enjoying herself."

Mildred shook her head as if speaking to someone of the lowest possible intellect. "Mr. Forester, you certainly know very little about women. I assure you that what I'm telling you is the truth, and what I'd like to know is, what do you intend to do about it?"

Gabriel stood up, his face red. "Madam," he said between clenched teeth, "this is quite extraordinary. I am not accustomed to being questioned in such a manner."

"Maybe it's time you were," Mildred said, completely unruffled by his outburst. "I understand from my good friend Eve that you have compromised this girl. Mr. Forester, in my day, my father would have taken a horsewhip to your shoulders for such actions. The least you can do is make good."

"Madam, please!" Gabriel turned to her, his eyes blazing. "I am well aware of what transpired between Jennifer and myself. I have proposed to her, but she declined. There really isn't anything else I can do."

"I see." Mildred speculated on this last remark, and sipped her tea quietly. "You proposed, you say? And, of course, assured Jennifer of your love and understanding for her . . . unusual occupation?"

Gabriel threw up his hands in resignation. "I told Jennifer that I forbade her to continue performing séances. I don't think it's unreasonable for a husband to insist that his wife not perform charlatan activities—"

"Young man, she is no charlatan!" Mildred put her teacup aside and faced him directly. Her old, razor-sharp eyes locked intensely with his. "I had a séance with Miss Appleton, and when I tell you a ghost appeared, you may take my word for it. Do you understand?"

Gabriel stared at her, and for the first time, the import of what Jennifer had tried to tell him sank in. "But that's impossible! There are no such things as ghosts—"

"I assure you, sir, that there are. What happened that night was a miracle. Surely you can't keep Jennifer from allowing the world to benefit from her talent. And surely, if you loved her, you wouldn't even try."

Everything that was once clear became muddled. Gabriel tried to sort out his thoughts, but found himself helpless to do so. He sank into his chair, shaking his head, desperately trying to compose himself. Jennifer really had conjured a ghost! It was incredible, to say the least. Although he knew Jennifer was convinced that such a thing had happened, he really hadn't believed it in his soul. But for a martinet like Mildred to testify that it did happen . . . He glanced up and saw Mildred watching him with a strange sort of understanding on her face.

"Young man, think about what I've said. Miss Appleton may have been reluctant to wed you because of your stance, but it is your duty to show her the error of her ways. She needs you, and if I am not very much mistaken, I think you need her. You don't know me, but I have wasted a considerable part of my life pining for a man I couldn't have. I let others interfere, you see, and as a result, lost the man I truly loved. Do not continue this foolishness any longer."

She rose to take her leave. When Gabriel started to rise with her, she shook her head, slipping into her coat. Her hat, a monstrous creation of dried fruit, birds, and butterflies, dipped precariously, but she straightened it instantly and gave him a piercing look.

"I will see myself out. I trust you to do the right thing. After all, I knew your father and, as a gentleman, he would insist on it also."

She strode from the room and was gone.

Gabriel shook his head in bewilderment, but he couldn't get past the truth of what she'd said. As outrageous as Mildred's delivery was, it didn't alter the fact that she was right. Shame coursed through Gabriel as he recalled accusing Jennifer of lying, when all the while she was telling him the truth. More important was Mildred's assurance that Jennifer did, indeed, still love him.

That thought burned like a spark in his breast. Gabriel realized that he'd been ten times a fool, and had allowed his own pride, his own outrage at Jennifer's refusal to obey him, to goad him into stupidity. He'd kept away from her in order to win the battle, and in doing so, had almost lost the war.

Sitting alone in his town house, Gabriel could finally admit the truth: He loved Jennifer and wanted her, no matter what. Even if it meant séances. Even if it meant ghosts. No matter what she brought into the relationship, it would be uniquely her own, and that he couldn't live without. She had been right in denying him, he realized with stunning clarity, for he hadn't been able to accept her.

Acceptance and love really were the same thing, and if it wasn't for an old society dowager, he might not have realized it even now.

Gabriel poured himself a brandy, hoping that tonight, at least, he could sleep. It would be the first night since he'd left her at the jail that he would be able to do so. Relief already coursed through him now that he'd made his decision. On the morrow, he would go see Jennifer, and try to explain.

He only prayed he wasn't too late.

JENNIFER ENTERED TWIN Gables, her bags stuffed under one of her arms, accolades under the other. She had just returned from her speaking engagement, and she smiled wanly as she surveyed the house. Goodness, it felt good to be home.

Collapsing into a chair, she realized she'd been gone since the day after the Christmas Ball. She was surprised to learn that since the ball, she'd become a spectacular success. Her innocence and directness were charming to the world-weary New Yorkers, while her burnished blond beauty was considered ethereal. She wasn't a sophisticate like the bored married women who summered in Europe when their husbands became too tedious, and she wasn't a giggling debutante who swooned at the first bawdy suggestion. She had an air of sexual sophistication, as if she'd taken a lover or two; yet, besides Gabriel, her name was linked with no one. Jennifer Appleton had become the apple of New York's eye.

While on tour, Jennifer discovered she had a talent for public speaking, for after her first engagement in Philadelphia, the Spiritualist Convention sponsored her enthusiastically, and with Josie Woods's blessing invited her everywhere. Elated, Jennifer found herself discussing politics with the political, and religion with leading ministers of their faith. Her presence was requested at the bedside of the dying, who wished her assurance that they would not simply leave this life for some everlasting sleep. Jennifer reassured them, gave hope to those whose grief overwhelmed them, and provided comfort to the comfortless.

Penelope and Winifred, far from languishing in her shadow, had become just as popular. Winifred had more than one assurance of college entrance, and Penelope had more beaux than she knew what to do with. Strangely enough, James McBride ceased to call. Penelope refused to say anything on the subject, to the relief of Aunt Eve, who had declared him unsuitable.

Now, their success was guaranteed. Donations for the Appletons began to pour in, and Jennifer invested the money, giving some to charities while carefully utilizing the rest. She had Twin Gables refurbished, and bought Aunt Eve new clothes. Winifred received a scholarship, to everyone's delight, and Charles agreed to help tutor her in the law. Penelope had her pick of rich men who all wanted to court her, even though she refused to show a preference for any man in particular.

Why, then, did Jennifer feel so empty?

Bone weary from her tour, Jennifer removed her hat and ran her fingers through her hair. Tossing her hat on the rack, she went upstairs and took a seat at the dressing table. Flipping through the cards from well-wishers, she knew that there was one person's writing she was looking for.

She had neither seen nor heard from Gabriel since the Christmas Ball. Her heart thudded painfully as she realized that, in all likelihood, he'd gone on with his life. He'd thrown down the gauntlet and she'd tossed it back in his face. In the process, they'd both lost.

Jennifer smiled sadly at how simple it all was, yet how ridiculously complicated they had made it. But while on tour, she had realized that her life without him in it was meaningless. There had to be a compromise, some way to work out their differences. And if not, she was ready to give it all up. Her sisters were on their way now, and they no longer needed her help. She'd had enough of fame and fortune to last ten lifetimes, and if it ended now, so be it. Something had changed inside her since seeing the ghost, and she understood now that life was more than this time spent on earth. It was eternal, she thought, and the love we nurture goes with us. The love she wanted was Gabriel's.

There wasn't a card from him, but she didn't let that get in the way of her plans. Slipping into her nightgown, she fell into bed, wanting nothing now but a good twelve hours sleep and forgetfulness. Tomorrow she would go to Gabriel, beg his forgiveness, and hope he would listen, but for tonight, she needed her rest.

Sometime around midnight, Jennifer woke. Penelope snored from the bed beside her, yet looked angelic as always, while Winifred slept quietly across from her. Glancing around the room, she wondered what had wakened her and listened intently.

Then she saw it. At first, a single spirit came into focus, then another, then another. Jennifer's scream caught in her throat as the room filled with ghosts, all of them sweeping around the room, just as they would in life. Some were dancing, one reading, another hurrying to market with a basket under her arm. Soldiers appeared, bloody and bandaged, while a beautiful woman kept searching for something and sobbing silently. Another ghost banged at a piano, music filling the room, and several more spirits joined him, one with a trumpet, another a trombone, until they formed a ghastly band.

"Dear God!" Jennifer managed to cry out, and Penelope and Winifred awakened at the same time the bizarre music started. Winifred stared, appalled, clutching her bedsheets to her chest as if for protection, while Penelope gasped in wonder at the sight before them. Aunt Eve rushed into the room, but the phantom party continued as if they weren't present.

The three girls looked at each other in astonishment, while Aunt Eve leaned against the wall to keep from fainting. Far below, in the parlor, Jennifer could hear the parrot squawk.

For the second time in its life, it spoke.

"It's a ghost! It's a ghost!"

CHAPTER 28

GABRIEL APPROACHED THE steps of Twin Gables with a bouquet of hothouse roses in one hand, and a surety in his heart. Maybe it was Mildred's little speech, or maybe he had finally woken up, but he never felt more certain about anything than he did about the decision to come here. Even if Jennifer said she no longer wanted him, he would plead his case and apologize, make her see that he understood that she was gifted, and had every right to use her talent. He loved her; no matter what it took, he would win her back.

The door swung open before he could knock. The maid ran screaming from the house, bounding down the stairs past him. Gabriel stared in astonishment, then entered the old mansion slowly. He stood in the foyer.

"Jennifer?" he called out, amazed to hear a cacophony of strange noises. Winifred must be experimenting with the harpsichord again, he thought wryly. Squeaks and whistles, groans and chords all echoed through the house like a drunken one-man band. There was something inexplicably eerie about the sounds, and he shuddered, feeling the response in his soul. Thankfully, Jennifer rushed down the stairs and ran directly into his arms.

"Gabriel! Thank God it's you! I was coming to see you today myself. You have to help us!"

She looked out of breath and completely wrung out. Gabriel held her tightly, amazed at how right it felt to have her in his arms once more. Yet he was alarmed by her demeanor.

"Jenny! My sweet girl, what is it? I came to tell you that I was wrong about everything, to beg your forgiveness . . . Good Lord, what is happening here?"

The sounds increased and Jennifer clung to him as if at her wit's end. "I don't know what to do! Gabriel, I need you. You weren't wrong, you were right, you were always right. I should never have played with this!"

To Gabriel's astonishment, Jennifer dissolved into tears, melting against him. He could feel her trembling, and knew that for once, she was really and truly frightened. He stroked her back, awkwardly trying to comfort her. She clung to him as if he contained the essence of life itself. That more than anything concerned him, for Jennifer had the courage of a lion.

"Jenny, my darling Jenny. Nothing can be that bad. I started to tell you, I love you. I realized a lot of things last night. You are gifted, and I had no right to try and stop you from using your talent . . . Good God, what's going on here?"

The noise increased tenfold, followed by renewed screaming. Jennifer clung to him again. "Gabriel, I was fooling with something I didn't understand, and now we're paying a terrible price. They're everywhere, and I can't get rid of them, no matter what I try. Poor Penelope can't even get dressed, and Winnie's books are floating in the parlor. Aunt Eve is beside herself, and I'm at a complete loss!"

"Jenny, calm down and tell me what is wrong. I'll help you, no matter what it is. Now what's everywhere? What has happened?"

Jennifer took a deep breath, then the words rushed out of her. "Twin Gables is haunted."

"What?" Gabriel didn't know what he'd expected, but certainly not this. "Haunted? As in ghosts?" His eyes looked past her into the dim hallway.

"Yes." Jennifer nodded, her eyes filled with terror. "Gabriel, I don't know what I've done! You were so right when you said that I didn't understand the occult, and that something awful could happen. We had the séance for Mildred, and our father's ghost appeared. Something happened as a result of that, and now the spirits are all over the house!"

"My God!" Gabriel disengaged from her and ruffled his hand through his hair. He stared at Jennifer in shock. "Are you sure?"

"Yes." She nodded. "It started a few days ago, and now this morning, the house is infested with them. Come look!"

As she dragged him into the parlor, Gabriel tried to tell himself that Jennifer was overreacting. It must have been a shadow, or a cloud of steam that had frightened her. Coming so soon after seeing a real ghost, Gabriel could easily see how it happened. Confident in his diagnosis, he followed her into the room. As he stood in the doorway, he was stunned by the vision before him.

They *were* everywhere. Wispy images of real people flew about the parlor, ducking beneath the doorway and into the next room. Couples danced on the rug, barely taking notice of the living around them, while another spirit girl walked the halls. Aunt Eve chased the ghost of an old man into the kitchen with her broom, while Penelope screamed upstairs. Winifred's books did a ghastly dance around the room, while a poltergeist opened drawers and scattered the contents of Jennifer's sewing basket.

Speechless, Gabriel glanced into the kitchen, and saw a vaporous chef preparing an invisible meal. An Irish maid, long dead, scrubbed the same pots she'd cleaned in her lifetime, and a ghost dog chased a spirit cat around the room. If he had any doubts about what he was seeing, the reaction of the real animals assured him otherwise. Angel hissed and spat, his back arched, his eyes narrowed to tiny slits, and the parrot paced the inside of his cage as a pirate specter attempted to feed it nuts split with his knife, and the mynah bird chattered in fright.

"My God," Gabriel whispered as Jennifer hugged him. It was a nightmare come to life, more vivid and more dreaded than the worst of his dreams. A wailing woman with long hair and a harp walked past him, sobbing as she played, and the hair on his neck stood straight up.

"Come this way. The library's the only room they don't like."

Gabriel followed Jennifer as if in a trance. He couldn't take his eyes off the ghosts, although they ignored his presence completely. Horror filled him, along with fascination, and when Jennifer closed the door, he sank into a chair, astonished to find that his hands were shaking.

"Here." Jennifer poured him a glass of water, her eyes full of understanding. She extended the glass to him, watching as he gulped the cool liquid. "It takes a little getting used to."

"Jennifer." He stared at her, feeling the clamminess of sweat beneath his collar. "We have to get you all out of here! It could be dangerous. The place is full of dead people, for God's sake!"

"They don't hurt us. They're more of a nuisance than anything else," Jennifer explained.

Gabriel rose, feeling his strength coming back. He closed his eyes, trying to rid himself of the incredible scene that lay just beyond the door, but to no avail. He could still hear their mournful wailings, the sound of ghostly music, laughter, and sobbing.

"A priest!" Gabriel said, relieved at the thought that

sprang into his head. "I'll send for the local priest. Maybe he can do an . . . exorcism or some such thing."

Jennifer laid a hand on his shoulder. "We've tried that. Father Ryan came this morning, and ran out screaming. No one seems inclined to stay in a house full of ghosts. Besides, the spirits seemed to laugh at him, so I don't think that even a more courageous representative of the church will have much effect."

"There has to be something!" Gabriel paced in agitation. "I've got it! How about another medium! Maybe another spiritualist will be able to undo what you've done. There are a few that are famous in the city—Tennessee Clafflin, for one."

"That fake!" Jennifer snorted. "Trust me, Gabriel, if psychic ability could fix this, it would be taken care of. I don't want to brag, but there isn't another medium in the city who's ever been able to do something like this. No, I think there's only one way to undo what I've done." She reached for the book of spells that lay on the table before her, and handed him the ancient tome.

Gabriel examined the strange volume, his finger tracing the pebbly leather cover in wonder. The book looked old and well worn, yet the pages were in remarkably good condition and even appeared to be trimmed in gold leaf. A strange vibration seemed to fill him as he examined the book, and he could swear he felt its power. His thoughts were interrupted as Penelope burst in, clad in a corset and chemise, her clothes pressed in front of her for modesty's sake.

"That's it! I'm getting dressed in here. They won't stay out of my bedroom. Why, I was standing behind our dressing screen, and three male ghosts were peering over the top, watching every move I made!"

Her sister huffed indignantly, and if Gabriel wasn't so concerned, he would have laughed at the idea that even after death, men still wanted Jennifer's gorgeous sister.

Turning his back to her, he heard the rustling of her skirts, while upstairs, bawdy hoots and laughter rang out.

"The nerve!" Penelope sniffed, while Jennifer repressed a giggle. She glanced at Gabriel, who still gazed at the book in perplexity.

"I found that in an old shop the day you ran into me in town, and used it during Mildred's séance," Jennifer explained, helping Penelope with her dress. "It was very effective. But look at the last page."

Gabriel ruffled through the book. Immediately, a hush seemed to fall over the house, as if the spirits were listening. As soon as he put the book down, the noise started again. He turned to the last page and as he read the spell, the cloud of doubt lifted from his brow. He turned to her in excitement.

"Jennifer, that's it. It has to be! Your chant is what brought the spirits here, and if so, this one could send them back!"

She gestured to the page. "Yes. This is a reversal spell, designed to undo whatever you have done. I discovered it last night while trying to figure out what went wrong. Strangely, the book was on the table—as if it were waiting for me, even though I swore I had locked it up with the other props. That spell isn't for the faint of heart, though. It requires black candles, hogwart, a dagger, and urine of a toad."

"Also hair of a cat, water from a stagnant pond, and bones of a black chicken." Penelope shuddered.

"And seed of a thistle, and teeth from a mouse." Gabriel continued, reading the ingredients.

"Ick!" Penelope cried. "This sounds really spooky. I'm getting nervous just talking about this."

Gabriel nodded, thumbing through the book. There were spells to gain money, spells to bind troublemakers. There were healing chants, chants to gain the gift of prophesy, and spells to raise the dead. As he stopped on the last page, he noticed that the energy of the house changed, and the spirits seemed to grow louder. He closed the book firmly. "I don't think we have much of a choice. What's spookier than a house full of phantoms?"

"You have a point," Jennifer conceded. "But you don't have to be involved in this. I know how you feel."

Gabriel looked at her incredulously. "Jennifer, if you think I'm letting you do this alone, you're mad. Besides, I have to be here. Look at this." He opened to the last page again and pointed to the spell.

Jennifer nodded and turned to him, smiling, knowing exactly what it said. The spell indicated that it had to be performed on the night of a full moon. And that there had to be true love present, for only love could cross between the worlds.

It was, after all, an irresistible force.

"IS EVERYONE READY?"

Jennifer glanced around the room and saw Aunt Eve light the candles. It had taken the girls all afternoon to gather the implements needed to perform the spell. The toad urine was the hardest, but unbelievably, Gabriel discovered a toad wintering in the basement. The little frog complied with his share of the ingredients as soon as Gabriel picked him up, and Jennifer had rushed with an eyedropper to gather up the liquid.

Penelope held Winifred's hand, and she, in turn, held Gabriel's. Jennifer took his other hand, surprised to find that it was warm and calm, unlike her own shaking nerves.

"Now we are." Eve took her seat and clasped Penelope's right hand. Penelope wrinkled her nose at the ghastly assortment of ingredients in the center of the table.

"I can't believe we had to get all these awful things! I sure hope this works."

"Hush," Winifred said impatiently. "Let's get on with it."

Gabriel nodded in agreement, obviously just as eager to be done with the bizarre ritual. Jennifer closed her eyes, ignoring the sounds of the ghosts in the house, the wailing, laughter, and eerie whispers that mingled with them. Concentrating, she allowed her mind to focus on the chant that she'd spent all afternoon memorizing.

> "Moon goddess bright, oh, silver light,
> Help these beings return this night.
> Lead the way, near and far,
> Guide them to your misty star."

Jennifer took up the cup that Eve had poured and drank of the wine inside, then passed it to Gabriel. He did likewise, then passed the cup to Winifred. A trembling began somewhere in the house, as if a strong wind was building and threatening to blow the mansion from its foundation. The chandelier danced overhead, and the phantom portraits swerved back and forth on their own. Ghosts appeared, dancing and singing, teasing and taunting, opening drawers and throwing the silver. Laughter and loud music resounded, and the four women held onto each other's hands in terror.

Suddenly, the room was filled with a strange light. Jennifer gasped, trying to keep her eyes closed, but the glowing luminescence penetrated beneath her lashes and she couldn't resist a peep.

Phantoms, different from those who'd been haunting the house, appeared one by one. They swirled about, dashing between Penelope and Winifred, hovering around the ghosts who were suddenly quiet, then wreathing above Aunt Eve who closed her eyes determinedly. One by one they paused, hovering overhead, until the room was a swirling mass of dissipated energy. It was beautiful, wonderful, and frightening, a glimpse into a valley of souls unfettered by beliefs or doctrine.

"My God!" Gabriel whispered as the spirits came into form. The faces that looked down at them were loving, and Jennifer knew that these were angels or spirit guides who would take the mischievous apparitions back to their own time and place. Some were male, others female. The visages that peered down at the humans were breathtakingly beautiful, wise and wonderful, and their presence made Jennifer want to cry.

"Read the next part," Penelope whispered, frightened. "Send them all back!"

Jennifer nodded, then flipped the book to the next page. When she looked up once more, she was astonished to see her parents, smiling at a distance. A childhood friend, cruelly drowned at a tender age, waved to them, as did other relatives long since dead. Eve opened her eyes and they filled with tears as she saw friends from her youth and relatives long departed.

"They've come to help," Winifred said, her voice rough with emotion. "I can feel their love."

Gabriel squeezed Jennifer's hand as he stared around the room and saw a face he'd never thought to see again. He rose, pointing, unable to speak. It was a long moment before he could force the words from his throat, and even then his voice was more of a croak. "My . . . father. He's here!"

Jennifer and her sisters turned quickly to the vision that seemed to grow stronger right before them. Jack Forester smiled, and his face was glowing with warmth and love. Dressed in a gentleman's suit, complete with hat and walking stick, he looked exactly as he must have in life. Jennifer saw the kindness in his eyes, the love that seemed to radiate from him. He reached out and touched his son, and Gabriel's face was streaked with tears.

"Father?"

"Yes, Gabriel, it is me. I want you to know something, son. I'm proud of you, proud of what you've done. Remember that always, and know that even in eternity, I love you."

"Father!" Gabriel reached toward the phantom, his voice overcome with emotion. "Please, don't go!"

But he was already disappearing. Jack Forester smiled once more, then slowly faded away. Jennifer felt Gabriel's hand clasp hers tightly as he slipped back into his chair, struggling with the torrent of feelings inside of him. Remembering the disagreements they'd had in life, Jennifer knew what it meant to Gabriel to see this man once more, and to realize, in one simple gesture, that all was forgiven. A moment later, Gabriel composed himself and nodded, then Jennifer continued with the chant.

"This I ask, our spell undone,
For the good of all, and the love of one."

The room slowly grew quiet. Penelope sobbed, Aunt Eve wept, and Gabriel sat still as a statue. The sound of the wind penetrated the séance chamber, and even the parrot stopped its dreadful squawking as a welcome silence filled the house.

"Is it over?" Penelope asked.

Jennifer slowly opened her eyes, almost afraid to believe that it had worked. Glancing around, she saw that the ghosts were gone. The wondrous guides had disappeared, and their bawdy guests along with them. The chandelier overhead was still, the birds watchful, and for the first time in days, the tiger cat settled down to sleep. Not a sound issued from the upstairs or the basement, and even the parlor was quiet.

"Yes," Jennifer said in awe. "It is over."

CHAPTER 29

THE FIRE CRACKLED in the hearth, and Jennifer sat with Gabriel, sipping Aunt Eve's tea, which was liberally laced with brandy. Snow fell softly outside, the white wispy flakes sifting through the trees like a cloudburst of feathers. The tiger cat slept peacefully, and even the parrot and the mynah had stopped squawking and had settled down for a night's rest. To all outward appearances, it was a quiet domestic scene. No one would have guessed that a battle with the occult had taken place less than an hour before.

"Gabriel, thank you so much for your help," Jennifer whispered, her voice rich with emotion. "I never could have done it without you. Listen to that." She gestured upstairs, to where her sisters slept.

"What?" Gabriel looked upward.

"Nothing. Silence. The most blessed sound in the world." Jennifer sighed in relief, leaning back against the parlor sofa. "After the last few days here, I never thought to hear it again."

"You were very brave, performing that spell," Gabriel commented, thinking back to the dreadful moment when the room had filled with specters. "Thank God it worked."

He glanced toward the table, then a puzzled frown creased his forehead. "Jenny, what happened to the book? I could have sworn it was right there."

Jennifer looked over at the table, then glanced beneath it. The book had been there—she was positive. Now it was gone, just as suddenly as it had appeared the day she'd bought it.

"That's strange. Maybe Aunt Eve or one of my sisters has it. In any case, I fully plan to retire. I've had enough of ghosts and phantoms and things that go bump in the night. Go ahead and say it, Gabriel, I deserve it. An 'I told you so' is the least I should get."

When Gabriel didn't respond, Jennifer sighed. Glancing at him, she saw that his face was troubled, as if he were struggling with something he didn't want to say. Her heart lurched painfully. Looking down at the rug so that he wouldn't see the tears in her eyes, she spoke softly, her voice nearly breaking.

"Gabriel, I know that after what happened tonight you probably want to run as far away from here as possible. Everything that you predicted came true, which is funny, as I'm supposed to be the fortune-teller. But you were right. The occult is something we never should have gotten involved with, and we've paid a terrible price. I endangered my sisters, myself, Aunt Eve . . ." Jennifer lifted her eyes and faced him, choking back tears. "It was thoughtless and dangerous. I'll understand if you want nothing else to do with me, and can only thank you for being, really and truly, a friend."

But Gabriel simply shook his head. Turning toward her, he took the teacup from her and firmly placed it aside, then took her hands in his own. His blue eyes burned with a deep intensity, and Jennifer's breath caught in fright. Surely he would tell her now he was through with her. In truth, she couldn't blame him.

Prepared for the worst, she was doubly shocked when

he spoke, his voice deep and compelling. "Jennifer, I want you to know how much I love you. If anything, this experience has made me a more complete, more spiritual man. Don't you understand? To see that we don't just die at the end of our existence, that we go on, that there is some purpose, some meaning to it all . . ."

He glanced away from her, as if the emotion were too much for him to control. Jennifer wanted to reach out to him, but knew he needed this moment to make sense of the incredible evening. When he looked back, his eyes were softer, filled with warmth and love. "And to see my own father, after fearing for so many years that he despised me, that I had been a disappointment to him. That was an ache I've carried with me, a painful wound that never completely healed. When he spoke to me, let me know that he understood and loved me . . . My God, do you know what that has done for me?"

Jennifer felt the tears welling in her eyes, but she quickly brushed them away, almost afraid to believe what she was hearing.

"I have lived my life very much in the moment," he continued softly. "I have collected payments from men who couldn't afford to pay, and have had little remorse about it. I have run a tight business, made a lot of money, and held my place in society. Yet, I realize now, it all means nothing."

"But, Gabriel, you aren't wrong to be successful," Jennifer protested.

"No, I know. But what have I done to make a lasting difference? I never gave a damn about my fellow man, never thought about helping anyone else until I met you. Strange as it may seem, in some ways I am the charlatan, for I've pretended that what I've done is important, and it really isn't. I've made money, but I've very seldom eased a burden from someone's shoulders, nor taken away their pain even for a brief moment. That's what you do all the time, dear, although it took me a long time to see it."

Jennifer smiled tremulously. "Are you sure? I don't embarrass you? You don't think I would cause you to lose business? I know what people think of me, and I know that we Appletons will never be entirely accepted. I would never want to hurt you, or cause you regret."

"Jenny." Gabriel smiled, and touched her cheek with his finger. "How could I ever regret any of this? As for society, remember that I am a merchant, and barely accepted myself. And as far as business goes, you've actually brought me more. The mayor came to see me after meeting you the other night. Apparently, he heard that you and I were . . . involved, and his curiosity got the better of him. In any case, it resulted in a nice deal. I won the city contract."

"Oh, Gabriel, I'm so glad!" Jennifer cried.

"I love you, Jennifer, and have from the first moment I met you. I fought against it, prayed against it, avoided you, and in general did everything I could to distance myself from you. But none of it worked. Every time I saw you I simply wanted you more. If you meant to get revenge, you got it in spades, for I spent endless nights thinking about you, wanting to feel you in my arms, wanting to see that incredible expression on your face the first time I kissed you. Even that should have told you where my priorities really were, for in the Barrymores' garden, I could no more resist you than a bee could a rose. I love you, Jennifer Appleton, every part of you, and wouldn't change a thing about you."

"Oh, Gabriel," Jennifer cried. Joy flooded through her, incomprehensible and stunning in its beauty. She hadn't realized until this moment how long she had ached to hear him say these things. But it was happening, it was real. "I will give it up, I promise! I never want to upset you or make you unhappy again. I love you, Gabriel, and only want your happiness."

"You don't have to give anything up. I admit, I'm glad to hear that you've decided against any more incantations, for I don't think I could sleep at night, knowing that ghosts were watching. But if you want to continue to help others, to see women who need your help, and men who come to you for spiritual guidance, I fully support that. I think I have to draw the line at the magnetic healing, however." At Jennifer's giggle, he continued. "I'm a little too jealous to have you laying your hands all over any man but me."

Jennifer wrapped her arms around him and hugged him fiercely. "I decided a long time ago to stop the healing. You were right about that, too. Gabriel, I love you! You've made me so happy!"

Having her this close was too much for him. Gabriel turned her in his arms, and her lips met his in a scorching kiss. Desire, long repressed, flamed quickly into being, and he groaned when Jennifer pressed herself fully against him, responding with an innocent ardor that set him on fire. His mouth opened over hers in a fierce demand, one that she answered so completely that he lost all control. His tongue met hers, wanting to taste the silken sweetness of her mouth, while his body sought more intimate contact. Jennifer rose on the parlor couch, her arms slipping up to his neck, her fingers buried in his hair as she lost herself in his kiss.

Aunt Eve's discreet cough from the next room was like a bucket of cold water thrown over the couple. Reluctantly, Gabriel eased from Jennifer's embrace, stunned by the realization that a simple kiss left him reeling. To his utter gratification, he saw that Jennifer's cheeks had turned a bright pink, and she smoothed her dress in confusion, as if trying to sort out what had happened. When she lifted her face to his, his breath caught in his throat.

"There is one more thing I am going to demand of you," he whispered, his voice aching and hoarse. When

Jennifer looked up at him shyly, he grinned, taking her in his arms. "You will refuse me until we are properly wed. I am going to take you as a decent man should, this time—*after* the wedding. Do you understand me?"

Jennifer's eyes melted and she smiled softly. "Yes, Gabriel. Oh, yes."

EPILOGUE

"JENNIFER, STOP FUSSING with that dress!" Aunt Eve scolded as Jennifer fidgeted uncomfortably in the ivory satin wedding gown. "You'll have wrinkles in every fold!"

The old woman's face softened even as she scolded, for Jennifer was a beautiful bride. Stepping back, she admired the simple gown, with its elegant scooped neckline, long sleeves, scalloped skirt, and fitted bodice. It was the new fashion, a Princess sheath dress which scandalously had no bustle. The dress fitted tightly to the hips, then flowed gracefully to the floor. A Worth original, the gown had cost Gabriel a small fortune, but he'd insisted in spite of Jennifer's protests. In retrospect, Eve could only admit that the man was right.

"I don't mind wrinkles," Jennifer said, giving her aunt a teasing sideways grin. "Especially like this." Reaching out, she startled her elderly relative with a fierce bear hug that left Aunt Eve slightly breathless.

"Whew! I daresay you are right." Aunt Eve fanned herself, but couldn't help the girlish giggle that escaped her. She reached out and pulled a few curls down from Jennifer's upswept hairstyle, to frame her face. "My dear, you look stunning. I've waited for this day, to see you so happy and well wed. I wish you and Gabriel would have given me more time to plan, but I suppose that couldn't be helped. A New Year's wedding! It is so unusual, yet special at the same time. You don't mind if I cry a little, do you?"

"Cry all you want," Jennifer said, fighting back her own tears. "Although I want today to be happy, and everyone to have a wonderful time. You know, Auntie, there is something that is troubling me. I have the impression that you and Mary Forester had more to do with all this than I've been led to believe. Is that true?"

"*Moi?*" Aunt Eve gazed at her in complete innocence, and Jennifer knew at once that her suspicions were correct. Before her elderly relative could feign a protest, Jennifer continued.

"And I think Mildred Adams was involved as well. I remember her saying something the night of the party about Gabriel."

"I know nothing of any of it," Eve said determinedly, although her eyes sparkled. "In any event, true love found a way, although you two were determined that it never happen."

Jennifer giggled, then hugged her again. When she broke the embrace, she glanced around the room. "Where is Winnie?"

"Here." Winifred stepped into the bedroom, holding a beautiful pearl necklace. "I thought this might be nice with your dress today," she said shyly. "It would please me if you'd wear it, but I understand if you'd prefer one of Auntie's necklaces, or that beautiful sapphire Gabriel gave you." Winifred glanced quickly at the lacquered jewel box on the table, where Gabriel's engagement gift resided.

"It's Mother's necklace," Jennifer breathed, looking at her sister with eyes full of love. "I know how much you treasure it. I'll be proud to wear it, dear, if you'll let me."

Winifred stepped behind Jennifer and hooked the intricate clasp. When she caught her reflection in the mirror, Jennifer reverently touched the pearls, remembering how Winifred used to caress the necklace nightly, thinking of their mother. Every pearl was filled with memories, and so much more beautiful to Jennifer than the finest of gems.

"I've got something, too." Penelope leaped up, determined not to be outdone by her sister. "It isn't as grand as Winifred's gift, but I do hope you'll carry it." Penelope pressed her prayer book into Jennifer's hands, the very one she'd carried when she'd made her First Communion. "I've kept it all these years for a special occasion, and I can think of nothing more special than this."

Jennifer touched her cheek in thanks, taking the book in her gloved hands. Aunt Eve dabbed at her eyes, taking in the vision of her three beautiful nieces. Penelope and Winifred, in burgundy velvet, looked wonderful, and Jennifer, the radiant bride, was like the brilliant diamond in their midst. "Are you ready, dear?"

Jennifer nodded, then followed her aunt out to the carriage. The church was beautiful, decorated with holly and pointsettias, and iced with snow. Disembarking from the carriage, Jennifer started down the aisle, her heart pounding as if it would escape from her body.

Gabriel stood waiting for her at the altar. In that second, it was as if time stood still. Everything she'd ever wanted culminated in this moment, and as the music began and she walked toward him, she could hear Penelope's sobbing and Aunt Eve's choked tears. She saw the Billings, Mrs. Hawthorne—holding the hand of her adopted child—Jonathan Wiseley, Mildred Adams with her handkerchief pressed to her face, and dozens more. Jennifer didn't want to cry; joy was bursting inside her, filling her with a sanctifying essence. Today she would be one with the only man she'd ever loved, and nothing could make her happier.

She reached the end of her journey and Gabriel took her hand in his warm one, giving her a reassuring squeeze. Jennifer stood beside him, repeating the vows. At the proper time, he slid the ring onto her finger, a magnificent diamond band that glinted beautifully in the dim candlelight. When she looked into his eyes, his expression took her breath away. He leaned down and kissed her and the minister coughed, for Gabriel didn't seem to want to let her go.

"There'll be plenty of time for that later, son," the pastor admonished him. Gabriel reluctantly eased from Jennifer's arms, amid good-natured laughter from the front pews. When he took Jennifer's hand, she felt the welcome pressure of the ring between her fingers, the symbol of eternity. Sensing a presence in the cathedral, she glanced up toward the rafters. There, amid the stunning light of the stained-glass windows, she could see her parents smiling down at her, Gabriel's father, and all those who had loved and crossed over to the other world. Tears stung her eyes and she smiled at the spirits, knowing that whether she could see them or not, they would be with her always.

Love, she knew for certain, was eternal.

And for her and Gabriel, it was just the beginning.

About the Author

Katie Rose is thrilled to be a part of Bantam's Fanfare program. A lifetime resident of South Jersey, Katie lives with her daughter in Marlton and spends much of her free time horseback riding, exploring old houses, and researching American history. She is fascinated with the Victorian period, and sees a distinct parallel in the industrial revolution and the technology revolution today. Katie has a degree in journalism, and has been published in book form, magazine, and newspapers.

Watch out for

A CASE FOR ROMANCE

the next magical romance
from wonderful new author

KATIE ROSE

On sale in the fall of 1998 from Bantam Books

Read on for a sneak preview of her work in progress. . . .

Emily rummaged in her pocket for her glasses, excitement coursing through her as she thought of seeing her new home for the first time. She put on her spectacles, and gasped in astonishment at the town outside.

It was a bawdy place; she could tell that immediately. The saloon was twice the size of the church, and the boardinghouse had the prosperous look of a booming business. The street thronged with life, cowboys and farmers, shopkeepers and miners. There was a dressmaker's shop, a shoemaker, a stable, and a blacksmith. Emily sighed in relief as she observed no milliner's shop, at least not on the main road. She was used to competition, but the less of it, the better. Even this consideration didn't distract her much. She was overwhelmed by the sights, smells, and noises of a real western town, and didn't want to miss a minute of it.

It was everything she'd expected. Where Boston was settled and dignified, Denver was alive, bustling and frenetic, filled with exuberance, like herself. Joyfully, she snatched up her carpetbag, unaware of the snubs of the women with her or the calculating survey of the cowboy who was just leaving the coach.

"Emily, I'd like to go with you to see the house, just to make sure you get there safely," the preacher volunteered. "Do you mind?"

"I ain't sure that's proper," the cowboy interrupted. He spat on the ground, the wet tobacco hitting the dirt with a tar-colored splat. He gave Emily a charming smile. "After all, this place has a reputation, and as a preacher, you need to keep that in mind. Ma'am, I'd be more than happy to provide an escort to your new home."

Emily was about to respond, when the preacher interrupted. "I must insist on being your escort. My mission is close by, and I have to go right past the house. Besides, Ewert Smith and I are friends, and he specifically asked me to direct Miss Potter should I meet her. That is why I made an introduction." He grinned at her winningly. "Do you mind?"

Emily shook her head. The cowboy seemed nice, but his spitting bothered her. Logically she realized that tobacco had to be expelled, but her feminine sensibility was still offended. Besides, there was something about this preacher that alerted her sleuth instincts, and she wanted to find out more about him.

Thomas looked at the cowboy with a sharp glance. The cowboy, tired of the game, shrugged and went off to the saloon. Emily smiled in appreciation as the preacher took her bag, then indicated the wooden boardwalk ahead.

"It's on the outskirts of town, if I remember right." The preacher gave her a reassuring smile. "Let's try this way."

Emily followed obediently, glad now that he was there to help. As Thomas walked in front of her, she thought once again of how he was so unlike any other preacher she'd ever known. There was a catlike grace to his walk, a sureness to his step. More than that, there was a presence about him that she wouldn't have expected. He tipped his hat in response to the nods that came his way, but she had a feeling that he would have gotten the same respect even without the collar.

The boardwalk ended, and was replaced by a well-worn path that led behind the saloon. Emily's eyes grew wider as they approached what looked like a Southern mansion. A beautiful white house rose out of the dirt like a castle in a dream, complete with graciously curved windows, green shutters, and gardens. As they approached the door with its bold brass knocker, Emily turned to the preacher in astonishment.

"This is it?"

"Try the door," he suggested, indicating the key that had been inside her letter.

Gingerly, she slid the key into the lock, more astonished than ever as it clicked and the door swung open. Thomas lit the gas, then turned up the flame, throwing the room into plain view. Emily polished her glasses, then put them back on, gasping in shock as she saw the parlor.

The place had obviously been ransacked, yet even in this dismal state, she could sense the opulence of the room, the scarlet and gilt decadence. Emily gasped as she saw the bar, the crimson chairs, the player piano, and the large portrait overlooking everything. And overhead were paintings, pictures like she had never seen before, depictions of scenes with men and women, doing things she couldn't even imagine. . . .

"My God!" She whispered, turning to the preacher in horror. "What . . . what was this place?"

"A house of sin." Thomas said, stifling his chuckles with obvious effort. Emily glanced at him quickly. She was not mistaken. There was a twinkle in his eye, and a suspicious grin played around his mouth. Odd for a preacher, she made a mental note. He indicated the portrait above the fireplace. "That was Rosie."

"But why—"

"I didn't know your father, but he probably never thought you'd come out here. Most women would have sold the property rather than face the dangers of the West. I guess he underestimated you."

"How incredible." The initial shock passed and left curiosity in its wake. Like most young women, Emily knew little about the dark side of men, the things whispered about between elderly women and always with disapproving tones. She stared at the ceiling in fascination. The paintings were incredible. Was it really possible for men and women to . . . ? Suddenly, she remembered her companion, and she tore her gaze away from the paintings, then glanced at the ruined chairs once more.

"Why would someone do this?" Emily questioned softly. "Do you think it was just vandals?"

"Possibly." Thomas shrugged. "But maybe they were looking for something. Something of value." He stared at Emily with a dark, piercing look.

"Like what?" Emily glanced up at him in confusion.

"I don't know. Didn't your father tell you anything about this place, or how he got his money? Maybe he left some indication in his will, or some other documentation?"

There was something about the way he was questioning her that made her uneasy. Emily sunk down into one of the least damaged chairs. Her gaze focused on the portrait hanging on the wall. "I know my father had secrets. He was very evasive in his letters about what he did for a living, who his friends were. My mother couldn't tolerate the idea of living on the frontier, so he went West to provide for us in the best way he could. She never said much about him, never indicated that anything was wrong. I don't think she ever imagined this!" Emily glanced once more at the bordello paintings.

"Then it seems you didn't know much about John Potter."

The preacher sounded disappointed, as if he was expecting some other answer. Emily shrugged. "It appears that there is more than one mystery here, if I am not very much mistaken. But it is a capital mistake to theorize without data. If you'll excuse me, I'll have to get started investigating." She rummaged through her carpetbag and withdrew the magnifying glass, then dropped to the floor.

Thomas stared in amazement as Emily, oblivious to his presence, began to examine every inch of the room. She crawled around the rug, grunting when she occasionally saw something that held some meaning for her, frowning when she saw the trampled condition of the room. She scooped up some ash near the fireplace, putting it carefully away in an envelope, then scraped some threads from the carpet. At one point she withdrew a tape from her bag, and measured some marks on the floor. She calculated some figures, then jotted some notes in her book. By the time she stood up, her hat askew, her nose smudged with dust, she looked as wretched as the room.

"Emily, what are you doing?" the preacher asked, seemingly astonished at her behavior.

"Collecting data," Emily replied, as if he were a fool. She sighed in disappointment. "Unfortunately, many people have been here since the murder. If only I had gotten here when the marks were fresh! I would have had him!"

The preacher's expression changed from amused to thunderous. "Emily, stay out of this. Whoever killed your father and Rosie has never been caught. The murderer is still out there."

"I know." Emily tried to smile at him, but saw no response in his eyes. "Don't worry. I'll be careful. I've read a hundred of these stories, and they all work the same way. Now I'll have to meet with the sheriff, read the papers, find out everything I can about my father and the girl—"

"Emily!" This time he shook her, choking off her words. The magnifying glass bounced to the floor and Emily's mouth dropped in stunned surprise. "This isn't a story we're talking about! This is real life! Whoever vandalized this place was looking for something, and they won't let a woman stop them! The very best thing you can do is get back on that stage and go home."

Emily squirmed, uncomfortably aware that she was

pressed right up against him, with one of his trouser clad legs between her own legs and his blackcloth rubbing against her blouse. Odd sensations started somewhere within her and she frowned, wondering what was wrong with her. She saw his gaze lower, and settle on her mouth, seemingly fascinated by something there. For the silliest moment, she thought he was going to kiss her, but he released her as quickly as if she was a scorpion that had climbed into his hand. Emily smoothed her dress, trying to make sense of everything. What in God's name was wrong with her? He was a preacher! Clearing her throat, she managed to speak coherently.

"I'm sorry, but like my great aunt Ester, I have to follow my destiny. I have to find out what happened, I have to discover who killed my father. In the meantime, I plan to stay here, and make this a good home again. You, as a preacher, should understand that. I'm going to fix up this house, plant a garden, meet other people, and have company. I'm going to church on Sundays, and maybe attend a dance. And I'm going to investigate. And no one is going to stop me."

Thomas wanted to fling his prayer book at the closest possible target in exasperation.

How the hell did this happen? He had wanted to question her, to get her to admit she knew something, but when she looked at him with those clear gray eyes, he seemed to forget all logic.

What was wrong with her, anyway? What decent woman would want to live in a bordello, let alone investigate a murder there? Didn't she understand the kind of danger she was in? It was obvious that the house had been deliberately ransacked. Of course she had to know why. Was there a reason she wasn't worried? How much of it did Emily know?

John Potter had been a clever man, more clever than most. After the robbery, he had successfully lost himself in the West, but the gold had never been found. The whorehouse was a self-maintaining entity, and not even the federal lawyers could prove otherwise. Concealing two million dollars must have been difficult, but somehow, Potter had done just that. There were no funds located in any bank in his name; the company had been able to ascertain that. Apparently, he'd sent some money to his wife and daughter back East, but it couldn't have been any huge fortune or they wouldn't have had to keep a millinery shop. No, the money was hidden somewhere, and Thomas was certain Emily knew where.

So what were her intentions? He stood outside, watching her shadow pass within the walls of the notorious house, rethinking everything he knew about her. Nothing about the woman seemed to add up. Her careful investigation of the room, while appalling, made sense. No one, not even the sheriff, had done such an examination. He'd have bet his life on that. And if they had, could they have found clues to the killer? It didn't seem that far off base.

So she was bright, yes, and incredibly naive. The incident with the cowboy had proven that. If he hadn't intervened, the man would have taken Emily home and probably to bed. But she obviously hadn't understood his intentions, nor what conclusions he'd jumped to upon hearing that she owned Shangri-La. No, Emily was odd, but she didn't seem to be sexually sophisticated, unless she was an incredible actress. . . .

Thomas frowned as he recalled the way she'd felt when he'd shaken her in exasperation. Up close, he'd noticed that her eyes were really remarkable, a strange, haunted silver that seemed to look right through him. And her mouth was pink and moist, and very kissable. For a brief moment, something had passed between them, something that would cause enormous complications, something that he didn't even want to think about.

He turned around and started toward Mrs. Haines's boardinghouse. Emily Potter was John Potter's daughter, and a factor in the case, nothing else. And he'd get the truth out of her, no matter what.

It had taken an additional hour of investigating before she felt satisfied that she had learned everything the parlor would yield. Emily slumped into a gilt chair, feeling totally and completely drained, and more than a little disconcerted.

The floor had revealed very little. She felt as frustrated as Holmes to realize that dozens of people had trod over the rug since the murders, clearly obliterating any trace of the killer. Still, she was able to fathom a few facts, and what she could deduce only confused her further.

There were boot marks, her father's she assumed, since she's found a pair of square toed Hessians in his closet. From his traces, he was standing facing the fireplace and smoking a good Cuban cigar. He had turned, and was extending a glass of whiskey to someone when the shots came. Emily could see where he'd fallen, the splashes of liquor and the broken glass, the blood stains that someone had tried to wipe up, and the stub of the cigar where it had rolled to land beside the fireplace. She shuddered when she thought of the blood, but forced the repugnance from her mind. This was a case, and Holmes would never let such feminine considerations stop him.

So, she surmised, forcing herself to review the facts, he'd been standing by the fireplace, enjoying a smoke, when someone walked in and shot him. It must have been someone familiar, for there were no signs of a scuffle, no indication that either her father or Rosie had struggled, and no signs of a break-in at the door. Yet the trampled flower beds and scuffed floor hid anything else she could have found with her glass. If only she could have been here earlier! Emily signed in frustration.

Rosie's part was a little more difficult to envision since her traces were not so obvious. She'd fallen near the steps; Emily remembered the newspaper accounts, and the positions of the bodies. Yet there were signs of a smaller pair of boots, much more feminine and pointed, which had left a trace in the cigar ash, and there were threads from a blue cotton dress. Had Rosie come down earlier, then returned? Emily's brow furrowed. The marks could have come from anyone, even one of the girls. If so, perhaps there was a material witness to the crime. From Rosie's position, it was probably safe to deduce that when she'd come down the stairs, she'd surprised the gunman. Having no choice, the man had shot her, too, then fled. But why? What had her father done to deserve such an end? And why Rosie?

Her eyes gazed once more at the ceiling, and she found herself blushing again. What kind of man had her father been? Emily's logical mind couldn't deny the fact that he must have been virile, and an opportunist. Was this how he'd gotten his money, the cash he had sent to them that was so welcomely received? Did it come from—

She couldn't think about that. Yet as she looked around the parlor, she could picture the women, some of them laughing and singing around the piano, others sipping drinks and flirting at the bar. She could see their gorgeous dresses, their sparkling plumes, their paste jewels and rouged faces as they took a man upstairs.

The paintings overhead seemed to laugh at her. Emily felt the color rise to her cheeks and was very glad no one else was present. It was foolishness, she knew that. Highly embarrassing. And, although she'd never admit it to anyone else, strangely erotic. She'd even felt a tingle when the preacher, Thomas Hall, had put his hands on her, to shake some sense into her. It was true, but the sensation had been there.

It was this house. Emily nodded, satisfied with that explanation. Dr. Watson climbed out of the bag and surveyed the new residence, mewing his confusion. Emily smiled and picked up the cat, softly stroking his fur. At least the little black and white was familiar and comforting.

"We can fix it," Emily spoke to the little feline, feeling a sense of peace come to her at last. "We just need some paint for the ceiling, some new chair covers, new curtains. It will look like a whole new place. In the meantime, we'll find out who did this, who killed my father and Rosie."

The house remained blessedly silent, but even voicing her thoughts out loud gave her strength. Dr. Watson mewed in agreement. She had a plan, and that was all that counted. Her eyes rose once more and met the beautiful gaze of the woman in the portrait.

Rosie. Without knowing why, Emily knew the woman staring back at her had been her father's mistress. She felt a warmth radiating from the woman's picture, and a strange sort of . . . acceptance? She really was losing her mind. Yet she couldn't help but admire the woman's beauty, and wonder to herself: Had Rosie loved her father, and had he loved Rosie?

A house full of mystery. Emily lowered the gas, then started upstairs with the letter, Dr. Watson hot on her trail. She had to take stock of the place before she could finish her plans. She never saw the curtains billow out from the windows downstairs, as if a cool breeze had ruffled them, then let them settle against the wall once more. Emily would have been thoroughly puzzled, for the windows had been firmly locked.

"Goodness, it is gloomy." Shuddering, Emily reached the great hall and discovered that the upstairs rooms appeared to have been ransacked as well. It was too dark to examine the rest of the house, but she made a mental note to do that the following day. Finding a candle, she lit the taper, then carried the guttering flame from room to room, looking for the least damaged. Dr. Watson mewed, as curious as herself, then halted before a door, refusing to enter.

"What is it? Oh, Watson, look at this room!"

The chamber must have been lovely at one time. Emily placed the candle on the nightstand and gazed in sincere appreciation at the cherry wood furnishings, the bureau with a mirror, the polished washstand. A gaslight flickered overhead, and the fixtures, made of cranberry glass, threw soft shadows everywhere. Green and pink flowered drapes had been pulled back at the window, showing lace undercurtains, and the same floral material covered the quilt. Emily tried hard not to look at the imposing poster bed that was the center and the focal point of the room.

Dr. Watson hissed and spat. Emily turned back to

fetch him, but the feline hunched his back and bared his teeth, refusing to enter the room. "You silly cat," Emily scolded the little animal, but Watson remained unconvinced. Reaching for her pet, she gazed in stunned surprise as the cat leapt out of her arms, remaining firmly on the other side of the hall.

"Fine. Stay there then. I've got to see this place." Turning around, she reentered the room, looking once more at the lovely surroundings.

Rosie's room. Emily felt it with a certainty that passed through her like a cold breeze. In spite of the vandalism, woman's jewelry still filled a glass casket on the dressing table. Emily picked up a silver hairbrush in wonder. Row after row of perfume bottles graced the table. She lifted a glass stopper, reveling in the flowery scent. It was strange touching another woman's toiletries, especially one who had been murdered. It was almost like seeing a ghost. Emily chuckled at the notion. Yet she couldn't help appreciating the perfumes. For a woman like herself who'd grown up in a spinsterish existence, this glimpse of the other side was intoxicating.

Finding fresh linens in the drawer, Emily made the bed, trying hard not to think of the activity that once took place here. Tomorrow, she would go through the room and donate the perfumes and Rosie's other belongings to charity. Someone could use these beautiful things, she thought, reluctantly putting on her own cotton nightdress. She would get fresh water and wash tomorrow. Tonight, she was just too tired.

She tumbled into bed. She didn't see the gaslight flicker overhead, nor the fixture slowly start to move, swinging over the bed in a circular motion. Shadows danced furiously over the walls, and downstairs, the piano played a bawdy tune.

Emily saw and heard nothing. She was asleep.

For current information on Bantam's
women's fiction, visit our Web site
Isn't It Romantic
at the following address:

http://www.bdd.com/romance

Bestselling Historical Women's Fiction

AMANDA QUICK

____28354-5 SEDUCTION ...$6.50/$8.99 Canada
____28932-2 SCANDAL ....$6.50/$8.99
____28594-7 SURRENDER ....$6.50/$8.99
____29325-7 RENDEZVOUS ....$6.50/$8.99
____29315-X RECKLESS ....$6.50/$8.99
____29316-8 RAVISHED ....$6.50/$8.99
____29317-6 DANGEROUS ....$6.50/$8.99
____56506-0 DECEPTION ....$6.50/$8.99
____56153-7 DESIRE ....$6.50/$8.99
____56940-6 MISTRESS ....$6.50/$8.99
____57159-1 MYSTIQUE ....$6.50/$7.99
____57190-7 MISCHIEF ....$6.50/$8.99
____57407-8 AFFAIR ....$6.99/$8.99

IRIS JOHANSEN

____29871-2 LAST BRIDGE HOME ...$5.50/$7.50
____29604-3 THE GOLDEN
            BARBARIAN ....$6.99/$8.99
____29244-7 REAP THE WIND .....$5.99/$7.50
____29032-0 STORM WINDS ....$6.99/$8.99

Ask for these books at your local bookstore or use this page to order.

Please send me the books I have checked above. I am enclosing $_____ (add $2.50 to cover postage and handling). Send check or money order, no cash or C.O.D.'s, please.

Name _____

Address _____

City/State/Zip _____

Send order to: Bantam Books, Dept. FN 16, 2451 S. Wolf Rd., Des Plaines, IL 60018
Allow four to six weeks for delivery.
Prices and availability subject to change without notice.

FN 16 3/98

Bestselling Historical Women's Fiction

Iris Johansen

- ___ 28855-5 THE WIND DANCER ...$5.99/$6.99
- ___ 29968-9 THE TIGER PRINCE ...$6.99/$8.99
- ___ 29944-1 THE MAGNIFICENT ROGUE ....$6.99/$8.99
- ___ 29945-X BELOVED SCOUNDREL .$6.99/$8.99
- ___ 29946-8 MIDNIGHT WARRIOR ..$6.99/$8.99
- ___ 29947-6 DARK RIDER ....$6.99/$8.99
- ___ 56990-2 LION'S BRIDE ....$6.99/$8.99
- ___ 56991-0 THE UGLY DUCKLING...$5.99/$7.99
- ___ 57181-8 LONG AFTER MIDNIGHT.$6.99/$8.99
- ___ 10616-3 AND THEN YOU DIE....$22.95/$29.95

Teresa Medeiros

- ___ 29407-5 HEATHER AND VELVET .$5.99/$7.50
- ___ 29409-1 ONCE AN ANGEL ......$5.99/$7.99
- ___ 29408-3 A WHISPER OF ROSES .$5.99/$7.99
- ___ 56332-7 THIEF OF HEARTS .....$5.50/$6.99
- ___ 56333-5 FAIREST OF THEM ALL .$5.99/$7.50
- ___ 56334-3 BREATH OF MAGIC ....$5.99/$7.99
- ___ 57623-2 SHADOWS AND LACE ...$5.99/$7.99
- ___ 57500-7 TOUCH OF ENCHANTMENT.........$5.99/$7.99

Ask for these books at your local bookstore or use this page to order.

Please send me the books I have checked above. I am enclosing $____ (add $2.50 to cover postage and handling). Send check or money order, no cash or C.O.D.'s, please.

Name _____

Address _____

City/State/Zip _____

Send order to: Bantam Books, Dept. FN 16, 2451 S. Wolf Rd., Des Plaines, IL 60018
Allow four to six weeks for delivery.
Prices and availability subject to change without notice.   FN 16 3/98

THE VERY BEST IN CONTEMPORARY WOMEN'S FICTION

SANDRA BROWN

___28951-9 Texas! Lucky $6.99/$9.99 in Canada
___28990-X Texas! Chase $6.99/$9.99
___29500-4 Texas! Sage $6.99/$9.99
___29085-1 22 Indigo Place $6.99/$8.99
___29783-X A Whole New Light $6.50/$8.99
___57158-3 Breakfast In Bed $5.99/$7.99
___56768-3 Adam's Fall $5.99/$7.99
___56045-X Temperatures Rising $6.50/$8.99
___56274-6 Fanta C $5.99/$7.99
___56278-9 Long Time Coming $5.99/$7.99
___57157-5 Heaven's Price $6.50/$8.99
___29751-1 Hawk O'Toole's Hostage $6.50/$8.99
___10403-9 Tidings of Great Joy $17.95/$24.95

TAMI HOAG

___29534-9 Lucky's Lady $6.50/$8.99
___29053-3 Magic $6.50/$8.99
___56050-6 Sarah's Sin $5.99/$7.99
___56451-x Night Sins $6.50/$8.99
___29272-2 Still Waters $6.50/$8.99
___56160-X Cry Wolf $6.50/$8.99
___56161-8 Dark Paradise $6.50/$8.99
___56452-8 Guilty As Sin $6.50/$8.99
___09960-4 A Thin Dark Line $22.95/$29.95

NORA ROBERTS

___10834-4 Genuine Lies $19.95/$27.95
___28578-5 Public Secrets $6.50/$8.99
___26461-3 Hot Ice $6.50/$8.99
___26574-1 Sacred Sins $6.50/$8.99
___27859-2 Sweet Revenge $6.50/$8.99
___27283-7 Brazen Virtue $6.50/$8.99
___29597-7 Carnal Innocence $6.50/$8.99
___29490-3 Divine Evil $6.50/$8.99

DEBORAH SMITH

___29107-6 Miracle $5.99/$7.99
___29092-4 Follow the Sun $4.99/$5.99
___29690-6 Blue Willow $5.99/$7.99
___29689-2 Silk and Stone $5.99/$6.99
___10334-2 A Place To Call Home $23.95/$29.95

Ask for these books at your local bookstore or use this page to order.

Please send me the books I have checked above. I am enclosing $_____ (add $2.50 to cover postage and handling). Send check or money order, no cash or C.O.D.'s, please.

Name _____
Address _____
City/State/Zip _____

Send order to: Bantam Books, Dept. FN 24, 2451 S. Wolf Rd., Des Plaines, IL 60018
Allow four to six weeks for delivery.
Prices and availability subject to change without notice.

FN 24 3/98